"*Sunday Clothes* is a timeless story of love and betrayal. Vivid and thought provoking."
—**Lyn Cote,** Author of *Summer's End*

"*Sunday Clothes* is engaging and well paced, while allowing the reader to become fully immersed in the story and its authentically flawed characters. Thom Lemmons does a masterful job of revealing the period, the people, and the frailties of religion, all without a hint of cynicism."
—**Steve Green,** President of Anvil Management

"A very realistic story, well written, perfect in historical detail, couldn't put it down."
—**Lois Gladys Leppard,** Author of "Mandie" Series

"Well written! Engaging! In *Sunday Clothes,* Thom Lemmons weaves a tale of consequences and hope in dark places. I found myself caught up in the characters' lives, dreams, and chances. Here's a book that will touch your heart and make you think about the choices that can change your life forever."
—**Marlo Schalesky,** Author of *Only the Wind Remembers, Cry Freedom, Freedom's Shadow,* and *Empty Womb, Aching Heart*

Sunday

CLOTHES

CLOTHES

A NOVEL

THOM LEMMONS

BROADMAN
&HOLMAN
PUBLISHERS

NASHVILLE, TENNESSEE

Published by Broadman & Holman Publishers,
Nashville, Tennessee

Dewey Decimal Classification: F
Subject Heading: CHURCH HISTORY—FICTION
UNITED STATES—HISTORY—1900–99
(20TH CENTURY)—FICTION

This is a work of fiction. Any similarity to actual persons, living or dead, except for certain recognizable historical characters, may be attributed only to coincidence.

1 2 3 4 5 6 7 8 9 10 08 07 06 05 04

Dedicated to the memory of
CYNTHIA JANE HATCHETT SIMMONS
1875–1964

Gold and all this world's wine
Is naught but Christ's rood;
I would be clad in Christ's skin
That ran so long with his blood,
And go to his heart, and give to him mine—
For he alone is a filling food.
Then I'd care little for kith or kin,
For in him alone is all that is good. Amen.
                    —Middle English lyrics
                    (translation by William Rankin)

Part I

August 1898

CHAPTER

1

*A*ddie shaded her eyes and stared up the dirt road for the tenth time in the last five minutes. There! And about time too.

A horse and buggy crested the hill up from Orchard Knob, trailing a cloud of dust that plumed off to the north, gilded by the westering sun.

She turned and leaned toward the screen door. "Papa, Zeb's coming up the lane. We'll be back after meeting's over." She didn't wait to hear his acknowledgment of her message. He'd be scowling.

Rose was sweeping at the other end of the front porch. "Rose, can you leave something out for Papa's supper before you go home?" Addie said. "I may not be back until after dark."

"Mmm-hmm." The broom never paused.

Addie looked at Rose. The old woman's plump arms moved rhythmically, twin metronomes keeping time to a well-worn tune. "Rose, you . . . you like Mr. Douglas, don't you?"

The broom made two strokes, then a third. Rose turned her head slightly toward Addie. "Ain't for me to say, Missy. He your man, not mine. Don't matter whether I like him or not." She went back to her sweeping.

Addie waited on the front porch as Zeb turned off the Orchard Knob road and into their lane. She smiled. How in the world had Zeb snagged the handsome, black-lacquered gig and the quick-stepping sorrel? He was always pulling off some dramatic gesture or other. It was one of the things she loved about him.

He drove up in the front yard, then pulled the horse around broadside and grinned up at her from the seat of the gig. "Well, did I tell you the truth?"

She smiled broadly and nodded. "Zeb, it's— Well, it's just something. How did you manage it—rob a bank?"

"I suppose so, in a manner of speaking," he said, pushing up his bowler to scratch his scalp. "I wrote three policies on a banker up in Murfreesboro, and that put me at the top of the production list for the week. The boss said whoever did that could use his rig for a day. And that's me! Now, are you gonna stand there gawking all evening, or are we going to meeting?"

She came down the steps, and he stood to hold her hand as she stepped into the carriage. She settled herself beside him, and he clicked his tongue while brushing the sorrel's flank with the buggy whip.

When they made the final turn into the lane, Addie glanced back over her shoulder at the house. Rose was standing still, staring after them.

Addie wished that Papa could at least try to like Zeb. He was polite, hard-working, and cut a handsome figure. She enjoyed the feel of his dark broadcloth suit where her hand rested on his forearm, the stark contrast of his crisp white shirt and black string tie. And Zeb was a thorough gentleman. He had never made any gesture toward her that was the least bit improper.

But Zeb was a salesman, and Papa didn't much approve of salesmen. He stayed put out with the daily stream of drummers that called on Caswell Mercantile Company, he said, and didn't see why he ought to be welcoming one into his house. Zeb sold life insurance, and that didn't help either: she'd heard Papa mutter about pigs in pokes.

Then, too, there was the fact that Zeb was a Democrat from Georgia, and Papa was Republican and didn't completely trust folks from Georgia. That was harder for Addie to understand. Why, from the top of Lookout Mountain you could just about spit on Georgia!

But worst of all, Papa was a strict Methodist, and Zeb was a Campbellite. As far as Papa was concerned, the Campbellites were Johnny-come-latelies who thought they were the only ones going to heaven. Papa said that any group so worked up over total immersion baptism was bound to be all wet about something else. They were worse than the Baptists, he said. At least you could talk to a Baptist, he said.

"Zeb, who's preaching tonight?" she asked, leaning a trifle closer to him as they turned onto the Orchard Knob road.

"Brother Charles McCrary, I believe. He's come all the way out from Nashville to hold this meeting."

"What's he like?"

"A mighty fine speaker, from what I hear. I've never heard him preach, but old Brother Houser once heard him debate some Baptist or other, and he said Brother McCrary like to brought fire from heaven, he was so good."

"Really?"

"Yep. Said he could quote whole books of the Bible from memory. Said he never once looked at a single note but just spoke extemporaneous. Said he whipped that Baptist like a tied-up goat and hardly broke a sweat."

They rode on in silence for some time. Behind them, the sun reddened toward the horizon. Cicadas slid up and down their two-note scale with a sound like miniature buzz saws. The horse tossed its head and snorted. Addie felt Zeb's arm encircle her shoulders, and she leaned into him a bit more.

"Addie, are you still my girl?"

"I guess so."

"Guess so?"

She laughed and jabbed him in the ribs with her elbow. "Zeb, you know good and well I am."

"Well, all right, then."

The wagonyard in front of the church house was three-quarters full by the time they arrived. The service hadn't begun, though, because several of the men still lingered outside the front door, chewing, spitting, and smoking. They all looked long in the direction of Zeb's borrowed rig as he pulled up the sorrel and looped the lines over the seat rail. Zeb helped Addie down, then unbuckled the bridle from the horse and clipped a tether to its halter. He pulled a grain-filled nosebag from the floor of the carriage, tied it behind the horse's ears, gave it a final pat on the withers, and offered Addie his arm as they walked toward the door of the church.

"Evenin', Zeb," called one of the men. They all touched their hat brims and nodded at Addie.

"Howdy, Pete," said Zeb. "Tom, Hershel. How y'all doing this evening?"

"Tolerable well," said Pete, "but I'd be a sight better if we got some rain." The others nodded.

"Well, like my daddy used to say, we're one day closer to rain than we ever have been," Zeb said.

"I guess that'd have to be right," Pete said, smiling.

Zeb and the other men talked a little more. They swapped opinions on the war with Spain. Hershel said it appeared to be winding down, now that Cuba had fallen.

Tom peeked through the open door of the church. "Boys, we better get on in. They're fixing to start." He held the door and motioned Addie and Zeb inside. "Y'all go ahead."

"Thank you, Mr. Hoskins," said Addie.

"Yes, ma'am."

Post Oak Hollow Church was a small one-room affair, its wood frame covered with whitewashed clapboard siding. There were windows down both sides and a raised platform across the front, in the center of which stood a sturdy oak pulpit. The two rows of pews on either side of the center aisle were constructed of rough-hewn hickory slats with no finish other than the gradual smoothing administered by the backsides of the congregation. The windows were raised, and a slight breeze wafted through, aided by the waving pasteboard fans wielded by many of the women. Most of the fans were from a local funeral parlor and bore an advertisement on one side and reproductions from the Doré Bible on the other. Even though the sun hovered above the horizon, the dale in which the church sat was already in shadow. The coal-oil lamps, in brackets along both side walls, were lit.

Brother Houser, a white-haired gentleman, stood and stepped carefully to a position on the platform just in front of the pulpit. He held a brown paperback book in his hand. "Folks, let's all get a song book and turn to number sixty-seven."

Addie and Zeb slid into a seat about halfway toward the front, on the left side next to the center aisle. With the rest of the congregation, they took a hymnal from the rack on the seat in front of them and rustled the pages to find the announced selection. In a reedy voice, Brother Houser began to sing.

I have found a friend in Jesus,
He's everything to me.
He's the fairest of ten thousand to my soul . . .

The congregation joined in with a vigor undimmed by the general lack of skill.

At first, Addie had thought it curious that the Post Oak Hollow congregation sang without a piano or organ. But Zeb had carefully pointed out to her that there was nothing in the New Testament that prescribed mechanical assistance to musical worship. "We try to follow the Bible as our only guide," he had said. "We wouldn't want to take a chance on doing anything where we don't have a New Testament example." Addie hadn't ever thought about it that way, but she had to admit there sure wasn't anything in the New Testament about pianos or organs.

"Silliest thing I ever heard tell of," Papa had said when she told him. "Course there ain't nothing in the New Testament about pianos and organs—nor hymnals printed on a printing press, nor ladies wearing corsets to church." He insisted it was just another case of useless, Campbellite hardheadedness. Addie had thought about pointing out to him that he was being just as dogmatic about his views as he was accusing them of being about theirs but decided discretion was the better part of valor.

After several songs and a prayer offered in an undulatory, singsong voice by one of the congregation's elders, Charles McCrary rose from his seat on the front pew and walked to the pulpit. His back was ramrod-straight; he carried nothing with him except a black leather Bible. He laid the well-worn Bible on the pulpit in front of him and swept his gaze over the assembly.

He was slight-built and balding. His face was clean-shaven, and wire-rimmed spectacles glittered on the bridge of his aquiline nose. The light glanced off the lenses, giving Addie the fleeting, disturbing impression that instead of eyes he had only featureless panes of glass. He had a thin-lipped, hawkish look; a man who brooked no foolishness. He appeared to be in his midforties, perhaps early fifties. And then he began to speak in a fine, strong baritone voice—almost startling, coming from such a small frame.

"It's good to be here with you, brethren in Christ," he said. "I bring you greetings from the church in Nashville and from all the faithful brethren throughout Middle Tennessee. When Brother Houser invited me to come and speak to you, I had no idea that the saints in and around Chattanooga numbered as many as they do. I'm truly pleased to see such a fine crowd here tonight and doubly pleased by the fine song service offered by Brother Houser.

"As my text for this evening, I have chosen a passage from the second epistle of the apostle Paul to Timothy . . ."

Addie noticed the long, drawn-out way Brother McCrary said "Paul"—as if he savored the name, was reluctant to release it from his lips. It sounded like "pole."

"In the fourth chapter, beginning in verse one, Paul says, 'I charge thee therefore before God, and the Lord Jesus Christ, who shall judge the quick and the dead at his appearing and his kingdom; preach the word; be instant in season, out of season; reprove, rebuke, exhort with all long-suffering and doctrine."

He never looked at his Bible, never made a move to open it. Addie watched, intrigued.

"'For the time will come'—now hear the next words carefully, brethren—'when they will not endure sound doctrine—'" He drove each word of the phrase home with special emphasis, as if hammering verbal nails into the lid of a coffin. He gripped the sides of the pulpit and leaned forward as he quoted the remaining verses. "'—but after their own lusts shall they heap to themselves teachers, having itching ears—'" He pronounced the last two words like a curse, or the name of an unspeakable disease. "'—And they shall turn away their ears from the truth, and shall be turned unto fables.'"

Two or three rows from the front, on the right-hand side of the meeting house, a toddler began to squall and fidget in her mother's lap. If Brother McCrary heard, he gave no sign. His face wore a pained expression, as if he felt personally responsible for the sorry state of fallen humanity. After a brief, reflective silence, he looked up.

"Brethren, as we look around us today, we see flagrant evidence of the truth of the apostle Paul's words, just read in your hearing. We see a landscape littered with so-called churches, where so-called Christians come together and profess their so-called allegiance to the Lord."

No beating around the bush, Addie thought. *He is going to wade right into it.*

"And in these so-called churches, brethren, what do we find? We find teaching that proclaims as doctrines the commandments of men—Matthew fifteen, nine. We find those who say 'Lord, Lord!' but do not the will of the Father in heaven—Matthew seven, twenty-one. We find those who have a form of godliness, but deny the power thereof—Second Timothy three, five. Who profess that they know God, but in works they deny him—Titus one, sixteen—"

Each time Brother McCrary cited a Scripture, he punched his Bible forward in the air, driving gospel spikes.

"In short, my brethren, we find those of whom the Lord will say in the last day, 'I never knew you: depart from me, ye that work iniquity,'—Matthew seven, twenty-three . . ."

For the next hour, he fired broadside barrages into every other church for miles around. He laid about with great, circular swipes of Scripture, hewing away at the false teachings and creeds of men that were, in his words, "leading astray the unsuspecting hordes of the sectarian world." He thrusted and parried with the sword of the Spirit, and he never mentioned any names; but as Addie heard him lambaste sprinkling and missionary societies and instrumental accompaniment to hymns and the christening of babies, she didn't need to wonder how Papa would feel about what she was hearing. If he walked in the back door before Brother McCrary finished, there might be a killing.

And yet, despite the relentlessness of Brother McCrary's onslaught, she was awed by his presentation. He never consulted an outline, never opened the covers of his Bible, but Addie never doubted that he was quoting his proof-texts verbatim. As he built his breastworks against the evil onslaught of denominationalism, Brother McCrary chinked each crack in the masonry with an appropriate New Testament citation. It was an impressive display of firepower. Addie had no idea the Bible was so hard on things she had previously thought proper, or at least harmless.

When Brother McCrary offered the altar call, Addie felt a tug within her. For some time, as she had been discussing various aspects of doctrine with Zeb, she had begun feeling curiously ambivalent toward her Methodist upbringing. Papa was a good man, although he'd seemed to grow harsher after Mama's death. They had always been a churchgoing family, and all of Addie's siblings—now with families of their own—were faithful members of their churches. One of her brothers had even been a class leader for some little church out in the country, before he and his wife moved back into town.

But something about the Campbellites appealed to her. Something, she told herself sternly, more than the charm and good looks of Zebediah Douglas. Something about their urgent appeal to Scripture. Something about their primitive, combative vitality. She had the sense that these folks really believed in something and were willing to fight for it. It gave them an identity that was clear-cut. It gave them a mission. Addie liked that.

But, oh! Papa would never forgive her.

From the corner of her eye, she studied Zeb. His face was intent, serious. He appeared to be hanging on every word that Brother McCrary spoke. So sincere . . . so handsome.

The congregation stood to sing the invitation hymn. Brother McCrary stood expectantly at the head of the center aisle, wiping his forehead with a handkerchief, ready to receive the penitents his sermon had quickened to contrition.

There's a great day coming;
A great day coming.

There's a great day coming, bye-and-bye;
When the saints and the sinners
Shall be parted right and left.
Are you ready for that day to come?

Are you ready? asked the chorus. *Are you ready for the Judgment Day?*
The day was coming, Addie felt sure. But it wasn't going to be today.

CHAPTER

2

"Well, do you love him?" Louisa peered at her younger sister, seated on the other side of the quilting frame. Addie ducked her head but not before Louisa saw the blush.

"Oh, Lou . . . I don't know," Addie said. "He's awful nice to me. He's a hard worker, and he makes good money."

"And he doesn't clean up too bad either," Louisa said. She felt the prick of the needle with her fingertip and pulled the stitch through from underneath. She pulled it tight, then placed the needle for the next stitch. "Zeb Douglas is a fine-looking man, and anyone who says otherwise would lie about something else."

Addie stitched in silence. Louisa thought she could see a faint smile at the corners of her younger sister's mouth.

"I tell you, I believe I've been working on this quilt all my life," Louisa said. "If I don't ever see another tree-of-life pattern, it'll be too soon. Cora Dickerson down the street got one of those new portable Singer sewing machines, and she's already started piecing tops with it."

"Does it do as well as hand piecing?"

"Why, I reckon. She could do three tops in the time it took me to get this one pieced. I've been telling Dub I need one. Course, I'll wind up ordering it from Sears & Roebuck's for Christmas and telling him he got it for me."

Addie laughed. "Lou, the way you talk about poor Dub! Anybody'd think you were mistreated, the way you carry on."

Louisa smiled. "Well, I know. Dub's a good man. I've got few complaints, really."

The silence stretched, broken only by the soft popping of the two quilting needles as they pierced the taut muslin.

"Lou?"

"Hmm?"

Addie's lips had that pinched-together, thinking look. Lou thought she knew what was coming next.

"Lou, I . . . I worry about Zeb and . . . Papa. Zeb's not— Well, he's not Methodist, you know, and—"

"Yes, I know," Louisa said. "Of course . . . there's always George Hutto."

"Oh, George Hutto!" Addie jabbed her needle through the cloth. "I'm so tired of everybody throwing George Hutto up in my face. I've known him ever since grade school, and I don't see what's so great about him, even if he does go to the right church!"

Louisa had reached the end of her thread. She looped the needle back through her last stitch and pulled the knot down into the batting, then snipped the extra off down close to the quilt. She reached for her spool of thread and wet the end of the thread between her lips, squinting as she tried to poke it through the eye of her needle. "Well, sounds to me like your mind's made up on that score, at least," she said.

"Honey, all I can tell you is this," Louisa said after awhile. "Comes a time when a woman has to do what's right for herself, and nobody can tell you what that is, except you. Not me, not Zeb . . . not Papa."

Addie's hands slowed, then stopped. "You mean . . . You think it might be all right if—"

"I didn't say that. I don't know about all right. All I know is you're a grown woman. This is the 1890s, Addie, and Chattanooga isn't Istanbul or Peking or someplace like that. A woman has to make her own way, best way she can. And if Zeb Douglas is the way for you, why then—" Louisa sat still for a few seconds, studying the backs of her hands. "Then, maybe that's what you have to do, that's all." She took a few stitches, then looked up, aiming an index finger at Addie. "Now mind, I'm not saying it's right, or wise."

Addie's eyes questioned.

"I'm just saying that you're eighteen years old, and you've got a right to have your say."

While she stitched, Addie began remembering what she used to do when she was a child. Sometimes, when she felt the need to get away from everyone, she used to climb to the top of one of the sweet gum trees that ringed the backyard of the house. She would climb way, way up to the highest branches, until every breeze that came along would cause her perch to sway and rock. When she was in the top of a tree, Addie could let herself feel freed from the pull of the earth. The thick green foliage hid the ground, creating a special apart-place for her.

Addie longed for a refuge just now. Louisa had made her see that she had the responsibility of choice, and her position frightened her. Maybe she had climbed too high this time. Maybe a storm was blowing up, rattling and shivering among the tops of the trees, tossing her back and forth, a storm that might throw her down from her safe place. Was there a safe place left? Could she really just do what she thought was best? Was it as simple as that? Or would there be other choices beyond this one, other responsibilities and other finalities that would spin off this moment, like the felling of the first domino? What other choices was she making right now, without a chance to see them?

Her vision refocused on the quilt beneath her fingers. Pursing her lips, she took up her needle and made another stitch across the tree-of-life.

Zeb Douglas felt like a long-tailed cat in a roomful of rockers. His horse was cresting the final ridge between Orchard Knob and the Caswell homestead. He could look down the slope to the place where their lane peeled off from the road.

He had proposed to Addie the week before as they strolled along the gaslit promenade beside the glassy pond in East Lake Park. It had been a fine Indian summer evening. They'd walked for a long time, her hand in his; the sweet twilight air had seemed like it was whispering secrets in his blood. Then one silence stretched a little long, and before he knew it he was speaking up.

"Addie, you know how I feel about you, don't you?" he said.

"Well . . . I think so."

"Addie, I . . . I love you. There, it's out. I want you to be my wife. I want to marry you, if you'll have me."

They had walked on slowly; that was the strangest thing, he thought later. To somebody standing on the other side of the pond, they were just two people walking together, moving along as smooth as silk. Who'd have known that his heart was slamming around inside his chest like a penned-up jaybird? He kept his eyes on the footpath, afraid to look at her, more afraid with every step. He started wishing he'd kept his mouth shut.

"All right," she said.

"What?"

She laughed a little and squeezed his hand. "I said all right. I'll marry you." He had looked at her then, and she was smiling. "I will," she repeated. She stopped walking and turned to face him, taking both his hands in hers.

Right then, he thought he might bust wide open. He felt his grin getting all long and rubbery. He wanted to jump up and down like a little kid on Christmas morning; he wanted to spin around in a circle and holler. He pulled her to him and squeezed her tight. Her wide-brimmed hat fell off, and he giggled like a schoolboy, snatching it up and planting it askew on her head.

"Oh, Addie, you don't know how you've just made me feel! I'm the happiest fellow in Hamilton County!" He planted a chaste but sincere kiss on her lips.

"Zebediah Douglas!" She pushed him away. "You'd best mind your manners!"

"Aw, I'm sorry, Addie," he said, grinning. "I just couldn't help it."

"Well," she said, a smile stealing across her face, "I guess I didn't really mind all that much. Just don't get too fresh, that's all," she said.

"Zeb," she said a few minutes later as they strolled on down the walk, "when are you going to tell Papa?"

And he hadn't drawn an easy breath since. His horse started down the curving slope of the Caswell's drive.

Jacob Caswell could sure do worse for a son-in-law. It wasn't as though Zeb didn't have prospects. He'd just been promoted to manager of the Murfreesboro office. He now had three other agents under him, and the company principals were very pleased with his work. He was an up-and-comer in the agency force.

You let your daughter marry me, and I guarantee you'll never see her taking in washing while her sorry husband's off running with his coon dogs . . .

But Jacob Caswell was a dyed-in-the-wool Methodist, and that was that. Every time Zeb called on Addie, he could feel her father's hostility to his religion chilling the back of his neck. Even when he didn't go in the house, he could sense Jacob's disapproval brooding over him like a summer thunderhead.

He tried to tell himself not to take it personally. Addie had warned him repeatedly of her father's uncompromising denominational compunctions.

She had told him about the time, one raw winter's night, when a knock came on the front door of their home. Outside was a man huddled against the sleet, clutching his collar about his neck. He told Addie's father that his wagon was broken down just beyond the crest of the rise; a wheel had come off the axle. Could he board himself and his horse for the night?

Addie's father had brought the man in and given him a cup of hot coffee. He was just about to pull on his mackintosh and go out into the night to help the stranger bring in his horse when he chanced to ask the fellow what brought him to these parts on such a bitter evening.

The man answered that he was a circuit preacher for the Church of Christ and that he had come to conduct a revival service.

"Papa got a sick look on his face," Addie said, "and started taking off his coat. The man looked at him kind of strange, and Papa said, 'Sir, my religious convictions prohibit me from rendering aid to a person I believe to be a teacher of heresy. I am deeply sorry, but I cannot help you this evening.'"

Addie told how her father sent that man back out into the sleet and shut the door behind him. Jacob Caswell leaned against the closed door for several minutes, then slumped down in the hall chair with his head in his hands. "He felt real bad for the man," Addie said, "but that's just how he is about what he believes."

Now Zeb was here. He reined his horse to a halt and eased down from the saddle. He looped the reins over the porch railing and straightened himself, staring at the front door of the house. He had to ask for Addie's hand; it was the only honorable thing to do. He knew she would marry him, but he also knew she wanted the proper forms observed. That's just the kind of girl she was.

He took a deep breath, then another. He dusted off his hat and put it back on his head. He straightened his tie and tugged his coat down all around. And then, like a man going to the gallows, he climbed the front steps.

He raised a knuckle to knock on the frame of the screen door, but before he could, the heavy inner door swung inward. Addie stood there, dressed in her newest crinoline-and-lace. At the sight of her, he almost forgot his nervousness. But then he saw the set of her eyes and the tense way she looked over her shoulder toward the parlor, and every trace of moisture instantly evaporated from his throat.

"Come on in," she said, standing aside and trying to smile. "Papa," she called, "Zeb's here."

Rose stepped into the hallway as he entered, drying her hands on a dish towel. Her eyes glinted from Zeb to Addie, then toward the parlor where Mr. Caswell waited. She ducked back into the kitchen.

Zeb had to concentrate on what his knees were doing as he paced toward the parlor. He expected Jacob Caswell to be seated in his red leather wingback chair, his face buried in the *Chattanooga Times* as he had been situated on the other rare occasions when Zeb had been admitted to the parlor. But this time he was standing, his hands clasped behind his back. He still wore his dark Sunday suit, his tie knotted at the throat. He was scowling at the floor, and he looked up as Zeb entered, with Addie following three paces behind.

"Papa," she said, "Zeb's here, and he wants—"

"I know why you're here," Jacob said. "I'm not blind, you know."

He glared at Zeb. Zeb felt his Adam's apple bobbing up and down like a fishing cork. Zeb thought of the words he had rehearsed on the way here. He drew a chest full of air and tried to square his shoulders. "Mr. Caswell, it must be apparent to you that your daughter and I—"

"It's apparent to me that my daughter has set her mind on marrying you, Mr. Douglas. Only a fool would think otherwise, and I don't much believe I'm a fool."

"No . . . no, sir. I expect not."

"She's eighteen years old," Jacob said, his eyes glittering toward Addie, "and I know better than to try to talk a woman out of something her mind's set on. That's the one piece of advice I'll give you, Mr. Douglas: don't try to reason a woman out of something she already wants to do."

Zeb swallowed. "Uh . . . thank you, sir."

"But I'll tell you this, young woman," Jacob said, aiming a finger at Addie. "You know how I feel about this man's religion. You were raised in a sensible Methodist family. If you choose to join this man's church—"

"Ah, we don't call it 'joining the church,' sir," Zeb said. "We believe God adds the obedient to—"

"Zeb! Not now!" Addie said.

"Never mind," said Jacob Caswell, his eyes still on his daughter. "You can call it joining, or being added, or whatever other fool thing you fancy, but I'll say this once and for all: if you follow him into this religious group of his, you best reckon all the consequences. You best make sure you love this fellow enough to live with the consequences."

No one spoke for a long time. Addie leaned against the doorframe, her hands behind her back. Zeb wondered if she was holding on to the woodwork to keep from falling. Her face was as white as the high lace collar of her dress, and her eyes looked big and dark as they flickered back and forth between him and her father.

Then Addie stood away from the doorframe. She walked toward Zeb and took his arm. She turned to face her father.

"Papa, I love him. I mean it."

Jacob Caswell grunted, shoved his hands into his vest pockets, and stalked past them. He grabbed his hat from the hall tree and yanked open the front door. They heard his rapid strides thump on the front porch and down the steps.

A long breath went out of Addie, and her head fell on Zeb's shoulder. "Well, that's that," she said.

Zeb couldn't speak. He put an arm around her and patted her. Twice.

CHAPTER
3

George Hutto stared at the marble top of the lamp table beside him. After a minute or two, he again picked up the society page of the *Times* and read the brief lines:

Mr. Jacob I. Caswell,
Proprietor of Caswell Mercantile Company, Orchard Knob,
Announces that his Daughter,
Adelaide Margaret Caswell
is
Engaged to be Married
to
Mr. Zebediah Acton Douglas
late of Chattanooga, recently moved to Murfreesboro
The Nuptials are Announced for
Sunday, the Twenty-fifth of June,
in the Year of Our Lord,
Eighteen Hundred and Ninety-Nine

When he finished the second reading, he started to wad the paper and hurl it into the fireplace. Instead, he crumpled it weakly in his lap and allowed it to fall onto the floor beside his chair. He stood up and paced toward the bay window, his hands clasped behind his back.

He had known Addie Caswell from the time they were kids in Sunday school class. He could never remember giving a plugged nickel for any other girl. He'd carried her books, endured her older brothers' taunts, and sent her valentines inscribed with pencil scrawls.

Well, it didn't matter now. She was engaged to this glad-talking Douglas fellow, and that was that. No sense crying over spilled milk.

He stared through the lace curtain. It was a gray day. Dry leaves scattered across the side yard, hurried along by the north wind. He shook his head, turning away from the window. Shoving his hands into his pockets, he slouched up the stairs toward his workroom.

His mother appeared at the bottom of the steps. "George, dear? You coming down to lunch, honey?"

He paused, glancing over his shoulder, then continued up the steps. "No, ma'am. Not hungry right now."

He heard her heels clomp on the wood floor, going toward the kitchen. "Mamie, just set two places," she said.

George entered his workroom and closed the door behind him. He went over to his table and picked up the painted hull of the frigate. Just about dry. He could go ahead and rig the masts. Placing the hull gently on the table, he took a paintbrush in one pudgy fist and a pair of tweezers in the other.

With a knuckle, he shoved his spectacles higher onto the bridge of his nose. He dipped the tip of the brush into the glue pot, then took the toothpick-sized mainmast in the tweezers. He applied two tiny dots of glue at equal distances from either end of the piece, then took another pair of tweezers and picked up the spar that bore the mainsail. He placed the spar on the mast, then reached for the topsail spar. Now he had to let the glue set for a few minutes.

If Addie truly loved the Douglas fellow, there wasn't much he could do about it. He'd never been one to force himself on folks or to act a fool, and he sure wasn't about to start. She was a grown woman, after all.

And besides, he was too plain, too dependable. Shoot, he knew it as well as anybody else. Most likely, Addie wanted someone with more . . . well, more gumption. Zeb Douglas was easy with words, never met a stranger. He could talk to you five minutes and you'd feel like you'd known him back to his grandparents on both sides. He just had that way with folks. Put you right at ease, and kept you there.

Compared to Zeb Douglas, George didn't make much of a show. He was just good old dependable George Hutto; never got in anybody's way, never said a cross word. Kind of fellow who'd never embarrass you. No surprises. No excuses.

He picked up the bottle that would soon house the frigate. As he'd done maybe fifteen times already, he compared the size of the neck opening to the width of the spars. He already knew they'd fit; he'd measured them four times before cutting them. That was the joke of the whole thing: the spars were far too narrow in proportion to the masts—completely out of whack. But once inside the bottle, safe behind the concealing curvature of the glass, no one would notice. Inside, the sails would belly forever out, full of nonexistent air. His frigate would sit on his or someone else's shelf, going nowhere at full sail across a motionless sea.

George set the bottle down and folded his hands in his lap. He sat for awhile. He scratched his face and sighed. The glue on the mast was about dry enough now. He bent back to his work.

Addie folded the table linens and patted them down into the cedar chest with the other things. She tallied the wedding gifts she had received so far: three hand-crocheted tablecloths, five place settings of silverware, several sets of serviettes and other assorted linens, and a brace of good, sturdy kitchen knives, each with a penny tied to the handle. And of course there was the album quilt presented to her by the ladies of the Methodist church. Made in the same style as the Baltimore album quilts Addie had seen pictured in *Butterick's Quarterly Delineator,* it was a floral quilt in dark blues and deep reds and rich greens on a background of white muslin. Each of the ladies had appliquéd a block and embroidered her name at its lower left corner. There were flower baskets, bird-and-flowers, rose trees, and other designs Addie had never seen before. The sashing between the blocks and around the border was a walnut brown. Addie ran her hand along the quilt and smiled.

But thinking of the Methodist ladies brought back the worry that had been nagging her like a toothache. She was going to have to decide something pretty soon about the church situation.

When she and Zeb talked, she felt her resistance wilting. It was just too hard to stand up to his constant scriptural salvos. And when she went back to her room and read the passages for herself, they did seem to point the direction Zeb aimed them.

She was coming to the uncomfortable conclusion that she'd never really known what she believed about the Bible. She'd just sort of gone along, without really studying for herself. Oh, she had been involved, even been a member of the Epworth League. But, somehow, she never got around to really looking into things on her own.

And there was no doubt in her mind that Zeb would insist they ought to go to the same church after they were married. "It just isn't right, Addie," he'd stress, "for a husband and wife to be divided over religion. A home ought to be of the same mind on that, 'cause if it isn't, why, there's no telling what else it'll be divided on."

That was true, she knew, but she was a little bothered by how the unity of their impending home was being achieved. Once, when she had asked him to come with her to the Methodist church on Sunday, he got an uncomfortable expression on his face and wouldn't look her in the eye. "Addie, I . . . well, I can't, honey. We've talked about what the Bible says, and . . ."

He wouldn't say anymore, but he didn't need to. Zeb couldn't find anything about the Methodist church he could use as a basis for compromise. She'd have to do all the compromising. But he seemed so convinced he was right.

As did Papa. She was stretched between the two of them like muslin on a quilting frame.

Quick steps pounded on the porch below her bedroom window, and someone rapped on the front door. "Is anybody home?" said a woman's voice. "Oh, Lordy, please be home, and hurry!" It was Martha Overby, who lived just around the shoulder of Tunnel Hill from their place, and her voice sounded to be unraveling with alarm. Addie rushed to the landing and down the stairs. She flung open the door. "Martha, what's—"

"Oh, Miss Caswell, please come quick! A rider just come up from the docks and said Perlie's johnboat washed ashore down below the Suck. They're a-looking for him right now, but it's just me and the babies at the house, and—" Her voice caught and she put a hand to her mouth.

Addie slammed the door and leapt down the steps, clutching her skirts with one hand. "You get on down there, Martha. I'll stay with your children until you get back." She didn't wait to see if Martha complied. She was already rounding the corner of the house and dashing uphill into the tree line.

Addie ran through the woods and over the shoulder of the hill. Soon she wished she had remembered to grab a shawl, at least. The cold air sliced into her breastbone as she dodged around fallen trunks and undergrowth. She got to the small house about five minutes later, her breath coming in pants. The Overbys lived in a ramshackle shotgun house that squatted at the foot of Tunnel Hill, squeezed between the river road and the railroad tracks of the Chattanooga-Atlanta line. Addie could hear the children howling almost before she rounded the bend of the hill, and as she neared the doorway of the tar-papered shack, she could smell the odor of stale coal smoke, bacon grease, and unwashed bodies. Two of the older children were standing just outside the front door, bawling as they stared at Addie. A dirty-faced toddler sat in the doorway and whimpered. And Addie was almost sure she could hear an infant's cries coming from somewhere inside the house.

She knelt down and pulled the two older ones to her. "Hush, now, y'all," she said. "You've got to help me take care of the little ones. You hear me? Your mama'll be here in a little bit, but she sent me to stay with you till she gets back. It'll be all right, now; just settle down." They calmed, a little at a time. The toddler put out a hand, and Addie pulled her close. Inside, the baby was still raising Cain.

"We better go inside. You'll catch a bad chill in this cold air. Does your mama have any milk for the baby?" The older boy, who looked about ten, shrugged his shoulders and dug the scarred toe of a brogan into the dust.

Addie disentangled herself from the grimy arms and fingers of the three children. She went into the house, fighting the urge to hold her breath, and beckoned them after her. She closed the rickety door against the chill.

A coal stove stood in the middle of one of the long walls; it doubled as a cooking oven. There were a few cane-bottomed chairs scattered about, all looking mostly the worse for wear. Pine planks laid across two sawhorses formed the kitchen table, and a few tack quilts, made out of feed sacks and backed with some of the homeliest homespun Addie had ever seen, spilled off the single shuck-mattressed bed onto the floor. The baby lay in a tangle of one of these, still squalling to beat blazes. Addie went to him.

"Now, you shush," she said. "You've just about kicked all your covers off, you little dickens." She scooped up the baby and tucked the quilt back around him. She rocked him in her arms as she scanned the shack for something to quiet him down.

She felt a tug at her skirts. The older girl, a finger stuck shyly in her mouth, held toward her a bottle half-full of milk.

"Thanks, honey! Where was it?"

The girl inclined her head toward the nearest chair. "Over there," she said in a barely audible voice. "Maw was feeding him when the man come."

Addie plugged the bottle into the tiny boy's mouth, and he pulled hard at the contents. "Well, nothing wrong with your appetite, at least," she said.

"They said Paw drowned in the Suck," the boy said, his chin beginning to quiver again.

"Now, that's not what your mama told me," Addie put in. "He just wasn't with his boat, is all. He's probably fine. I bet they'll find him. You don't go giving yourself such notions, all right? You've got to be brave for your sisters and your little brother."

The toddler, her eyes as round as teacups, edged closer to where Addie was seated. *Lord, please let these children's daddy be all right,* she prayed silently as the baby squirmed, fussed once or twice, and settled back into his consumption of the milk.

The sound was faint, and at first Addie thought she'd just imagined it. But gradually, she realized a man was approaching the house. She began to make out the words of the song he was singing at the top of an untuneful voice:

Hot corn, cold corn, bring along a demijohn
Hot corn, cold corn, bring along a demijohn
Hot corn, cold corn, bring along a demijohn
Farewell Uncle Bill, see you in the mornin', yes, sir!

Seconds later, the boy's head jerked up from the place he slumped beside the bed. "That's Paw!" he shouted, springing up and racing across the room to the door. He flung it open and dashed outside. "Paw! Paw!"

Through the door, Addie could see Perlie Overby striding toward the house, bellowing at the top of his lungs. He paused as the boy dashed toward him.

"Hold on there, boy! You're liable to knock—"

The two went down in a tangle as the son flung himself at his father. "Paw, the man said you was drowned! He said you was drowned in the Suck!"

"Well, I ain't," said Perlie, "so git up offa me before I jerk a knot in your tail!"

By this time the older girl was rushing outside, and the toddler was standing in the door, once again whimpering in confusion.

"I wish somebody'd shut the door," Addie said, left in the chair with the nursing baby. Feeling the cold draft, she pulled the dirty quilt closer about the slurping infant.

The three Overbys shuffled closer to the open doorway. "Well, I was settin' a new trap down there on the other side of Moccasin Point, by Brown's Ferry," Perlie said to his tightly clinging offspring. "Right on the bank is where I was. The rocks is real mossy and slick right there at the edge, and just as I was a leanin' over to pull back the jaws of the trap, my foot slipped. I went down like a ton of bricks, made the biggest splash you ever heard, and my foot kicked the gunwale of the boat and knocked her just far enough out for the current to catch her, and by the time I could stand up and dump all the fish outta my pockets—whoa, now! Who's this here?"

Perlie stood in the doorway, one damp boot on the threshold. Peering into the dark interior of the shack, he straightened. "Well, I'll be! I believe that's Miss Addie, yonder!"

"Hello, Mr. Overby. Your wife came to the house and was real scared, so I told her I'd come tend the children while she went down to the docks."

Perlie had swept his battered plug hat off his head as he came inside.

He held it in both hands at chest level, like a shield. "Well, now, Miss Addie, that was mighty kind of you, mighty kind. I shore appreciate you watchin' the young 'uns, but this here old dirty place ain't a proper—"

"She told us you was all right, Paw," the boy said. "She told us all the time you was all right." He aimed an admiring look at Addie.

"Well, course I was all right," said Perlie, crumpling his hat between his fists. "Just got a little wet, is all. And I reckon I'll have to walk all the way down to the Suck now and get my johnboat back. And a course I lost a half-day's work and still got traps to check, but— Scuse me, Miss Addie! There I go, lettin' my mouth run off again, and you settin' there without a coat on. Boy! Go shut that door!"

"I'm all right, Mr. Overby, really."

"Now, Miss Addie, you just let me have that little 'un there, and you can go on back to your house, you hear?"

"Oh, I don't mind—"

"Nope. I'm back now, and I can tend my own young 'uns."

"But—you're wet! Don't you want to get some dry clothes on?"

Perlie shrugged and grinned. "Why, land's sakes, Miss Addie! These here's the only britches I got. They'll dry out directly. Come on, now, hand him over here."

"Paw, did you really catch fish in your pockets when you fell in?" the boy said.

"Why, course I did! But they was all too little to keep, so I put 'em back in till they was growed up some. Move on over now, boy, so Miss Addie can hand me your little brother."

Addie rose and offered the baby to his father, careful to keep the bottle in the hungry mouth. Perlie murmured and whispered to the tiny boy as he took him. Addie would never have suspected that the rough, tobacco-stained man could show such tenderness toward anything, but as he rocked and coddled the baby in his arms, she knew she wasn't needed any longer. Perlie sidled over to the chair and eased himself into it. The boy moved in beside him on one side, and the older girl on the other, while the toddler came between his knees and laid her head on his grimy, wet pant leg. Addie could see the baby's eyelids flutter, then droop closed.

"Well, if you're sure you don't need me," she whispered.

"No, you go ahead on," Perlie said in a low voice. "And take one a them quilts with you. That north wind's colder than gouge."

"No, I'll be all right," she said, glancing at the stained quilts piled on the floor. "I'll just leave, then. Bye."

"Bye, Miss Addie. I'm much obliged to you," he said.

As she walked toward the door, she heard him singing softly, but no more tunefully than before:

Upstairs, downstairs, out in the kitchen
Upstairs, downstairs, out in the kitchen
Upstairs, downstairs, out in the kitchen
See Uncle Bill just a-rarin' and a-pitchin', yes sir.
Hot corn, cold corn, bring along a demijohn . . .

CHAPTER
4

*T*he spanking two-wheeled sulky and neat-stepping bay were cost-
ing Zeb more than he cared to admit, but this weekend he wanted
to cut the best figure he could.

Zeb figured Addie's father was doing everything he could to throw a
wet blanket on their marriage. Surely Jacob Caswell wouldn't disinherit
his daughter for marrying outside the Methodist church. But lately
Addie's letters had dwelled more and more on his opposition. Zeb wondered if she was trying to let him down easy. Or maybe there was another
reason.

George Hutto, for example. Did he think Zeb didn't notice the way
his eyes lingered on Addie when they met in the street? And George
Hutto was here in Chattanooga, while Zeb was in Murfreesboro, trying
to improve his lot in life—and Addie's. George Hutto would solve Addie's
problems in neat fashion: the family was Methodist and old Deacon
Hutto had held onto the money he'd made. Unlike most of the leading
citizens of Hamilton County, he'd avoided wild speculation during the
panic of '93. Zeb had tried more than once to get an appointment with
old man Hutto to discuss financial matters, but was always bluntly
rebuffed.

Zeb pulled up in the yard of Post Oak Hollow Church. The
thrushes and blue jays were holding their own noisy prayer meeting in

the greening branches of the surrounding trees. He stepped down from the sulky and looped the reins over the hitching post, then turned to hand Addie down. He gave her his best smile. Her gaze slid across him without so much as a howdy.

Addie rested her hand on Zeb's arm as they walked toward the church door. He was working too hard at his good mood, and it made her nervous and aggravated at the same time. Why couldn't he just let her be? Since when did a person have to grin every time somebody else wanted her to?

The fact was, she was getting scared. She still honestly believed she loved Zeb, and when she was with him, things seemed to be the same as always. But it was so hard to remember that during the long weeks when he was in Murfreesboro and she was here. On the other hand, Papa's disapproval was every day. The silent drag pulled at her like a trotline weight.

Would Zeb stand up to everyday life? Till death do us part is a long time, she told herself as they went up the steps into the meeting house.

"Brother Zeb, good to see you!" said the toothy deacon at the door. "Say, could I get you to lead a prayer for us today?"

They found a seat just before the service started. Old Brother Houser stepped to the front. The congregation quieted amid the rustle and thump of hymnals grabbed from the racks on the backs of the pews. "Let's all get a song book and turn to number one-oh-five," he announced. He hummed to himself to get the starting pitch.

Have you been to Jesus for the cleansing pow'r?
Are you washed in the blood of the Lamb?
Are you fully trusting in his grace this hour?
Are you washed in the blood of the Lamb?

Brother Houser led out in his raspy warble, waving his right hand in the air to keep the time. The congregation chimed in by degrees.

Addie felt nervous, as if she could see and hear too much. The man seated behind her sang in a booming bass, almost on key. She could smell his tobacco-tinted breath, hear him belt out the words of the chorus.

Are you washed in the blood?
In the soul-cleansing blood of the Lamb?
Are your garments spotless,
Are they white as snow?
Are you washed in the blood of the Lamb?

She tried to concentrate on the words of the hymn, but she found her thoughts drifting toward the unseen man behind her. In her mind's eye, she constructed a vision that resembled Perlie Overby, with his stained, ragged clothing, his bushy beard, and his rough-hewn courtliness. As far as she knew, neither Perlie nor his family had ever darkened the doorway of any church. But the man sounded like Perlie Overby would, if Perlie were singing this hymn. Except maybe this man was a little closer to the tune.

Addie thought about the pitiful way Perlie and his family lived. And about the tender way he held his infant son, how he had crooned to him in his unmelodious voice. About the way the older children had gathered to him.

Addie realized her heart was pounding in double time. Why was she so restless today? She felt like one of the squirming children, impatient to be somewhere else, anywhere else. On the outside she was still, but inwardly she was fretting and hot and distracted.

A middle-aged man walked toward the front to lead the congregation in prayer. Dink Gilliam—he had a blacksmith shop and livery on the eastern edge of Chattanooga, just down the street from her father's store. Dink was a square-cut slab of a man with a thick neck bulging over the restraint of the buttoned white collar of his Sunday shirt. As he reached the pulpit and prepared to launch into his prayer, Addie could see the dirt between the split calluses on his fingers. He had a ruddy face and a wide-lipped mouth. "Let us pray," he said, ducking his head as if he was dodging something.

"Our father which art in heaven, we thank thee for this day, when we can come together to worship thee in spirit and in truth. We pray that thou'd bless us as we gather, and that all that's done here'd be pleasing and acceptable to thee . . ."

A little boy on the second row from the front began to fidget and fuss, but if Dink heard, his only sign was to raise his voice and plow ahead.

"Lord, we'd ask thee to bless the sick and afflicted wherever they may be, especially those of our number, that they might soon be returned to their muchly wanted health, if it be thy will, and if not, thy will be done in all things . . ."

The man behind her shifted in his seat and the pew creaked. Some man in the back of the church cleared his throat.

"Lord, we'd pray thy blessin's on Brother J. D. as he breaks unto us the bread of life. We'd ask that thou grant him a happy recollection of the things he's learned, and that we might take it into our hearts and apply it to our lives . . ."

A mud dauber wasp hummed through one of the open windows and buzzed among the open rafters.

"Lord, be with us now through the rest of this service and the rest of the day. We ask all these things in Jesus' name. Amen."

"Amen," chorused several of the men seated about her. Dink, looking relieved, made his way back to his seat, and Brother Houser returned to the front. "Number twenty-three," he said.

Sing them over again to me,
Wonderful words of life;
Let me more of their beauty see,
Wonderful words of life . . .

The hymn concluded and J. D. Carson stood from the front row and took his place behind the pulpit. He had a shock of unruly brown hair, trimmed close on the sides of his head but blossoming in profusion everywhere else. His farmer's hands were rough and nicked, and his face was a weathered brown up to a line that ran just above his eyebrows. Above that, his forehead was stark white. His wife and two young daughters sat on the right-hand front pew.

"Brethren, it's good to be with you on this Lord's Day morning," he said. He flipped through the pages of his Bible to locate his text for the day. "I'm especially glad to see Sister Hawkins able to be back with us after her long sickness." He smiled and nodded toward an older woman seated in the second row on the aisle. Sister Hawkins gave a little cough into a crumpled handkerchief.

"This morning, brethren, I want to talk about last words. Some of you know what it means to say good-bye to a mother or a father. Some of you know about saying good-bye to a husband or a wife. And if you've ever said that final good-bye to someone like that, you know you'll always remember the last words that loved one spoke to you while they were here on this earth.

"Last words are something that can't ever be forgot, brethren, because they're the most important words we'll ever hear. They're important because of the person speaking 'em. They're important because of what that person means to us. And they're important because they're what stays with us. They're what we remember.

"Well, there's lots of last words in the Bible. This morning, I want to look at a few of those last words, and let's see what we can learn from 'em that might help us live more like the Lord wants us to . . ."

Addie's vision drifted in the empty air just above the preacher's head. She was remembering the last hours of her mother. Mama had languished for months as the cancer gnawed at her vitals. There was nothing Dr. Phipps could do for her but gradually increase the dosage of morphine. One day in summer, Mama sent for her. Addie could still see the brilliant June sky as it had appeared through the window of Mama's room, could still hear the fluting of the mockingbirds and cardinals in the trees outside.

But the warmth and gaiety of summer halted at Mama's windowpane. Her sickness dimmed the sunlight to a dull haze as it came inside. Mama lay propped up against the headboard of her bed, a dried-out husk. Every so often a spasm took her and her eyes would squint with the pain. Her hair hung dank and limp. Her eyes were dulled by the torture of the disease and the drugs that sometimes held the misery at bay. Addie went to her bedside and took her hand. Mama opened her eyes and looked at her for a long time before saying anything.

"Addie, honey. Pull my curtains for me, would you, darling? The light hurts my eyes." Her voice was a gray glimmer of what it had once been.

"Yes, Mama."

"Sweetheart," Mama said, "I want you to know how much I love you."

"Yes, ma'am. I love you, too, Mama."

Mama had patted her hand—once, twice. Her palm felt pasty and insubstantial. Addie wanted to cry, but Mama was trying to say something else. Addie leaned closer to catch the whisper.

"Addie . . . take care of your papa. He'll need you more than ever when I'm . . . gone."

It hadn't occurred to Addie to question Mama's words. Or perhaps she had been too grieved to take issue, to make the weary, obligatory protest against her mother's assessment.

"Yes, ma'am."

Mama died that night, during the wee hours. Addie was thirteen. She could still feel the knot of anguish she carried in her chest for months and months afterward. If she hadn't had Rose's ample lap to cry into, she probably couldn't have survived at all. The colored maid seemed to know when Addie was longing most for her mother. Addie could still feel Rose's warm, dry hand gathering and sifting her hair, rubbing along the back of her neck, patting her shoulders.

"Hush, now, baby," Rose said. "Your mama with Jesus, honey. You can make it. It just take time, baby. It just take time."

Addie could still smell the starch in Rose's apron, could still remember its feel against her cheek as she wet it with her tears.

She tried to remember a time when she had been able to share her grief with Papa, but there was nothing to remember.

Take care of your papa . . . Last words. Impossible words.

J. D. Carson held his open Bible aloft. "So when Joshua had all the people of Israel gathered together, he gave them a speech. And what did he say? He said this, brethren: 'Choose you this day whom ye will serve; whether the gods which your fathers served that were on the other side of the flood, or the gods of the Amorites, in whose land ye dwell: but as for me and my house, we will serve the LORD'—Joshua twenty-four and verse fifteen."

J. D. lowered his Bible. "Mighty strong words, brethren, and a question that still bears asking: 'Choose you this day whom ye will serve.' Think about it. Who are you gonna serve? God? Or something else?"

Zeb nodded, his eyes fastened on J. D. He hoped Addie was listening. J. D. was a little rough around the edges, but he was sincere, and Zeb knew where he was headed with this first point. Addie needed to decide if she was going to continue to serve her family's traditions or follow the truth of the Bible as he'd tried to lay it out for her. He tried hard to be patient with her, tried not to force too much on her at once. But often he despaired of ever winning her completely from the domination of her father's sectarian attitude.

Sometimes he wondered why it was so hard for people to agree on what the Bible said about things that seemed so plain. As a boy, he'd assumed it was just because folks hadn't had the opportunity to hear the truth. But now, he knew that some people were just too attached to their own traditions to turn loose, even when they'd had the chance to listen to correct doctrine being taught.

He remembered once, when he was a boy, being at the feed store with Daddy on a Saturday morning in midwinter. It was a year or two before Daddy died, he remembered. A bunch of men were gathered around the stove, and Zeb was eyeing the horehound candy in a jar on the counter. The men were talking low and lazy. Then, for whatever reason, the subject of religion came up.

"By the way, Gus," one of them said to Daddy, "ain't you one a them Campbellites? Outfit that believes you're the only ones goin' to heaven?"

The lull in the talk by the stove pulled Zeb's attention from the candy jar, drew his eyes to his father's face. Daddy was staring into the grate of the stove, a little smile on his lips. But his eyes weren't smiling. "Now, Shep," he said, "that ain't exactly a fair way to put it—"

"Why not?" said one of the others. "That's what I've always heard about y'all too—that everyone that don't believe the same way y'all do about everything is going to hell."

There was a silence. The inside of the feed store, so cozy only moments before, had suddenly become uncertain, menacing.

"Tell you what, boys," Daddy said, "I ain't sure what minded y'all to get on this subject, but . . ." He shifted on the nail keg where he was seated. He glanced at them, then back to the orange glow in the stove grate. "It's true that we believe the Bible teaches a right way to do things. And we believe that folks ought to try to—"

"Try to do everything like y'all do, right?" said one of the men. "Ain't that what you're trying to say, without saying it? That y'all have figured out what the Bible says, and anybody that don't agree with you is wrong?"

"Say, now, fellas," said John Hatchell, the store owner. "It's winter, all right, but I don't believe we need this much heat inside here, do y'all?"

Daddy gave Mr. Hatchell a grateful glance. The others left off at that, but Zeb still remembered how, just a few minutes later, he and Daddy loaded their ground sorghum onto the wagon and drove back out to the house, huddled against the cold. Daddy kept quiet all the way home. And Zeb never said anything about the horehound.

Those men were the type J. D. was talking about. They weren't interested in hearing the true word of God. They were only interested in guarding what they already knew—whether it was right or not. Men like Addie's father.

"Now, then. Take a look over in the book of Acts, the twentieth chapter and verse twenty-eight. The apostle Paul is just about to leave for Jerusalem, and he knows he'll never again see the Christians at Ephesus. A course he's sad about that, and they are, too, but even more important, he's got some things he needs to tell 'em. Some things they need to know to keep their faith sound, 'cause Paul knows there's plenty of trouble ahead. Listen to what he says . . ."

Trouble ahead. Addie wondered if J. D. had just given her a private prophecy. Sometimes she thought Zeb had no appreciation at all for the sacrifice he was asking her to make. It looked as if he thought her joining his church was no more rigorous than changing the style of her hat.

Oh, she knew he took his faith seriously. And there was no question of his devotion to the teachings of the Bible as he understood them. But he acted as if she should just immediately see things the way he did. As if his views were so self-evidently correct that only a simpleton or a reprobate would reject them. As if it were that easy to turn her back on her upbringing. On Papa. She knew Papa was neither a simpleton nor a reprobate. Where did he fit into Zeb's scheme of things?

She thought just maybe she had a clearer idea of the size of her step of faith than Zeb did. She knew he meant to be there for her no matter what happened, but it wasn't the same for him; he wasn't closing a door on anything. And she didn't think he had the slightest idea how she felt about it. He was asking her to give away her entire world and accept a world she didn't know anything about. If Zeb was right about everything, God would make it all come out, somehow. But what if Zeb was wrong? And even if he was right, would God give her back the family, the past, she would lose?

Mama, I wish you were here. I need to talk to you right now.

"'. . . for I know this, that after my departing shall grievous wolves enter in among you, not sparing the flock. Also'—now get this, brethren—'*of your own selves* shall men arise, speaking perverse things, to draw away disciples after them.'" J. D. lowered the Bible, his brow furled. "Brethren, we sure need to pay attention to what Paul is saying here. He's saying that not only will false teachers come from outside the church, they'll also come from inside. There's not any of us that's immune to error, brethren. We got to study and pray, and watch ourselves all the time, to make sure we stay pleasing to the Lord . . ."

Zeb recrossed his legs and fussed with the knot in his tie. He flicked an imaginary speck of lint from his trousers and glanced at the rafters above J. D.'s head, where a mud dauber made lazy forays against the wood. From the corner of his eye, he glanced at Addie, sitting so still beside him in her high-collared dress and flower-trimmed hat. Before he could forbid it, a vision sprang into his mind: he was wrapping her in a passionate embrace, her face turned up to his, her eyes closed, her lips parted in rapture. His chest constricted in a rush of tenderest desire.

He pulled himself back toward the present. It wouldn't do to torture himself with dreams of what wasn't yet to be—what might not happen at all, he thought. Besides, this wasn't the time and place for daydreaming. He needed to be paying attention to the sermon.

J. D. was right. You had to stay on guard. If you didn't, you might drift into error and sin, like countless thousands throughout the ages. God was merciful and good, but he still had certain expectations. He gave his will to men in the pages of the Bible, and he expected obedience. Obedience wasn't an easy matter. It was like walking a greased plank, and you had to give it all you had to keep your balance. Fine and dandy for the Methodists and the Baptists to talk about God's grace and "once saved always saved," but Zeb knew the Bible also said that faith without works was dead—James two, twenty-six.

"Last of all, brethren, let's look in the Gospel of Mark, chapter sixteen." J. D. licked his thumb and turned several pages in his Bible. He scanned the page to find his place. "These are some of the last words the Lord spoke to his apostles before he went back up into heaven. Listen to what he says. 'Go ye into all the world, and preach the gospel to every creature. He that believeth and is baptized—' Let me repeat that last phrase, brethren. It says, 'He that believeth *and is baptized* shall be saved; but he that believeth not shall be damned.'"

Addie heard two older girls at the far end of the pew snickering into their hands as J. D. pronounced the closing word of the verse. Again she was conscious of her heart hammering against her breastbone. *He that believeth and is baptized.* What about she that believeth? She might be saved, but what then? And then she knew the true name of her vague agitation. It was the disguise she had constructed to cloak the anger she felt at Zeb, at her father, at herself, at the Church of Christ—even at Mama. It was the way she hid from herself her useless rage at the unfairness of everything and everyone that she cared about, her rage at her own inability to find a way to be completely happy. Why did it have to be so hard for her? Why did she have to be the one to reconcile comfort, truth, and love within herself? It was like trying to catch rain in a sieve. It was like trying to crochet with baling wire.

"Now, brethren," J. D. was saying, "we all know that there's lots of good folks out there in the sectarian world, lots of sincere folks who think they're following the Bible. But the Lord said 'he that *believeth* and is *baptized*,' in that order. It ain't enough to be sincere, brethren. You got to do right. Jesus said, 'Not every one that saith unto me, Lord, Lord, shall enter into the kingdom of heaven; but he that *doeth* the will of my Father which is in heaven,'—Matthew seven, twenty-one. And what is that will, brethren? Listen again to the Lord's last words: 'he that believeth and is baptized shall be saved . . .'"

Addie's mind was a stump in Zeb's pasture and he'd jammed a pry bar beneath it. With J. D.'s proof-texts as his fulcrum, he was prying, prying, trying to break her loose. Her thoughts of Papa screamed out against the dislocation, clung to the soil of her past with weakening tendrils. She felt as if everyone in Post Oak Hollow Church was staring at her. *Well, does she understand or not? When is she going to come around?*

"If you're here today and you're not a member of the Lord's church, you need to make it right," said J. D. "You need to come down front and confess Jesus as your Lord. We'll go this very hour down to Chickamauga Creek and baptize you for the forgiveness of your sins, and you'll be washed clean in the blood of the Lamb. If you're already a Christian and you haven't lived right, you need to come and ask for the prayers of the church. Whatever your need is today, won't you come forward this morning while we stand and sing?"

Brother Houser led into the altar call.

While Jesus whispers to you,
Come, sinner, come!
While we are praying for you,
Come, sinner, come . . .

Zeb felt Addie's hand on his arm. He glanced at her and he felt a thrill along his spine. She was moving past him, toward the center aisle! Was she at last going to make the commitment for which he'd pleaded these last months? Was she going down front to get baptized? If she was, that could only mean . . .

Addie's face felt hot. The inside of the church was a blur as she moved toward the aisle. She felt every eye on her as she sidled past Zeb and stepped into the center. With her hand covering the sob trying to escape from her lips, she strode down the aisle and out the back door of the church as the congregation sang the final words of the verse.

Now is the time to own Him:
Come, sinner, come!
Now is the time to know Him:
Come, sinner, come . . .

CHAPTER

5

❦

*T*he drive back to the Caswell homestead was as long as a dreaded chore, and very quiet.

Addie sat in the sulky and sobbed as the service wound to its conclusion. Zeb, of course, had stayed inside through the communion service and offering until the very end, to lead the final prayer requested of him. That suited Addie fine because she really didn't want to have to explain to him feelings she didn't fully understand herself.

When the congregation was finally dismissed, Zeb stepped briskly from the church door, striding toward the sulky. His expression was a mixture of embarrassment, concern, and confusion. But at that moment, Addie couldn't bring herself to care about what he was thinking. She was too busy with trying to organize and understand her own thoughts.

They were almost halfway back to Orchard Knob before either of them spoke.

"Addie—what's wrong?" Zeb finally blurted as they neared the one-lane bridge across Cellico Creek.

She shook her head and stared away from him, across the flats toward the Tennessee River, glittering in the noonday sun. She didn't know how to begin to tell him what she felt. Or maybe she was afraid of what she might say if she tried.

"Honey, I— Is it something I did that upset you?" he asked in a limp voice as they clattered over the tiny wooden bridge.

She turned in her seat and stared at him, unbelieving. Could he really be in some doubt about what was bothering her? Was he that blind? Again she could summon no words suitable to her purpose, and turned away.

After another eternity, they arrived at her house. He stopped the sulky in front of the porch steps just as Rose, still wearing her Sunday dress with a white apron tied around her waist, stepped out of the front door with a broom in her hand. As if the sulky and its occupants did not exist, she began methodically sweeping the porch.

"Well . . . I, uh . . . I wonder what's for dinner today?" Zeb stammered into the stony silence.

For the first time since leaving the church house, Addie found her voice. "I don't think you'd better come in for dinner today, Zeb," she said, staring straight ahead. "I think you might ought to go on back to Murfreesboro for awhile. I . . ." Her tone wavered, then caught again. "I think it might be best if we didn't see each other for awhile." She placed her hand on his arm to steady herself, then caught up her skirts as she stepped down from the sulky.

"Do what?" he asked, incredulous. "Addie, why won't you tell me what—"

But she had already gone up the steps and was crossing the porch and reaching for the front door. And then, as he stared after her, she was inside, and gone.

Rose grunted softly as she placed the platter of fried chicken in the center of the table. She glanced at Mr. Caswell, then backed into the corner and bowed her head.

Jacob glanced at Addie, who sat listlessly in her chair, staring at a vacant corner of the dining room.

"Shall we pray? Our gracious heavenly Father, we thank thee for this thy bounty that we are about to receive, and for all thy many blessings. Amen."

Reaching for a thigh piece, Jacob again glanced at his daughter. "Where's your beau? He not joining us today?"

For a long moment he thought she hadn't heard him. "What's that, Papa?" she responded, finally. "Oh, Zeb . . . No, he's not coming in today. He . . . he had to go on back to . . . to Murfreesboro."

Jacob received this news with a lift of his eyebrows. He spooned a heavy dollop of mashed potatoes onto his plate and reached for the bowl of cream gravy.

"Guess maybe he decided Methodist chicken was off his menu."

Addie stared sharply at her father, then turned away. She grabbed for the bowl of green beans and flicked a spoonful onto her plate.

Rose poured buttermilk into Jacob's glass from a large crockery pitcher. "Rose, pass me that plate of corn while you're here, would you?" he said. He selected an ear from the platter.

"Still, I guess it makes sense. After all, there ain't nothing in the Bible that says it's all right to eat fried chicken on Sunday."

"Papa!" Addie flung her napkin from her lap and vaulted to her feet, glaring at him.

"What? I was just making conversation, is all. Nobody else at the table seemed to much want to talk to me."

"Neither one of you understands a thing! Not a blessed thing!" Addie whirled about and knocked over her chair as she stomped into the hallway and up the stairs.

Jacob stared after her. As Addie's footsteps pounded up the staircase, he peered questioningly at Rose, who returned his look with a flat, judging glint in her eye.

"What did I say, Rose?" he asked. "I was just going on; she knows that, doesn't she?"

Rose moved to Addie's place and began removing her plate and silverware. "Ain't what you said," the black woman replied without looking at him. "That child beggin' you for help, but you ain't listenin'."

The train ride back to Murfreesboro barely registered in Zeb's consciousness. He felt as if he were in a black, muffled box, and the sounds and sights of the outside world reached him only as vague bumps and muted murmurs.

He couldn't believe Addie was going to call it quits with him. He just couldn't bring himself to accept it. And the hardest part of it all was that he didn't have the faintest notion what had set her off. The more he thought about it, the more maddening it became.

On Monday morning, he flung himself into the work of the agency: canvassing residential and commercial districts for prospects, going on appointments with junior agents, making calls on policy holders who were late with premium payments. He kept himself busy, trying to crowd out the numb place at the center of his chest.

But it was no use. When he went back to his boarding house at night, the answerless questions came rushing back to nag at him. He followed them round and round inside his head, mesmerized by the pain and confusion like a bird charmed by a snake. Some of the other bachelors at the house invited him to join them at their evening roisters, but Zeb had no taste for such activity, even if his convictions had permitted it. Instead, he sat in his room and read the psalms of lament from his Bible and tortured himself with his impossible longing.

The year turned the corner into May, and an unseasonable hot spell settled down onto Chattanooga like an unexpected visit from a free-loading relative. Addie spent her days searching for a cool draft and her nights tossing on sweat-dampened sheets. You expected to be hot and distracted by, say, mid-July or August. But in May you expected to be enjoying cool night breezes and days just warm enough to make a glass of lemonade taste really good. But these days, a glass of lemonade didn't seem to do anything but emphasize the discomfort.

She sat on the front porch one morning, already worn out from fanning herself. She heard the telephone rattle, just inside the front door. It was still a new enough sound to startle her. This past spring Papa had grudgingly placed the order and had the line run out from the nearest trunk, in Orchard Knob. Addie puffed a stray lock of hair out of her face and pushed herself up out of the rocking chair.

She reached the apparatus, pulled the black earpiece from its brass hook, and stood on tiptoe to get her mouth near the mouthpiece.

"Hello? Who's there?"

"Addie? Is that you?"

Addie thought she recognized Louisa's voice through the static. "Yeah, Lou, it's me. How are you?"

"Fine, honey. Can you come over this afternoon? I'm having a quilting—" Louisa's voice dissolved in a burst of static and electric squeals, and Addie waited patiently until the noise on the line subsided.

"—someone to watch the babies so I can get everything done," Louisa was saying.

"When did you say you wanted me to come over?" Addie said, mentally filling in the gaps.

"Sometime this afternoon, if you can."

"All right. I'll see you after lunch. Bye." She hung up the earpiece without waiting to hear Louisa's farewell. As bad as the lines were, it probably wouldn't have mattered anyway.

Louisa and Dub had recently moved to the newly fashionable Cameron Hill neighborhood. When Addie stepped down from the horse-drawn trolley at the foot of the hill where they lived, she was already drenched in perspiration. By the time she had climbed to the top of the street, she thought she might drown standing up.

The door swung open. "Hi, Aunt Addie."

It was Robert, her sister's oldest. The six-year-old grabbed her around the waist in a fierce hug. Patting his back, Addie asked, "Where's your mama?"

"She's in the carriage house, looking for her parasol. We're going to town! And you're coming with us!"

Some time later, they trooped inside the open doorway of Peabody's Dry Goods Emporium on Market Street.

"Now, Robert," Louisa said, "you keep your hands to yourself while we're in here. I don't need you handling every string of licorice in the store, you hear?"

"Yes, ma'am." The boy made a beeline for the candy counters.

Louisa shook her head as she shifted the baby from the crook of one arm to the other. "That young 'un says all the right things, but I don't think he listens to himself."

Little Katherine tugged on Addie's hand. "Aunt Addie, can we go look at the bowth and thingth?"

"Sure, honey. Just let's keep our hands to ourselves, all right?" The four-year-old nodded solemnly.

"I hate not going to Papa's store anymore," Louisa said as they moved among the bolts of cloth and barrels of molasses and other staples stacked on the pine-planked floor. "But it's just so far over there from where we— Robert Eugene Dawkins! What did I just tell you?"

Robert yanked his hand away from the lid of the jar holding the peppermint sticks. He rubbed his palm on his backside as he peered over his shoulder at his mother.

"Well, anyway," Louisa said as she began inspecting a stack of bunting, "how's Papa these days?"

"Oh, he's . . . fine, I guess." Addie hoisted Katherine up so she could see the satin bows on the top shelf of the glass display. "I . . . I don't talk to him much these days."

"You spoken to Zeb since last time?"

Addie shook her head.

Mr. Peabody approached. He wore black sleeve garters and sported a pencil in the band that held his eye patch in place. He had lost an eye during the siege of '63, and for as long as Addie could remember, there had been a persistent rumor among the children of Chattanooga that he led a secret life as a pirate. The chance of maybe seeing what really lay beneath the patch, along with his well-stocked candy cases, drew many a young boy into his establishment.

"Can we help you with some bunting today, Mrs. Dawkins?"

"How much is this a yard?"

He peered at the material. "Believe it's twenty cents."

"All right, let me have . . . five yards, I guess."

"Yes, ma'am." He went behind the counter to get a pair of shears.

"Well, Addie, you're going to have to tell Zeb something before too much longer. Your wedding is announced for June, and—"

"I know, I know," Addie said. "What else do you think I've been doing the last few weeks, except going round and round about all this? Oh, Lou! I don't know what to do!"

"About Zeb, or about the church?" Louisa said. She picked up a paper sack and started shoveling navy beans into it from the bin where they now stood.

"It's all the same thing, Lou," Addie said. "I can't marry Zeb unless I'm willing to join the Church of Christ. I can't just decide on marrying the man I love—I have to marry his church too. And you know what that'll mean. It's just too much for me to think about. Have you . . . have you talked to Bob or Junior about this at all? What do they think about it?"

Louisa set the sack on the scales, noted the weight, then placed it on the counter. "Two and a half," she said to Mr. Peabody, who waited, pad in hand. He scribbled down a figure. She turned back to her younger sister.

"Well, Addie, they feel kind of the same way I do. The boys think you've got to make up your own mind about this and do what you think is right. Junior says you ought to pray about it." Junior was the oldest brother, the lay minister.

"Don't think I haven't been," Addie said. "And I keep waiting for God to give me an answer. But he just listens, I guess. So far, I don't feel any closer to knowing what to do."

"Addie, maybe he's waiting for you to decide. Maybe he doesn't care which way you go on this, just so you give yourself the go-ahead, one way or the other."

"Lou! That almost sounds—blasphemous!"

"Why? Getting married is an honorable thing, and not getting married is too. Why should God care which one you do, as long as you get on with it and quit bothering him about it?"

Addie stared at her sister. "Well, Lou," she said finally, "this is my life, and things don't look so cut and dried from where I stand." She whirled away and stalked to the other side of the store. "Robert," she called in warning to her nephew who stood, fingers twitching in desire, before the toy shelves, "you better not mess with that stuff. Remember what your mama said."

Louisa made several more selections and waited for Mr. Peabody to figure the total. She signed her ticket and gave instructions for the goods to be delivered that afternoon. They were almost halfway back to the house, trudging with the children up the side of Cameron Hill, before anything else was said.

"Oh, I'm sorry, Addie," Louisa said. "I didn't mean to sound so hard and all. I just wish you could get on with your life, either way. That's all I meant."

Addie took several steps before answering. "I know. You're just trying to help. Everybody's just trying to help, though. Well . . . almost everybody. That's part of what makes it so hard—"

At that moment, George Hutto came around the corner, headed straight toward them down the hill. He walked in his usual slow gait, his eyes on the ground in front of his feet, but since they were downhill from him, they came into his field of vision anyway. He glanced up at them and, seeing Addie, stopped in his tracks. After a moment, he swept his bowler from his head.

"Hello, Mrs. Dawkins," he said. "Hello . . . Addie."

"Hello, George!" Louisa said in a hearty voice. "How are you today, other than it being too hot?"

"Yes, ma'am, it is awful hot, isn't it?" He was answering Louisa, but his eyes stayed on Addie as she bore down on him.

"Hello," Addie said, following her words with a curt nod. She never broke stride as she drew even with him and then she was past, marching up the hill like Sherman through Georgia.

"Aunt Addie, slow down!" said Katherine, trailing along at the end of Addie's arm like a dinghy on a tow rope.

As she strode up the hill toward her sister's house, Addie knew what she must do. As much as she hated to admit it, Lou was right. It was time to quit mealymouthing. It was time to do something.

Addie stared long at the letter she held in her hand. Then, with elaborate care, she blotted it and folded it and slid it into an envelope. She sealed the flap and carefully inscribed Zeb's name and the address of his Murfreesboro boarding house. Before she could change her mind again, she walked quickly to the postal clerk's window and purchased the two-cent stamp that would take her missive to its destination.

CHAPTER
6

May 28, 1899

My Dearest Zeb,

    I hope you can find it in your heart to forgive me for seeming so cruel in dismissing you last month. I assure you it was not done with malice or without extreme soul-searching on my part. Since then, I have shed many tears and spent much time in prayer. Zeb, I have decided that we should marry without further delay, if you still will have me. I do not think that we should wait until the announced date in June as I am not sure my nerves can withstand the tension of the weeks involved. I hope you will not think me immodest or forward in this. I realize this may rush things a bit, but I truly believe it will be best to have the entire business done at the earliest opportunity.

    Awaiting your quick reply, I am

Your own,
Adelaide M. Caswell

The window squeaked against its track. Addie winced. Slowly, with many glances over her shoulder, she raised it as high as it would go. A cool puff of night air brushed against her cheek, and the insects' chorus trebled in volume. She hoisted her carpetbag to the sill and eased it out onto the roof of the front porch. Moving as stealthily as her skirts would allow, she climbed through the window and onto the shake-shingled roof. She turned around to close her window, then changed her mind. *Let them find it open. They'll know soon enough anyway.*

She looked around. The stillness and the moonlight turned the home place into an old-fashioned daguerreotype, frozen in place for this silent moment, for her eyes only. Something to be looked at. To stand outside of.

Moving out to the edge of the roof, she reached cautiously around the corner of the house and felt her fingers slide over Papa's fifteen-foot ladder. Normally the ladder stayed farther along the side of the house, but she had been inching it toward the front porch over the past several days. She dragged the ladder to her, careful not to allow it to bump the side of the house. She dropped the carpetbag over the side of the porch roof. It thumped into the thick bluegrass of the side yard. She held her breath, waiting for one of the dogs to bark, or for the front door to open below her. After maybe a minute, she swung herself onto the ladder.

Reaching the ground, she gripped the handle of the carpetbag and set off toward the hill behind the house. There was a three-quarter moon, plenty of light for her to find the path that led over the shoulder of the hill and down toward the river road. As the carpetbag's weight dragged at her shoulder, she half-regretted telling Zeb she'd meet him by the old abandoned springhouse on the river road. This was the only way though. If Zeb had tried to slip up close to the house, the dogs would've raised Cain.

"Kinda late for a stroll, ain't it?"

The voice came from just inside the tree line, ahead and to her left. A figure stepped out into the moonlight.

It was Papa.

She stopped, her body ramrod-stiff. Her fist gripped the handle of the carpetbag so tightly that her fingernails dug into her palms.

"I expect you're going to meet your fella," he said. Her tongue seemed locked behind her teeth. Finally, she nodded her head.

He snorted, shoving his hands into his pockets. He looked away from her.

"How'd you know?"

"Ladders don't walk down the wall by themselves," he said without looking at her.

A long hush grew stale and heavy between them.

"I'm glad your mama didn't live to see this happen," he said. His voice sounded strange.

"Papa, that's not fair," she said, barely controlling her voice. "What Mama asked me to do—it was too much."

"What are you talking about?"

"I did my best, Papa, but you—" She swayed with the effort of holding in the sob that needed to be released. "I did my best to take care of you, but you— You didn't want to be taken care of. You didn't want to understand or listen."

"Addie, I don't know what you're—"

"I've got to make my own way now, Papa," she said through clenched teeth. "I can't live your life anymore, nor Mama's. I've got to live my own now. Try to see that. Try to understand."

They stared at each other for a moment that lasted forever. And then she walked past him, toward the hillside.

"Addie, I hope you understand what's going to happen."

"You do what you think is best, Papa," she said without turning around or breaking her stride. "And I'll do the same." Squaring her shoulders, she strode into the shadows beneath the trees.

Jacob watched her go until the trees hid her from him. Then he crumpled to his knees and held his face in his hands.

Zeb was waiting at the agreed place. He beamed at her as she came out of the trees, and she did her best imitation of happiness as she lifted the carpetbag up to him. She didn't start crying until the buggy was moving down the road toward Chattanooga.

"What's the matter, honey?" Zeb asked. He pulled up the horse and turned toward her.

"Papa," she said through her sobs. "He caught me leaving."

"Addie, did he hurt you?"

She shook her head. "He didn't try to stop me. It's just hard, Zeb. It's real hard."

He placed his hands on her shoulders. "Addie, look at me. Honey, look at me. I'm going to take care of you now. You aren't in your father's house anymore. You're going to be my wife, and I'm going to do right by you. You hear me?"

After a second or two, she nodded her head.

"All right, then. I want you to dry those eyes and stop worrying. It's gonna be all right, honey. Do you believe me?"

Another pause, and then she nodded.

"You sure you believe me?"

She nodded again, sooner this time.

"All right. Then how about a smile. Just a little one, huh?" He chucked her lightly under the chin. At last he coaxed a quavering half-smile from her. "There you go. Now you just sit back and let's get into town and find the preacher, all right?"

They drove into town to the house of a minister that Zeb knew. Addie would have preferred that J. D. Carson perform the ceremony since she at least knew him slightly, but it was seven or eight miles to his place over by Harrison.

Though the man was about to retire for the evening, he agreed to perform the ceremony. His wife witnessed. The impromptu wedding party gathered in the small parlor of the minister's house, the minister's four nightgowned children ranging big-eyed in the background, and Zeb and Addie were joined in matrimony.

With Zeb's first kiss still moist on her lips, she turned to the minister and said, "Now I need another favor. I want you to baptize me."

The man stared at her, at Zeb, then at his wife.

"Well, Arliss," his wife said, "didn't you hear the young woman?"

"Of course I heard her, Mother," he said. "But I don't know anything about this . . . situation." He looked at Zeb. "Does she understand what she's doing?"

Zeb looked at Addie, and his smile was as wide as she'd ever seen. But as he opened his mouth to answer the preacher, Addie said, "Yes, sir, I believe I do. I'd like to be baptized. Tonight."

Half an hour later, Zeb was holding aloft a coal-oil lamp and watching with the minister's wife as Addie and the minister stepped gingerly into the waters of the Tennessee River below the Walnut Street bridge. Addie was wearing an old shift that the minister's wife had found in a trunk.

Addie stared at the blackness of the water and tried not to shiver as it rose higher and higher up her legs; stared at it, trying to read some message there. But it was only water, and it was night. The lamp Zeb held aloft glimmered and rippled on the surface, and it seemed to her that its faint light only darkened the unseen. It was only water. But she was here now, and it was too far back to the bank. Much too far.

They waded out until the waters reached to their waists, and the minister turned toward Addie. He murmured a few instructions. He placed one hand on her shoulder.

"Addie, do you believe that Jesus Christ is the Son of God, and that he died for your sins and rose on the third day to ascend to the right hand of God?"

"Yes, I do."

He raised his other hand. "Then, because of your confession of faith, I now baptize you in the name of the Father and the Son and the Holy

Ghost, for the remission of your sins and that you might receive the gift of the Holy Ghost." He placed one hand between Addie's shoulder blades and cupped the other over her hands, covering her face. He tilted her backwards into the dark, swirling water and then raised her up again. She gasped as she came out of the water, then began wiping the water and hair out of her face. She felt the minister take her arm. He led her back toward the bank.

Zeb handed the lamp to the minister's wife and stepped into the water to meet her.

"Zeb! Your boots!"

"Never mind about that." He took her into his arms.

Some moments later, after hugs and smiles all around, they climbed into the minister's buggy. Addie was wrapped in the towels they had brought.

"Where will you go?" the minister's wife asked.

Addie looked at Zeb. She just now realized that she hadn't given the first thought to where they'd spend their first night as man and wife.

"Well, I believe we'll go spend a little time in Nashville," Zeb said after a few seconds. "Then, I guess we'll go back to Murfreesboro. I'm in the insurance business there." Zeb fished a business card out of his vest pocket and handed it to the minister's wife.

"Well," she said, beaming at them, "it's a fine way to begin your lives together—with a new birth into Christ! I'm so happy and proud for you both."

"Thank you, ma'am," Zeb said. He grinned from ear to ear as he pulled Addie closer to him.

There was no train out of Chattanooga until morning. Addie knew they'd have to stay in a hotel, but she was surprised when Zeb pulled up in front of the gleaming, just-completed Patten. The yellow glow from the lobby's electric lights gave her a feeling of comfort as Zeb helped her down from the buggy.

They went inside. Addie was at once taken aback and thrilled to hear

Zeb casually inform the desk clerk that he needed a room for the night for Mr. and Mrs. Z. A. Douglas.

She tried the name in her mind. *Mrs. Zebediah Douglas. Addie Douglas. Adelaide Caswell Douglas.* She smiled, savoring the newness, the adventure of it. The bellboy came and collected their bags, and the clerk handed Zeb a gleaming brass skeleton key. "Room two-twelve," he said. "Top of the stairs and halfway down the hall to your left."

Addie stirred and woke. There was a momentary sense of dislocation as she stared at the unfamiliar ceiling. A movement in the bed caused her to turn her head and see Zeb's back and shoulders, still rising and falling in sleep.

For a few seconds everything seemed unreal, off-kilter. *What am I doing here? Am I really supposed to be in bed with Zeb, really supposed to be married? Is this my real life? How can I manage this?*

But then, as she lay still and allowed her waking to reorient her, she knew with a warm certainty that this was real, was her life; that Zeb was her husband—and that everything was just as it should be.

The wedding night was a rush of images and sensations—unfamiliar, anticipated, splendid, and dreaded, all at once. Louisa had told her some things, of course, and hinted at others. But she was still nervous about being alone with Zeb, her ignorance of what was expected of her.

But Zeb was so gentle, so loving. As his arms enfolded her and his lips pressed against her face, her hair, her neck, she found herself worrying less about what should happen next than savoring what was happening now. Something bloomed inside her, responded with a warm uncoiling to Zeb's tender urgency. She knew, as they clung to each other, that she would give willingly whatever was required to sustain this timeless moment, this sudden need, this enfolding nowness.

There was pain, for which she was not quite prepared. But she almost laughed at the dismay on Zeb's face when she cried out. He was consoling almost to the point of silliness. "It's all right, honey," she said, gentling his concern with her voice, her arms, her hands. "I think it'll be better now." And it was.

Now, watching him sleep, she smiled at the memories. So many changes, so many things she had learned in the space of two weeks. She felt wise now, miles and ages away from the girl who hiked over the hill with her carpetbag in her hand. How could life come so far, so fast?

Zeb snorted and jerked. She reached over and patted his shoulder. He rolled over to face her.

"Good morning, Mrs. Douglas." He smiled, his eyes still half-lidded with sleep.

"Morning, sir. About time you woke up, I guess."

He raised himself on one elbow and looked at her.

"What? What's the matter?" she asked.

"Nothing. Nothing at all." He leaned over and kissed her on the forehead. "I'm just thinking about how lucky I am, that's all."

She felt her face go warm. "Oh, Zeb. You better go on and get ready for work."

He placed his palm on her cheek and turned her face toward his.

"Zeb, what are you doing? You'll be late for work. Zeb, this isn't exactly the time—"

But it was, all the same.

Later, she sat in front of the mirror, basking in the afterglow as she brushed out her hair and listened to Zeb in the next room, whistling as he worked at his cravat.

"Zeb?"

"Yes, ma'am?"

"Do you think we might find us a little house to let? The folks here at the boarding house are nice and all, but . . . I guess I'm not used to so many people living all around me."

He came into the room, a thoughtful look on his face. "Well, now, Mrs. Douglas, I don't guess I'd thought about that. Not since last night on my way home, when I signed the papers on the cutest little bungalow you ever saw, just about three streets over."

"Zeb! Did you really find a place?"

A slow grin spread across his lips as he nodded.

It crossed her mind that she'd like to have seen the house before they were obligated. She hushed the thought and reached out to grab his hand. "You do beat all, Mr. Douglas! You sure do beat all!"

He held her hand a moment more, then went back into the next room.

"Better finish up, honey," he said. "It's almost seven o'clock. If we don't hurry up and get downstairs to the dining room, the grits'll all be gone."

Jacob Caswell trudged up the steps and into the offices of Haynes and Sutherland, Attorneys-at-Law. A clerk seated near the front door stood from behind his oak rolltop desk and extended a hand. "Good morning, Mr. Caswell! How can we—"

"Dan here today?"

"Uh—yes, sir, I believe so. Did you have an app—"

"Tell him Caswell's here and I need to see him right away."

The clerk excused himself and went through the low swinging gate in the banister that divided the front area from the lawyer's offices. Jacob heard the quiet knock, heard the creak of hinges, heard the low murmuring. He started walking toward the swinging gate while the clerk was still turning around to invite him in. He marched into Dan Sutherland's office and pulled the door shut behind him.

Dan Sutherland had just seated himself behind his massive mahogany desk when Jacob came in.

"Morning, Jacob. Nice to see you in such a good mood."

"I don't have time for your folderol today, Dan. I got something on my mind to do, and I want it done proper and quick."

Dan leaned forward in his chair as Jacob thumped into one of the chairs across the desk.

"Well, I can see you're in a hurry, Jacob, so why don't you just give me a quick once-over?"

Jacob reached into his inside coat pocket and produced a set of papers about a quarter-inch in thickness. He slapped the sheaf onto the inset leather pad atop Dan's desk. "That's a copy of the will you drew up for me after Mary died," he said, thumping the papers with his index finger. "I want it changed. Now."

CHAPTER

7

*T*he lawyer arched his eyebrows and leaned forward onto his elbows, bridging his fingertips together. "Well, all right, Jacob. What exactly did you want changed in here?"

Caswell huddled into himself for a spell.

"I want my youngest daughter written out of the will."

Dan made himself count to ten, then on up to fifteen, just for good measure.

"Jacob, you and I've known each other a long time, and you know good and well I don't often give my clients advice on much of anything outside the law. But I think you better be mighty careful about what you're fixing to do."

Caswell sat with his arms crossed on his chest.

"Now, Dan, I been all over this in my mind, so don't you start preaching to me about—"

"All I'm saying is that I've never seen any good come from something like this."

"Dan, I didn't come here to—"

"I know why you came, Jacob, and I'm trying to make you see sense, which would probably be a flat-out miracle. Don't worry, I won't charge you extra for the breath I waste on your bullheadedness."

By now both of them were half out of their chairs. Dan glared at Jacob for a few seconds, and Jacob finally blinked.

"Dan, she's betrayed the family," he said as he sank back into his seat. "She's ground her heel into her mother's memory, and she's turned her back on the way she was raised. I don't see why she ought to benefit from what belongs to the family when I'm gone."

Dan studied his fingernails. "Are you sure the rest of the family feels the same way you do?"

"I don't care what they feel!" Jacob slapped the desk and jumped to his feet. He stalked three paces toward the door, then whirled, aiming a finger at the attorney. "I'm the one that made the money! I'm the one that'll blamed well decide who gets it when I die."

"Now, you know I'm not much of a churchgoing man myself," Dan said, "but I'd be careful about making free with what's gonna happen when you die. The courts of Tennessee don't have jurisdiction in the sweet by-and-by—assuming that's where you end up."

"Fine one you are to be lecturing me about the hereafter," Jacob said, jamming his fists into his pockets. "Maybe I'll find me another lawyer who's willing to spend more time lawyering and less time preaching."

"That's up to you, Jacob. But you know all-fired well I'd be less than a friend if I didn't say what I thought about this."

"I hired a lawyer, not a friend."

Sutherland stared hard at the other man for a full fifteen seconds.

"No, I guess you're right, Jacob. You can hire a lawyer. But you sure as blazes can't hire a friend."

"Now, Dan, you know how I feel about strong language—"

"What did she do that was so unforgivable? Marry a hard-working, good-looking boy from over the state line? You'd disinherit her for that?"

"No! Not just for that! Is that all you think this is about? Well, let me tell you something, Dan. Let me just tell you something." Jacob was leaning on the desk, looking like he might leap across it into Dan's face.

"When Mary was on her deathbed, I made her a promise. I promised her I'd raise Addie the way we would've done it together. I—"

Jacob's mouth moved, but the words hung in his throat. The line of his lips blurred. Dan looked away.

"I told her I'd raise Addie to make her proud," Jacob said a few seconds later. He stared into a dark corner of the room. "It was the only promise I ever made to Mary that I didn't keep."

"Jacob, that's not true. You did the best you could. No one in Chattanooga that knows you would say otherwise. You provided for Addie, and you did your best by her—"

"And what thanks do I get? She runs off with some fella that looks more than half Cherokee—"

"Now, Jacob, there's not a family in Hamilton County that's been here very long that doesn't have a speck or two of Cherokee blood—"

"Who goes to some backwoods church that thinks folks like me are hell-bound! Well, no sir! I'll not have it! I'll not let her shame me and get by with it!"

Sutherland flung his hands in the air and came out from behind his desk. He strode to his door and opened it.

"Jacob, I don't believe there's anymore I can do for you today. If you want to estrange yourself from your own flesh and blood, I can't stop you. But I won't be a party to it!"

Jacob Caswell's eyes bulged, his face flooded with crimson. He snatched the will in his fist and stalked from the office. He strode past the clerk and slammed the door, making the window panes shudder.

"Mr. Caswell! You forgot your hat!" the clerk said.

"Let him go," said Dan from the doorway of his office. "Man that hotheaded got little enough use for a hat anyway."

The ginger tom leaned against George Hutto's leg, and he glanced down, then back to the hull he held in his fingers. He maneuvered the piece through the bottleneck and settled it onto the wet glue on the platform inside.

Again the cat twined its body against his shin, giving a small, interrogative meow. George lifted the bottle to eye level and studied the alignment of the hull on the base. The man-o'-war was large enough that there was little margin for error. If the hull wasn't centered just right, the three masts might not have clearance. He kicked at the cat. "Cut it out, Sam."

But the cat rubbed against him again, then rose on its hind legs and placed its forepaws on his thigh. The cat flexed its claws just enough to let George feel the prick, all the while peering into his face.

George huffed and glared at the cat, then caught himself chuckling at the insistent expression on the feline face. "Well, you're not one to let a body ignore you, are you, fella?" George placed the bottle on the table and scratched the cat behind the ears. "All right. I'll let you out, if nobody else will."

As he reached the bottom of the staircase, he pulled his watch from his vest pocket. Ten minutes to two. Almost time to walk back down to the office. He unrolled his shirt sleeves and fished his cufflinks out of the other vest pocket. He went through the kitchen to the back door, unlatched the screen to let the cat outside, then walked back into the parlor to fetch his jacket from the armchair.

It was nice and cool inside the house. He dreaded the thought of the hot walk downtown and the dreary afternoon in the office. He sometimes could have sworn the columns in his ledger grew when he wasn't looking.

He stepped to the doorway of the library and peered into the darkened room. Mother was dozing in one of the leather armchairs. He turned to go and a board squeaked under his foot.

"George, honey? That you?"

"Yes, ma'am. I'm going back now."

"All right, dear. Ask Mamie to come in here before you go, would you?"

"Yes, ma'am." He settled his panama on his head and walked down the hall toward the front door. Mamie was dusting the crystal in the sitting room, singing quietly to herself.

"Mamie, Mrs. Hutto needs you in the library, please."

"Yessuh. She be wanting her headache powders, I imagine. Bye, Mister George."

The first person George saw when he reached the office was Matthew Capshaw. He and Daddy had known each other since they served on opposite sides in the Civil War. He never tired of telling the story of how he and Daddy had met. He was doing it now, in fact.

"Yep, me and old Hutto was in the war together," Uncle Matt said, "but one of us—I won't say who—was wearin' the wrong colors."

George felt sorry for the young man Uncle Matt had trapped. He was a courier for one of the Nashville firms they dealt with. In fact, George could have sworn Uncle Matt had told this same fellow this same story within the last year. Uncle Matt had a hard time remembering whom he had favored with which one of his tales. Most likely it wouldn't have mattered anyway; when Uncle Matt took a notion to tell a story, there wasn't much you could do.

"Well, like I was sayin', I was on picket duty, back in the fall of '63 durin' the siege. It was late at night, you see, and I was wore plumb down to a nub. I'm a-leanin' up against a tree—big ol' elm, I believe it was— and I say, kinda out loud, but talkin' to myself, I say, 'Lordy, I'd give a five-dollar gold piece for a chaw a tobacco.' And then this voice from the dark says, 'Well, here, soldier. I'll give you a chaw, and I won't charge you but six bits.'" Uncle Matt slapped his knee and guffawed.

George smiled politely, trying to slip around Uncle Matt and the courier. As he walked past, Elizabeth, Uncle Matt's youngest daughter, rounded the corner from the back with an armful of file folders. She rammed into George, spilling the folders onto the floor.

"Oh, my goodness! I'm sorry, George, I didn't see you!"

"No, it's my fault, Betsy. I should've been watching where I was going." He knelt down and began scooping up the scattered sheets of foolscap.

Uncle Matt barreled ahead. "Well, when I heard that voice out of the dark thataway, I like to of—" He broke off, glancing at the figure of his daughter. "Well, anyhow . . . I was mighty startled. And then this ol' boy comes towards me and I can see he's wearin' blue. 'Here you go, soldier,' he says to me. 'Unless you're afraid to take a bite from a Union plug.' And that was how me and ol' Hutto met, and I still ain't convinced him the North was just luckier than the South . . ."

George handed Betsy the last handful of papers. As she reached to take them, the backs of their hands brushed. "Thank you, George," she said.

Her voice stopped him. It sounded low and buttery. George knew she was looking at him. He felt the blood burning his cheeks. Without meeting her eyes, he touched the brim of his panama and retreated quickly to his tiny office at the back of the warehouse.

He removed his hat and coat and filled his pen from the inkwell at his desk. The problem of Betsy Capshaw tugged at his mind. She was a dozen years his junior, and he had always thought of her pretty much like a younger sister. But in the last few years it had become more and more difficult to ignore the fact that she didn't reciprocate his perception.

He was at a loss about how to discourage her and spare her feelings at the same time. He'd thought for a long time that the best course was to say nothing, acknowledge nothing. Then, when he married . . .

The image of Addie Caswell—*Addie Douglas*—flashed across his mind, and he paused in his addition of the column. He put down his pen and rubbed his eyes.

He wondered how she was getting on. He'd heard rumors of her father's wrath at her marriage, and he hoped they weren't true. Zeb

Douglas was a good fellow, if a little flashy, and he hoped for Addie's sake that Jacob could come to accept that fact, at least. Addie shouldn't be blamed for choosing a fellow like Zeb, instead of . . .

He sighed and picked up his pen. He couldn't find the place he'd left off, and the sum had gone clean out of his head, so he began again at the top of the column.

There was a shuffle of feet outside his door and a knock at the frame. He glanced up. "Come on in," he said. He laid his pen aside.

Ben Thomas and Joe Whitehead stepped in. "Hello, fellas." George smiled. He stood and extended a hand to the nearest. The two men shook his hand and greeted him, then took the seats in front of his desk. The office was small, so they had to scoot carefully between the wall and the desk to keep from banging their knees. Whitehead, especially, with his gangly build, looked cramped.

"Sorry, Joe. I've been meaning to talk to Dad about getting a little more space, but—"

"Don't worry about it, George," Joe said.

"What brings you boys down here today?"

Whitehead glanced at Thomas, who cleared his throat. "George, Joe and me—and John Lupton, too; you know him, don't you?—well, the three of us are starting a little business venture, and we were just wondering if you might be interested in coming in with us."

George leaned back in his chair and scratched his chin. "Well, ah . . . I don't know, boys. What've you got in mind?"

"You know who Asa Candler is, don't you, George?"

"You mean that druggist down in Atlanta, the Coca-Cola man?"

"Yeah. Well, right now, the only place you can get Coca-Cola is in a drugstore or a soda fountain, right?"

"Well, yeah, but where else would you—"

"What if you could buy Coca-Cola in a bottle, premixed?" Ben Thomas said. "What if you could bottle it and put it in an ice chest—say, at a grocer's or a livery stable or . . . anywhere! Anywhere there might be thirsty people."

George peered at the top of his desk.

"Think about all the people already drinking Coca-Cola," said Whitehead. "This thing could go national, George."

"What thing? All I've heard so far is an idea."

Thomas leaned forward. "Me and Joe and John Lupton have been talking to Candler about getting the sole rights to bottle Coca-Cola. We think he'll come around to our way of thinking, once we convince him we're serious. We want to bottle premixed Coca-Cola, seal it in a pressurized container, and sell it in stores for a nickel a bottle."

"What's to keep some old boy in the next county from doing the same thing?"

"I don't know, for sure," Whitehead said. "Maybe we'll come up with some unique design for the bottle. We'll have patent protection, once we get going. But think of the possibilities, George! Chattanooga is a rail hub. We could ship Coca-Cola anywhere in the country from our bottling plant! The iron business isn't going to make it around here, and you can see that, if you'll just look. Birmingham's going to wind up with most of the business because they've got better grade ore down there. Shipping hasn't got a prayer until they do something about the lower Tennessee. The best opportunity a man's got right now is for something that's portable, something he can sell anywhere at a price that anyone can afford. Something he can pay somebody else to sell for him, and rake some profit off the top. Coca-Cola in bottles! Just think about it, George!"

George massaged the bridge of his nose. "Sounds to me like you fellas already have everything worked out. What I haven't figured out yet is why you need me."

Ben Thomas thumped an imaginary piece of lint off the crown of his hat. "Well, strictly speaking, George . . . we need money. It'll take money to set up the plant and buy the equipment. When we go back to talk with

Candler, it'd be nice to show him some deep pockets, convince him we mean to stick to this thing till it's done right. We were sort of hoping—" Thomas cut his eyes at Whitehead, then back to George "—hoping you might could come in with us, maybe talk to your dad . . ."

George leaned back to stare at the ceiling, cupping his chin and rubbing his cheek with the tips of his fingers. "I don't know, boys, I just don't know. Sounds like a pretty risky proposition to me. I don't know how Dad'll feel about something like this."

"We understand, George," said Whitehead. "It's something new. Course, we think it'll work. But it takes some getting used to, no two ways about it. Why don't you give it some thought, talk it over with your dad, and we'll check back with you?"

"We'd sure like to have you for a partner, George," said Thomas. "You and your family are real fine folks, and we'd like to have you on our side of the fence."

"Well, thanks, fellas. I appreciate your interest, anyway. And I will give it some thought, I promise you."

"Well, good," said Thomas, standing and extending his hand. "Thanks for talking to us, anyway."

"Sure, Ben, sure, Joe," he nodded to Whitehead, taking his hand in turn. The two men replaced their hats and walked out the door.

George sat back down and peered into space, his arms crossed across his chest. He liked Whitehead, Thomas, and Lupton, all three. He'd known them for a number of years. But . . . putting Coca-Cola in bottles and shipping it all over the country? He sighed. This business was doing all right. His family was comfortable, well respected. Why would he want to take a chance?

He found his pen, inspected the tip, and bent back to his column of figures. Maybe he ought to stop by Peabody's on the way home and order more ship bottles. He'd been thinking about building a steamer.

CHAPTER

8

Nashville, Tennessee
October 18, 1899

Dearest Lou,

Well, I guess there's not much doubt about it. I haven't had my time of the month for two months now. I haven't told Zeb yet, but I guess I won't wait too much longer as he needs to know.

I trust this finds you and yours well. We are fine here. I'm finally getting settled in since our move. The men here at the home office seem real proud of Zeb and the work he did with the Murfreesboro office, and he assures me that this move is a real first-rate thing for him, so I guess I'm happy about it. But it does seem a bit hard, just being a newlywed and all and having to up and move so soon.

In a way, I hate to tell Zeb about the baby. Is that terrible of me? Sometimes I fancy I can feel that little life down inside me, and the privacy of it comforts me somehow. But I know these are foolish thoughts. Zeb will be so proud and happy to know he will soon be a papa.

Addie held the pen suspended above the paper. Her eyes left the page and wandered to an empty space somewhere between her bureau and the window. She ran her other hand over her belly, trying to imagine what was happening inside her body. If a new person was growing inside her, why did she feel so much like she always did? Why wasn't she shining like the sun, or laughing all the time? There ought to be some extravagance. But, no; this was quiet and slow. She smiled.

> *How are your Robert and Katherine? And baby Ewell? Is he still gaining weight as fast as he was at first? I know they keep you plenty busy, and I guess I'm fixing to find out just how busy, here in a few months.*
>
> *I don't suppose there's been any change with Papa, has there? I'd like to at least let him know about his future grandchild. That is, if he'd really want to know.*
>
> *Your loving sister,*
Adelaide C. Douglas

She sealed the envelope and affixed the stamp. She placed it on the edge of the bureau so Zeb would see it on his way out in the morning.

A horseless carriage clattered and banged past the front window. Addie glanced at it on her way to the tiny kitchen. There were more horseless carriages here than in Murfreesboro or Chattanooga. Granny White Pike was a busy thoroughfare. Sometimes carloads of youngsters woke them at night with their hollering.

She scooted the cane-bottomed chair under the bureau. She smiled at herself. Youngsters! Here she was, an old lady of nineteen, thinking such things. She paused and passed her hand absently across her belly, imagining the curvature that would become more and more pronounced in the weeks to come.

Ten steps away from the bureau and Addie was in the small kitchen. She had a dutch oven full of white beans simmering on one back burner of the Crown stove and a pan of chopped potatoes stewing on the other.

She wrapped a dish towel around her hand. She opened the oven door and removed a pan of cornbread, setting it on top of the stove to cool. Addie went to the cupboard above the sink and removed two plates. She scattered the silverware beside the plates, humming under her breath.

Yonder over the rolling river,
Where the shining mansions rise,
Soon will be our home forever,
And the smile of the blessed Giver
Gladdens all our longing eyes . . .

It wouldn't take a mansion to make her happy. Even this little cracker box of a place would be fine if she could just stay in it for awhile, see the same scenery for longer than a three-month stretch.

Zeb came in at a quarter past six, his tie loosened and his collar unbuttoned. Despite the slightly cool evening air, his face had a sheen of sweat.

"Had to walk all the way uphill from the Edgehill Street stop." He brushed her cheek with his lips as he set his briefcase on the floor.

"Why didn't you get off at the regular place?"

Zeb smiled and ducked his head. "Well, I got to studying about a proposition Mr. Griffs made me, and I guess I just forgot where the trolley was. Good thing I looked up when I did. I like to went clear to the other side of Vanderbilt."

"Must've been pretty serious, then."

He looked at her a moment, then resumed peeling off his coat and yanking loose the knot in his tie. "Yeah, I guess you might say so."

Addie set a blue-striped crockery bowl of stewed potatoes on the table, then turned to look at him, wiping her hands on her apron.

He folded his coat over the back of a kitchen chair and draped his tie atop it. He shoved his hands into his pockets. "Addie, they want me to open a new district office."

She raised her eyebrows.

"In Little Rock."

"Arkansas?"

He grinned. "Yes, ma'am."

She went toward the stove, bunching her apron in her hands to pick up the pan of cornbread.

"What's wrong, honey? It'll be a real—"

"Opportunity? Like Murfreesboro and here?"

"Addie, what—what's the matter?"

The cornbread clattered to the tabletop, and she covered her face with her hands. She felt his arms around her, and she pushed him away. "No, don't, Zeb! I'll be all right in a minute, so just . . . don't."

When she looked up at him, his shoulders were slumped. She regretted her loss of control. She daubed at her eyes with a corner of the apron.

"Zeb, I'm sorry. I'm just a little upset right now, and . . . I'm expecting."

His forehead wrinkled, like he was trying to work a cipher in his head. And then, something took off behind his eyes, and he jerked himself up straight, like a puppet when somebody twitches the string.

"You're what?"

She had to smile. "I'm expecting," she said in a quieter voice. "In a family way, Zeb. You're fixing to be a daddy."

He still didn't move, except for his eyes. They were popping and jerking all around the room. He reminded her of some little boy who'd just been asked a hard geography question by the teacher. He stood there with his hands still in his pockets, looking like he was trying to figure out the right answer.

And then, he grabbed the chair with his coat lying across the back, pulled it out from the table, and sat down like a boxer after a rough round. She didn't know what to do, so she went to the icebox for the but-termilk pitcher.

"How do you know? Are you sure?" His eyes still weren't focusing on anything in particular; his arms hung loose at his sides.

"Well, yes, dear, I'm sure. Women know these things."

Then the smile came, rounding the side of his face and spreading in all directions like molasses on an empty plate.

"A daddy," he said. His grin went rubbery around the edges. "I'm gonna be a daddy." He got up from his chair and dropped to his knees in front of her. He placed his arms tenderly about her waist. "Oh, honey. I don't know what to say."

A warm gush of love welled up in her. She placed a palm on the crown of his head, stroking gently down the back of his neck, over and over.

"Well, I guess we better eat this before it gets too cold."

He sat as if he hadn't heard. "Addie, I love you."

"I love you, too, Mr. Douglas, but if you don't get out of my lap, your supper won't be fit to eat."

Later, as he spooned a helping of potatoes onto his plate, he said, "When do you reckon the baby might come?"

She put down her fork and thought for half a minute. "I guess about springtime—maybe sometime in April." She toyed with her napkin, then asked him, straight out. "Zeb, how soon do you think we'll have to go to Arkansas?"

He didn't answer right away. He chewed his potatoes and took a slow drink of the frothy white buttermilk. He daubed the corners of his lips with his napkin. "Well, today they sounded like it might be pretty soon, but what with you being in a family way and all, I just don't know . . ."

"Zeb, I'd sure like to have Louisa with me when my time comes. That'd be a lot easier here than in Little Rock."

He nodded. "Yes, that's a fact." He buttered a slice of cornbread. "I'll talk to 'em tomorrow and see what I can work out."

A hundred questions crowded onto the back of her tongue. *What if they don't care about me and the baby? Why does it have to be right now? Why Little Rock instead of someplace closer: Lebanon or Manchester or even Memphis, for goodness sake? There must be one or two people in a place the size of Memphis who don't have enough insurance. Why can't we stay someplace long enough to see the seasons change?*

But she sat silent, with her left hand properly folded in her lap, lifting her fork to her lips and sliding the food into her mouth without letting it scrape against her teeth. She would wait and see what Zeb arranged with the company. He'd be able to manage something. And she did love him so. Surely everything would work out.

CHAPTER
9
❧

So, anyway, like I was sayin', these ol' boys went to this fancy hunting lodge and man, they was just made outta money. So they says to the feller at the lodge, 'We don't care how much it costs, we want the best quail dog you got on the place . . .'"

Will Counts was fairly shouting in the front seat, but Addie still could barely hear him over the commotion of the horseless carriage. She held on to her hat with one hand and tried to brace herself against the bumps and swerves with the other. She gritted her teeth and prayed they'd get to church in one piece.

"Will is so proud of this silly thing," Beulah Counts shouted in Addie's ear. "He figured out a way to build a backseat out over the engine, so us and the boys could go driving together. They'll be just sick when they get home from my brother's and find out they missed out on a trip in the horseless carriage. Will don't take it out every Sunday, you know." Beulah's smile testified that she held a far higher opinion of Will's generosity than Addie.

"And the feller says, 'Well, boys, the best thing for quail around here ain't a dog.' And they say, 'What you talking about?' And he says, 'Well, ol' Uncle Jake here can find a covey quicker'n any pointer this side of the mountains.' And they's this old feller setting in the corner, half asleep. And the hunters says, 'How much?' And the feller says, 'Five dollars a day per gun, and y'all have to buy Uncle Jake a plug of tobacco.' And the hunters says, 'Well, all right, then, if you ain't pulling our legs.' And they pay their money and go to hunting . . ."

The Duryea clattered down Granny White Pike, and Addie's insides curdled with each jolt. She wished she and Zeb had taken the trolley, as usual. Compared to this rattletrap, the trolley was like a leisurely afternoon on a still pond. But Will had been anxious to show Zeb his new toy, and she hadn't known until this morning of the perilous invitation he'd accepted.

"Well, I mean to tell you, them boys went through the quail like you-know-what through a goose. They limited out that day, and the next day, and the next. They'd go along, and ol' Uncle Jake would stop, all of a sudden. He'd point at a little scrap of cover and say, 'They's a brace right there,' or, 'they's four of 'em settin' under this 'simmin bush right here.' The gunners 'd get all set and Uncle Jake 'd step in there and put up the birds, and blam! blam! Ol' Jake'd pick up their birds and hand 'em to 'em and they'd go on to the next place. These ol' boys was in some tall cotton. I mean, they was just tickled sick . . ."

"Now, how you feeling these days, honey?" Beulah's meaty hand thumped on Addie's arm. "Having any morning sickness?"

"Not too much," Addie said. "Some days are worse than others." She squeezed a wan smile onto her face.

"Well, now don't you worry about it, honey," Beulah said. "You know what they say: 'sick mother, healthy baby.'"

This young 'un ought to be stouter than garlic.

"Now, for the whole next year, all these ol' boys can talk about is getting back to that place and shooting birds over ol' Uncle Jake. They walk into the place the next season and go straight to the feller and say, 'We're here to hunt with Uncle Jake.' And the feller gets sorta sad-looking and says, 'Boys, I'm sorry, but Uncle Jake passed on.' Well, the hunters are just dumbstruck, you know, and finally, one of 'em asks, 'How'd it happen?'

And the feller says, 'Well, he got to running the chickens, and we had to shoot him.'"

Zeb's sudden guffaw splashed back over Addie. When she glanced up, she could see the approaching spire of the church. She clenched her jaws and gripped the arm rail. She sucked deep draughts of the cool autumn air into her nostrils and allowed it to escape from between her lips. At last, the end was in sight. *Lord, if you'll let me get there without heaving up my insides, I promise you I'll never ride in one of these hellish machines again.*

Will herded the Duryea against a curb near the front door and set the brake. They all clambered out as several knickered boys broke away from their families and raced over to the machine, eyeing it and pointing at it. Zeb offered her his arm and they walked up the five steps onto the portico, blending with the rest of the faithful going into the building.

The Twelfth Avenue Church of Christ met in a red-brick church house purchased from a Baptist congregation that went out of business. Their first act upon assuming ownership was to remove the bell from the steeple since they held that bells, like pianos and organs, had no scriptural authorization and were mostly for show, anyway. They sold the bell to some Methodists and used the twenty dollars to buy a new front door and a sign to hang above it. "Church of Christ," the sign proclaimed in terse block letters, black on a field of unspotted white, and the members all agreed the twenty dollars had been well spent.

When Addie and Zeb got inside, the elders were already seated in the two large chairs on either side of the pulpit. Addie and Zeb scooted into their customary place about halfway up on the right side of the aisle, just as the song leader strode to the front to announce the first hymn.

Hark! the gentle voice of Jesus falleth
Tenderly upon your ear;
Sweet his cry of love and pity calleth:
Turn and listen, stay and hear.

Ye that labor and are heavy-laden,
Lean upon your dear Lord's breast;
Ye that labor and are heavy-laden,
Come, and I will give you rest.

Heavy-laden—that about summed it up for Addie. If Louisa were here, things would be better. Someone to talk with, really talk with, not just pass pleasantries while the men amused themselves. Someone to understand without needing everything spelled out. Someone Addie could trust to tell her what was happening to her body, to her feelings, to her life. Someone to give her a hint of what might lie ahead.

Take his yoke, for he is meek and lowly;
Bear his burden, to him turn;
He who calleth is the Master holy:
He will teach if you will learn.
Ye that labor and are heavy-laden . . .

Though he was mouthing the words of the chorus, they barely registered in Zeb's mind. He needed to decide what to do about the offer Mr. Griffs and Mr. Carleton had made him. He knew he could turn the Little Rock agency around and make it a paying proposition. He knew he was being given these challenges for a reason, and he knew one day his consistent successes would be rewarded by a plush home office position. He had to think of the future—now more than ever. Surely Addie could understand that.

And then he thought of her tears, of the flat, scared look in her eyes when he had first mentioned the promotion. It had knocked the wind out of him, that look. He thought she'd be proud of him, excited by the possibilities before him—before them. But all she could see was the uncertainty.

He knew as sure as sunrise he shouldn't turn his back on this new chance to prove himself. But he couldn't figure out how to bring Addie around. He'd promised to take care of her. And he was doing that, wasn't he? He was bringing home more money now than he ever had. And the prospect Griffs and Carleton offered him promised even more. But Addie . . .

His glance fell on the sloping shoulders of Will Counts and his wife. Beulah Counts sure seemed like a good woman. Seemed like she doted on Will and everything he did. Zeb wondered if Beulah might be able to talk to Addie. Zeb liked Will just fine. He might see what Will thought about the idea. Maybe all Addie needed was another woman to talk to her, to help her see things.

They sang two songs, and then one of the men led a prayer. Another song, and it was time for the sermon. Brother McCrary went to the pulpit and stood with his head bowed for a moment. He took a firm grip on the sides of the lectern and leaned into his text for the day. The light glittered from the lenses of his wire-rimmed spectacles.

"In James the second chapter and verse fourteen, the writer says, 'What doth it profit, my brethren, though a man say he hath faith, and have not works? Can faith save him? If a brother or sister be naked, and destitute of daily food, and one of you say unto them, Depart in peace, be ye warmed and filled; notwithstanding ye give them not those things which are needful to the body; what doth it profit?

"'Even so faith, if it hath not works, is dead, being alone . . .'"

He quoted more of the passage, never looking down at the open Bible on the lectern. He engaged the eyes of the congregation one by one, as if he had handpicked each verse as a personal oracle for the individuals in the pews.

"Brethren, it's easy to talk good religion. It's easy to say all the right things and put up a good front for the eyes of men. What's hard," he said, his voice dropping a half-tone, "is living good religion. James knew this, brethren. And that's why he gives us this warning. We all need to listen, to pay attention to his words. And we all need to obey. Error waits on every side to snare the careless, the heedless. The only way to keep your feet on the strait and narrow path of our Lord is to be constantly vigilant . . ."

Addie tried to get interested in Brother McCrary's sermon, but her mind slipped off his words like ice skidding on a hot skillet. Her eyes wandered the sanctuary. She and Zeb hadn't really gotten to know anyone at Twelfth Avenue. Of course, they'd only been here for a month and a half or so. Beulah and Will Counts were the only people they'd visited with at all, other than when they came to this building on Sundays. She tried to let herself really see the individual people around her. She knew scarcely a handful of them, but she tried to imagine what they might be like.

Two rows in front of her and across the aisle sat a desiccated old woman, her back bent nearly double with a dowager's hump. She reminded Addie of old Miss Ruthie at Centenary Methodist in Chattanooga. Miss Ruthie had never married, never even been seen with a man. Once, at a church social, Addie and several of her friends were gathered around Miss Ruthie. One of them asked her why she'd never taken a husband. Addie, a little embarrassed by her companion's cheek, watched as the frail old maid smiled and stroked the girl's pinafore with her twiglike, bent fingers. "Well, sweetie," she said in her high, airy voice, "the fact is, I was in love once."

Addie and her friends drew closer, as if Miss Ruthie were about to reveal a great and necessary secret no one else could tell them.

"Oh, it was many years ago," Miss Ruthie said. Her eyes closed in reverie. "Long before the war. He was the sweetest boy I'd ever seen. His daddy had a grist mill down on Chattanooga Creek, just down the riverbank from Brown's Ferry. He was just the kindest thing, and so polite, even though he'd never had much schooling at all.

"Oh, my papa wasn't too happy about the whole thing." The color rose on Miss Ruthie's withered cheek. "But Mama wouldn't allow him to scold me." Her thin, bluish lips parted in a smile as she removed a lilac-scented kerchief from the front of her dress. Addie noticed the trembling of her brown-spotted hand as she daubed at her lips. "I never said anything to Mama about it, but somehow she knew."

There was a long silence. A group of young boys rioted past, but the girls didn't even blink in their direction.

"I thought he was the most wonderful thing in the world," Miss Ruthie said finally, folding her hands in her lap.

When she could stand it no longer, Addie asked, "Well? What happened, Miss Ruthie?"

The old woman pursed her lips and turned her head slightly to the left. She wasn't looking at them now. "He died of typhoid during the autumn of '32. It broke my heart."

And that was all she would say.

Addie remembered that one of her friends went and got Miss Ruthie a glass of iced lemonade from the table where the church ladies were setting out drinks—as if that might help, somehow. She remembered how Miss Ruthie's story stayed with her in the days that followed. Like a sad, sweet, old song, it echoed around in her mind at the oddest times—when she was doing chores or skipping rope, playing with dolls or working on her lessons.

She remembered thinking there was a sort of mystery about old men and women. They knew things, had seen and remembered things. They were harder to surprise. She remembered trying to imagine herself as an old woman; she could never conjure up any image other than a slightly wrinkled version of her own ten-year-old face, still capped by the same chestnut hair in ribboned braids.

These days, she was starting to understand a little bit of why she couldn't see the old woman she would become: a child can't comprehend all the different kinds of living there are. A child thinks mostly about the visible differences. She doesn't imagine that all the really important differences are on the inside, tucked away where they can't be seen. Everybody was like that. Much of the real truth about people was hidden from view—sometimes until it was too late. You mostly just had to wait and see.

"A lot of people will tell you that it's more important to be a good person than to follow the teachings of the gospel," Brother McCrary was saying. "They'll tell you it doesn't matter much whether you pay attention to the Scriptures or not, as long as you're living a good, moral life. But these words of James's stand in contradiction to that sort of thinking, brethren. It's not enough to say 'Lord, Lord,' and do not the will of the Father in heaven—Matthew seven, twenty-one . . ."

The thought of traveling to Little Rock gave Zeb an odd, secret feeling of excitement. For all his seriousness about his business, there was still a towheaded, eager part of him that stood on tiptoe and watched as he did new things, gained admittance to better and higher circles. *Successful men travel on business,* this part of him whispered, goggle-eyed and breathless. He was becoming important to the company, or they wouldn't send him so far away.

He thought of seeing new country, eating new food in places he'd never been. Zeb had never crossed the Mississippi River. He thought of all that wide water, sheeted brown beneath him as he rumbled over the new bridge at Memphis. Strangeness and distance chanted to him, pulled at him.

And it was, after all, an opportunity. It wasn't just some lark he'd made up for himself. Griffs and Carleton were depending on him. He couldn't afford to disappoint them, to let the company down. He really ought to take the bull by the horns.

Zeb sensed the faint, sour taste of resentment. A man couldn't be shackled to his wife's uncertainties, could he? If he was to be the provider, shouldn't he do it in the way he saw best?

But her anxious face, the bluntness of her apprehension . . .

The baby in her womb.

It wasn't fair. How could a man argue with a woman when she was carrying his offspring? She was proof against any attempt at logic or persuasion. It was almost as if she held a hostage and was, in turn, held hostage. And there was a kind of selfishness about her, too, as if she now contained inside herself her own final reason for everything.

He knew he ought to go. But how could he?

"Brethren, is there someone here today who is ready to shoulder the task our Lord has set? Is there someone who is ready to answer, as the prophet Isaiah, 'Here am I; send me'?"

The congregation sensed the approaching end of Brother McCrary's sermon and began reaching for the hymnals in the racks.

"If you're ready to get busy for God, if you're tired of carrying the useless load of sin and are ready to be washed in the blood of the Lamb and begin walking in the footsteps of Jesus, won't you come down front today, while we stand and sing?"

The two elders rose from their chairs and paced to the front of the dais as the congregation stood. The song leader strode to the front, singing the opening notes of the altar call.

What can wash away my sin?
Nothing but the blood of Jesus.
What can make me whole again?
Nothing but the blood of Jesus . . .

CHAPTER
10

*A*ddie knotted the stitch and leaned over to bite the thread with her teeth. She squinted at the piecing, turning it this way and that. She reached over to the gas lamp and brightened it a bit, then continued inspecting her work. Satisfied with the stitching, she removed the straight pin. She laid the completed "bow tie" on the stack with the two dozen others she had finished.

She felt a dull ache starting behind her eyes. She had been piecing for most of two hours. It was time to get up and move around a little. She levered herself out of the kitchen chair, putting a hand to her back as she stood. Standing was getting harder and harder, along with everything else—she was now almost in her seventh month. The morning sickness had abated, however, which was a blessing. Beulah Counts had assured her of that, recounting in uncomfortable detail the story of her sister, who had "been sicker 'n a bloated mule" for the entire duration of her pregnancy. Addie dared not complain in Beulah's presence after hearing that.

Beulah had also let it be known that it was foolish to be making a bow tie quilt for the baby. "What if you have a little girl?"

Addie had shrugged. "I guess the bow tie'll keep her just as warm."

Beulah had mumbled something about crowing hens.

Addie didn't care. She liked the bow tie. She had decided to alternate pink and blue ties, but it had nothing to do with Beulah and her opinions.

Addie had begun to notice an odd effect Beulah had on her. Beulah was so plainspoken, so cut-and-dried about everything, and, above all, so bumptious and rough in her manner that Addie felt she had to compensate by going the other way. Lately, it had seemed that the longer Beulah lolled on the settee, the more primly Addie perched on the edge of her seat. The more Beulah swilled her tea or coffee, the straighter Addie's little finger extended from her own cup handle. The more blunt Beulah's speech became, the more Addie found herself searching for the most delicate and proper language possible. Addie hated herself for doing it, but she didn't seem capable of stopping; it just seemed to irritate Beulah so.

There was a quiet tap at the front door. Addie pulled aside the curtain, peering into the early spring dusk. Mr. Chester stood on the doorstep, blowing into his cupped hands. She undid the latch and opened the door. Her landlord smiled at her and touched the brim of his derby. "Evenin' Mrs. Douglas! Just checking by to see if you're needing anything."

"Thank you, no, Mr. Chester. Won't you come inside? It's pretty nippy out."

"Oh, no, I spect I'll be getting back, ma'am. Mrs. Chester thought I oughta look in on you, make sure everything's all right."

"Yes, sir, I'm fine, thank you."

"Well, all right, then. Good night." He touched his hat brim again as he backed away from the door.

"Good night, and thank you." She closed the door and latched it. She hugged herself against the cold draft from outside, rubbing her upper arms. And that was another thing. . . . Her feet hadn't been warm since January, what with the baby taking more and more of the right-of-way. She could pile on ten quilts at night, and though her face and neck might be sheathed in sweat, her feet would still feel like two chunks of ice.

She never felt cold at night when Zeb was at home. . . . She glanced at the bureau, where his last letter lay open, read twice since its receipt this morning. It was on the stationery of his hotel in Little Rock, dated one week previous. It was scrawled in the curvaceous, elegant hand of which he was so proud and began, as did all his letters, with the salutation, "My Darling Addie."

> *I trust this finds you & our (son? daughter? ha) well. Have had good success this week, hope to close two contracts within the next few days. Have several promising leads on prospective agents for Area. All else pretty good here.*
>
> *Will plan to leave in three weeks (Mar. 20th) on the ten o'clock (morn.) train. Should pull into Nashville, barring anything out of the ordinary, by about ten o'clock that night. Am most anxious to once again see my lovely Wife.*
>
> > *Much love,*
> > *Zeb. A. Douglas*

Addie sighed. Another two weeks to wait.

The days seemed ages long these last few weeks. She had almost reached the point of looking forward to Beulah's social calls. Beulah, for all her bluster and unsolicited advice, was at least nearby and could be depended on for some diversion every once in awhile; a little conversation—however one-sided. Why hadn't Louisa answered her last letter? Addie wondered. She had written her what seemed weeks ago, asking her to consider coming to Nashville to help in the days following the baby's arrival. She really thought she'd have heard something from her sister by now.

Massaging the small of her back, she paced slowly into the ten-by-twelve bedroom that opened off the parlor. She ran her hand around the new cradle that sat on the floor beside their bed. It had just come a few days ago. Zeb had ordered it from the Sears & Roebuck catalog and had it delivered. She and Zeb had looked at a few cradles, had briefly discussed their various merits and faults, but she had never really made up her mind which one she wanted for the baby.

She sighed. It didn't much seem to matter now. The cradle was here and it would do just fine, she supposed. It was good of Zeb, really, to go ahead and make the decision. She would probably have just dawdled needlessly over details that wouldn't matter to anyone but herself. She could almost imagine Beulah's assessment of the situation: "Honey, that baby'd sleep just as good in an egg crate, long as it had plenty of padding . . ." And a bow tie quilt would keep her just as warm, she told Beulah in her mind.

"All in favor, say 'aye.'" There was a tired murmur of responses. "Opposed, same sign." Silence. "All right, the motion carries."

George Hutto leaned back from the long walnut table. With what he hoped was an unobtrusive motion, he eased his pocket watch out and thumbed the cover latch. He suppressed a wince. Nine-thirty! They'd been at it for more than two hours, and Clem Osgood didn't show any signs of stopping. Not for the first time, he scolded himself for allowing Dad to talk him into being on the board of Baroness Erlanger's new hospital. He was as grateful for the baroness's generosity as anyone else, but there were plenty of things he'd have preferred to be doing at nine-thirty on a Tuesday evening, rather than sitting in this hard chair and waiting for Clem to put things to a vote. And with a new hospital, there seemed to be no end of things on which to vote.

As Clem made full steam ahead into the next item on the agenda, George's tired mind wandered. He had a new book at home that he'd been wanting to read, but at the rate this meeting was going, he'd be too tired to enjoy reading when he got there. And then, his attention was commandeered by the words "three more deaths this week."

"Where?" one of the board members was asking.

"One up in Lookout. One out in the county, and one in Cameron Hill. This is the worst spell of scarlet fever we've had since I don't know when."

"Cameron Hill . . . Who was that?"

"Little girl—Dub and Louisa Dawkins's daughter."

A shock of recognition jabbed at George's midsection. "Little Katherine?" he blurted, the first words he'd said all evening, other than "aye."

Clem looked at him and nodded. "Yeah, I think that was her name. You know the family?"

George's face reddened. Was Clem mocking him? No, probably not. He doubted anyone in the room would know that the mother of the dead child was Addie's older sister. Probably no one in the whole blessed state knew he had ever cared for Addie in the first place—including Addie. "I, uh— Yes. I'm . . . acquainted with some of them. From church."

"Heard it was a mighty sad thing," one of the other board members offered. "Heard that toward the end the fever turned her mind. Heard she hollered about angels coming for her, and such."

"How old was she?" someone asked.

Clem shrugged. "I read the obituary, but I forgot."

There was a moment or two of silence before Clem cleared his throat. "Next item: staff wants two more beds in Convalescent Ward C . . ."

As the talk droned on, George came to the guilty realization that he had already forgotten about Katherine Dawkins, except for speculating whether Addie would be attending her funeral. He removed his spectacles and pulled a wrinkled handkerchief from his vest pocket to clean the lenses. Resettling his glasses on the bridge of his nose, he risked another glance at his watch. Nine-thirty-eight. He sighed.

W. G. Dawkins walked the elderly couple to the door. "Thank you for coming over, Brother Wilks. You, too, Sister Wilks. I know Louisa appreciates it too."

The old woman was sniffling into a well-moistened lilac kerchief. "So young," she murmured over and over, shaking her head. "So very young."

They were at the door, and the husband turned to shake Dub's hand. Without looking him directly in the eye, he said, "Dub, she's better off now."

"Yes, Brother Wilks, I know. Well . . . thanks again." The old people went into the night, and Dub leaned wearily against the door, latching it behind these, the last two callers of a very long and very difficult day.

He had started back toward the parlor, knowing Louisa would be maintaining her ceaseless vigil beside the small casket, when a quiet knock came at the kitchen door.

Oh, Lord! he thought. *Who in the world, this late of an evening?* He stepped across the plank floor of the kitchen and parted the shade slightly, at first seeing no one. Then, peering downward, he realized the knock belonged to the shortened form of old black Rose, the housekeeper of Louisa's father. *Now why would she be coming around again?* he wondered. *She already brought that platter of chicken this morning . . .*

He parted the door a foot. "Evening, Rose. What can I do for you?"

"Mister Dub, I sure am sorry 'bout coming so late, but I sure needs to talk to you."

He sighed. "Rose, it's nearly ten o'clock. Are you sure it can't wait till in the morning?"

"No, sir. 'Fraid not. I needs to talk to you tonight."

Rose showed about as much likelihood of budging as an oak stump. She wouldn't look at him, but neither would she back up an inch. Dub had been around Louisa's family long enough to recognize that Rose had something on her mind. He could shut the door in her face, even lock it; she'd still be standing there the next morning, waiting to say what she came to say. Wishing desperately he could sit down somewhere, he let the door fall open. Rose stepped inside. A dark, threadbare shawl was wrapped round her shoulders.

"Mister Dub, I needs fifteen dollars."

"Rose, good Lord! Why at this, of all times—"

"I got to buy a train ticket to Nashville, and I needs fifteen dollars. I got some money saved up, but I needs that much more than what I got, to do what I got to do when I gets there."

"Rose, why do you need to go to Nashville right now?" he asked, rubbing his temples. "Why can't you wait till after the funeral, at least?"

"Miz Addie," came the instant reply. "She in a family way, and somebody got to tell her what happened to her sister's child. She find out from a telegram, she liable to lose that baby. And somebody got to do for her, now she gettin' along toward her time. Miz Louisa woulda done it, but she can't now. Somebody got to do it, Mister Dub. You the only one close by I can ask. I needs fifteen dollars."

Dub studied her squat, unmoving figure for several moments. "I don't reckon you've told Lou's daddy what you're fixing to do?"

Rose's eyes flickered toward him, then went back toward their resting place somewhere between the chair rail and the kitchen floor. Her face was as immobile as ever, but that single glance had told Dub all he needed to know.

He had to admit, he hadn't thought about Addie in the time since Katherine's death. She would certainly need to know, and Rose was correct about something else: the news shouldn't just be dropped on a woman as far along as Addie was. Too bad Zeb was still in Arkansas.

"I guess you're right, Rose," he said slowly, reaching into his coat pocket for his wallet. "Let's see, here . . . Five, ten . . ." He dug about in his pants pocket and felt the contours of a five-dollar gold piece. "That'd about make fifteen—"

She snatched the money from his hand and walked out the door. Just like that. He smiled faintly, despite his crushing weariness. "You're welcome," he said to the closed door.

He went into the parlor, and Lou appeared not to have moved since he had last seen her. She stood beside the open casket, staring down into the face of their dead daughter. The expression on her face was that of someone trying to recognize someone who looked familiar—yet not quite. Walking toward his wife, Dub averted his eyes from Katherine's—no, *its*—face. It *didn't* look just like her, no matter what the well-meaning visitors said. Everything that made her Katherine was gone; this was just what was left behind. This wasn't what he wanted to remember.

"Lou, they've all gone," he said softly, placing his hands on his wife's shoulders. "Why don't you come to bed? You've been right here all day, on your feet."

"Who was at the kitchen door?" she asked him, without taking her eyes off her child's face.

"Just old Rose," he said, surprised that Louisa had been aware enough to ask the question. "She wants to go to Nashville. To be with Addie."

After a pause, Louisa nodded. Then turned and walked away, toward the stairs.

"Where you going, honey?" Dub asked.

"To bed, I guess. Maybe if I lie down, I can let myself cry."

Rose sat on the hard bench in the colored car, staring out the window as the night rushed past, featureless and punctuated only by the frequent glowing cinders from the smokestack.

The colored car was right behind the engine, so the air in the car was uncomfortably full of smoke and coal dust, and the noise and bumps and shakes were more noticeable. It was an old, ramshackle wooden coach, in sharp contrast to the sleek, upholstered, well-equipped steel coaches available to the white passengers of the Nashville, Chattanooga, and St. Louis line. Rose would have liked to use the toilet, but the smell was unpleasant, even from where she was seated at the other end of the car. She wasn't that uncomfortable—yet.

Not many folks, colored or otherwise, rode the late train to Nashville. There was a young, bright-skinned woman with a brand-new basket in her lap, seated two rows up and across the aisle, to Rose's left. A little closer to the front and on the same side as Rose, there was an old man and two young boys, about seven and twelve, Rose figured. The man's skin was the hue of water-stained chestnuts, and the boys were somewhat lighter. The boys were sprawled asleep on two of the benches, so soundly asleep that even when the train's rough motion jogged them onto the floor, they crawled back onto their plank resting places without opening their eyes.

Rose watched the dark roll by and thought about everything that was happening. It was too bad about Louisa's little girl. Addie would take the news awful hard, Rose knew; Katherine had been her favorite. She was a sweet little child, always so happy and content. Seemed like those were the ones that took bad sick most often. Maybe not, though, she reasoned. Maybe with them you just noticed more. But children were surely hardest to lose or to see lost. It was out of order; the wrong of it showed up more plainly. "Lord Jesus, please come 'longside Miz Louisa and Mister Dub," Rose mouthed silently. "You know what they needin'—give it to 'em, Lord, amen."

Rose thought about the bits of news she had gleaned about Addie during her errands to the Dawkins's home during Katherine's illness. *Her stuck there in Nashville, coming to her time in the middle of a bunch of strangers, and that husband of hers way off somewhere . . .* Rose shifted slightly to ease her lower back. Not that a man was much good when the time came, anyway. Rose had borne seven children and seen five of them raised to adulthood, and never once had her man been in the room with her to watch the birthing of his offspring. But Rose had been among friends, and the women of the church had always been there to aid as only those who also knew the sweet, grinding agony of childbirth could. Her man would come in when the blood and struggle was out of sight, and he'd look at the life he'd sired, and he'd maybe smile, maybe not. She'd had a good man—better than many—but there were some times that were just beyond a man.

The bright-skinned girl set the basket carefully on the bench beside her and stood, stretching the kinks out of her cramped legs. She turned and glanced at Rose, smiling briefly.

Rose had cousins in Nashville. She could stay with them and come during the day to do for Addie. *Someone* had to do for her. Louisa would have done it, if things had been different. Addie should have been able to draw comfort from the bosom of her kin, but . . .

Rose had worked for Jacob Caswell's family since he was a young man, and it pained her soul to see his spirit shriveled by his bitterness toward Addie. "Sweet Jesus, won't you change that man's heart?" she mouthed, still looking out the window. "Won't you soften him toward his own flesh and blood, for the sake of thy Word, which say, 'he that trouble his own house shall inherit the wind'?"

The train rolled on through the night and into the dawn, winding up and down grades and in and out of tunnels carved into the flanks of the steep hillsides. At about seven in the morning, it ground slowly to a hissing halt in the Nashville station. Gripping her battered and creased cardboard valise in one hand, Rose stepped down onto the platform, glad her cousin's place wasn't too far from the station. Even if the trolley had been running at that hour, she doubted she could have managed to locate a colored car. As it was, she'd have to walk. Rose didn't mind. She'd gotten where she had to go in life mostly on her own two feet.

The persistent knocking finally penetrated Addie's slumber. She worked herself to the side of the bed and managed to lever herself into a sitting position. Pushing her hair out of her eyes, she felt blindly with the other hand for her dressing robe, draped on a chair beside the bed. She sashed her robe and parted the curtains, peering out into the gray morning to see who was standing on her doorstep. At first, she didn't recognize the short, broad shape. Then, as the caller reached toward the door to knock again, she turned her face slightly toward the window where Addie stood. Rose! With a gasp of joy, Addie weaved her way around the bed in the tiny room and stepped as quickly as she could across the parlor, toward the front door.

She yanked open the door and threw wide her arms to receive Rose's squat form. The two women embraced in the open doorway. "Oh, now honey, we got to be careful," Rose said a moment later, placing a hand on Addie's protruding belly. "Way you done swole up, two be a crowd!"

"Come in out of this cold air," Addie said, smiling. "I just can't believe you're here! How long can you stay?"

Rose pulled the door to, then turned to look carefully at Addie. "Long as you need me, honey. I'm here to do for you till your baby come."

Addie stared at her, placing a hand to her mouth. "Oh, but . . . Papa. How did you manage—"

"Don't make no difference," Rose said. "I'm here, and I'm stayin' till I ain't needed no more or you tell me to clear out. Set yourself down, now! Ain't no call for you to be standin' up all this time." Rose fussed over her, getting her seated and propped up just so, mumbling and clucking all the while. Addie sighed under the ministrations, feeling more comforted and at home than she had since . . .

"Now, Rose, you must tell me all about Lou and all the others. I was expecting to hear from her anytime, but she hasn't written in the longest."

Rose paused in her bustling about, giving Addie a slow, careful look. She straightened slowly, arms akimbo, and fixed Addie with a sad look, her head cocked slightly to one side. "Honey, that's the other reason I'm here. Your sister ain't going to be able to come."

Addie's eyes went wide. "Why? What's wrong? Is it Dub? Or . . . or Lou herself?"

Rose shook her head and stooped again to lay a hand on Addie's arm. "No, honey. Ain't none of the grown folk. It's your niece, Katherine, sugar. The scarlet fever done took her. She done passed."

CHAPTER
11

❧

*T*here was a moment of shocked silence. Then Addie covered her face with her hands. The sobs started in short, silent bursts, then deepened and broadened into a river of grief, pouring from her in huge gasps and loud moans. She felt Rose's arms around her, smelled the dusky, warm scent of her, and for a moment she was again that bewildered, abandoned child of thirteen, buffeted by a loss that could never be fathomed, only endured. And again, Rose crooned her untiring incantation of comfort: "It's all right, Missy. You can make it. It's going to be all right, by 'n' by."

In the days that followed, they settled into a routine. Rose would come midmorning, after Addie had gotten herself out of bed and in some semblance of order. She would stay through early afternoon, leaving only after she had prepared something that Addie could warm up for supper. On the fine days, if Addie felt up to it, they would go for short walks up and down the streets of the neighborhood. If Addie needed anything from the grocer or butcher, Rose would go around and give orders to have it delivered. She heated towels on the stove and made hot packs to ease Addie's aching lower back muscles. She massaged Addie's calves when the frequent cramps would tie them in knots. She helped in piecing the baby's quilt.

They would sit for long stretches of time without speaking—Addie in her overstuffed armchair, Rose in the cane-bottomed rocker. During the day, the light from the parlor windows was more than adequate to piece or sew by. Addie felt no need for speech, no need to hold up either end of a conversation. Every so often, Rose would ask, in her low, monosyllabic way, if Addie needed anything. And Addie felt not the slightest hesitation about making any request. This, after all, was Rose. Her presence was like the feel of an old, well-worn quilt on a cold night.

Addie sometimes wondered how Rose had managed to get Papa's permission to come and help out, but she could never make herself ask. Even more, she longed to ask Rose if Papa ever mentioned her, if he ever thought of her. But she was terrified of the answer to that question and left it well alone. And besides, thinking of home invariably led her thoughts back to little Katherine—her adorable lisp; the silken feel of her cinnamon-colored hair as Addie brushed it out for her; the beautiful, perfect curve of her chubby cheek; the sound of her laugh . . . No, it was better not to speak of the things of home. For now, it was enough that Rose was here. The nights were less lonely, knowing she would see a familiar, caring face the next day.

About a week after Rose's arrival, Beulah Counts came to call. She blustered in on the coattails of an unseasonably warm south wind. "Lord-y, I tell you that wind like to blew the hair off my head. How you doin', honey? Mercy, I never seen such a wind as—"

She stopped in midsentence, staring at Rose, who was just then coming from the tiny kitchen bearing two steaming cups of coffee.

"Who's that?" Beulah blurted.

"This is Rose, my— She's come to help me out these last few days," Addie explained, glancing nervously from Rose to Beulah. Rose gave no sign of recognizing Beulah's presence, carefully placing first one coffee cup, then the other, on the two crocheted coasters on the small table by Addie's elbow. "She's . . . Rose has been with my family for years, and it's so kind of her to come when I needed her," Addie said, smiling sweetly, first at Rose, then at Beulah.

"Uh-*huh*," Beulah snorted, placing a hand on her hip. "Well, thank you for the coffee, Addie. I guess I wouldn't mind a taste, even on a day like—" Beulah's hand, stretched toward the coffee cup farthest from Addie on the table, froze in midgesture as she watched Rose nonchalantly grasp the cup and bring it to her lips, sip noisily, and replace it on the coaster, never once looking in Beulah's direction.

"Yes, that's a good idea," chirped Addie into the awkward silence. "Rose, why don't you bring Mrs. Counts a cup of coffee? How do you like it, Beulah dear?"

Beulah's jaw hung slack on its hinges as she turned to regard Addie. "Addie!" she began in a stage whisper, "do you honestly think it's proper—"

"Why, of course, Beulah!" piped Addie, at once flustered and secretly delighted at Beulah's discomfiture. "I think if you want a cup of coffee, it's perfectly proper for you to have it. How do you like it? Cream, sugar, . . . or both?"

Beulah stared at Rose's broad, disappearing back, momentarily framed by the kitchen door. "Both," she said, finally, pinching her lips together like a miser closing a purse.

"Rose, did you hear?" asked Addie.

"*Mmm*-hmm."

Beulah seated herself, perching uncharacteristically on the edge of the small settee, accepting from Rose the coffee cup as though it were a live rodent. She balanced the cup and saucer carefully on her knees and strove gallantly to ignore Rose's presence while she made several abortive attempts at chitchat. She never separated the cup from the saucer.

In a few minutes, Rose took her own cup to the kitchen and came back out wearing her old, ratty shawl and a nondescript kerchief over her head. Without a word to anyone, she walked toward the door.

"Rose, are you leaving?" Addie asked.

"Yes'm. I be back in the mornin'."

"Well . . . All right, then. Good-bye—and thank you."

"*Mmm*-hmm." And then she was gone.

"Who is that old nigger woman?" Beulah demanded as soon as the door was shut. "And why on earth were you . . . drinking coffee with her?" she continued, her lip curled in contempt. "Having her to wait on you is one thing, but that's so, so . . . familiar!"

"Oh, Beulah!" Addie laughed. "Rose just about raised me! In fact, she did raise me after my mama died. And I'll tell you what else: she cares more for me than—" The words *my own father* died in Addie's throat. "—than lots of folks who've known me as long," she said. "She's just . . . Rose, that's all. You can't let her get to you. She's just like that, is all."

"Well, you better listen to me, Adelaide Douglas," Beulah lectured, shaking an admonitory finger, "she's a little too big for her old britches, is what I think, don't matter how long you've known her. And people in Nashville ain't like some might be in Chattanooga."

No, I guess not, Addie thought.

"You let her keep carrying on like that around you and you'll be sorry, mark my words. You give 'em an inch, and they'll take a mile!"

Despite her best efforts, Addie began to smile while trying to calculate all the inches Rose had accumulated during her lifetime. "Well, anyway, Beulah, I'm so glad you came. Your hand is so much steadier than mine—would you please help me baste the batting into a quilt?"

"I guess so," she sighed, leaning over to place the cup and saucer on the side table. "Where is it?"

"At the end of the settee, by the door. The bow tie."

"Yes, I remember the bow tie," Beulah said. "This room's not big enough to cuss a cat without gettin' fur in your mouth. How in the world you gonna set a quilt frame in here?"

"Oh, it's just a baby quilt," Addie said. "I didn't figure on using a frame. I thought I'd probably just lap-quilt it."

"Well," Beulah said, shaking her head, "where's your needles and thread?"

Despite Addie's fretful impatience, March 20 did finally arrive—the day on which Zeb was to return. She was nervous and agitated all day, picking things up and immediately setting them down again, pacing the small parlor like a lion in a cage, staring habitually out the windows, though she knew Zeb's train wouldn't arrive in Nashville until ten o'clock that night.

"You better set down and rest, Missy," Rose said. She was seated in the rocker, and she had the bow tie quilt spread across her lap, taking fine stitches through the cotton batting into the backing, then back through the top. "You gonna wear yourself plumb out before your man even get home."

"Oh, Rose, I'm sorry. Here, I'll sit down and talk to you. I'm acting just like a schoolgirl today!"

"*Mmm*-hmm," came the murmured reply. Rose kept her eyes on her stitching as she asked, "How long he been gone, honey?"

"Oh, it seems like forever! But, I guess it's really only been . . . about a month."

Rose made no reply.

"He's doing very well in Little Rock, really," Addie went on. "His bosses are real proud of him. And . . . and so am I."

"*Mmm*-hmm."

"Oh, but I wish it were ten o'clock already!" Addie pushed herself out of the chair and paced toward the front door, then back, hugging herself. "I miss him so much!"

"You ain't going to hurry that train none, wearin' out this here floor," Rose said. She brought the thread to her lips to bite off an end. "He be home pretty soon, and then you be wishin' you save your strength for somethin' besides walkin' around all day."

"Rose! You crude old thing! I'm—I'm expecting!"

"Yeah, you is." She grinned at Addie. "And so is he!"

Addie stared at her, mouth agape.

"Honey, I done had seven babies," Rose went on, squinting one eye to rethread the needle, "and I knows how mens thinks, and what they thinks about. He been gone from home a solid month, and he be needin' you. Don't worry about that baby; you ain't gonna hurt him. De good Lord know what he doin' when he made us the way he do."

A flush was creeping up Addie's neck, and a smile twitched the corners of her lips. She turned away, unwilling for Rose to see the effect her advice was having.

The day wore on toward afternoon, and presently Rose stood and walked into the kitchen. She came back, carrying her shawl and kerchief.

"Oh, Rose, don't go!" Addie urged. "Please! Stay with me until Zeb— until Mr. Douglas gets home. I don't think I could stand being by myself today, as fidgety as I am. Will you stay? Please?"

Rose looked at her a long moment, then smiled slowly. "Well, all right. I reckon I can stay a little while more, at least. I don't know if I can catch a trolley after ten o'clock, though—"

"Oh, thank you, Rose! I need someone to talk to, to make the time pass faster."

"Well, I don't know about that," Rose said, tossing her wraps on the settee and slowly settling herself back in the rocker. "Seem to me like time pass on its own lookout; don't make no difference whether folks be tryin' to pass it or not."

"Now, Rose, you know what I meant. There's something I've been wanting to ask you these last few days. I've been wondering: what was it like for you when you had your first baby? How did things change for you?"

Rose rocked slowly back and forth, her hands folded on her bosom. Her face was angled to one side; she appeared to be looking beyond Addie, out the window toward Granny White Pike. For several moments she stayed like that—rocking and looking and saying nothing.

"James come into this world during the worst thunderstorm of the spring, back in '57, I guess it woulda been," she said. "He was my first, an' I guess I was plenty scared, not much knowin' what was happenin'. Oh, I done helped at lots o' birthins, but this one was mine, see, and that make everythin' different."

Addie shifted in her chair, moving the pillows at the small of her back so she could face Rose with more ease. The afternoon sun bathed the room in warm, languid light. The traffic on the street outside was infrequent, and the ticking of the Ingraham mantle clock loaned a settled, comfortable feeling to the small parlor. Rose's well-worn voice droned along the paths of her memory. Addie felt the pull of the voice, felt it summoning her steadily and pleasurably into the reminiscence, like a firm, sure hand on the drawstring of a well bucket, bringing water from a deep, sweet source.

"It was nearly midnight when I felt the pains comin' on, and I sent my man Leland down to Sister Hattie's house—oh, I guess maybe a quarter mile or more." She let out a deep, bubbly chuckle. "Honey, I ain't never gonna forget the look on that man's face when I told him it was time. I done had to jab him in the ribs four or five times with my elbow to get him awake enough to 'tend what I was sayin'. Directly, he set up. 'What you doin', woman?' he say, like I done stabbed him.

"'It's time,' I say, 'the baby comin'.'

"For a minute, I think he don't hear me. He just sit there, rubbin' his face and yawnin'. Den his eyes, they pop like *this!*" Rose laughed again, shaking her head at the memory. "'What you say, woman?' he holler. He like to fall out the bed trying to get his britches on.

"We was stayin' down by the freight yards in them days, and the closest help was Sister Hattie Sorrels. Leland light out for her house like the devil hisself was on him. He ain't no more than go out the door when the lightnin' flash so close by you could hear it crack like a whip, and right on its heels a clap o' thunder that like to wake the dead."

"Oh, Rose! Weren't you scared?"

Rose shrugged. "I guess . . . maybe. But it was too late to do much more dan wait. And pray. I done plenty o' both."

Several quiet moments passed.

"How long has your husband been—gone?"

"Fourteen years, the tenth of next month," Rose answered instantly.

"Was . . . was he sick?"

Rose shook her head. "He got hurt workin' on the incline railway up on Lookout. He was standin' behind a car loaded with blast rock, and a couplin' bust, and he get run over. He live about three days." Rose mused a few seconds. "Leland was a crew boss, so the company pay for the funeral, and they give me fifty dollars."

The clock ticked patiently. An electric trolley clattered past on the street. "How long did it take before you got over it?" Addie asked in a half-whisper.

"You don't never get over it, honey," Rose said in a creased voice as low as a moan. "You just learns to live with it, that's all. And the Lord give strength for the day."

The afternoon wore on, and despite Addie's objections, Rose had to leave. The Nashville negroes were boycotting the traction company just then, but Rose's cousins had told her about a group of blacks who were attempting to run a hack service to compete with the trolleys. The hack picked up not too far from Addie's house, but it stopped running after dark.

"I got to get on, honey," Rose said, gathering her things. "I'm too old to walk all the way to Freeman's house, and I'm too scared to try it at night."

"Of course, Rose. Thank you so much for staying with me a little longer."

"Yes'm. Don't get up, now. I can make it out the door by my own self. You don't worry about your man; he be here soon's he can, I imagine. You just take it easy, and send for me, you be needin' anythin'."

Addie watched Rose talk herself out the door, watched the door close firmly behind her, watched her amble off down Granny White Pike with her back-and-forth, purposeful gait.

Addie looked at the mantle clock and sighed. Only a quarter till five . . .

The brakes jolted the car, shaking Zeb awake. He blinked groggily, wincing as he rubbed the back of his stiff neck. He must have fallen asleep somewhere just this side of Jackson, he guessed. He peered with bleary eyes through the window and watched the Nashville station platform crawl past; slowing, slowing, and stopping with a far-off hissing of steam. "*Naysh*ville, folks, this is *Naysh*ville," sang the conductor as he walked back through the car. Zeb creaked to his feet and reached into the luggage rack for his valise.

He felt kinked and crusty from the journey, but despite his weariness, a warm anticipation bloomed within him. He was anxious to get to the house, to see Addie. It had been a long month. A corner of his mind teased at the question of whether she'd be glad to see him, whether she'd be at all inclined toward—

No! Mustn't be thinking about such things, he lectured himself. After all, Addie was approaching her time. Such things weren't decent to contemplate, and it would surely harm the child anyway. Addie was a fine, upstanding woman, and she deserved the utmost respect, especially from a husband who had been so long absent. Especially in her delicate condition.

He shuffled down the aisle of the car. The air coming through the open doors was chilly, after the comfort of the heated coach. He pulled his watch from his vest pocket and flicked open the cover. Ten-oh-seven. Just about right. The trolleys wouldn't be running, but he could probably hire a hack to take him home.

He found a slightly dilapidated hansom waiting in front of the station, the horse champing noisily in a nosebag and the cabbie dozing in the seat. "Say, there," he called, tapping the side of the cab, "you for hire?"

"Yes, sir," the cabbie replied through a yawn. "Just climb in and tell me where to."

"Granny White, up past Vanderbilt. You know where Edgehill is?"

"Yes, sir, sure do," the cabbie answered, untying the nosebag. "Have you there in a jiffy."

Half an hour later, Zeb got out of the hansom and flipped a fifty-cent piece up at the driver. "Thank *you,* sir!" he heard as the cab clattered off. He realized he probably shouldn't have tipped so much, but he was glad to be home, and he felt generous. *Besides,* he thought as he strode toward the front gate, *I can afford it!* He felt his pulse quickening as he opened the gate. The gaslights in the parlor were glowing through the windows, so Addie was waiting up for him. It would be so good to see her again.

An instant after the gate catch banged home behind him, the front door flew open. She was striding toward him, as fast as her girth would allow. He set his valise down and she was in his arms, and he was smelling the sweet scent of lilac soap and feeling her silken hair and drinking a long, glad draught from her lips.

"Well, we better get in the house," he grinned at her a moment later. "Folks'll talk."

"Oh, let 'em," she sighed, putting her arm around him as they walked toward the front door. "I've missed you so, Zeb."

"And I've missed you," he replied, opening the door for her.

They went inside. He dropped his valise beside the settee and tossed his derby on the lamp table by the door. Addie took his hand and pulled him forward. Toward the bedroom. He stared at her.

"Addie, what . . . Are you sure . . . Is this—all right?" Despite his protests, his voice was thickening with onrushing desire, and her eyes said everything he wanted to hear.

"Why, we ain't gonna hurt that baby none," she said in a weak imitation of Rose's gutteral voice. "The Lord know what he doin' . . ."

Half an hour later, he remembered to come back into the parlor and douse the gaslights.

CHAPTER
12

*L*ouisa noticed a buttercup blooming in the tall grass just beside the front steps. Without exactly knowing why, she approached the simple little yellow blossom and knelt down, touching its petals gently with a gloved finger. Rising and looking about somewhat self-consciously, she realized it was the first thing since Katherine's death that she had perceived for its own sake.

The automobile was still coughing its death throes when Dub joined her on the front porch. "Don't understand what's wrong with that cotton picking thing," he muttered. "Guy at the livery said he adjusted the carburetor—whatever in thunder that is."

"Place looks kinda bad, doesn't it?" she said, looking about her. A tread on one of the front porch steps gaped loose from its stringer, and paint was flaking in numerous places from the porch railing and trim. The grass in the front yard of her father's house appeared not to have been cut since last summer. In several places, jimsonweeds and cockleburs reared almost knee-high above the unruly lawn.

"Well, he's never been the tidy one in the family," Dub observed, pushing his hat back on his head.

"It didn't have to be this way, Dub," she insisted in a low voice. Her husband made no reply.

She went to the front door and rapped. "Papa, it's Lou and Dub! Papa, you home?"

They heard steps coming down the hallway inside, approaching the front door. The door opened, and Jacob Caswell stepped out onto the front porch, carefully pulling the door shut behind him. "Hello, Lou," he nodded to his daughter. He shook hands with his son-in-law. "Dub."

"Jacob."

"Papa, will you come eat lunch with us after church tomorrow?" Her eyes raced over him as she asked the question, spotting details with a woman's trained eye: the missing button on the waistcoat, the soiled cuff, the wrinkled trousers. It wasn't hard to imagine what the inside of the house looked like. *No wonder he pulled the door to,* she thought. *He still has some pride.*

"Yeah, hon, I guess that'd be all right," he answered, his hands jammed in his pants pockets. He rocked on his heels, staring out across the road, recently covered with fresh, orange gravel. "Thank you. I'll be there. Dub, how's the hardware business these days?"

"Not too bad, I don't guess. Summer coming on, the farmers are coming in, getting ready for . . ."

Louisa strolled away, the men's voices fading to a nondescript hum in her mind. She went down the steps and paced slowly around the side of the house, looking at everything and nothing, feeling inside herself the gradual swelling of the familiar empty space. It wasn't as bad now as right after the funeral, after everybody went home. Those few days were the worst, when there wasn't even the prospect of a public service to prop her up, only the remainder of a lifetime with a Katherine-shaped void. No, it was some better now. Not easier, exactly. Maybe she was learning to accept the numbness in her heart. Maybe she was learning to expect less.

She sat down on a stump about halfway between the back door of the house and the tree line of the wood covering Tunnel Hill. When she was still living here, this was a hoary old ash tree whose shade had accommodated many a quilt-top tea party, attended by herself and Addie, then barely more than a toddler.

Addie. I should be with you now, helping you and doing for you. Or you should be here, staying with me while Zeb goes off and does whatever it is that takes him away for so long at a time. But . . .

There used to be a soft cushion of bluegrass beneath the old ash, she remembered. But now the ground around the stump was mostly worn bare, with a few scraggly clumps of dandelion and wild rye scattered here and there. The tree had been struck by lightning one night during a wild summer thunderstorm when she still lived here. Louisa still remembered the searing crash that pounded her chest and sounded like the roof being ripped off the house. The next morning, the old ash tree was a smoking, charred splinter. No more tea parties.

Hearing footfalls, she looked up to see Papa walking toward her, his hands still jammed in his pockets. Seeing her glance at him, his eyes dodged to a spot on the ground beside the stump.

"Lou. How . . . how you doing?"

"Fine, Papa. 'Bout the same, I reckon."

"Dub says business is good."

"I guess. I wouldn't know."

He scuffed the toe of his shoe beneath a tuft of rye grass and started idly trying to root it from the ground. "Boys all right?"

"Yes. Robert still mopes some, and the baby's too little to know much."

"Well, I expect they'll be fine. Just take some time."

"Yes. Just time."

He pulled a hand from his pocket, wiping it hesitantly on his pant leg. He walked up beside her, finally, and laid it on her shoulder. "Lou, I . . . I'm sorry. Real sorry."

She sat perfectly still and expressionless, for so long that he removed his hand. He rubbed his face and stuck his hand back in his pocket. He looked away, toward the trees. Just beneath the eaves of the wood stood a sprig of dogwood, halfway through the change from blooms to leaves.

"I'm sorry, too, Papa."

It was such an odd thing for her to say, dropped without warning into the silence, that he forgot his diffidence and stared at her. "What?"

"I'm sorry too." She looked up at him. "We both lost a daughter, Papa. The Lord took mine, and there wasn't anything to be done about it."

She stood, staring into his shocked face.

"What's your excuse, Papa?"

She turned and walked back toward the house.

She could hear Dub grunting as he tried to crank the motor car. As she rounded the corner by the front porch, she glanced over her shoulder. Her father was still standing by the stump, staring at the place where she had sat.

As she entered the final month of her pregnancy, Addie began to feel more and more like a beached whale, and Zeb just couldn't seem to understand—although she thought he wanted to. This morning, for example, she felt his irritation at her slowness in getting ready for church. She could hear him pacing the parlor, hear the click of his watch cover every two or three minutes. He might blame her sloth, but he wouldn't allow it past his lips. That was something, at least.

She snapped home the last clip on the last garter, sighing as she straightened her skirts. Then she gazed hopelessly at her stockinged feet, so far away, and the high-topped shoes on the floor beside them. Bending over to fasten the buttons on her shoes was far beyond her ability this morning, even allowing that her puffy, swollen feet could be coaxed into the strict confines of the lace-up boots. "Zeb, dear, could you please come help me?" she called, unable to think of any better plan.

Zeb walked into the bedroom, his mouth a tight line of impatience. He looked at her. She handed him the buttonhook. "I can't do my shoes," she said with a shrug. "I'm really sorry, dear, but . . ."

Without saying anything, he knelt before her and held up one of the shoes. She pointed her toes and pushed, and he wriggled it back and forth until her foot was encased in leather. Then he began working the button-hook in and out of the fasteners.

They were just finishing the other shoe when they heard the slowing chug of an automobile, the squealing of brakes, followed closely by the obnoxious, gooselike honking of the brass horn. "Beulah and Will are here," he said in a terse voice. "You ready now?"

She stood. "Just hand me my purse, over there by the dresser." They went to the front door. Addie noticed that Zeb slapped a grin on his face as soon as they stepped outside.

What a fellowship, what a joy divine,
Leaning on the everlasting arms;
What a blessedness, what a peace is mine,
Leaning on the everlasting arms.

Leaning, leaning, safe and secure from all alarms;
Leaning, leaning, leaning on the everlasting arms . . .

Addie wished she could lean on something. The burst of energy she had felt a day or two previous had by now completely evaporated, and she felt all used up. The congregation arrived at the end of the song, and Brother McCrary motioned from the pulpit for them to sit down. Scarcely had she settled herself into the pew when she felt a wet spot. She was horrified to think she might have soiled her undergarments. The baby had settled awkwardly in the past few days, and sometimes, lately, she had barely been able to control her elimination functions. She felt her face burning with humiliation. How on earth could she politely excuse herself during the sermon without embarrassing herself and Zeb?

Just then, a sharp pain speared her midsection, starting from just beneath her breastbone and rippling down her stomach like cascading fire. It felt like the time her calf muscle had cramped while dog-paddling across the deep hole in Cellico Creek—but much, much worse. Despite her best efforts, a gasp escaped her lips, and her hands went to her belly.

Zeb looked at her, his face confused at first, then wide-eyed. "Is it time?" he asked in a half-whisper, grabbing her elbow.

She nodded, biting her lower lip. "I think so," she managed.

Zeb stood, stepping over the ankles and knees of the other startled worshippers seated on the pew, making his way toward the aisle. He pulled her after him. "Scuse me. Pardon me," he said in a low voice, keeping his eyes carefully averted from the surprised faces of those he was stepping over. Addie trailed behind him as fast as she could, one hand holding his, one hand gripping her abdomen, her nostrils flaring in and out as she grappled with the pain clamped like a vise on her stomach.

Beulah Counts, seated two rows behind Addie and Zeb, punched Will in the ribs. Will jerked his head up, saw the Douglases threading their way toward the center aisle, and half-leaped from his seat. The four of them paced hurriedly toward the front door of the church.

And all the while, Brother Charles McCrary never paused in his delivery, never faltered in the rhythm of his homily.

Pacing quickly toward the Duryea, Zeb asked Will, "How far is it to the closest hospital?"

"No!" grunted Addie, walking half-doubled over. "Take . . . me . . . home!"

"Now, honey, it may be fine and dandy," Beulah lectured, "for them hillbilly women in Chattanooga to drop their babies in the cabin with nothing but a granny woman, but here in Nashville, we got doctors and hospitals for such things! You just get in the car and we'll get you to—"

Her pain made Addie reckless. "Beulah, hush!" She turned to look at Zeb. "I want to go home. And I want you to go get Rose."

"Oh, Lordy! The old nigger!" howled Beulah. "What next?"

Zeb looked at his wife, panting and hanging on to his shoulder. Then he glanced at Will, who was staring back at him, trying to avoid his wife's angry glare. "Will, I believe you better get us to the house, quick as you can," Zeb said. "And then—I guess you better go get Rose."

Seated beside the bed, Zeb watched helplessly as his wife's grip suddenly intensified on his hand. She pulled her knees up and rolled to one side, letting go of a long, low moan.

He prayed harder than he ever remembered praying in his life. How much longer could Addie hold on? Where in the name of heaven was Will Counts? He half suspected Beulah had talked him into driving to the hospital and trying to convince someone to come back to the house, even though Addie had given him the piece of paper with the address of Rose's cousin scrawled in the old black woman's spidery hand.

He looked on as his wife wrestled alone with her misery, feeling as helpless and lost as an abandoned child. In her agony, she seemed distant and locked away from him. He was frightened by it but had no words with which to resist, even had she been able to hear through the fearfully intimate cords of travail that separated her from him, from knowing, from everything that had been before now. She was far, far beyond his help or even his recognition, and he was bewildered, defenseless, and insufficient.

He heard the backfiring of an automobile and craned his neck to peer around the doorway into the parlor and out the windows facing the street. His heart leaped into his throat as he saw Rose stepping out of the car almost before Will could get it stopped by the curb, and striding in short, side-to-side steps toward the front door.

"Honey, Rose is here! Hang on, all right? She's here, Addie. Can you hear me, darling?"

"I'm having a baby, Zeb, I'm not deaf! Go on and let her in the house!"

Gratefully, he rose from his chair and strode to the door, but before he could reach it, the door flew open and Rose marched past him as if he were a hatrack, shoving her purse, hat, and coat at him as she went by. "Get some water boilin'," she commanded, "and bring me some clean towels. We in for a long haul, so you might as well get comfortable."

Beulah stood in the doorway, arms akimbo, a tight-lipped, disapproving expression on her face. Will was standing a pace or so behind, hands in his pockets, peering sheepishly in at him. Zeb came to himself and tossed Rose's things on the rocking chair. "Will, thanks for everything."

Will waved his hand in dismissal. "Weren't nothin' atall," he said. "You need us to do anything else?"

Zeb looked into the bedroom, where Rose leaned over Addie, murmuring low and smiling, wiping her face with a cloth moistened in the washbasin on the bureau. Carefully avoiding eye contact with Beulah, he replied, "No, I don't guess. I think we're all right now. We'll send word when . . . when the baby comes."

"Well, all right, then," Will said, backing gratefully away from the door. He glanced at his wife's stiff, unmoving back. "Beulah," he said in a low voice, "I don't believe we're needed here now."

She drew a loud breath through her nose and let it back out the same way. "No, I'd say not," she huffed, picking up her skirts and flouncing past her husband. Zeb closed the door as Will turned to follow.

"Let's get you outta them skirts and into somethin' more practical," Rose said, raising Addie to a sitting position. She took her feet and carefully swung them down to rest on the floor.

"Oh, Rose, I don't think I can manage! Do you think there's time?"

"Honey, this your first child. We gonna be here awhile before anythin' much happen, other than some hurtin' and some strainin'. Next time, it'll be some easier, but this time you got lots o' work to do."

"If I have to hurt this much for very long, I don't think I'm gonna make it," Addie despaired.

Rose chuckled deep in her throat as she unbuttoned Addie's dress and slid it off her shoulders. "Oh, I imagine you make it," she smiled. "Besides, you in too deep now, honey. Ain't no backin' out."

"Will it really be as long an ordeal as all that?" Addie asked quietly. "Are you sure?"

Rose shrugged as she pulled a fresh nightgown from a bureau drawer. "Ain't no one sure but the good Lord," she said. "But I done had seven of my own and helped a sight more into this world. If your baby here by sundown, you be better off than some I know."

Addie heaved a deep sigh as she settled the nightgown around her. Then she felt a warm, familiar hand on her shoulder. "I be here with you, honey," Rose said, patting gently. "I be here till you don't need me no more. Ain't much in the way of birthin' babies I ain't seen."

And then another contraction ripped downward from Addie's breastbone and clenched her belly in a steel band.

For the next eight hours, Zeb alternated between pacing the shrinking confines of the parlor and fetching various items at Rose's command. When the early spasms came, he was frightened by the sounds coming from the partially closed bedroom door. He wanted to either go in and hold his wife or run out the door and down the street, to return when it was all over.

As if divining his thoughts, Rose had poked her head into the parlor during that time. "You the only help I got," she said. "You stay close by where I can call you easy and quick. Now, go warm me a towel on the stove!"

He carried to the doorway a dizzying succession of warm towels, cold cloths, ice chips, steaming water, cups, saucers, blankets, and other assorted paraphernalia. Each element disappeared in a flash of brown hands and arms into the birthing chamber. These instant errands were interspersed with bouts of pacing and an inner turmoil that mounted with each agonized moan from his wife's tortured body. She sounded like she was dying! Maybe Beulah was right; maybe she needed a doctor. Once, during an apparent lull in Addie's labor, he crept to the door and timidly raised a knuckle to tap and inquire whether anything was needed. Scarcely had he rapped once when Rose's head thrust from inside. "Scald a big dishpan and bring it to me," she ordered, shutting the door in his face. And so it went.

As the afternoon light began to slant long and golden with the coming of evening, the sound and activity in the bedroom reached a flurrying crescendo. Zeb's blood ran cold as he heard the brutish grunts and growls coming from Addie's throat.

He heard Rose chanting in a low, insistent voice: "Come on, now, honey. Push for me, baby, *push* for me. Come on now, *puuuuush* for me, baby. That's it, that's it. All right, let go for a minute, let go . . . Now! *Puuuuush,* honey! *Come* on, now . . ." Sounding now like a mule skinner, now like a revival preacher, Rose cajoled and urged and scolded to the rising and falling accompaniment of his wife's groans and exhalations and half-articulate cries.

"Just a little more! Just a little more now, baby!" he heard, Rose's voice rising half an octave, as Addie panted loud and rhythmically. "Just a little—there you is, you little dickens!" Rose cried in triumph. A few seconds later, Zeb heard a sound that made his knees wobble: the thin, high wail of a baby exhaling its first lungful of air in a cry of protest.

He would have gone to the door if he thought he could take the five or six paces without falling. His heart was yammering in his chest like a thing gone mad. Without realizing it, he had collapsed onto the divan and sat there, staring at the partially closed bedroom door as if it were suddenly the gateway to a foreign country.

CHAPTER
13

Rose sat heavily in the chair beside the bed as she wiped the last traces of blood from her hands and forearms. "We get you cleaned up, Missy," she said, "before your man come in here. He see you like this, he liable to fall out."

Addie looked up from the head of her nuzzling baby long enough to give the older woman a wan smile. "I guess I don't exactly look fit for polite company, do I?"

"Honey, after what you just done, ain't nobody gonna expect lace and spit curls. But we don't wanna scare your man, neither. Most men can stand nearly anythin' 'cept birthin' blood. I think it must remind 'em of what it done took they mamas to get 'em here. I think they feels bad about it but can't say so."

Addie caressed the child's downy head. She was starting to get the hang of nursing now and her little mouth was pulling greedily at the nipple. Addie felt the twinge of afterpangs now and again, but compared to the ordeal of the birth, they were barely worth noting.

"Raise up a little on this side, honey." She leaned as Rose directed, feeling the sheets slide from beneath her. "Now the other side, sugar. Your nightgown don't look too bad, since we kept it up out the way. We get some clean sheets on this here bed and then we be ready for the new papa to come have a look at this here fine young 'un."

Addie peered down at the tiny profile, still nursing eagerly. The baby's eyes were open, their hue a dark blue bordering on purple, and now and again Addie thought she cut her eyes upward, trying to see. "My sweet baby," Addie murmured, stroking the still-moist cheek. "My beautiful, perfect child." She felt dizzied by the dense reality of the suckling child in her arms, by the unfamiliar, stunning fact of her presence. All during the nine months leading up to this moment, Addie had known her more as idea than actuality. But now . . . This thing that had issued from her in tides of pain and blood was a *person,* endowed with every perfect detail in breathtaking miniature. There now existed a living, breathing human being who had never before been! The simple wonder of it rose far beyond the reach of her mind's vision, swelling unutterable within her until she thought her heart must burst. She used a finger to heft the tiny hand with its five miniscule fingernails, and suddenly she knew: her heart wasn't bursting. It was stretching to bear her love for this child, just as her muscles and sinews and flesh had stretched and groaned to deliver such a miracle into the light of day.

Rose tossed a clean, crisp sheet into the air and it settled down over them like a gently falling cloud. She tucked the corners in and propped Addie up just so. Casting a final critical glance at the tableau, she went to the door and called out to Zeb. "Well? You ready to see your new baby?"

Addie heard his steps slowly traverse the parlor. He stepped into the doorway, his face as drawn and void as an empty poke. He looked at her, then down at the tiny head bobbing at her breast, and his eyes flared open. The sight breathed life back into him; his whole body bloomed and stretched and widened with joy, and a grin clasped his face. "Why, Addie," he breathed, "it's . . . it's beautiful!"

"Not an 'it.' It's a 'she,'" Addie beamed.

"A girl?"

"Yeah. Is that all right?"

"Why—why, I imagine so! I imagine *so!*"

"What you doin', standin' in that door like you's company?" Rose said. "Get on over there and hold that baby!"

Nervously rubbing his hands on his wrinkled shirt front, Zeb sidled toward the bed. He reached forward to receive the wrapped bundle.

"Don't worry, you ain't fixin' to break her," came Rose's voice, soft at his elbow. "Just let her head rest in the crook o' your arm; there—just like that. Looky there, she cuttin' her eyes at you. You see your daddy, li'l Missy? This here your papa, honey."

Zeb peered into his daughter's face, hardly daring to breathe. "Her . . . her mouth looks like yours," he told Addie in a stage whisper.

"Yeah, but she got your eyes, that's for sure," Rose said.

"You really think so?"

"Mmm-hmm. I expect they be green this time next year, just like yours. What you gonna name her?"

Zeb and Addie stared at each other. "I thought we'd name her Mary Alice," Addie said, "after both our mothers. If . . . that'd be—all right."

Zeb's eyes were drawn back to the tiny, red face peering from the blankets. "Well, Miss Mary Alice Douglas. How do you do?"

In the days that followed, Zeb became more practiced at holding his daughter, but he never quite felt comfortable doing it. Addie or Rose would place the baby in his arms, and he would struggle manfully to relax—mostly to no effect. But Mary Alice didn't seem to mind; she seemed fully as contented to be in one set of arms as another. Unless, of course, she was hungry or soiled. Then Zeb yielded gratefully to the experts.

He couldn't talk about the way he felt toward the child because he didn't understand it himself. Looking at her, he felt an odd mixture of awe, delight, confusion, pride, fear, and pleasure. Protective zeal surged through him, and on its heels came intense bouts of anxiety. It was at once a wonder and a worry to him that he must now portion his consciousness, not in halves, but in thirds. "Daughter" became an exotic taste for him, a new sensation that he caressed in his mind, standing back and watching himself admire its novelty—and fret over its ramifications.

Sometimes, as he sat, he would catch one of the women watching him. Addie's eyes were always soft and cherishing, loving him from where she sat, glowing with an adoration that seemed to radiate to him from the baby when he held her. These days, he basked in a reflected light.

Rose, on the other hand, used a more veiled look. Sometimes she would smile at him a little and nod her head, but her eyes never dropped their guarded assessment. She reminded Zeb of an insurance prospect, listening patiently to the sales pitch and constantly wondering how much the payments will be.

He sometimes thought he was outside the fence, looking in at Rose and Addie. The two women shared something he couldn't calculate or understand. It was the same when callers came, the women all aflutter and the men—when they couldn't avoid coming—with hats in hand, smiling gravely down at Mary Alice, who appeared completely indifferent to all the attention. The women had so much to say about the whole matter; the men seemed more intent on failing to notice it. They would talk to Zeb about the weather, about automobiles, about dogs and guns and Congress. They would have discussed business, he guessed, but for their knowledge of the line Zeb was in. Maintaining a proper distance was the thing.

A few days after Mary Alice's birth, a delivery boy came bearing a stylishly wrapped package with a card from the men at the home office. "Congratulations, Zeb and Addie," it read. Along with the package, the boy handed Zeb a small note in a separate envelope. "So pleased to hear of your new arrival," it read in Mr. Griffs' back-slanted hand, "and looking forward to your return to the field. Little Rock needs your steady hand on the tiller."

Reading the note again, Zeb—to his surprise—felt an odd sense of relief. In the back of his mind, he had been wondering how to broach the subject of his return to work, but there hadn't seemed to be a right time to mention it. Now, Mr. Griffs had handled it for him. After all, the bosses were plainly ready to have him back in action. Surely no one could fault him for that! And, with the new responsibility of a child to feed and clothe, it was only right that he return to the serious business of making a living. Addie would understand.

"Oh, Zeb, look!" Addie cried, holding up from the ruin of the decorated box a shining silver cup and saucer. "It's got her name engraved on it, and her date of birth!" Addie turned the set this way and that.

"Sure is pretty," said Rose, cradling Mary in one meaty arm.

"Zeb, you must tell Mr. Griffs and the others how delightful this is!"

"Well, now that you mention it," he said in his most carefully casual voice, "I had thought about checking in at the office here in the next day or so."

"Yes, I suppose it's about time for you to think about getting back," Addie said. The dip in her voice was so slight, Zeb would never have noticed it, had he not been looking for it.

The next morning he rose and quietly washed and dressed in the half-light that trickled through the closed window shades. His eyes felt gritty, and there was a dull pressure in his forehead. He figured he'd slept perhaps three hours all night.

Sleeping with an infant in the tiny bedroom was a mounting frustration. Each time Mary would gurgle or stir, Addie would sit up or rise from the bed to stand over her and peer intently at her in the dimness. And then, every three hours or so, the baby would get hungry and begin the clucking and chirping that would eventually erupt into a full-blown demand to be fed. Usually, before she could get up a full head of steam, Addie would reach into the crib and gather her up, murmuring sleepily to her and bringing her to the breast.

Amid such a commotion and bouncing of mattresses and rustling of bedclothes, slumber would have been impossible to any but a dead man, Zeb surmised. He had always been a light sleeper in the first place, and the nightly program was certainly not geared to his rest patterns. Addie could catnap during the day when Mary was asleep, but he had never been able to doze when the sun was up.

As he fastened the cuffs on his shirt, he looked over at the tangled bundle on the bed sighing deeply in rhythmic, slow breaths. *Best not to disturb Addie,* he thought. Lifting his coat from the bedpost, he tiptoed from the room. He took one last glance at the two sleepers and backed quietly through the door, latching it behind him.

In the kitchen was Rose, who had slept on the settee. She sat at the small table, blowing softly on a steaming cup of coffee. She looked tired, crumpled. As he came in, she got up to get the coffeepot. She poured a cup and set it in front of him.

"Thanks."

She seated herself again without replying. They both sipped gingerly at the black, near-boiling brew.

"They's toast in the skillet," she said, a few moments later.

He went over to the stove and carefully plucked a crisp slice of buttered bread from the flat iron skillet. He took a bite, then another.

"How come you didn't go back to your cousin's last night?" he asked around his second mouthful.

Rose sipped, then shrugged. "Got too late. Thought y'all might need some help."

"Sure was a short night," he admitted.

"Mmm-hmm."

She tilted her cup and allowed a little coffee to dribble down its side into her saucer to cool. In a bit, she picked up the saucer and slurped. Setting it down slowly, she glanced at him. "Ain't nobody's fault, though."

He looked at her. "Do what?"

"Ain't the baby's fault. She don't know no better. And Miz Addie bound to be restless with her for a little while, till she get used to it."

"I know that."

She looked down at her saucer. "Yessuh. I'm just sayin' . . ."

He took a few more sips of his coffee, then poured the remainder down the sink. He crossed the parlor and took his hat from the lamp table, pulled on his coat, and walked out the front door.

Rose watched him leave, then studied the tabletop for a long while. "Lord, tell me I'm wrong about that man," she prayed softly.

Perhaps forty-five minutes later, Addie stumbled into the kitchen.

"Mornin'," said Rose.

"Good morning. I don't know why I'm up, the baby's still asleep."

"You better get your rest while you can," Rose said. "You want some coffee?"

"Oh, nothing right now, Rose, thanks." She peered around. "Where's Zeb?"

"He gone, honey. He left before you got up."

"Oh. Well, I . . . I guess he needed to get an early start."

"Mmm-hmm. I guess so."

CHAPTER
14

*T*he band struck up Sousa's "Liberty Bell" march, and George Hutto smiled as a group of young children near the front formed an impromptu marching corps. They tromped up and down in front of the crowd by the bandstand, wriggling their fingers and swinging their arms in imitation of clarinetists, trombonists, and cymbal players. They kept at it, too, for the entire march. No one really minded, George guessed, since it was the final piece on the program. It was a gorgeous, sunny Fourth of July afternoon, and surely no one expected children to sit in one place and fidget indefinitely.

George wandered from his place toward the back of the crowd, meaning to head for the nearest lemonade stand. It looked as if nearly everyone in Hamilton County was in Olympia Park today, and most of them were smiling, as far as he could tell. So far, the reputation of the Chamber of Commerce was secure for another year. George only hoped this evening's fireworks display was a success. He had felt deep misgivings about letting the Chamber talk him into chairing the entertainment committee, but when the mayor had asked him, he hadn't been able to find a handy excuse. And, indeed, things were going well. The children's patriotic skit this morning had been met with enthusiastic—if slightly partisan—applause, and the community band had done a real nice job just now. Once the fireworks went off without difficulty, he could rest easy.

For perhaps the twentieth time that day, he scanned the sky to the west and southwest, looking for any telltale stacks of cumulus clouds that might be gathering into thunderheads. All clear, so far. Of course, it was still early afternoon.

The First Methodist Church lemonade stand was in an elm grove, just south of the grandstand for the racetrack. As he approached, George could hear the roaring, popping, and wheezing of the racing cars as their drivers made last-minute adjustments before the preliminary heats began. They had intended to hold the automobile races earlier in the day, but the noise and smell of the machines kept the horses in such a continual uproar, they'd been forced to delay the motorized events until after the end of the harness racing and draft competitions.

George fished a nickel out of his pocket and laid it on the plank counter. "How about a glass with lots of ice?" he asked the nearest attendant.

"Coming right up, George," she answered. Hearing his name, he looked up at her. "Well, hello, Louisa! Excuse me for not noticing who I was talking to."

"That's quite all right," she smiled, setting down a glass full of chipped ice and pouring into it from a crockery pitcher so large she had to wrestle it with both hands. "Everybody seems to be having a real nice time today. Y'all did a good job, looks like."

George smiled shyly, dabbing his forehead with a handkerchief. "Well, thanks. Wouldn't be proper not to throw a big Fourth of July, though, would it? Church making lots of money today?"

"Doing pretty well, long as the weather stays warm."

"Well, here's hoping it does, at least till after the fireworks," he said, saluting the sky with his glass and taking several deep swallows. "Say, uh, Louisa," he continued, hesitantly, "what do you hear from . . . from over Nashville way?" He sipped again at his lemonade, tilting his panama back on his head.

"Oh, I don't guess you heard. Addie and Zeb had a little girl."

"You don't say! What'd they name her?"

"Mary Alice, after both grandmothers."

"Well, I'll say! That's just fine, isn't it! Just fine! Guess everybody's doing well?"

"Far as I know." Her smile was quick, and George thought maybe it never got as far as her eyes. She turned away to drop his nickel in the till and put the lemonade pitcher back on the work table. He felt awkward. Maybe he shouldn't have brought up the subject of children to her.

He cleared his throat, trying to think of something to chink the gap in the conversation. "Louisa, it's . . . it's real good to see you out, working with the other women from the church, and . . . and getting on so well and all."

She shrugged and looked away. "Some days are better than others, George. You just keep putting one foot in front of the other, somehow."

There was a long silence, and this time George didn't have the nerve to try and fill it.

"But we'll manage, I guess," she finished finally, giving him another smile and doing better with it this time. "And thank you for saying something. Most folks just ignore it, pretend everything's like it always was."

He blushed and pulled off his glasses, ducking into his collar as he polished the lenses with his slightly damp handkerchief. "Well, I . . . I'm awful fond of your family, is all, and—"

"Yes. I know you are, George." Her eyes were still on him, but now they were full of something besides pain.

He peered at his lemonade, then took an extra-long, thoughtful sip. "I reckon your daddy was tickled," he said, trying to quickly cover his befuddlement, "to hear about Addie's new—"

George cringed inside. *Of all the stupid things to say!* "Louisa, I'm sorry, I wasn't thinking—"

"It's all right, George," she said. "You're not to be faulted. Any right-thinking man *would* be proud and happy about a healthy new granddaughter. Papa's just not too good at admitting he might be wrong about some things. He's got more pride than any one man needs."

George clunked his empty glass down on the plank. He gave her a nervous smile and touched the brim of his hat. "Well, good to see you again," he managed, backing away. "I guess I better go see how those boys are doing with the race cars. Tell Dub I said hello."

"I sure will. Nice talking to you, George."

He nodded and smiled again, then turned and strode purposefully off toward the grandstand.

As the western sky began to redden, the crowd started to gather in and around the grandstand. Chamber of Commerce officials had roped off a large area of the infield, just inside the far turn, where the fireworks would be detonated. Families sprawled on quilts in the rest of the infield, staking out space from which to observe the much-anticipated display.

George paced the enclosure, frequently wiping his brow as he observed the preparations of the pyrotechnician. The man had set up a long, narrow table, crisscrossed by scorch marks. He was laying on it a collection of tubes, rockets, and canisters. He made numerous trips to the interior of his painted wagon, always returning with another armload of mysterious and imposing articles. The wagon was painted a brilliant red, and on its side it advertised the name and vocation of the owner. "Horatio P. Folger, Esq.: Explosives Expert, Fireworks, Rainmaking, & Etc.," it announced in ornate gold-highlighted black letters that followed each other round in an elaborate oval. In the center of the oval were the words "Atlanta, Georgia, United States of America (God Bless the USA)." Beneath, in finer, more sedate black print and straight lines, was an amplification: Available for Civic Events . . . Private Celebrations . . . Land Clearing . . . Demolition . . . and Various & Sundry Other Uses."

George had been watching Horatio P. Folger since his arrival in the midafternoon. Folger had a florid complexion and a prodigious moustache with waxed handlebars. He wore a derby that apparently never left his skull, despite the summer heat. Predictably, a train of boys had trailed him into the fairgrounds and loitered about his wagon, occasionally making half-hopeful offers to assist, which were refused with a chuckle and a shake of the head. And, of course, under his watchful eye, no one dared approach the wagon for a closer look. Horatio P. Folger had evidently been at this for some time.

George was considerably relieved to lay eyes at last on this man. Upon the skill and provision of Horatio P. Folger hung the success or failure of Chattanooga's Independence Day festivities. George well knew that six months from now very few would remember who had won the cake-baking contest or the horseshoe tournament, but everyone would recollect and discuss at length any perceived inadequacy of this, the capstone event.

Folger went methodically about his business, now and again casting a quick eye at the western horizon. At the center of the roped-off staging area he had placed five or six metal tubes, arranging them in a ten-foot circle. To George, they suspiciously resembled artillery mortars. In a concentric arc fifteen feet outside the circle, Folger had deployed three metal racks that appeared to be frames for launching skyrockets. Each rack could hold four rockets.

During a lull in the preparations, George approached. "Ah, excuse me, Mr. Folger?"

"Yeah, that's me. What can I do for you?"

George had expected the voice to be a bass boom, but it was actually a rather high-pitched, soft tone that greeted him. "Ah, I'm George Hutto. I'm the fellow who wrote you . . . hired you?"

"Why sure! Glad to make your acquaintance, Mr. Hutto!" As he pumped his hand vigorously, George noted with some satisfaction that Horatio P. Folger had all his fingers and thumbs.

George pulled out his wallet and peeled off a number of bills. "Let's see. I think it was a hundred, wasn't it?" He offered the bills, but Folger shook his head.

"Just half now, then half when the show's over, if you're satisfied."

George raised his eyebrows. "Why, I, ah . . . I just assumed—"

"No, Mr. Hutto," said Horatio P. Folger, "I don't want nobody to pay a hundred dollars for a show that don't meet expectations. Half now, then we'll talk later." He held out his hand.

Feeling a cautious, hopeful glow spreading inside him, George counted out fifty dollars on the waiting palm.

"Oh, and one more thing," added the fireworks man. "Reckon you 'n' 'bout two other fellas could run for me during the show?"

George frowned doubtfully. "Run?"

"Yeah. I'll have all the charges and rockets laid out on that table yonder, in order from left to right. All you gotta do is bring me the next thing, wherever I'm standing. Rockets'll be yonder," he said, pointing at the three racks, "and charges come over here, to the mortars."

"Well, I don't know who I can get—"

"Anybody's fine; you 'n' two other men oughta be plenty. Just don't ask no kids. I don't trust kids. They're too clumsy, or too excited. Either one can get you into trouble with this stuff."

George nodded solemnly, feeling a tiny ache beginning in the center of his forehead. "I'll see what I can do."

"Fine." Folger squinted at the western sky. "I imagine we'll start here in about . . . oh, say twenty minutes. Oughta be good and dark by then."

George wandered off. *Good and dark . . . don't trust kids . . . charges . . . rockets . . .* He wished he had some headache powders. He wished he hadn't allowed the mayor to talk him into this job. He wished above all that he hadn't made the acquaintance of Horatio P. Folger, Esq.

Twenty minutes later, George stood by the scorched table and craned his neck skyward to see the huge, floral burst of reds and greens and brilliant whites that announced the opening of the fireworks show. As he heard the *boom!* closely followed by the long, collective *ahhhh!* from the gathered populace, his apprehensions evaporated like a raindrop on a hot sidewalk. He and the two other men ran for Horatio P. Folger and observed at close hand the work of a master.

Folger seemed to be following a sort of secret choreography as he skipped in and out of the circle of mortars and placed the rockets in their launching frames. As he lit the fuse of one rocket, George could hear him softly count, "One, two, three," before lighting the next fuse. And the rockets would ascend in graduated cohesion, flinging across his black velvet canvas the shimmering, cascading, supremely transient compositions of Horatio P. Folger, Esq.

He danced back and forth, loading two or three of the mortars to toss aloft a violet starburst in combination with a scurrying tangle of red-and-white poppers, with maybe a shower of golden stars thrown in for good measure. Then he would be at the nearest frame, setting the rockets brought to him by his half-mesmerized assistants.

George and the other two runners fell into his rhythm, pulled in irresistibly by their leader as, from left to right, they slowly denuded the scorched table of its carefully organized cargo. Folger never looked at them, never gave them any instruction other than his reaching hand awaiting the next explosive pigment for his aerial palette. There was no time for chatter, nor any need. There was only time to retrieve the next charge, the next rocket, and perhaps to glance upward at the breathtaking, disappearing beauty.

For the grand finale, there was a storm of red, white, and blue starbursts, underlined by thundercracking white shells that exploded barely a hundred feet off the ground. Folger dashed and sprinted to and fro like a man gone mad, firing mortars, lighting rockets, and setting the next pieces with absolute, sure-handed precision. George and the other two men were huffing and puffing, trying to keep pace with the dashing figure of their taskmaster. The cannonade went on and on, seemingly beyond endurance, beyond what was possible for a human to maintain or to watch. And when the last explosion rolled away over the Tennessee River and into the hollows between the hills, when the curtain of silence had settled over Olympia Park for ten seconds, then twenty, then a minute, when even the little children knew that nothing could possibly follow such magnificence, there erupted from the exhausted, thrilled, drained crowd a groundswell of applause, accompanied here and there by spontaneous choruses of Ward's "Materna" and "Columbia, the Gem of the Ocean."

George stepped over and gratefully pressed fifty dollars into the hand of Horatio P. Folger, Esq.

George was pleased to realize that he hadn't thought at all of being nervous during the fireworks show. As he walked back toward town, he heard many favorable comments from other homeward-bound folks, and each compliment gave him a tiny, pleasant glow. The mayor even found him along the way, came up to him, and clapped him on the shoulder. "Fine fireworks this year, George, just fine!" he said in his big, glad voice. "Where was it that fellow was from? Atlanta?"

"Yes, sir, I believe he was," George replied.

"Well, fine. We ought to try and hire him again next year, don't you reckon?"

"Well, I'll let somebody else worry about it next year."

"Oh, now, George, don't be so modest! You did a real fine job on the entertainment! Everybody says so, and I wouldn't be surprised if you weren't asked again!"

George felt his insides give a kind of half-regretful shrug. "Well . . . I guess we'll have to wait and see," he said, finally.

He climbed the hill toward home, thinking about his conversation with Addie's sister at the lemonade stand. It was too bad about her father. A corner of his mind tried to toy with a slight, guilty pleasure at her misfortune, but he sternly resisted. Such uncharitable thoughts weren't Christian, and he well knew it. If Jacob Caswell wanted to be famous for mulishness, that was his lookout.

He had reached the gaslit streets of Cameron Hill. He looked about him at the folks wending homeward, talking and laughing softly among themselves, some carrying the small, sleeping forms of those overcome by the strenuous task of being children on a holiday. George wondered what it must be like to have a family, to have children. The quiet, homeward talk went on all about him, but he caught only snatches of words here and there. It was as if those around him were speaking a dialect that was just foreign enough to be puzzling. He could hear tone and inflection, sense the smiles, arguments, caresses, and frustrations lying just beneath the surface of the muted syllables pattering about him in the humid summer darkness—but he couldn't quite seem to make sense of the words. George wondered what, exactly, he had missed.

"Good evening, George," called a female voice to his right. He glanced over to see Elizabeth Capshaw walking arm-in-arm with young Jeff Hinson. "Evening, Betsy, Jeff," he replied as they passed, nodding and touching the brim of his hat. He stared after them for a moment. Jeff had been squiring Betsy around ever since Easter. Looked like they were getting to be thick as thieves. They walked ahead of him, hurrying along to be somewhere else.

Perlie Overby waited, his dirty plug hat crumpled in one fist. After a few seconds, the front door swung open. "Well, hello, Perlie! I didn't hear you come up. Sorry it took me so long to get to the door."

"That's all right, Mr. Caswell, I shoulda made more noise, I guess. I kinda figured your dogs'd bark at me, but I reckon they've smelled my durned ol' hide so much here lately, I'm just part of the furniture anymore."

Jacob laughed.

"I come by to let you know I'll finish the scraping down at the store by tomorrow noon. I guess I'll be ready to start painting then."

"Fine, Perlie. Just tell Gus or one of the boys to get you what you need."

"Well . . . All right, then. Uh, say, Mr. Caswell?"

Jacob had already started back inside. His hand on the doorknob, he turned back toward the ragged figure on his porch. "Yeah, Perlie?"

Perlie was twisting his hat in his two grimy fists, and his eyes watched the gouged toes of his battered boots. "Uh, Mr. Caswell, I know it ain't been a week yet, but we run plumb outta beans last night at our place, and I was just wondering if they was any way I could go ahead and maybe get my day's wages so I could—"

"Sure, Perlie, sure. Why didn't you say so? Wait right here and I'll be back directly." He ducked back inside the doorway of the big house while Perlie waited, alone on the wide porch. When Jacob reappeared a minute or two later, he held out a silver dollar in one hand and a cloth sack in the other. "Here's a day's pay, plus a little extra, and here's some cornmeal. I've got more than I can use right now, so why don't you take this on home, and your wife can cook up some griddle cakes or something for your young 'uns till you get a chance to get by the store."

"Well, that's mighty generous, Mr. Caswell, mighty generous for sure!" Perlie's head bobbed up and down in gratitude as he took the limp sack from Jacob's hand. "If you're sure you ain't got no use for this here, I imagine we can take care of it for you."

"Well, that's all right. You take it, and welcome."

Perlie turned to go, then faced Jacob once more. "Say, Mr. Caswell, I hate to be a nuisance, but I got to thinking today, I ain't seen Miss Addie around here fer awhile. She git married off, or something?"

Jacob's jaw clenched and his brow clouded over. Staring over Perlie's left shoulder, he said in a grudging voice, "Yeah. She married and left town."

"Well, that's real fine. I always did like Miss Addie. You know, one time a coupla winters ago, she come to my place and set with my young 'uns while me 'n' the missus was out of pocket. She was real kind to them young 'uns, too, and I ain't never forgot it. Where'd she move off to?"

Jacob peered across the road for a second or two more, then lanced Perlie with a direct look. "I really couldn't say." And then he was gone.

Perlie gaped at the closed door. He thoughtfully hefted the sack of cornmeal a time or two. Finally, settling his hat on his head, he eased down the steps and turned toward home.

CHAPTER

15

Zeb stepped off the train into the midafternoon heat and bustle of Union Station in Little Rock. He set down his valise and motioned with his free hand for a nearby porter. The uniformed negro approached, trundling a hand truck in front of him. Zeb pointed at his suitcase, then handed him the valise. "Is there a hack that can take me to the Gleason Hotel?"

"Yessuh. Right this way."

Ducking through the shouldering crowd as he followed the porter, Zeb noticed a poster advertising a traveling Chautauqua troupe. There was a show at seven o'clock that evening in the city park. He wasn't in the mood to sit up in the room and brood. Might be good for him to get out, be in a crowd, hear some music and talk and laughter. He decided to go, after a nap, a bath, and supper.

When the bellboy set his luggage down on the lumpy bed, Zeb dropped two half dimes into the waiting hand, tossed his hat on top of the suitcase, and stepped across the room to open the curtains. He heard the door close behind him. Zeb stood with his hands in his pockets, staring down from his third-story window onto Markham Street. Just across the way rose the dome of the state capitol building.

He wondered how Addie and the baby were doing. He hated to leave only two weeks after Mary Alice's birth, but the days of inactivity had begun to chafe more and more. He was worried about his new agents here. A couple of them seemed like real good men, but there were others who wanted constant propping up. He couldn't afford for the Little Rock agency to falter, now that Griffs and Carleton were beginning to take such a personal interest in his career. If he could keep things going here, it might be the next step to a home office assignment—and he had yet to reach his thirtieth birthday.

Addie had started to tear up some when he was taking his leave. She'd been standing in the front door, holding the baby in her arms.

"Well," he'd said, looking away, "I guess if I wanna catch my train, I better get going." The hack was standing in the street, the driver staring fixedly over his horse's rump.

"Yeah," she said, or he'd thought she said. Her voice was soft and airy. Her chin was dimpling, as if she were trying to hold it still.

He'd leaned over and kissed Mary Alice on the forehead, then did the same to Addie. He turned and walked away, toward the hack.

"I'll write as soon as I get there," he'd called over his shoulder, afraid to look at her, afraid she'd burst into tears in front of the hack driver. He'd thrown his bags into the cab, and the driver clicked his tongue, and he was away, wishing he could ignore the dull ache in his throat.

But he was feeling better now, thinking about all that needed to be done here, all the opportunity waiting for him. It was his responsibility to make a good life for his family. It was his God-given duty, if it came to that, and he was determined to make the most of this chance. Addie would understand. When he had a home office job in Nashville, he'd buy her a nice, roomy house with a big nursery for Mary Alice. He'd be home every night, and they would have nice things—the kinds of things his mother had never had.

He felt a heaviness around his eyes and remembered he'd promised himself a nap. He loosened his cravat and unbuttoned his collar. Setting his luggage on the faded carpet, he stretched out on the single bed with his hands behind his head and closed his eyes.

After tossing and turning for quite awhile, Zeb finally accepted his failure at the attempt to actually sleep. He sat up, rubbing his face, and realized the shadows in the room told him dusk was approaching. No time to bathe now if he wanted to get something to eat and get to the Chautauqua show on time. He ran a hand through his hair and straightened his collar and tie. Giving himself a final once-over in the streaked mirror on the opposite wall, he walked out, locking the door behind him and pocketing the skeleton key.

By the time he arrived at the park, a crowd was already pooling under the tent. A brass band was thumping out some march or other; the muffling of the tent and the crowd made the tune indistinct. Zeb hurried up and snagged one of the last rickety wooden chairs on the end of the back row just as the band collided with the final note of the march. The crowd applauded politely, and a large, pot-bellied man with luxuriant sideburns and a florid complexion mounted the steps to the podium and approached the lectern.

Slowly and dramatically, he unbuttoned his coat to reveal a brocaded waistcoat. He took a deep breath and looked at the audience. "I shall perform Antony's funeral oration from *Julius Caesar,* by William Shakespeare," he announced in a booming bass voice. He gripped the sides of the lectern and gazed out over the heads of the crowd. Taking three paces away from the lectern, he raised his right hand in a graceful, beckoning gesture.

"Friends, Romans, countrymen, lend me your ears! I come to bury Caesar, not to praise him . . ."

There was a slight disturbance by Zeb's elbow, and he glanced up to see an older man and a young woman standing beside him. The man pointed at the two empty seats to Zeb's left and asked with his eyebrows if they were taken. Zeb shook his head and stood to let them pass. The man entered first, followed by the woman. They settled themselves, and Zeb resumed his seat.

"... The noble Brutus hath told you Caesar was ambitious; if it were so, it was a grievous fault ..."

From the corner of his eye, Zeb saw the woman pull a fan from her handbag. The short, soft drafts bore the scent of her perfume: lilac. In an instant, he was carried back to a moonlit promenade beside the pond in East Lake Park, in Chattanooga. Addie always wore lilac perfume in those days, and the smell made him long for her with a sudden, bodily ache.

" ... ambition should be made of sterner stuff ..."

She had seemed like an angel to him in those days; her every movement had enchanted him, had hinted at secrets, suggested the possibility of delightful discoveries. He could look at her for hours on end and never grow tired. She dispensed happiness to him, simply by being in his presence. He thought he could never again lack for anything if only he might have her.

And then he had won her. Over Jacob Caswell's disapproval and the entangling ties of her Methodist upbringing, he had won her. He, the outsider, the poor boy from the hardscrabble farm in north Georgia. The one with the ambition and the drive and the determination—he had won her. And for a time, the sweetness of his life had been everything her enchantment had intimated. She was like the magic pan of gingerbread in the fairy tale; each day he fed on her love until he was satisfied; and the next morning she was still there, fully as beautiful and charming and delightful as the day before.

When had he first noticed the fading of the sweetness? Was it something he had done that had broken the spell? How had he failed her? He had been a faithful husband and a diligent provider. He didn't run with the drinking crowd, didn't gamble or carouse. He had based every decision on what he believed to be best for them in the long run. He didn't like all the moving around and traveling, but what else could he do? This was his opportunity—their opportunity.

He thought of her face in the moonlight of East Lake Park, then remembered the drained, resigned, suffering expression she'd worn yesterday as he walked out the front gate. Where had he gone wrong?

". . . O judgment! Thou art fled to brutish beasts, and men have lost their reason . . ."

The woman beside him stopped fanning for a moment, leaned over and whispered something to the older man. Zeb heard their chuckles mingle softly. He cut his eyes to the left without moving his head. She was well dressed, and he could see strands of blonde peeking from beneath her lace bonnet. She bore a slight resemblance to her companion, and Zeb wondered if she might be his daughter. She was fair-complexioned, but there was a sprinkling of faint freckles across the bridge of her nose. She resumed fanning, and Zeb returned his eyes to the podium.

After the orator, there was a handbell choir, and after that, a male quartet dressed in wooden shoes and knee breeches and singing in Dutch. Then a man made up like Abe Lincoln gave the Gettysburg Address, and a woman dressed as the Statue of Liberty recited "The New Colossus," by Emma Lazarus. Finally, the pot-bellied Antony came back and gave a long-winded, stentorian benediction, and the program was officially over.

Zeb stood and tried to work the kinks out of his legs. He turned to go, and felt a hand on his arm.

"Thank you for saving the seats for us," said the young woman, smiling playfully. "I told Daddy we'd be so late we'd have to stand, and if it hadn't been for you, we would have."

The man stuck out a hand. "Pete Norwich."

Zeb shook his hand firmly. "Zeb Douglas. Pleased to meet you."

"Yes, indeed. And this is my daughter, Rebecca. She drags me to these cotton-pickin' cultural sessions, whether I want to come or not."

Zeb chuckled with them and took her proffered fingers gently. "Pleased to meet you, Ma'am."

"It's 'Miss,'" she corrected him, "and the pleasure is mutual."

He looked at her a trifle longer than was strictly necessary. "Well, folks, I'd best be getting back," he said. He touched the brim of his hat and walked away toward the park entrance. He decided to write a letter to Addie just as soon as he reached his room.

Rose deftly slid the diaper under Mary Alice's tiny, elevated behind and gently lowered her onto it. She folded and tucked it around the baby's waist and legs and fastened it with safety pins. "There you go, Missy. I reckon that'll hold you for awhile, at least." She rearranged the little white Alençon lace gown and carefully picked up the child, bringing her to her ample bosom. Humming a tune under her breath, she paced slowly toward the parlor, bouncing the baby in a soothing, easy motion.

"Do you really have to go back?" Addie asked. Her expression was wistful as she sat in the cane-bottomed rocker and watched Rose with her daughter.

"Mmm-hmm. 'Fraid so, Missy. I done wore out my welcome at Freeman's place, and you ain't got room for me here."

"When does your train leave?"

"In the mornin', 'bout eight."

"I'll miss you, Rose. You've been so good for me—and for Mary Alice."

"Well, you gettin' stronger now. You can manage just fine by yourself, I imagine. I'm a old woman, and I been gone from my own place just about as long as I can stand." Rose eased herself into the overstuffed chair, still gently bouncing the baby and humming softly.

Addie leaned her head back and closed her eyes, rocking slowly and listening to the husky half-whisper of Rose's voice.

"What's that song you're singing?"

Rose increased the volume just enough for Addie to make out the words.

Come and go with me, to my father's house,
to my father's house;
Come and go with me, to my father's house,
to my father's house.
There'll be no dying there,
There'll be no crying there,
No sorrow there, in my father's house,
in my father's house.

There was barely enough contour in the tune for it to be called a melody; it was more like a chant. Nudged along by Rose's voice, it rolled forward and forward, the words barely changing from verse to verse, hypnotic and comforting as the well-worn creases in Rose's hands.

All will be well, in my father's house, in my father's house . . .

The slight creaking of the rocker made a sort of plaintive counterpoint to Rose's soft singing. Addie felt her mind bobbing aimlessly along the slow, thick current of the tune, whirling lazily in the eddy of the refrain.

In my father's house, in my father's house . . .

Addie thought about her father, imagined him sitting alone in his red leather chair in the parlor, sequestered behind the *Chattanooga Times*. She wondered if he even knew about her baby; he hadn't written or sent any word since her marriage. She thought about the things he had said to her when Zeb proposed. Addie questioned whether he still considered her part of the family. In her worst moments, she doubted it. But sometimes, she held out some small hope that Papa would relent, would see that she was still his daughter, no matter what church she attended on Sundays.

Mary Alice's eyelids fluttered a final time, then closed. Rose peered at her a moment, then eased herself out of the chair and padded to the bedroom. A moment later, she came back into the parlor, having deposited the sleeping baby in her crib.

"Rose, you never did tell me how you talked Papa into letting you come here to help me."

Rose glanced at her, then seated herself heavily in the chair. "Slave days is over, honey," she said, looking down as she arranged her skirts. "Don't reckon I need your daddy's say-so to come to Nashville if I got a mind to."

"Then he didn't send you to me," Addie said in a sinking voice. She'd known all along, really, but she'd beguiled herself with the faint hope that Papa had at least given grudging permission for Rose to come and help his daughter in her time of need.

Rose studied her a moment, then looked out the window. "Honey, your daddy done changed when your mama died. I seen death do that to folks—make 'em hard inside, make 'em forget how to love them that's left."

"I wish Papa could at least try to understand how I feel," Addie said softly.

"I wish he could, too, honey," Rose replied. "But sometimes, when somebody hurting—even somebody who love you, deep down—they can't see nothin' but they own hurt. It ain't right, and it ain't fair, but there it is anyway."

Several silent moments passed; the mantle clock ticked sedately. Addie's rocking slowed, then stopped. She crossed her hands on her lap and stared out at Granny White Pike. "I wish Zeb could come home this weekend."

"Mmm-hmm."

"He works so hard, Rose. Sometimes . . . sometimes I worry about him."

Rose said nothing.

Zeb peered again at the piece of paper in his hand. "Eleven-oh-seven Ninth Street," he said aloud. He looked around him, scratching his head, until he spied a knot of people walking up the steps of a small rock building in the middle of the block. "Must be it," he muttered, and stepped quickly toward them.

It was Sunday morning, and he had really intended to go home this weekend, but at the last minute, one of his agents had requested his help to close an important sale. They hadn't been able to see their prospect until late yesterday afternoon, long after the last convenient train to Memphis had pulled out from the station.

He had been meaning for some time to try to locate the local congregation of the church, but today was the first time he had been able to find the meeting place. Two or three days earlier, he had been idly thumbing through the newspaper and noticed a small advertisement for a "gospel meeting" to commence the next Sunday morning. The evangelist was some Texas fellow Zeb had never heard of, but the way his name was printed in large, bold letters, he figured to be really something.

Zeb mounted the steps to the building and entered the small, cramped vestibule. It appeared the church house was packed to the limit. Evidently the Texas preacher commanded quite a following in these parts. He spotted a vacant place on the last pew, against the wall, and immediately made for it. A bonneted woman was seated next to the open place. Zeb touched her shoulder. "Scuse me, ma'am, but are you saving this for anybody?"

She turned to him, and the first thing he noticed was her good-natured smile. The second thing he noticed was the spray of freckles across the bridge of her nose, and the third thing he noticed was the lock of golden hair that fell from beneath her bonnet to the middle of her forehead. "Well, I guess I get to return the favor, Mr. Douglas. But, it's 'Miss,' remember?"

"Yes, Miss Norwich. I won't make that mistake again."

"Fine. Then I guess you can have a seat."

Part II

September 1902

CHAPTER
16

*A*ddie hadn't heard anything from Mary Alice for some time, so she paced back through the house, trying to locate the too-quiet toddler. When Zeb had moved them into this new, larger place, she'd thought she'd enjoy the increased room, but at times like this she found herself missing the little servant's cottage on Granny White Pike: there was less space there for a toddler to wander.

She rounded a corner into her bedroom and spied her daughter in the act of plucking one of her crystal figurines from the top of the dressing table.

"No, ma'am!"

Mary Alice's head wheeled about, her eyes big with guilty surprise. Addie paced quickly to her and snatched the figurine from her chubby fist with one hand, spatting the child's hand sharply with the other.

"You are not to bother these! No, no!"

The baby's face quickly clouded up and began to rain. Addie picked her up and marched back toward the front of the house, plopping the squalling infant down in the parlor in front of a pile of rag dolls and brightly painted toys.

"If you'd stay in here and play with your own things," she said, "you wouldn't get into trouble."

Mary Alice, the very picture of wronged innocence, bawled unabated at her mother.

Addie sighed and rolled her eyes and searched beside the chair for the mail-order catalog she'd been perusing just before. She thumbed it back open to the jewelry section and began again to look at the men's rings. She'd decided to buy Zeb a wedding ring for Christmas this year. She'd always felt a little guilty for never having procured him a band. He claimed it didn't matter to him, but it did to her. He'd gotten her a fine, stylish gold band for their first anniversary, and she intended to have a ring for him by Christmas. She had almost enough money hidden in the pantry Mason jar to pay for the ring she'd chosen. She enjoyed looking at the picture and imagining how it would look on Zeb's finger. She thought he'd like the ring. It was a gold band, about a quarter-inch wide, with a bead of finely inlaid silver on each border. It would look elegant on his hand, set off by his clean, crisp white cuffs and the dark suits he favored.

Her eyes stayed on the pictures of the rings, but her mind wandered toward Little Rock. In the beginning, Zeb had assured her that success-fully turning around the Little Rock agency was the final stepping-stone to his home office position here in Nashville, but it had been more than a year now, and he was still spending at least two weeks each month in the Arkansas capital city—sometimes, like this month, even more. From his talk of things there, it seemed the agency was doing well. She won-dered why the men in the home office couldn't be satisfied with Zeb's work and offer him the Nashville job he said he wanted. But, on the few occasions when she'd tried to ask him about it, he'd become distant, almost annoyed. "There's still a lot to do there, Addie," he would assure her. "Griffs and Carleton are depending on me to leave Little Rock in good shape. I can't just walk off—not until the job's finished."

There were times when Addie wondered what had changed between her and her husband. When they were courting and first married, he couldn't seem to get enough of her presence. She smiled wistfully as she thought of some of the grand surprises he'd manufactured "for no rea-son," as he sometimes said, "but to see that dimple on your right cheek."

It had seemed so easy to enjoy each other in those simpler days: a sun-shiny afternoon was a good enough excuse to walk hand-in-hand up Cameron Hill; a night with a full moon carried a honey-scented enchantment that made words unnecessary; seeing the look on his face when she came down the front porch steps was like the secret opening of a longed-for gift.

When had the little joys begun to disappear? What was it about the daily friction of living together that rubbed so much of the shine off two people who thought they loved each other? And could they get it back?

She hoped Zeb got that home office job real soon.

Mary Alice's sobs had subsided to an occasional sniffle and whimper by the time Addie saw the postman walk past the front window. She laid aside the catalog and went to the door. The bright Indian summer after-noon sun was warm on her forearms as she opened the mailbox and removed the contents: a solicitation from someone running for county magistrate, a circular from a sewing notions company, and a letter addressed in a familiar hand . . . from Lou!

Smiling, she went quickly inside and tossed aside the other two pieces, eagerly running a finger beneath the flap of Lou's envelope.

Dearest sister Addie,

I suppose you thought I dropped off the face of the earth, since you haven't heard from me for nearly two months now. I am some better each day, it seems, altho there are still days when I'm not sure I want to make the effort to keep going, but those seem to be fewer and farther between, thank the Lord. It has now been twenty months since my precious Katherine's death, and tho I never thought life could go on without her, it seems to, just the same. I still miss her terribly, but things aren't quite so dark anymore, some-how. Then again, sometimes the most unexpected things will set me off. I might see a little girl about her size and coloring, or I might hear a snatch of a song she used to sing. And I still can't bear it at church when they do "Safe in the Arms of Jesus," like they did at her service. Dub tries his best but he just doesn't understand a mother's heart and I guess no man does, not really. He's got to where he doesn't like to go out to her grave with me anymore.

Well, how are things with you? I'll bet Mary Alice is just tearing up Jack by now at her age and getting into everything, but just try and remember that you'll miss these times someday. Oh, goodness, I better not get started that way again or before you know it I'll get back around to Katherine and be all down in the dumps again. How is Zeb? Did he ever get moved back to Nashville, like you thought he might? It'd be a shame for him not to get to be around Mary Alice these next few months as she'll be changing so fast and you miss something if you're gone for even a day, seems like. I sure would like to see that little sweet thing, tho I know it will make me sad. I hope we can come to Nashville before long but Dub stays so busy down at the store and with Robert in school and all it seems like the time just isn't ever right.

Oh, I almost forgot to tell you that George Hutto said he was mighty proud to hear about Mary Alice and he knew she had to be a beautiful baby with you being her mama. I wonder how long it took him to work up the nerve to say that much about you at one time. He looked about like a little boy at his first recital.

Well, I guess I've rattled on long enough and should close now. You give that sweet baby girl a hug from her Aunt Lou and write me back when you can.

> *Your loving sister,*
> *Louisa C. Dawkins*

Addie laid the letter on the table beside her and smiled into the middle distance. What she wouldn't give to spend an afternoon in the parlor with her older sister, just talking about this and that, like two old married women.

But, of course, it wouldn't do, not with Papa's disapproval hanging over them like a curse. Addie noticed Lou had avoided any suggestion that she and Zeb should come to Chattanooga. They both knew it would be too hard, that Papa would be the invisible participant in every conversation. She would have to work so hard to ignore him that it was almost inevitable he would be the only thing she thought about. And Addie couldn't imagine much good coming from that.

Mary Alice tugged at her skirt. Addie looked down and the child held up her arms. "All right, Miss, come on up," she said, lifting the baby into her lap. Mary Alice snuggled close, the first knuckle of her fist in her mouth. Addie squeezed her gently and rubbed her cheek against the silky brown wisps on the crown of Mary Alice's head. "Mama doesn't like to get on to you," she said, "but you have to learn to leave things alone, little dumplin'. Here you go," she continued, giving her daughter a sudden squeeze. "That's from your Aunt Lou."

The baby giggled at the sudden movement. Addie squeezed her again, she chuckled louder, and so it went for several moments. Soon, the laughter of her little one had banished most of the trailing tatters of Addie's hovering melancholy. She looked at the mantle clock and realized it was nearly three o'clock. "Come on, young 'un," she smiled at Mary Alice. "Let's find you and me a piece of shortbread. I'm just about hungry!" Mary Alice babbled happily at her mother and clung to her shoulder as they walked toward the kitchen.

Nothing was said when, after an absence of nearly three months, Rose resumed her duties at Jacob Caswell's house. If he was surprised to find her standing on his doorstep on the July morning she returned, he gave no sign. If he was at all curious as to her whereabouts during her time away, he gave her no evidence, and he knew Rose wasn't inclined to any unnecessary explanation. And so, with no more to-do than a slight nod from each, the two of them resumed their former arrangement.

Most of the time, Rose moved about the house as dispassionately as the shadows of clouds move across the landscape. She dusted, swept, straightened, cooked, and cleaned with the impersonal efficiency of a force of nature. Jacob, on the rare occasions when he noticed her at all, thought that sharing a room with her was about like sharing it with a piece of moving furniture.

But every once in a great while he would feel something brush against his awareness; a tingle on the back of his neck; an impalpable sense of being watched, or thought about, or disliked . . . or pitied. He would look up, and if Rose did happen to be in the room, he would generally see no more than the flicker of an eye or the slight turning of her head as she attended to whatever task engaged her. Sometimes, he would peer at her thoughtfully for some minutes. If she ever noticed his gaze, it wasn't apparent.

One day, as Rose was setting his lunch before him, he could have sworn she spoke. "What?" he asked.

She cut her eyes at him as she placed the gravy tureen in front of him, then turned to go back toward the kitchen. "Didn't say nothin'," she mumbled as she ambled away from him. When she came back a few seconds later bearing a platter of freshly baked cat-head biscuits, he said, "I sure thought you said something to me."

She shook her head as she poured his coffee.

The silence lengthened, broken only by the taps of his spoon against the sides of his cup as he stirred in his cream and sugar.

"Well, Rose, I guess I never did ask you where you went this spring. I don't recall being asked for time off."

"Can't nobody remember what they ain't been asked. I went on my own and I didn't ask no leave. You don't want me around no more, all you got to do is say so."

"Now, Rose, don't go getting touchy on me. I didn't mean anything by it. I was just curious, is all."

She walked back toward the kitchen, muttering under her breath. When she returned, carrying a plate of cold sliced roast beef, she was still going. She clanked the plate onto the table in front of him and turned away. As she did, he was pretty sure he made out the words, ". . . ain't got as much sense as God give a goose . . ."

"Rose, why don't you just turn around here and tell me what's on your mind?" he said. "All this grumbling and mumbling's about to give me the indigestion, anyway. You might as well have your say, all at once, and get it over with."

She came about to face him, her hands on her hips and her face tightly set in a scowl of disapproval. "I done been at this house for more than eight years, and every time I think you can't get no more bullheaded and hardhearted, you up and shows me how wrong I is!"

He stared at her, mouth agape. "Rose, what in thunder are you—"

"You let that child walk outta your life with no more thought than if you was turnin' out a stray dog! You really think you gonna make out any better on the Judgment Day than that boy she married? Or is you so busy feelin' sorry for yourself about losing Miz Mary that you ain't got no time to try to understand somebody else's feelin's?"

"Now, Rose, that's just about enough!" he shouted, slamming his fist on the table and rattling the dinnerware. "The Good Book says, 'Honor thy father and mother!' She—"

"The Good Book also say, 'He that trouble his own house shall inherit the wind!'" she said.

"What about, 'Children, obey thy parents'?"

"'Fathers, provoke not thy childrens to wrath!'"

"I'll not sit here and be lectured about my own children by a nigger maid!" Jacob wadded his napkin and flung it on the floor as he shoved back his chair and stood. "It's none of your business what I do or don't do about Addie!" he shouted, pointing an accusing finger at her. "She's the one who left, not me. I provided her a home, and she showed her gratitude by turning her back on me—and her mother's memory! Don't you stand there all holier-than-thou and condemn me for following my God-given conscience. It like to killed me to see her leave like she did! Do you think she's the only one who's hurt over all this?"

"You be a sight better off to listen to this old nigger instead of diggin' yourself a deeper hole than you already in! You didn't no more know that young 'un than if she was a stranger, but you so bound up in yourself, you couldn't see who she was!"

She turned her head sidelong and shook it at him as she spoke, as if admonishing a wayward child.

"She ain't in pigtails and pantaloons no more! She a grown woman, and she got to find her own way, and you got to let her! But what did you do? You good as told her your way was the only way! She your daughter in more ways than one, can't you see that? You tell that child to jump, she naturally going to squat! You tell her to gee, she'll haw every time! You tell her she can't have the man she got her eye on, you just as well be tellin' her he the only man in the world! That child didn't leave you—you run her off, only you too blind to see it!"

Jacob glared at her. He felt his fingers curling into claws. He spun away, swaying against the edge of the table and knocking his coffee cup sideways. He stalked out of the dining room into the hallway and half ran to the front door, flung it open and was gone.

Rose stood perfectly still, hands on hips, her eyes fixed on the space where he had been. Slowly, her head began to shake, and her eyes brimmed with tears.

"Sweet Jesus, help that man. He dyin' and don't know how to tell nobody."

CHAPTER
17

*A*nd the old fella says to the doctor, 'Who says Grandpaw *wanted* to get married?'" As soon as the punch line was out of his mouth, Pete Norwich guffawed loudly.

"Pete! Honestly!" his wife said in a shocked tone, but Zeb noticed she was smiling behind her napkin.

Becky shook her head, grinning despite her slight blush. "Daddy, I've got half a mind not to let you speak at the table anymore if all you're going to do is embarrass us in front of our guests."

"Oh, now Becky, come on! Mr. Douglas here didn't take offense at my little joke. Sakes, I've told that one at church before!"

"Not when I've been around, you haven't!" his wife said.

Zeb chuckled politely, more at the reactions of Pete's wife and daughter than at the joke itself. It was slightly off-color, but, Zeb had to admit, pretty funny.

"Mrs. Norwich, could you please pass some more of that delicious corn?"

"That's the way—duck out on me right when I need reinforcements," Pete Norwich said. "Well, as long as you're at it, pass that corn on around here when you're done."

"Mr. Douglas, would you please hand me the potatoes?" Becky said. Zeb passed the bowl of mashed potatoes to her, seated to his left.

"Here you go," he said. As he handed her the bowl, her fingers brushed across the back of his hand. He was almost sure it was unintentional.

Zeb had caught himself wondering about her age, about why she was still living with her parents when her two younger brothers were already out making their own ways in the world. Zeb had caught himself thinking other things about Rebecca Norwich, too; things that he did his best to shoo from his mind as soon as they entered—things about her easygoing manner, her quick smile, the freckles scattered like brown sugar across her cheeks and the bridge of her nose, the way the sunlight glinted in her blonde hair, the way that blonde hair might feel between his fingers . . .

"Pete, why don't you let me come down to your office tomorrow and show you what our company can do for your savings?" Zeb said. "We've got some of the best guarantees in the business, and I think we could—"

"Oh, land sakes, here he goes again!" Pete said. "Have the boy over for Sunday dinner and he starts twisting my arm about insurance before the chicken's even cold! Makes a body reluctant to show hospitality to strangers."

"Now, Pete, you hush!" said Ruth. "Zeb's not going to finagle you out of any money—and besides that, he's not a stranger. I don't know why you won't at least hear out his proposition."

"Lord a' mighty! He's got to my own wife now! What's a fellow to do?"

"Sounds to me like you ought to just buy something from him, Daddy," Becky said. "I'd bet that'd be the best way to get him off on somebody else."

"'Fraid not, Miss," Zeb said. "Soon as I sell this old mossback one policy, I'll be after him for something else. Any boy in knickers can tell you it's easier to keep a wheel rim rolling after you get up some momentum."

"Well, at least he's honest!" Pete said. "I like that in a swindler."

"To tell the truth, Mr. Douglas," Becky said, "I must confess I don't see how you do what you do."

"What's that?"

"Walk up to perfect strangers and convince them to trust you enough to buy a life insurance policy from you; give you their hard-earned money in exchange for something they'll never even see."

"Well—"

"It's 'cause he's got a silver tongue and a line of malarkey that'll reach from here to the top of the capitol dome," said Pete.

"Pete! Hush!"

Zeb grinned. "In all fairness, Mrs. Norwich, your husband's got a point. Being able to talk to folks is a pretty big help. But, of course, you've also got to know what you're talking about, and you've got to sincerely believe that you've got the answer to their biggest problem—"

"And do you?" Becky interrupted.

Zeb looked at her. "Do I—what?"

"Have the answer to their biggest problem?" She smiled.

Zeb felt an odd tension in his chest, but he tried to shove it out of his awareness. "Well, every man's gonna die, but not every man's got enough money saved up for his family to live on after he's gone. So . . . yes, I guess I do." He looked at her as he finished. Her strange smile puzzled him, intimated that he'd answered a different question than the one she'd asked.

"Well, I think I'll go out and spend all mine while I'm still kicking," said Pete, "and let Ruth and Becky makeshift for themselves when I'm pushing up daisies."

Zeb winked at Ruth. "Mrs. Norwich, it sounds like I better write him up today and not wait till tomorrow."

"Absolutely!" she said. Pete grabbed his heart and moaned while everyone else laughed.

Walking back toward the hotel, Zeb stared at the sidewalk in front of his feet and thought about the Norwiches. They were such nice folks. This was the third Sunday in a row Zeb had eaten lunch with them. Pete Norwich was a most companionable fellow, and Ruth, his wife, was as gracious as she was hospitable. Zeb truly enjoyed the cordiality and open, easy manner of this family. They had immediately made him feel welcome at church, for which he was grateful.

And . . . Becky. Zeb felt a twinge of something that might have been guilt—but why? he asked himself. He hadn't behaved any less than properly toward her. Could he help it if the family had taken a shine to him? He was a married man, after all, and wasn't about to do anything foolish.

Now that he thought of it, had anyone at the Norwich household ever asked him about his home and family? Absently, he rubbed the third finger of his left hand. Lots of men he knew didn't wear wedding bands, he thought, a little defensively. Besides, that was Addie's lookout. He'd bought her a ring; she could get one for him if she wanted him to wear it.

Becky's question stayed with him. Not so much the question, really, as the interest it implied. He wished Addie would show evidence of some interest in what he did to put bread on the table and a roof over their heads. She had never really asked him about his business, never shown much curiosity about what he did all the time he was away from her. But he noticed she never turned down any of the things it bought for her.

And then an unmistakable sense of guilt jabbed at his insides. He shouldn't throw off on Addie so! After all, she was the mother of his child! He had courted her and won her and promised to take care of her when her own father had pushed her out. He thought of her, standing on the doorstep of their new house, holding Mary Alice and waving good-bye to him as he left to catch his train. He thought of her as she lay beside him in their bed at night, recalled the smell of her hair, the softness of her neck against his cheek. A warm, penitent glow of protectiveness spread through his chest.

He decided to go home the very next weekend. He might even try to find time to go by that notions shop around the corner from the Gleason, try to find something nice for Addie and Mary Alice. Thinking of this made him feel better, and by the time he got to the front door of the hotel, he was whistling a jaunty tune and tipping his hat at passersby.

The look on her face when she opened the door and saw him was worth a thousand dollars at least. Her eyes went wide and her face lit up with a surprised joy that made him wish he could go away and come back again right now, just to see it.

"Well, hello!" she said, and opened her arms to him. Their embrace lasted a long time but not long enough.

Mary Alice bobbed into the room, attracted by the commotion. Zeb's heart turned over when he saw her. She stood with a finger in her mouth, trailing a rag doll along behind her by one soiled, unkempt pigtail. He knelt down and held out his arms.

"Hello, little lady," he smiled. "Come give your daddy a hug."

She stared at him doubtfully.

"Come on, sweetie," urged Addie. "You better give Daddy a hug." The child made a few tentative steps toward him before he swooped upon her and grabbed her to him, kissing her loudly several times on each cheek. He set her back down and she stepped quickly to her mother, holding on to her skirts and looking back at him—not exactly in fear, but not in amusement either.

"She'll get used to you," Addie said, looking down at her and stroking her hair. "Besides, it's been, what? Nearly three weeks this time?"

He willed himself not to display annoyance at his daughter's caution or his wife's veiled rebuke.

"Well, maybe this'll warm her up some," he said, producing a brightly wrapped parcel from the pocket of his greatcoat. He knelt and held it out to Mary Alice. "I brought you something, sugar," he said, coaxing her. "Something you can use to fix up that dolly's hair."

Mary Alice's eyes went to the package like a moth to a candle flame. It was wrapped in bright blue paper and tied with a red satin bow that gleamed like the day before Christmas. She paced slowly toward it. When she reached him, her gaze shifted from the parcel to his face, making sure he wasn't about to pounce again. She took the package and retreated a step or two, then plopped down on the floor and began worrying at the bow.

Zeb stood and walked over to Addie. "And here's something for her mama," he said, handing her a slightly larger package done up like the first, in blue and white. As she took it from him, he kissed her on the cheek and began removing his coat.

"Oh, Zeb!" Addie withdrew from the unwrapped box a shimmering silver chain attached to a gold-filigreed silver locket. "It's so pretty!"

"Aren't you gonna open it?"

She pried open the catch. Inside was a tiny photograph of her husband. She smiled at him.

He shrugged and grinned. "Don't want you to forget what I look like while I'm gone."

Mary Alice made a frustrated whimper.

"Here, dumplin', let me help," Zeb said. He squatted beside her and tugged the ribbons off the corners of the box and started a small tear in the paper. In the tentative manner of children more interested in the wrapping than the contents, Mary Alice slowly tore off one corner of the paper, then another. Gradually, she revealed a small rectangular box, which proved to contain a miniature comb fashioned of tortoiseshell.

When he again looked up at Addie, she was clutching the locket to her with both hands and regarding him with a fond, glistening expression that quickened his pulse.

Charles McCrary stood in the vestibule of Twelfth Avenue Church of Christ, his Bible tucked beneath one elbow, and spoke to each member of his flock—*Christ's flock,* he reminded himself—as they passed him on their way out the door. "Good to see you, Sister Crenshaw; glad you're doing better . . . Morning, C. L. Your knee giving you anymore trouble? Hello, there, Janey! I sure like that bonnet your mama put on you today!" His facial expression was much relaxed from the professional scowl he usually affected in the pulpit. In the vestibule, he tried to be more accessible to the congregation.

As he stood here on Sunday mornings, he imagined himself as one of the sheep tenders of the Lord's homeland: carefully watching each beast as it stepped over the threshold of the fold on its way to pasture, looking for signs of disease or infirmity that required the healing hands of the shepherd. Did this one have an infected cut that needed binding? Did that one need the burrs picked out of its coat? Was that lamb gaining weight as it should?

But sometimes he wondered how much he really knew. Sometimes, as he smiled into their faces and shook their hands and laughed at their childrens' comments, he wondered what hidden hurts haunted their dreams at night, what silent sins nagged at them in secret. There were times when he wished he could do more than warn them from the pulpit. But he was, after all, only a minister of the gospel, an earthen vessel—Second Corinthians four, seven. There was only so much he could do.

Addie shuffled along toward the vestibule, holding Mary Alice on one hip with Beulah Counts at her other side murmuring in her ear, ". . . thought I was absolutely going to fall asleep if he didn't finish pretty soon—" Beulah's face brightened and her voice increased in volume as she extended her hand to Brother McCrary. "That sure was a good lesson today, Brother McCrary!" she said as the preacher smiled at her.

"Well, Sister Counts, thank you. Sister Douglas, good to see you," he said, turning to Addie.

As he shifted his attention to her, Addie noticed the light glancing off his spectacles.

"You, too," she replied, nodding.

"Is Zeb gone back to Little Rock?" the minister said. "Noticed he wasn't here this morning."

"Yes, sir. He left last Wednesday to go back."

"Well, fine. Good morning, Brother Chandler," he said, reaching past Addie toward the next person in line.

"Addie, why don't you and the baby come on home with us and eat dinner?" Beulah suggested as they stepped out into the gray light of the overcast autumn day.

Addie sighed. "Oh, Beulah, I hate to impose on you again—"

"Don't be silly, honey, it's no trouble! I'll just set an extra place and we'll fix Mary a little pallet for her to take her nap, and you and I can sit and get caught up on . . ."

The afternoon's itinerary droned on, but Addie stopped listening. It was no use. Once Beulah decided to do you a charity, there was no escape. It was just easier to go along with her. Moments ago, Addie had been puzzling over what she would fix for herself and Mary Alice to eat, but now she was gazing wistfully in her mind at her quiet parlor, with only Mary Alice's baby jabber to put up with.

Addie managed an occasional nod or indistinct murmur of agreement, so as to keep Beulah's conversational skids greased. She was vaguely grateful Beulah's husband had not driven the horseless carriage to church this morning. Instead of having to balance Mary Alice on her lap and endure its jostling and stench, they could have a nice, sane walk for the ten or twelve blocks between the church house and the Counts' home.

She wondered how Zeb was doing, and what he was doing. He hadn't talked much about Little Rock this last time, which was both a relief and a curiosity. In the past, he had talked so much about the "good things happening with the agency" that she had grown mortally weary. It was hard to preserve the appearance of calm, detached interest—the only way she had found to negotiate the shoals of Zeb's professional enthusiasm. "Why don't you ask me how I feel about something?" she often wanted to say. "Why don't you at least try to talk about something I want to talk about, something that's interesting to me?" She felt like one of Zeb's prospects sometimes—like she was being sold on something she'd already bought and paid for. Still, he was her husband and a good provider for her and Mary Alice. The funds he deposited in their bank account on his trips home were more than adequate to keep them all fed and clothed, and supply some nice things, besides. It almost made her ashamed to be impatient with Zeb, as hard as he worked and as easy as she had it. So, out of consideration, instead of showing how she really felt, she tried to be just a shade more than polite—without being so encouraging that he went on and on and on.

She glanced over her shoulder at Will Counts, stepping along behind them with his sons. Will was usually a quiet man—with Beulah as his wife, how could it be otherwise? Addie had the fleeting thought that perhaps Will suggested her invitation to Beulah, to give her someone besides himself to talk at. But, at least Beulah and Will were home together at night. At least Beulah didn't have to stare up at her bedroom ceiling, missing her husband and wondering how he was, or whether he was giving any thought to her. There was something to be said, after all, for just being together.

A tiny smile fluttered on her lips as she reflected on Zeb's last furlough. He had been—how could she put it?—*here*—really here with her, she decided, at last. He'd hardly mentioned Little Rock at all. She'd be busy in the kitchen or taking care of the baby, and she'd turn around and find him leaning in a doorway, looking at her and smiling. He'd told her at least a dozen times he loved her. And . . . he had been so passionate.

Her cheeks flushed with remembered pleasure as she thought of his wide, warm hands, strong on the small of her back as he pressed her urgently to him—

". . . going to answer me, girl?" Beulah was saying, jogging her elbow.

"Do what?" Addie said.

"I been trying for the last half mile to get you to tell me what you'd rather have for dinner—butter beans or purple hulls. I got both, and I'll be glad to—" She peered intently at Addie's face. "You all right, honey? Your face is sure red all of a sudden."

"I'm fine, Beulah. Purple hulls, I guess."

CHAPTER
18

Zeb had only intended to stay home for the weekend, but he talked himself into changing his plans. His time with his wife and daughter seemed especially sweet those few days. Mary Alice soon overcame her reticence about him, and in their bed at night, he and Addie made ardent love to each other. On Monday morning, he decided, rather than catching an early train back, he would go in to the home office and make a report to Griffs or Carleton—whomever he could find. He would hang around the office for awhile, then come back home for a long lunch. He'd done a good job in Little Rock, and he knew Griffs and Carleton wouldn't begrudge him a little extra time with his family.

The fact was, there was something about going back to Little Rock that made him restive. When he tried to make himself plan his departure, it just seemed easier to get distracted. His leave-taking, when it could finally be avoided no longer, was more arduous for him than it had ever been.

Still, he was feeling better by the time his train reached Memphis. By the time they rolled into Union Station in Little Rock, he was positively eager to get back to work. He decided that the best antidote for the homesick blues was a dose of good, honest, hard work. He'd enjoyed being home, but he was back now, and it was time to get down to business.

Thursday morning, when he walked into the cramped, two-room office he had rented for the agency, his secretary handed him a note written in a diagonal scrawl across a torn scrap of paper. "Dere Zeb," it read, "im sorry, but i cant do no more. rekin i just want cut out for this binniss. yr. frend, Luke C. Cutler." Zeb looked at the secretary.

"Brought it by here Monday morning, first thing," Abner told him with a shrug. "Looked like he was kinda glad you weren't here."

Zeb shook his head in disgust. "Well, Ab, you can lead 'em to water, but you can't make 'em drink. Cutler would've been all right, if he'd just had as much gumption as his wife told me he had." Luke Cutler had answered a notice Zeb placed in the newspaper, announcing the hiring of "Enterprising Men for Financially Rewarding Opportunities in this Area." More properly, Cutler's wife had answered the advertisement: she had done most of the talking in the interview; Cutler himself seemed less than enthusiastic about the whole matter.

Abner grinned. He was a slight-built, youngish fellow Zeb had hired the first week he'd been here. He managed the office work and correspondence for the agency. He'd had a brief career as a schoolteacher that had ended abruptly, for a reason Zeb had never learned and decided not to be curious about. Ab was clean, fairly literate, had a reasonably neat hand, and he didn't need much money to live on, which was perhaps his greatest asset, given what the home office was willing to pay for clerical help. "I told myself the first time she drug him in here, 'This man don't want to be here for no reason of his own.'"

Zeb sighed and smiled wryly. "Well, it appears her ambition didn't last him long in the heat of the day." He pushed his hat up in the back, scratching his head. "Guess I'll have to find another man for the north Saline County debit."

"Yeah. Some a those policies are a week behind already."

Zeb wadded up the note and tossed it at a wastepaper basket. As he strode toward his desk, he felt his chagrin giving way to a kind of calm eagerness. He was embracing the challenge, welcoming it as a familiar, satisfying adversary. He would manage this difficulty, and the next, and the next, and the next, because that was what he was good at. His determination was stronger than anything that stood in his way, and he would prove it, one more time.

For the next several days he was immersed in the duties of the agency. First, he busied himself with finding Luke C. Cutler's replacement: he set about visiting northern Saline County policyholders, at once encouraging continued payment and collecting premiums but also finding out who knew whom in the area, who was trusted, who needed work, who had higher goals in life than growing corn and cotton on ten acres of river bottomland.

Zeb relished the power over others granted him by his gift of gab. He could walk up to any sharecropper's shack and strike up a conversation. Likewise, he could stroll along the courthouse square and engage some vested, bejowled lawyer in a lengthy exchange of views. The trick, he had learned, was to figure out what the other person was interested in and evidence an interest in that himself. Folks just naturally opened up to him.

Zeb knew he could talk to anyone, at any time, in any place. If good humor and an easygoing manner was what the situation required, he had a vast store of jokes and the familiar style in which to frame them. If, on the other hand, a somber, earnest tone seemed more appropriate, Zeb could instantly become sincere, as easily as taking off one hat and putting on another. He could be anyone he needed to be, a gift not shared by many other people. It was his protection and his advantage. He prided himself on being able to do what most folks were unwilling or unable to do, and to keep on doing it as long as he had to.

Within two weeks he had hired a man to run the debit vacated by Luke C. Cutler. Most of the policies in the vacant debit were paid up to date, and the new agent seemed of a temperament more suited to the insurance business than that of Cutler. Zeb had made contact with his other three agents and assured himself that they were being productive. The stack of new-policy applications to be processed by Abner and forwarded to the home office was holding steady. He even had the leisure to consider whether it might be time to expand the agency by adding another debit just across the Arkansas River, in Argenta.

The burst of activity generated by Cutler's abdication carried Zeb to a new height of expansiveness. His prospects here were good, and that was so because of his own efforts; there was no feeling of indebtedness or obligation to a predecessor to abate his self-satisfaction. This agency was his; he had built it from the ground up, with no assistance from anyone else. He was becoming known and respected in this place and among these people. No one here knew or cared that he was born and raised on a bare patch of red clay in north Georgia, that his father had died with three young children in the house, and that his mother had been too poor to refuse the suit of the first man who held out the prospect of keeping a roof over their heads.

He had carved his own niche out of Little Rock, and, somewhat to his own surprise, the thought of going back to the home office was losing much of the aura it once had. What did Nashville have to offer, other than more money and a bit of stability? Nashville was someone else's domain, not his. He wondered what Addie would say if he told her he wanted to move here. He was afraid he already knew the answer, and he didn't like to let himself think about it.

Becky totaled the column of figures and made an entry in the ledger. Before reaching for another account book, she allowed her eyes to roam from the second-floor office area down the stairway and out over her father's department store, resting them for a moment from the close work with which she had been occupied most of her morning. For a few moments she watched the sales clerks and customers milling about the counters below. It was a Monday morning, and there weren't many shoppers in the store. For that very reason, she usually chose Mondays to get the accounts up-to-date.

I wonder what he's doing right now, she thought, and immediately chided herself. *Rebecca Norwich, you are not a schoolgirl anymore, and you know much better than to sit about mooning over some man you know as little as you know Zeb Douglas.* She shook her head and took up the next batch of sales receipts. *But I wonder if he ever thinks about me,* her mind whispered. With an exasperated sigh, she flung down the tickets and tossed the pen onto her desk.

She got up from her oak swivel chair and paced the length of the office area, then back again. She wondered, not for the first time, what it was about Zeb Douglas that hung so in her mind. She hardly knew anything about him, other than his easy smile, his lovely manners, and his familiar, friendly way of speaking to her and her parents. He never talked about anything or anyone in Nashville, where he went every second or third weekend, other than vague references to "the home office." She had no idea about his family, where he came from, or what he was like during the week at his small office near the capitol building.

But she found herself thinking of him more and more. When she came to the store, she sometimes found herself detouring needlessly by the opening of the street where the insurance office was located, more than half-hoping their paths would cross. She had almost nerved herself, once or twice, to walk into the office and pass the time of day, but so far she had managed to restrain herself from such brazen assertiveness. It was about time for Zeb Douglas to eat Sunday dinner with them again, she decided. She'd say something to Mother.

George huddled as deeply as he could inside his greatcoat, trying vainly to dodge the raw north wind. It was cold, the sky was spitting snow, and he was tramping up and down the streets of Chattanooga trying to secure signatures on a letter of solicitation to Mr. Andrew Carnegie of New York asking him to build a library in this city.

How did he allow himself to be goaded into these situations? He'd heard vague rumors of some of the society ladies forming a committee, and the next thing he knew he was being badgered by his mother into knocking on the doors of perfect strangers and asking them to endorse this fine community effort. Didn't anyone think he had work to do? Did they think Hutto & Company ran all by itself?

Well, he was sick and tired of the whole thing, that's all. Let somebody else get out and catch pneumonia on Mr. Carnegie's behalf. He'd knock on one more door and then he was going home, and the Library Boosters could all go hang, which would suit him, plumb to the ground.

He shuffled onto the front porch of a single-story frame house and tapped gently, hoping no one was home, but the latch began turning almost before his hand had fallen to his side. George waited for the door to open, clamping his portfolio under one elbow and blowing on his hands.

"Yes?" The woman who had opened the door had a black shawl wrapped around her shoulders and was clearly not happy about standing in her doorway with such a brisk north wind blowing.

George touched the brim of his bowler. "Ma'am. I'm George Hutto, and I'm working on behalf of the Chattanooga Library Boosters—"

"Lord a'mighty! On a day like this? Well, come on in before we both freeze slap to death!"

"Yes, ma'am. Thank you." George stepped across her threshold and removed his hat. He stood in a small foyer with a knotty pine plank floor covered by a slightly threadbare Persian rug. As he warmed up, he was able to allow his face to relax from the squint it had assumed while he was walking into the frigid blast outside. His eyes moved about the portion of the adjoining parlor that he could see until they came to rest on a huge oil painting above the fireplace mantle—a painting of a clipper ship cutting through rough waters under full sail. "Oh!" he said, the word slipping out softly without his realization.

"What? Oh, the ship. My daddy painted that years ago."

George took a hesitant step or two toward the painting, then stopped and shook his head. "Sorry, ma'am, I didn't come here to look at—"

"It's all right, go ahead. It's kind of an interesting old painting, if you like that sorta thing."

"Well . . . thanks. I believe I will look at it a bit, if you don't mind," George said, giving a little smile to no one in particular. He paced closer to the painting and tilted his head this way and that, peering at the ship and her rigging. "I guess I'm kinda interested in old ships," he remarked. "I build them as a hobby. Well, that is, I build models. Not real ships, of course."

"Is that so?" George could hear her stepping quietly over to stand just behind his left shoulder. Without moving his head, he cut his eyes toward her. She was looking at the picture also, not saying anything.

"Well," he said, clearing his throat, "I guess I don't need to take up too much more of your time." He faced about and pulled a sheaf of papers from his portfolio. "As I said, I'm with the Library Boosters, and—"

"How many have you built? Just curious."

He stared at her a moment. "Oh, ships!" he said after a few seconds. "Well, I don't really know, let's see—"

"How long does it take? To build one?"

He peered at her again. She was no longer clutching the shawl about her, but it still hung over her shoulders. Her hair was a sandy brown and pulled back into a tight, no-nonsense bun on the back of her head. Her eyes were a chestnut brown—almost black—and she wore a high-necked green linen blouse with a tightly pleated front and a heavy skirt of the same color.

"Well . . . about a week, usually," he answered. "Anyway, we're trying to get a Carnegie library built here in Chattanooga, and—"

"Would you like some hot coffee?"

Again, he wore the puzzled look of an old dog interrupted in mid-trick. "Pardon?"

"Coffee. It's hot, and you must be half frozen if you've been tramping up and down streets all morning."

"Well . . . I . . . I suppose so. Yes, ma'am, that'd be nice."

"May I take your coat and hat?" She held out her hands for his wraps.

George handed her his bowler and removed his greatcoat. She gestured vaguely toward a settee near the grate and then wheeled about, vanishing into another room.

George seated himself gingerly on the settee, his hands on his knees, and looked around the room. The scarcity of knick-knacks surprised him, somehow, as did the relative absence of typical feminine touches in the general decor: no doilies on the furniture, no lace on the curtains, nothing extra or added on. Everything in the room looked as if it was there for a reason.

A log settled on the grate, sending a shower of sparks up the flue. George was glad for the warmth. He squatted in front of the hearth and worked the fire with a poker. He heard her come in behind him. George turned around and moved back toward the settee just as she placed a steaming cup in its saucer on the low table in front of his place. She took a seat in an overstuffed armchair across from him.

He took a careful sip of the coffee and risked a glance at her. She was staring frankly at him, though the expression on her face was considerably more toward pleasant than it had been when he had knocked on her door. With her dark eyes, her gaze reminded him uncomfortably of a crow's, intent and unblinking. He quickly dropped his eyes to his cup.

"You aren't having any coffee?"

"Nope. Had my two cups already, don't need anymore. I keep it on, though. Most of the day. Just in case."

After another careful sip, George asked, "Does your husband work near here?"

"Widowed three years. Consumption."

"Oh, I'm . . . I'm sorry."

She shrugged. "Lord giveth, Lord taketh away."

He nodded somberly.

"Least he left me well fixed," she went on, still peering at George with those forthright, burnt-sepia eyes. "That, plus my inheritance from my family. Long as I'm careful, I don't have to do anything I don't want to do."

There was an awkward pause.

"Well . . . that's a blessing." George blew on his coffee.

"You told me your name, but I forgot," she said.

"George Hutto. And I don't guess I know your name either," he said, feeling an odd sort of embarrassment steal over him. Here he was, sitting in the parlor and drinking the coffee of a woman whose name he didn't even know!

"Breck. Laura Sanders Breck. My husband's people were from Kentucky, but I'm out of the McMinnville Sanderses."

George nodded thoughtfully, though he had never in his life met another person from McMinnville, as far as he knew.

"Lord never blessed us with children," she said. "Couldn't understand why, but there you go."

She had thin lips that were almost the same color as the rest of her face. Her frame appeared to be somewhat on the spare side, although she was not so thin as to be gaunt. As she spoke, her eyes flickered here and there, always coming back to rest on his face. The rest of her stayed very still, though: her hands rested in her lap and never moved; she held her head motionless; she never changed position in the deep cushions of her chair.

George sipped politely at his coffee a few more moments, and Laura Sanders Breck watched him. He cleared his throat, placed his cup in the saucer, and gently set it on the table. "Well, Mrs. Breck, I certainly—"

"Laura." Her crow-eyes glittered at him as she said it. Like an invitation, or a challenge.

"I certainly thank you . . . Laura . . . for the coffee and the seat by your fire," he said. "And now, if I might have my hat and coat, I'll be on my way."

Without a word, she sprang from her overstuffed chair and dashed out of the room, returning seconds later with his things.

"Thank you," he said, placing the bowler on his head and shrugging on the greatcoat. He glanced a final time at the clipper over the fireplace, studying it with a slight squint. She preceded him to the entrance, clasping the shawl about her neck with one hand and opening the front door with the other. He took a deep breath and shouldered into the cold air on the front porch. "Thank you again," he said as he passed her. Her only reply was a quick, curt nod.

As the door closed behind him and he thumped down the front steps, he realized he had completely forgotten to ask her to sign Carnegie's petition.

CHAPTER
19

. . . Anywhere with Jesus I can go to sleep,
When the dark'ning shadows 'round about me creep,
Knowing I shall waken never more to roam;
Anywhere with Jesus will be home, sweet home.
Anywhere, anywhere! Fear I cannot know;
Anywhere with Jesus I can safely go.

The song coasted to a halt, and the noise of hymnals sliding into pew racks momentarily filled the church house. Then the room quieted as the worshippers stood, waiting for the benediction.

"Our Father in heaven, we thank thee for the blessin's a this hour," the gangly, bespectacled man prayed in a singsong voice, "and for the truths spoken unto us by Brother Woodrow. We ask thy blessin's upon each that's here, and that thou'd bring us back at the next appointed time. In Christ's name, amen."

A chorus of male "amens" answered, and the racket of conversation swelled as the congregation shuffled along the pews toward the center aisle and the front door. Zeb moved with the others, laughing and talking. A firm, meaty hand clapped him on the shoulder, and he turned around.

"Zeb, my wife has fixed up the biggest ol' mess a chicken and dumplings you ever saw, and I figure you're just the man to help us eat it," said Pete Norwich. "Whaddya say?"

And Zeb knew immediately the source of his malaise before his last return to Little Rock: it rose up in him instantly now, flared into a klaxon of danger, blaring away inside his head. He was a married man, and the tendrils of guilty pleasure that beckoned him to accept this opportunity to be with Becky Norwich were forbidden to him, and he knew it. He shouldn't go. He should decline Pete's invitation as gracefully as possible, and he should go back to his rooms and pack his things and get on the next train to Nashville, and he should never come back to Little Rock again.

But . . . he was in charge of his own life, wasn't he? He'd managed things in Little Rock very well, and he was in control of himself, and what was wrong with having lunch with some of the new friends he'd made for himself in this place that was his own? Why should he turn tail and run, why raise all kinds of awkward questions with Griffs and Carleton—not to mention worrying Addie needlessly? He could handle it. He was equal to this challenge too. And these were church folks, for Pete's sake. What could happen?

He grinned at Pete Norwich and said, "Sure, Pete! I'll be there! Thanks!"

Zeb leaned comfortably back in the chair and patted his stomach. "Pete, I'll tell you one thing: Ruth knows her way around the kitchen. How in the world have you kept from getting big as the side of a barn, way that woman cooks?"

"Self-control, son. Nothing but self-control."

"Yeah, but I'm talking about you, not her."

"Watch it, boy. I'll toss you out on your ear, you keep that up."

Pete rustled the newspaper, and Zeb listened to the women's voices coming low from the kitchen, just audible above the noises of splashing water and the clink of dinnerware. Becky's voice was lighter in timbre than her mother's, though much the same pitch. Zeb imagined her, sleeves rolled to her elbows, perhaps a wisp of blonde hair falling to her shoulder as she washed and dried . . .

Norwich made a disgusted sound. "I tell you, Zeb, I don't understand what Roosevelt thinks he's gonna accomplish with this Labor and Commerce Department foolishness. Sounds to me like just another way for some Washington bureaucrat to get his hands on the public funds."

Zeb made a noncommittal reply. It was almost reflexive with him: he seldom allowed himself to be drawn into political or religious discussions with prospects. Just as Pete was launching into a diatribe against the wasteful ways of the federal government, Mrs. Norwich came in from the kitchen, bent over the back of his chair, and whispered something in his ear.

"Huh? Why? I've just started my paper, Ruth! Can't a man at least—"

"Pete."

He stared at her for maybe five seconds and gave in with a shrug. "Yes, ma'am. I'll be right there." He looked at Zeb, shook his head, and sighed. Zeb gave him a small, sympathetic smile in return as Pete laid aside the newspaper and followed his wife from the room.

No sooner had they left than Becky came in. Zeb looked at her and smiled. She ducked her head and seated herself in the chair her father had just vacated. She lifted a corner of the newspaper, smiling fondly. "Daddy and his Sunday afternoon rituals." She shook her head.

"Sure was a good lunch, Becky. Your mama knows how to rearrange the groceries, that's for sure."

"Glad you enjoyed it." She wouldn't look at him. He couldn't stop looking at her.

There was a longish silence. Becky took a deep breath, patted her palms on her knees, and turned her face toward him. "It's a nice, bright afternoon. Why don't we put on our coats and go for a stroll?"

Zeb nodded. "That'd be all right, I guess." He got up from his chair as she went to fetch their wraps. She handed him her coat, and he held it for her. As she slid her arms into the sleeves, she leaned back against him, ever so slightly. His heart hammered at his rib cage like a wild thing.

They walked out into the brilliant blue afternoon. The wind was still and every breath of fresh, cool air entered Zeb's lungs like a shout of joy. He ambled along with his hands in his pockets. "Nice day, like you said," he offered.

She murmured in agreement.

"Glad you mentioned a walk."

She said nothing.

They strolled along for almost a hundred yards without speaking. "Excuse me for asking," Zeb said finally, "but how come a woman as nice looking as you never found a husband?"

She made no reply for a long time, and Zeb feared he had transgressed. Just as he was about to attempt an apology, she said, "I haven't been in a hurry about such things." Out of the corner of his eye, he saw her glance at him, then away. "I'm still not," she said.

They walked on. Ahead and to the right, the capitol dome glistened in the crystalline air. "How'd you come to work for your daddy?" Zeb asked.

"I've always enjoyed the company of men more than women. Guess it comes of being raised with brothers. I've never much been able to abide quilting parties and so forth. I'd rather be working on the store's books than gossiping about chintz."

Zeb looked at her and grinned. He could see the smile starting, watched with amusement as she tried to suppress it. At last, it broke free across her face and she looked at him, laughing.

"That's the most words you've said in a row all day. I'd about decided the cat had your tongue for good."

She shook her head and grinned at the ground. "I don't know what's got into me today. I'm usually not nearly so reserved." She looked at him. "Especially around friends."

They stopped walking and looked at each other. At the same instant, their hands reached out and found each other. "Friends," Zeb nodded. They walked on.

December 15, 1902

My Dear Husband Zeb,

How anxious I am for you to come home for Christmas! I think you'll like the way the house looks, at least I hope so. The wreath is real pretty, I think. Mary Alice is about to worry me to death, trying to keep her out of the Xmas tree.

I hope all is well with the agency. It sounds to me like you've really got things going your way. I know you work so hard & I'm very happy it's paying off. Maybe the men at the Home Office will soon figure out what a go-getter you are & give you that position you've been looking for so long. I certainly hope so.

Had a letter from Lou the other day, she seems pretty good, right now. Says Daddy doesn't hardly come out of the house at all anymore. It makes me sad, thinking of him in that big old house all alone, with just Rose for company, & her only part of the day. I know he did wrong by you and me, but my heart aches for him. I guess I can't help it since he is my father, after all.

Well, I'll close this for now. I love you with all my heart & I'm looking forward to meeting you under the mistletoe (ha!). Hurry home as soon as you can.

Your own,
Adelaide C. Douglas

Addie read the letter one last time before folding it. She gazed wistfully for a moment at the envelope, thinking about Zeb's hands holding it. She wanted to feel those hands again, to look into his face. She briefly considered adding a postscript to that effect but thought better of it. Zeb might think she was being affected—too romantic and gushy. He might think she wasn't being brave.

Besides, if she started putting down on paper everything she wanted to say to Zeb but couldn't, she'd never have time for doing anything else. How could she tell him how desperately lonely she was much of the time? How could she say how it made her feel sitting in church with Mary Alice on her lap and looking about at the other families, the children ranked in the pews between their parents like books between bookends? It took two parents to do that. And how could she tell him how she longed to cook for him, to put three plates on the table in the evenings, to hear him breathing beside her in the dark of their bedroom? How could she explain how badly she wished he were here with her, hearing Mary Alice's babbled attempts at new words, smiling at the new things she was doing each day, marveling at the way their daughter's personality was already bursting into bloom? Hardest of all, how could she give vent to her darkest suspicion: that Little Rock had stolen her husband from her?

No, it wouldn't do. He would think she was trying to tether him to her with guilt. He would resent her interference in the pursuit of his dream. He would sigh and shake his head and secretly rue the day he had taken such a weak woman for a wife, and though he might accede to her wishes, there would be a hurt place in his heart that could never be hers again.

Stop it, she told herself. There was no point in thinking such things: Zeb loved her and Mary Alice. He was a good man, and he had more to do during the day than mope over her. He wrote faithfully, and besides, he was just trying to make his way in the world the best way he knew, and she should be ashamed of herself for being so selfish. He'd come back to Nashville soon enough, and their future would be secure, and all would be well, and he wouldn't have to spend so much time away from home ever again. "Just try and stand it for a little while longer," he'd told her the last time he was home. "And I promise some day it'll pay off." Someday. That was what she'd think about—how it would be, someday.

Nodding to herself, she affixed the stamp and sealed the envelope. She stood and suddenly felt the room whirling about her head. She had to grab the back of the chair to keep from falling over. In a moment, the spell passed and the room got still again. She'd been having some dizziness lately, for some reason. That, and feeling tired all the time.

Before Addie posted the letter, she just had to look again at the ring. She slid out the lap drawer of the secretary and fished around in the back until her fingers closed on the small, square box from Sears & Roebuck's. She removed the lid and admired the smooth, shining gold of the center section and the elegant, beaded line of the silver borders. The ring was even more beautiful than the picture in the catalog. She knew Zeb would be proud of it, and that he would be surprised. She tried to imagine the look on his face when he unwrapped it. Feeling a small glow of pleasure, she replaced the cotton padding atop the ring and put the lid back on the box.

She stepped out on the porch and clipped the letter to her mailbox with a clothes pin. It was a cold, bright day, and the blue sky was thickly littered with gray shreds of cloud, scudding along before the north wind. Gripping her elbows against the chill, she glanced up and down the street. Then her eyes fell on the bare branches of the two large hickory trees standing guard in her front lawn. She stood a moment, looking up to their tops, which swayed slowly back and forth. Even if she could climb them, she thought, there was no hiding place now, no concealing safety where she could sit and dream. Only the tossing, indifferent wind of December. *I hope Zeb comes home soon,* she thought, and went quickly back inside.

CHAPTER
20

*E*ven as George Hutto walked up the front steps of Laura Breck's house, he still couldn't figure out exactly what he was doing there. Last week, as much to his own surprise as anyone else's, he had heard himself invite her to accompany him to Baroness Erlanger's Christmas social. Her black eyes blinked at him twice, then she accepted with a quick nod and a sharp, decisive, "Yes." That was all, just "yes."

George still hadn't been able to pinpoint when he had precisely understood that he was "calling on" Mrs. Breck. He had visited her that bitterly cold day, admired her father's ship painting, said barely twenty words to her, and left the premises without even concluding the business that had placed him there. Then a week or so later, he found himself again walking up her street for no reason that he could readily recall. He was almost chagrined when she spotted him from her seat on the front porch swing. It was a rather cool afternoon, after all. Why would anyone be sitting in a porch swing on such a day?

He couldn't remember the substance of a single conversation they'd had. Once or twice a week, he would turn up at her door and she would invite him inside. She would always have coffee or tea just ready, and a cake or some cookies to go with it. They would usually sit in the parlor. Sometimes he would stare at the ship painting and they would make random comments to each other. Other times they would just sit in her small kitchen and sip their tea and stare out the window at the side yard. Once, they had even ventured into the backyard. He had paced up and down with his hands in his pockets, and she had sat in a whitewashed wrought-iron chair, gathered about herself like an owl on a fencepost.

He tapped at the door and she opened it almost instantly. "Good evening," he intoned, touching the brim of his bowler. "If you're ready . . ."

Without replying, she scooted outside and closed the door behind her. She bent over the skeleton key in her hand, carefully inserting it into the lock and turning it. She dropped the key into her handbag and straightened to face him. As they started down the porch steps, he felt her slip her gloved hand into the crook of his arm. He wasn't quite sure what to do with his hand while keeping his elbow at the proper angle to allow her hand to rest comfortably. He felt a little like Napoleon Bonaparte, but for some reason he didn't want to do anything that might make her move her hand.

All of proper Chattanooga was at the social. George and Laura Sanders Breck glided about at the fringes of the crowd; he introducing her with painstaking propriety to those of his acquaintance, she responding suitably, even emitting a slight smile on occasion. As they moved on past those with whom such formalities were impossible to avoid, puzzled eyes inevitably followed the near-silent duo on their polite, grave voyage through the evening's festivities. Cloaked in a sort of stately embarrass-ment, they passed among the celebrants, creating hardly a ripple, other than a questioning smile here and there.

Once, as George carefully dipped some punch for himself and Laura, he felt an elbow in his side. Uncle Matt Capshaw had sidled up to him and was leering at something above his head. "Better kiss that lady friend a yours," he winked, "'fore I do." Puzzled, George's eyes followed Matt's up to the bundle of mistletoe, festooned with a red-and-silver bow, that hung from the ceiling, strategically positioned above the punch bowl. George felt his cheeks stinging and hurriedly finished filling the cups, hoping wildly Mrs. Breck, standing beside him, hadn't noticed. Even worse—what if she thought he'd intentionally lured her to the punch bowl for some clandestine purpose! "Here you are," he said, offering her the punch, and was horrified to see her looking above him—at the mistletoe.

"Thank you," she said, taking the punch from him. Their eyes met. Her lips tightened a notch, a very faint pink tint brushed her cheeks, and she turned away, going back toward their place on one of the benches against the wall of the salon. George followed her, unable to take his eyes off the tops of his shoes. He thought he heard Uncle Matt snickering behind him.

Perlie Overby tramped through the thickly drifted snow on the way to Jacob Caswell's house, humming tunelessly under his breath. It was Christmas morning, and he was happy. His youngsters had rolled out of bed at the crack of dawn, tousle-headed and eager to see what surprises awaited them.

"Look like ol' Santy left some stuff over by the stove," Perlie had directed them, grinning from his and Martha's bed. His wife was just then stirring sleepily toward awareness, but he had come wide awake in the predawn darkness when he heard the first whispers from the children's pallets.

There were four paper sacks by the stove, with four names scrawled in pencil. Ned, the oldest, immediately took charge. "Percy first," he said, bringing the baby's parcel to his parents' bed, where the three-year-old still lay sleeping in his place between the two adults.

"Hey, young 'un!" Perlie prodded, gently rocking the sleeping infant. "Better wake up, boy, and see what Santy brought." The child made no response, other than a reflexive, fending gesture. "Leave him alone, Daddy," Martha murmured. "He's the only one in the house got enough sense to know it ain't time to get up yet."

Perlie had chuckled at this. "What's he got, Paw?" Ned inquired. Perlie had reached into the sack and produced a bright red apple. Gently he laid it in the crook of the sleeping toddler's arm. The little boy hugged it to him without so much as the flash of an eyelid.

Next, Ned handed her sack to six-year-old Sally. She produced a fistful of dark brown lozenges. "Horehound," she said with a shy smile. Mary, the older girl, was not content to allow her big brother to dole out her surprise. Grabbing it away from him, she eagerly looked inside. There was a white comb and about a foot of bright red ribbon. She immediately began attending to her tangled hair. "Hey, boy," Perlie beckoned to Ned, "You better see what you got this year, ain't you?"

"I guess so," Ned replied, reaching with calculated casualness for the final sack. Perlie nudged his wife, who sat up on one elbow to watch her son's expression.

The intake of breath and the rapt look was all the confirmation Ned's parents needed. "A knife!" he breathed, holding it up like a rare jewel. "A real Barlow!"

Perlie smiled again as he kicked his way through a snowdrift. The Barlow had been a chore to get hold of, but it was worth every penny. A bubble of cheer rose in his breast, and he sang a little to himself.

She churned her butter in Paw's old boot,
With a risselty-rasselty, hey, John dobbelty
Rusty co-pollity neigh, neigh, neigh!
And for the dasher she used her foot.
With a risselty-rasselty, hey, John dobbelty
Rusty co-pollity neigh, neigh, neigh!

She sold her butter in my home town,
With a risselty-rasselty, hey, John dobbelty

Rusty co-pollity neigh, neigh, neigh!
And the print of her heel was on each pound.
With a risselty-rasselty . . .

He cleared the tree line and entered Jacob Caswell's backyard. The dogs must have been curled up under the house somewhere, because no barking challenged his approach. A wisp of smoke rose from one of the chimneys. He rounded the house and tromped up the front steps, kicking his boots against the risers to shake off the loose snow. He knocked on the door.

Jacob opened the door, still wearing his dressing gown.

"Christmas gift, Mr. Caswell!" Perlie hoisted the flour sack he had toted from his shack.

"Christmas gift back to you, Perlie. Santa Claus find your house, I guess?"

"Sure did, Mr. Caswell, sure did! And ol' Santy left something there for you too!" He handed Jacob the sack.

Jacob peered inside the sack with a puzzled expression. "Well, now, Perlie, what in thunder . . . You sure didn't need to go to any trouble—"

"Why, shoot, it wasn't no trouble, Mr. Caswell, no trouble atall. I just 'preciate the work you've slid my way the last few months, and, well . . . it ain't much, but me 'n' Martha just wanted to say 'thanks,' that's all."

Jacob had extracted the pungent bundle from the grimy flour sack and held it at arm's length.

"Martha figgered, this being winter and all, with all the sickness and such going around, you might could use you a as'fiddity bag."

Jacob continued to eye the bag. A piece of thick homespun was wrapped around the highly aromatic contents and tied at the top with several rounds of grayish yarn, the whole package dangling from a rawhide strap.

"You wear it around your neck—"

"Yes, an asafetida bag," Jacob said. "I haven't had one of these in . . . quite some time. Well, Perlie, you . . . you tell Martha I said, 'thanks,' all right?"

Perlie's head bobbed gratefully. "I sure will, Mr. Caswell! And Merry Christmas to you!"

"Merry Christmas to you, Perlie."

Jacob backed slowly toward the door, still holding the asafetida bag in front of him like a talisman. He went into the house and closed the door. Being careful not to allow the high-smelling package to touch him, he watched out a side window as Perlie Overby tramped in his own tracks, whistling his way back across the side yard toward the tree-covered hillside. He shook his head as Perlie disappeared among the tangle of bare branches. *Crazy fool, tramping all the way over here in the snow just to hand me this nasty thing.*

He took the asafetida bag to the back porch, hanging it carefully on a nail. He wondered what Christmas morning could have been like at the Overby's shack. *That bunch is so poor they can't even pay attention. Yet there he goes, whistling like a meadowlark on Christmas morning, out before breakfast to bring me a present. Crazy fool.*

Jacob went into the parlor and poked at the fire, trying to rouse it a little more. He straightened and looked about him. Time was when this room would have been filled with laughter and the sound of ripping paper. When he would have sat in that chair, right over there, with his feet propped on that ottoman, and endured, with good-natured grousing, all the fuss his wife and children were making. When there would have been four stockings hanging on the mantelpiece, the toes rounded with the obligatory orange or apple. When, at the end of the day, after all the visiting and fighting over the new toys and "Christmas-gifting" of friends and neighbors were concluded, when the children were at last in their beds and the fires were all banked for the night, he and Mary would have smiled at each other and climbed the stairs, arms around each others' waists, up to their own bedroom, tired and happy and relieved and eager.

He hadn't even put up a tree this year. What was the point? Nobody here but him, and he'd just have to sweep up all the dropped needles, come tomorrow. Too much trouble, with nobody in the house to care one way or the other anyhow.

Unbidden, the image of seven-year-old Addie entered his mind. She wore her hair long in those days, streaming in a chestnut cascade down her back, sometimes tied with an emerald-green ribbon to match her eyes. Addie was always quieter on Christmas mornings than he expected her to be, he remembered. As if she were thinking of something else; as if she were doing sums in her mind.

He closed his eyes and shook his head just as the big clock in the entry hall chimed the quarter hour. Jacob glanced out a frost-rimmed window, guessing the hour by the color of the daylight. Looked like it was going to be a pretty nice day. He was due at Lou's by nine. He stirred the fire a final time and hung the poker on the rack.

Rose coughed as Bishop Jefferson rose from his chair beside her bed. "I sure thank you for coming over, Reverend," she said.

The white-haired pastor took her hand and patted it. "Sister Rose, it was a pleasure. I just hope you get to feeling better real quick."

"Lord willin'. It's in his hands." She covered her mouth and gave another rattling cough. "They's a lot o' sickness goin' round. I expect you got other folks to see today. You done spent enough time on me."

Lila, Rose's daughter-in-law, came into the bedroom. "Mama, you better try an' rest now," she said, smiling at Bishop Jefferson. "Thank you again for coming, Reverend. I know you're awful busy, and this being Christmas Day and all . . ."

He made a placating gesture. "Now, Lila, you know I been knowing this lady here a long time. Don't make no difference about how busy I am.

When I heard she took sick, I just had to come, that's all. You folks need anything, you let me know, you hear?"

"Yes, sir." Lila went to her mother-in-law's bedside. "You want some more water, Mama? You warm enough?" Lila tugged at the worn, faded, nine-patch quilt that covered the sagging shuck mattress.

"I'm fine, honey. You go on back in there with your childrens. Bye, Reverend."

The pastor waved as he closed the door behind him. Rose took Lila's hand.

"Honey, get one of your boys to run over to Mister Jacob's house and tell him I won't be in tomorrow. I don't think I'm gonna to be well enough to work for a few more days."

"Don't you worry about that, Mama. I'll go to Mister Jacob's for you till you doing better."

"Thank you, honey. I sure appreciate all you doin'. You so good to me, bringin' me over here and all . . ."

"Hush now. You better rest."

Rose nodded and rolled over on her side, heaving another clattering cough. Lila tiptoed out of the room. As she closed the door and turned around, Mason, her husband, was standing behind her.

"How's Mama?"

"I don't know. She seem awful weak, and her cough sound pretty rough to me."

"She ain't never spent this many days in bed," Mason said softly, shaking his head. "I don't know . . ."

Lila patted his arm and went to see about the children.

Becky listlessly pulled the wrapping paper from her package. She noted the contents of the box and forced a smile onto her face.

"Thanks, Mother. The brooch is lovely." She paused, then added, "It'll look real nice with my new dress."

Ruth Norwich gave her husband a worried glance, but he was engrossed in the James Fenimore Cooper novel he had just unwrapped. Heaving a mental sigh, she smiled back at her daughter.

"Well, I hoped you'd like it, dear." *The scoundrel. Why, any man with one eye and half sense could see the way this girl feels about him! Why in the world didn't he have the gumption to get her something—anything? Zeb Douglas, if I had you here right now, I do declare I'd skin you alive.*

"Well, I guess we'd better start cleaning up all this," Becky was saying, gathering scraps of tissue paper into her lap. "Ray and Fred and their bunch'll be here before much longer, and—"

"I'll take care of this, honey," Ruth interjected. "Why don't you just gather your things and get them put away?"

"Oh. All right." Becky drifted down the hallway toward her bedroom.

Why hadn't he at least told her he was going back to Nashville for Christmas? Becky wondered as she allowed the things in her arms to fall onto her bed. They'd gone for one of their long walks one day, and the next day he was gone on the morning train. No note, no telegraph—nothing. Almost as if he didn't want her to know he was leaving. Why?

It was funny how people could surprise you, she thought, idly patting the new clothes into a bureau drawer. You were with someone, and you liked it—very much. You thought he did too. You could feel things inside yourself beginning to loosen, things you had held in check for a long time. You sensed the same thing happening with the other person, sensed his unfolding enjoyment of simple talk and unguided conversation. Sensed the gladness with which he took your hand when you walked with him.

And then he did something you didn't expect—like leaving town with no notice. Like forgetting a simple thing like a Christmas gift for someone whose company he seemed to relish. It was *Christmas*, for Pete's sake! A flash of anger flared in her mind for an instant, and she tried to hold it, tried to fan it into something stronger, something to brace her and stiffen her backbone. But even as she clutched at it, big dollops of melancholy splashed on it and doused its heat. Fact was, she didn't want to be angry at Zeb. She just wanted to understand. And she wanted—part of her hated to admit it—to see him again.

Her mother came in. Becky could hear her bustling innocuously behind her, waiting to be invited into a conversation. She wasn't sure she had the energy to maintain her side of the talk, but it would be nice to think someone understood.

"Mother?"

"Yes, honey."

"You reckon men do things on purpose to irritate us, or do they just not know any better?"

Her mother's laugh was low and conspiratorial as she came to her and took both her hands. They looked at each other for a moment, and Mother glanced over her shoulder, back down the hall toward the parlor where Daddy still sat, probably still traipsing in his mind through the forest primeval with Hawkeye and Natty Bumppo.

"You care a great deal for him, don't you?" Mother said.

Becky shrugged and nodded. "And I thought he felt the same, but . . ."

"Sweetheart, you have to remember one thing about a man: things that are plain as custard to you don't make a lick of sense to him. Your daddy says it works the other way, too, but that's just because I don't let on how much I know about him."

Becky gave her mother a shy smile. "So, you mean . . . maybe he just—"

"Took off to Nashville with no more forethought than a goose. Probably didn't anymore mean to hurt your feelin's than a rock means to mash your toe if you drop it on your bare foot. He'll probably show up back here in the next few days with a box all wrapped nice and think that's good enough. 'After all, didn't I bring her a present?' he'll think. 'Not exactly on Christmas, but, shoot, it's not like I forgot or anything . . .'"

"And I'm supposed to sugar right up to him, just like that?" Becky asked, a skeptical scowl hooding her face.

"Oh, now, honey! I didn't say *that*, did I?"

Pete Norwich stood in the doorway of his daughter's bedroom looking quizzically at his wife and daughter seated on the bed and giggling together like two schoolgirls. "What in thunder are y'all laughing about?"

They looked up, almost as if they'd been caught with their hands in the cookie jar. "Oh, nothing, honey. Just girl talk, is all," Ruth said, dismissing him with a wave. "Go on back and read your book."

Mary Alice giggled and buried herself in the pile of crumpled wrapping paper. She had been awake for less than a half hour, but already all her Christmas gifts had been examined and discarded as she turned her attention to the gaily colored litter on the floor of the parlor.

Zeb yawned and stretched. "Well, that's it, I guess. Now that the presents are all opened, I believe I could use a cup of coffee."

"There's one more, Zeb."

He peered around the messy room. "Where? I don't see anything but opened boxes and about a bale-and-a-half of torn paper."

She gave him a nervous little smile, biting a corner of her lip. "Right here." She brought the ring box out of the pocket of her nightrobe.

She had dreamed and dreamed of this moment. Perhaps it would redeem the strangeness she had been sensing from him since his arrival two days ago. Perhaps the sight of his wedding ring, so long overdue, would bring back some hint of what she had once felt from him. Addie felt her heart hammering in her throat as she handed him the small, rounded, red velvet box.

Zeb opened the hinged lid. His expression never changed one bit, not even as he took the ring out and slipped it on the third finger of his left hand. After a moment or two, he looked up at her and said, "It's real pretty, honey. Thanks."

She felt dashed; she wanted to cry. Day after day, as she had stared at the ring's likeness in the mail-order catalog, she had imagined how pleased he'd be when he saw it. She had imagined, over and over, how glad he would be, at last, to wear the gold band that said he was hers, forever. She had fancied his grateful smile, the big, warm hug he'd give her. He would appreciate the time she had spent choosing this ring, this very ring. He would understand that she had thought and thought of how it would look on his hand, and of how good it would make her feel to give it to him. And maybe—somewhere deep inside, so deep she had not allowed herself to put words to the thoughts—she had hoped this ring could buy him back, could ransom him from Little Rock and break, with its shiny, golden magic, the spell of otherness that had grown stronger and stronger in him since he took that first train across the Mississippi River.

But all he could do was look at her with that polite expression and say, "Thanks." He didn't see any of it, did he? No, he had no idea. She had his thanks and nothing more. Her hopes crumpled inside her like an overused handkerchief.

"I'm glad you like it," she said, trying and failing to keep the hurt from drawing taut the line of her words. "I'll go get us some coffee."

Zeb watched her leave the room. He sighed and looked out the front window while Mary Alice played with innocent abandon among the torn paper.

What have I done now?

CHAPTER
21

*M*ount Moriah African Methodist Episcopal Church was crammed full. More than three hundred people had braved the January wind to wedge themselves into the tiny frame building. Inside, there was barely enough space at the front of the sanctuary for the Reverend Bishop Florissant T. Jefferson to stand in front of the pine plank box that held the earthly husk of Rose Lewis.

With tears streaming down her cheeks, Sister Alma Weeks was pounding out the final chorus of "My Father's House" on the battered, ill-tuned old upright piano as the congregation rattled the rafters with the refrain.

> *There'll be no crying there* (no, Lord!)
> *There'll be no dying there* (Thank you, Jesus!)
> *No sorrow there, in my Father's house,*
> *In my Father's house . . .*

As they came to the end of the song, the mourners drew the final words of the chorus out into a long, broadening rallentando, profusely ornamented by impromptu vocal flourishes from all over the church house and loud tremolo chords from Sister Alma. When the last flurries of the piano and the final amens had faded and ground to a halt,

Bishop Jefferson raised his long arms up and out, his Bible clasped in one hand.

"My brothers and sisters, we are gathered here today on this sorrowful occasion to say good-bye and Godspeed to our dearly departed sister, Rose Lewis."

A chorus of assent arose from the crowd. "Yes, Lord." "That's right." "Mmmm-hmmm." "Yes, sir." "Well, then."

"Shall we pray? Our Father that art in heaven, *holy* and *blessed* be thy name—"

(Yes, Lord . . . Well . . . Go ahead, brother . . . Tell it . . .)

"—we invite thy presence with us here today, as with *sorrowful* hearts, and *bitter* weeping, we lay to rest this good sister here—"

(Oh, yes, Jesus . . . That's right . . .)

"—a woman of *noble* character—"

(Yes, yes . . .)

"—a woman of *godly* and *pleasing* conduct—"

(Sure is . . .)

"—a faithful and *tireless* servant of yours, holy *Father*, thank you, Jesus . . ."

(Oh, Lord, that's surely right . . . Amen, and amen . . .)

"Our Father, we ask that you look down in mercy and tenderness upon our brothers Mason, James, and William, and our sisters Ruthie and Clarice, and their families as they mourn the passing of their dear mother—"

There was a loud moan on the front pew from Clarice, the oldest daughter. She leaned against her husband, a long-shanked, thin man with skin the color of black coffee. He put his arm around her and patted her shoulder.

"—And, Lord, we know that even now, Leland, Charles, and little Esther are welcoming a beloved wife and mother into the *bosom* of Father Abraham, praise the Lord—"

(Well, then . . . That's all right . . . Yes, Lord . . .)

"—and Lord, we know that just as thou hast *raised* Jesus Christ from the dead, so shall Sister Rose enter into thy *joys*, as will *all* of us here, if we *faint* not, nor grow *weary* in well-doing—"

(Thank, you, Lord Jesus . . . Hallelujah! Yes, sir!)

Dub and Louisa Dawkins sat about two-thirds of the way down the center aisle on the left-hand side, the only white faces in the pews. Louisa was a trifle uncomfortable, but she had insisted this was an obligation that could not be avoided. As the funeral service swirled about her, her mind was inevitably drawn back toward the solemn, quiet ceremony that had ushered her daughter Katherine into eternity. She remembered sitting with Dub on the front pew, with the children ranged beside them. She remembered feeling as if she were frozen into a block of ice, sundered from everyone and everything else by the grief that was her food, her breath, her every waking thought. She had felt so alone, so cut off. And the funeral service at First Methodist Church had utterly failed to touch her. She had endured it, allowed it to run off her mind like rainwater off a roof. When someone had instructed her to sit, she had sat. When told to rise, she rose. She was not a participant. She was barely a presence.

But here every person in the church building seemed drawn toward Rose and her family by the rowdy cadence of the give-and-take between the minister and the mourners. This was a ceremony that enveloped the participants, made them partners in the dance. Despite her discomfiture, Louisa felt herself joining in with Rose's family and friends to sing and weep and pray her into the arms of God. It touched something deep and quick within her, gave her a keen pang of longing for all that was lost.

Bishop Jefferson had finished praying. As he lowered his face to peer out over the audience, Louisa could see the beads of sweat on his broad forehead, just below the cottony line of his white, close-cropped hair. She could also see the tear tracks down both his cheeks.

"Brothers and sisters, Rose Lewis was a good woman."

(Amen . . . That's right . . .)

"She was a woman who loved God, and loved her neighbor as herself."

(Mmm-hmm . . . Sure did . . .)

"She cared for her husband and did him good, and not harm, *all* the days of his life."

(Well, then . . . Yes, indeed . . .)

"And, my brothers and sisters, I say, with so many of you here today . . ."

For the first time, Bishop Jefferson's voice faltered. Louisa stared in fascinated sympathy as he swallowed and blinked rapidly.

"I say to you . . . that Rose Lewis was—my friend."

(Amen. Thank you, Jesus.)

"And is that not why there are so many of us here today?"

(Yes, sure is . . .)

"Look around you at those gathered here," he said. "Not many of us rich—"

(No, indeed . . . That's the truth . . .)

"—not *many* of us wise—"

(Preach it, brother! Go ahead!)

"—not *many* of us mighty according to the deeds of this world—"

(That's right! The man is mighty right!)

Louisa sensed the bishop gathering himself, flexing his mind and heart for a great rush toward glory. She felt her pulse accelerating.

"We are the *weak*—"

(Amen!)

"—the broken-*hearted*—"

(Yes! Yes!)

"—*some* would even call us *'fools'*—"

(Oh, yes, Lord!)

"And yet, I *say* unto you, that God hath chosen the foolish things of this world, that he might shame the wise—"

(Thank you, Lord Jesus!)

"He hath placed his treasures in jars of clay, that through the foolishness of the gospel he might call *all* men everywhere unto himself—"

The minister heaped phrase upon phrase, like a man throwing dry wood on a bonfire.

"And I *say* unto you, my brothers and sisters—"

(Tell it! Tell it!)

"—that this woman here, our departed Sister Rose—"

(Thank you, Jesus! Thank you, Lord!)

"—was surely a minister of the gospel—"

(Oh, yes! Hallelujah!)

"—in her humble service—"

(Amen!)

"—and her faithful life—"

(That's right!)

"—and the spirit of the Lord was *surely* upon her—"

(That's the truth! That's the Lord's own truth!)

"—and she shall surely have her reward—"

(Thank you, Lord!)

"—and shall hear the Master say, on that great and *terrible* day—"

(Praise Jesus! Thank you, sweet Lord!)

"—'Well done, thou good and faithful servant'—"

(Oh, yes! Yes, yes, yes!)

"—'enter thou into the *joys* of thy Lord.'"

(Hallelujah! Thank you, Lord!)

"Amen. Amen. Shall we sing?"

The pianist banged out the opening chords of "My Lord, What a Morning." Bishop Jefferson fished a handkerchief out of his hip pocket and mopped his forehead and cheeks.

My Lord, what a morning,
My Lord, what a morning,
My Lord, what a morning,
When the stars begin to fall . . .

When the service was over, Rose's family lined up on either side of the back door of the church and everyone filed past them. Louisa found the exercise in odd contrast to the noisy service; the well-wishers were somber, almost shy as they shuffled past, offering handshakes or, in rare cases, hugs to the bereaved. Were these reserved people the same as those who, with shouts and cries of hallelujah, had ridden the crests of Florissant T. Jefferson's zeal?

Louisa recognized Mason, Rose's youngest child, and his wife, Lila. She knew she'd have to be the one to speak; Dub kept his eyes fixed on the toes of his shoes and his hands in his pockets as he shuffled along beside her.

She took Mason's hand. "Mason, I'm Louisa Dawkins—Jacob Caswell is my daddy. We're real sorry. Rose was like a part of our family. I'll never forget all she did for my little sister."

A light of recognition swept away the veiled look with which Mason had been regarding her. Louisa thought he looked uncomfortable, unaccustomed to the buttoned collar and tightly cinched tie he was wearing.

"Miz Lou? I sure appreciate you coming today. Mama was awful fond of Miz Addie."

"I know she was. Daddy would've been here, too, but him being sick and all . . ."

Mason nodded. Louisa held his eyes a moment longer, then stepped back. He was already reaching for the next person in line. As she turned away, Louisa noticed the faded stains on the cuffs of the trousers of his suit. Then they were outside, and Dub was guiding her away, stepping quickly in the brittle January sunlight.

It was even worse than he'd thought it would be.

The Memphis-to-Little Rock train jostled across the alluvial plain between West Memphis and the village of Forrest City. Zeb stared out the window at the bleak, gray winter landscape filing slowly past his window.

Yesterday, as he began packing his valise, the vague fear came upon him again. He sensed something was coming toward him, some threat he could not escape. He had a sudden, unexpected longing to stay in Nashville, an odd sense that he would be safe here. But he couldn't! He had a place there, and he had to return to it. What if Addie and Mary Alice were to come back with him?

That night at supper, he broke a long silence by mentioning casually that there were some nice houses in Little Rock, plenty big enough for their family but not too expensive.

He watched her as she stopped chewing and stared at him. She put down her fork and swallowed.

"What?" she said in a low tone that was both a question and a threat.

He shrugged, ignoring the alarms going off inside his head. "Well, I was just thinking that things are going pretty well for me there, and—"

"I thought you were up for a job at the home office, here in Nashville."

"Well, I still am, as far as I know, but . . . I . . . well, I sorta like it there." The words sounded weak, even to him.

She sat with her arms folded across her chest, hugging her elbows with both hands. He could see the muscles working at the sides of her jaws.

"Zeb, I'm tired of up and moving every time you think you've got a better deal. I don't know anybody in Little Rock, and I only put up with you going there because you said it was the last step to getting a settled job back here in the home office, where you wouldn't be dragging Mary Alice and me from pillar to post anymore. I put up with it because I thought it was just for awhile."

She looked away from him and he could see her chest heaving beneath her crossed arms, could hear the angry puffs of breath coming from her nostrils. He stared at the tabletop.

"Addie, I . . . it wouldn't have to be—"

"Have you ever stopped to think about what I might want, Zeb? What might be best for Mary Alice?"

He sat silently, bowing his head to receive her angry blows. Couldn't she see that he was sorry? Didn't she care how bad he felt?

"I don't want to move to Little Rock," she said in a voice as flat as the backside of an axe. "I want to stay here, or—go back to Chattanooga."

So that was it! Addie had never really left Chattanooga, had she? He had promised to take care of her, to make a new life for them, and he had kept his end of the bargain, but she—she had never stopped pining for the security of her own people and her own place! She didn't trust him, even after all he'd done! He felt the dull ache of anger in his throat; a wordless anger, and blunt. If she could be hard, he could too.

"Well, all right, then," he said. "Just forget it." He picked up his fork and put another bite of food in his mouth. It tasted like sawdust.

The train heaved itself up the grade to the top of Crowley's Ridge and now rolled toward the drab, tree-lined fields of central Arkansas. A mist was falling from the gray sky. Zeb began trying to occupy his mind with what needed to be done in the office upon his return. He tried to put Addie out of his thoughts.

Addie watched Mary Alice dabble her fingers in her cereal, but this morning she didn't have the energy to correct her daughter. Thinking about the argument with Zeb and the fierce silences that followed it drained her, sapped her desire.

There was a dull fear about the way she had felt during much of Zeb's time at home—his "visit," as she now thought of his times at home. His place within her was much like that of a visitor—a person she recognized but didn't really know all that well. Even though he shared her bed, he was, in many strange ways, unknown to her—and she to him.

He just didn't see her. He saw a picture—a portrait he had painted in his mind and labeled "wife." She honestly believed he could no more conceive of her as having volition and desire, of wanting one thing and not wanting another, than he could lay an egg. It simply hadn't occurred to him that she wouldn't jump at the chance to join him in his beloved Little Rock.

She had seen the dejected way he hung his head when the resentment began spilling from her, but it hadn't mattered. She couldn't stop, couldn't stem the flow that spilled from her, fueled by every frustration and every moment of lost loneliness she had felt since he had uprooted her life with his promises of care and security. What did he know of security? He thought it was something in an account at the bank. He had no idea. If she had said everything in her mind, he'd have had something to feel bad about, all right!

But now that her anger was spent and Zeb was gone and the house was filled with the melancholy quiet of a drab winter morning, she wondered if she had done the right thing after all. Maybe it would have been better to keep still. Maybe it would have been the Christian thing to do. She'd half-expected him to yell at her, to fight back. Instead, he just finished his supper and went into the parlor to hide behind a newspaper. He hadn't bothered to try to kiss her good-bye when he left the next morning. At the time, that suited Addie fine. But now, she wondered . . .

CHAPTER

22

George held Laura Sanders Breck's elbow as she stepped into the buggy. Even though it was early February, George felt sweaty beneath his collar. The weather was fair, at least—one of those rare winter afternoons that made spring seem like more than a vague hope. He gave the hired rig a final inspection as he walked around to climb up on the seat. He didn't exactly know what he was looking for, but he thought he ought to appear accustomed to doing such things. Bill Cray, the livery-man, was a friend of the Hutto family. Surely he wouldn't allow George to take Laura Sanders Breck out in an unsafe rig. George clambered up into the seat and managed to get the reins gathered into his hands. He glanced over at Mrs. Breck and aimed a smile at her that he hoped appeared friendly and relaxed. "All set?" he asked.

She stared straight ahead and nodded sharply. Once.

George clicked his tongue and the horse leaned into the collar, then stopped. George clicked louder and brushed the bay's flank with the buggy whip, but the horse made no response other than an annoyed flick of the tail. "Oh," George said, looking down beside him, "the brake." He released the brake and clicked his tongue, and the horse moved obedi-ently forward. "Good old Bill," George said. "Looks like he gave us an experienced horse." Mrs. Breck made no reply. As they made the final turn out of the wagonyard, George noticed Bill Cray leaning against the door of the barn, hands in his pockets, grinning at them.

They were going on a drive to the top of Lookout Mountain, a favorite activity for courting couples. George had been embarrassed in extending the invitation, half hoping Mrs. Breck would decline. She hadn't, though, and here they were, clip-clopping down Ninth Street in the broad light of a Saturday afternoon. George felt very conspicuous. He kept his eyes straight ahead, sighting between the bay's ears at a spot on the road about ten feet in front of them. He hoped Mrs. Breck wasn't too uncomfortable with the whole town staring at them, as he thought it must surely be, but he didn't dare turn his head to look at her.

Just after they had rattled across the plank bridge spanning Chattanooga Creek, George decided he really ought to break the silence. He cleared his throat.

"Nice day for a drive, anyhow."

"Quite pleasant."

"I think it does a person good to get some fresh air once in awhile."

"I just hope some fool in one of those motor cars doesn't come along and scare the horse."

George slumped a little lower in his seat. "Well, so far we haven't seen any."

"I noticed your livery friend had them stacked all around his place."

"Bill works on them now. Says it's the wave of the future. Says one day, there won't be anymore livery business, just motor cars."

Laura Sanders Breck gave a skeptical grunt. "It'll be too bad if he's right."

George thought so, too, but he wanted to talk about something else—if he could only think of what that might be. The road was starting to rise up on the flanks of the mountain now, and the horse was leaning more heavily into the collar. George stole a glance at Mrs. Breck. She was sitting ramrod-straight on her side, holding on with a gloved fist to steady herself against the tilting road. She looked as if she was having an awful time. George felt his heart sinking down into his shoes. She was a nice lady, but when he was around her, he felt even more tongue-tied than usual. Still, she seemed not to mind his company; she had yet to refuse any invitation he'd offered. It was confusing. He had the vague sense that there was something they were missing, but he had no idea what it was.

The road turned up more steeply, and the muscles in the horse's hindquarters bunched tighter. Just as George was about to ask Laura Sanders Breck if she would care to get out and walk around a bit, the horse, straining mightily with the load and the severity of the grade, squeezed off a long, low, quivering flatulence.

George felt his face and neck burning with embarrassment. The sound seemed to go on and on. Without realizing it, he scrunched his chin into his chest. The bay was still pressing forward, and every step produced a staccato aftershock. George wished he could just disappear. How in the world could he ever again face a proper lady like Mrs. Breck when such a mortifying indelicacy clogged the air between them? Not to mention the rather unpleasant smell. And then he heard her speaking.

"Sounds like your livery friend's been feeding 'em plenty of oats."

George felt a laugh bubbling up inside him. No, not now! He clenched his jaw against it and willed it to go away. He felt it surge against the dam of his teeth and force its way upward, squeezing tears from his eyes. Still he held himself in check.

And then the horse erupted once more. It was no use. George threw back his head and guffawed. He laughed all the way from the soles of his feet, laughed so hard the crown of his head ached. Laura Sanders Breck would probably never let him in her sight again. When he finally got a lasso on the runaway laughter, he risked a glance at her, wiping his eyes on his coatsleeve.

And she was smiling. Staring straight ahead but smiling. She turned her head to look at him, and the crow-black eyes twinkled with amusement. She started giggling, and it was all up with him again. Soon, they were both howling at the top of their lungs. Somewhere amid the cleansing flood of merriment, he felt her fingers brush his. They held hands the rest of the way up the mountain.

It was Sunday morning, and Zeb Douglas felt wretched. He looked in the mirror a final time, adjusted his cravat and smoothed back his hair. It was time to be leaving if he didn't want to be late to church, but he was having a hard time getting himself to walk out the door.

He'd avoided Becky Norwich and her family since arriving from Nashville three weeks ago. When he considered her, his thoughts were tangled and troubled. In his mind, her image was perpetually bathed in a golden light. Becky was good-natured and confident. She had learned that it was all right to have firm opinions on things, and Zeb loved to hear her express them. He never had to wonder what she was thinking. She gave every evidence of being tremendously interested in him and everything he did. Being with her was a heady draught.

But he was a married man! He'd made promises to Addie and sired a child with her. Even though she was dour so much of the time, even though she'd never understand why he didn't want to leave Little Rock, even though he never seemed to quite measure up to her expectations or her approved way of managing life, she was his lawful wife.

As he paced back and forth across the tiny front room, he stuck a hand down in the side pocket of his coat. His fingers encountered a round, smooth object. He drew it out and looked at it. It was the ring Addie had given him at Christmas. On the train, he had been wearing this suit and had, without thinking, dropped the ring off his finger and into this pocket, where it had apparently stayed these last few weeks.

Several times he slipped the ring on and off the third finger of his left hand. Then, slowly, he pulled out the top drawer of a bureau and placed the ring in the bottom, beneath his clean handkerchiefs. He turned around and walked out the front door, closing it behind him. When he reached Ninth Street, he paused long. Finally, instead of turning west toward the rock church building, he turned eastward, pacing slowly toward City Park. He wasn't ready yet to face her. Not this morning.

He walked around the mostly deserted park with his hands thrust in his pockets. Apparently, most of Little Rock's citizens were in church this morning—as he should have been. He felt like a great coward, felt guilty for abandoning his Sabbath duties because he couldn't order his own thoughts and feelings. He tried to pray, but no worthwhile words would come to his mind. He wasn't sure God wanted to listen to the likes of him, anyway, right now.

He decided to go back to his rooms. He had taken a flat above a dry goods store on Izard Street, about half a block off Fifth. It was small, but he didn't need much room just for himself. It was also a lot more economical than staying at the Gleason. He had several city blocks to negotiate on the way to the office each day, which he didn't mind—the walk gave him time to think. He arrived at his front door and was about to put the key in the lock when he heard quick footsteps coming up the stairs behind him. He looked back and felt his heart fall into his stomach. It was Becky Norwich.

"Becky, what . . . why aren't you—"

"In church? Well, I guess I might ask you the same thing."

She stepped onto the landing at the head of the stairs. "And while I'm at it, I might just ask you this: who in the world do you think you are, anyway?"

His door fell open and she barged past him, into his apartment. "Becky, this isn't . . . I don't think—"

"Don't worry, I'm not going to stay long enough to start any talk," she said, standing in the middle of his parlor. "Mother and Daddy are visiting my uncle in Hot Springs, and as far as they know I'm at church this morning, like a good little girl."

He stepped into the room and closed the door. "Becky, I'm sorry. I know you must think—"

"Let me just tell you what I think, Zeb Douglas. I think you're about the most ignorant, unfeeling man I've ever been around. I think you don't know what's going on right under your nose, and I think I've just about had a belly full of it, is what I think." She jabbed the air in front of his face with her index finger.

"You lead me to believe you enjoy my company, you hold my hand and say we're friends, and then you leave for Nashville at Christmas without so much as a fare-thee-well. You've been back in town for at least three weeks and you didn't call, didn't send a note, didn't act like you've ever even made my acquaintance. I'm hurt and embarrassed, Zeb, is what I am. I thought you cared about me, but I guess you're just not the man I thought you were."

She had apparently run out of breath. "Becky, I'm awful sorry," he said. "You just don't know what I've been going through." He tried to look at her, but he couldn't. He kept his eyes on a spot on the rug to the left of where she stood.

"Well, I know what I've been going through," she said. "I've been in torment, wondering what I did, what I said, how I had possibly offended you to the point that—"

"No, Becky, that's not it at all," he said, looking at her for the first time. "It's not you. It's . . . it's me. Like you said, I'm not the man you think I am."

Scores of words clogged his throat. He had to tell her! *I'm married, Becky, and I feel things for you I'm not supposed to feel! There's a wife and a daughter in Nashville, Becky. A wife who's angry with me most of the time, who doesn't understand me half as well as you do, who confuses me and upsets me—but a wife, Becky. No, I'm sure not the man you think I am.*

He tried to swallow past the knot in his throat. He felt a tear well slowly from his eye and roll down his cheek. She moved toward him and touched the tear with a fingertip. Becky peered into his eyes. He wanted to say something but just didn't know how to start.

"Oh, Zeb," she whispered, her face inches from his. "Why can't you just tell me?"

He felt his arms encircling her waist. He pulled her to him, half expecting her to slap him, to scream. Instead, he felt her hands on the back of his head, pulling his mouth hungrily to hers.

At first, he heard a voice in the back of his head chanting over and over, "This is wrong, this is wrong, this is wrong . . ." But her breath felt sweet on his neck and her soft blonde hair tumbled down around his hands and the hot blood shouted in his ears as it coursed through his body. Presently the voice was an echo, then a whisper . . . then gone.

Addie nibbled at the dry toast and waited for her morning nausea to subside. This stage had run much longer this time than with her first pregnancy. Surely, though, she ought to be mostly past the sickness part within a few more weeks.

Mary Alice padded into the kitchen, waving the letter she'd received yesterday from Louisa. "Honey, put Mama's letter down," she admonished her daughter. "Put down Aunt Lou's letter."

"An' Loo?"

"Yes, honey, that's from Aunt Lou, and Mama wants you to give it here." She held out her hand. Mary Alice reluctantly placed the envelope in Addie's hand. "Thank you, sweetie. Now go on back in your room and play, all right?"

Mary Alice immediately plopped down in the floor and began fiddling with the lace at the hem of her nightgown. Addie sighed. She ought to dress herself and the baby, but she just didn't have a lot of extra energy these days, and the news from Chattanooga hadn't made things any easier.

She had cried most of yesterday after reading about Rose's death and funeral. In her grief over Rose, she had barely noticed Lou's worried postscript about Papa's persistent cough.

Right then, it seemed to Addie that loss was all she'd ever known. Her mind viewed the landscape of her life and found it a bleak and barren place. At this moment, she longed with everything in her for one person who would really listen to her, but it looked like there was no one available for the job. She had never felt more lacking and alone than when she found out Rose was gone. At least when Mama died, there was Rose's lap. Who was left?

Addie wondered if she was the only person in the world who had sustained such dreadful damage. The people she saw on the street and in the stores gave no sign of such wreckage in their lives as she was finding in hers. Surely others had survived abandonment and bereavement. When would her rescue come? When would the good days return? Or wasn't she entitled?

"Well, Rose," she said aloud, "Guess what? I'm gonna have to deliver this baby without you. Reckon how I'll manage?"

"Mama ha' bebby," Mary Alice said, standing and placing a chubby hand on her mother's belly. "Ha' bebby."

CHAPTER
23

*D*ub, I'm worried about Papa."

"What's the matter, Lou?"

Dub slapped at his pillow. It had been a hard day at the store; he'd caught one of the new clerks stealing from the till. Dub hated conflict and avoided it whenever possible, but he couldn't tolerate theft for one instant. He'd had to confront the clerk, who had denied everything and turned surly. He'd had to have some of the other men remove the fellow from the store. He'd decided not to press charges, but the whole matter had given him a headache that had lasted the rest of the day. He was hoping that he could go to sleep tonight and wake up tomorrow without a tenpenny nail in the center of his forehead.

"Well, he won't go to the doctor, and he's been coughing like a lunger for two weeks now. I'm afraid he's got walking pneumonia but won't do anything about it."

Dub sighed. He rolled from his side to his back, staring at the ceiling of their bedroom.

"He won't stay at home," Louisa said. "He gets up every morning of the world and goes in to that store. He's trying to kill himself is what I think."

Dub knew he had to try to make some sort of reply. "Well, honey, surely if he felt that bad he'd stay home."

Her silence was not that of a satisfied person who was ready to let things drop and allow her husband to go to sleep. He waited, blinking at the darkness above his head.

"Dub, I can't help worrying about him. Course he won't let anyone close to him, but I'm his daughter, after all."

"Lou, if you're that worried, why don't you say something to him?"

"Why, Dub, you know good and well he won't listen to anything I say. That's about the most hardheaded man in the world, and you know it as well as I do."

And he's got at least one hardheaded daughter. "Honey, I don't know what else to say."

She sighed. "Well . . . Good night, dear."

"Night." He rolled back onto his side and pulled the quilt over his shoulder. He waited.

"Would you go with me to see him, Dub?"

"If I thought it would do any good, which I don't."

She sighed again. He felt the mattress rock as she leaned over to blow out her bedside lamp. He waited.

"I sure wish you'd get this bedroom wired for electricity."

"Yes, ma'am. I'll tend to it one of these days."

Another sigh. The light went out and Dub closed his eyes at last.

Louisa sent the boys off to school the next morning, then put on her coat, gloves, and hat before she could talk herself out of her mission. The hack deposited her on the boardwalk in front of Caswell's Dry Goods, and she paid the driver, squared her shoulders, and marched up the front steps.

She tramped up the stairs at the back of the store and pushed through the swinging gate into the office area. Her father's desk was unoccupied. She was about to ask Mr. Sloan, the bookkeeper, for Papa's whereabouts when a rasping, rattling cough from the vault told her. She went into the vault. Jacob was standing and turning around with a box of receipts in his arms when she saw his face. Before she could stop herself, she let out a gasp.

His face was ashen, and his eyes looked like tunnels in the side of a washed-out clay bank. He wheezed with every breath. He looked at her, and for an instant he wore a guilty expression, before he remembered himself.

"Well, what are you staring at?" He tried to draw himself a bit straighter.

"Papa, you're going home right this minute! You're in no condition to be—"

"Last time I checked, I was still your daddy, and I can still—" A coughing fit took him, and he nearly dropped the box. Louisa thought he was about to fall, but he leaned against the vault wall until the spell passed. "I can still look out for myself, without your help," he finally managed in a half-choked voice before another cough shook him.

"Besides," he said, "there's nobody back there at the house anyway. I'm as well off here as I would be there."

She moved to him and pulled the box from his grasp. "What are you talking about? I thought Lila was—"

"I ran her off."

"What?"

"She didn't suit me," he said as he pushed past her. "If you're gonna stand there gawking, you might as well bring that box to Abe." He shuffled out of the vault and turned toward his desk.

Mr. Sloan appeared in the vault doorway. He glanced over his shoulder at Jacob's receding back, then at Louisa. "Lou, he don't need to be here," he said quietly, bending over to pick up the box of receipts. "He's mortal sick, if you'll pardon my saying so, and I wish he'd go to the doctor, but he won't listen to nothing nobody here says to him about it."

Louisa closed her eyes, massaging her temples with one hand and cradling her elbow with the other.

"I was glad to see you coming up those stairs, 'cause I figured if anybody could talk sense to him, it'd be you."

"Abe, he won't listen to me either," she said. "At least, not yet."

Abe Sloan shook his head and turned to go back to his desk. "I sure wish he'd listen to somebody. He don't need to be here, and that's the Lord's truth."

She walked out of the vault and turned the corner toward her father's desk. Jacob sat slumped in his swivel chair. He appeared shriveled, shrunken within himself. He was looking away from her, out over the sales floor. She pulled a cane-bottomed chair over and sat across the desk.

"Papa, why are you doing this?"

"Doing what?"

"Killing yourself."

"Just got a bad cold, is all."

"Papa, you and I both know better than that. Why is it you've decided to quit living?"

He flicked an angry glance at her, then turned away again. He started to cough and scrabbled hastily in the lap drawer of his desk for a handkerchief. Though he tried to hold it crumpled in his fist as he brought it to his mouth, Louisa saw the rusty speckling of dried blood.

"I don't know what you're talking about," he said, wiping his lips. "I'll be all right. If you came down here to henpeck, why don't you just go on back home?"

"Papa, don't you know I love you?" she said, trying to keep her voice even. "Don't you think I care about what happens to you? I can't just let you sit down here and die and act like it doesn't matter to me one way or the other! Why won't you let somebody help you?"

"I don't need anybody's help!"

He immediately went into another coughing spasm. Out of the corner of her eye, she saw some of the customers on the sales floor stare up at the office. She started to come around and hold his shoulders, but he waved her off.

When he could speak again, he said, "I've been alone since your mother died, and here lately I've decided that suits me just fine. Nobody to tell me to pick up my stuff, nobody to get in my way around the place, nobody to worry about whether I come or go. Nobody to lecture me about what I ought to do, nobody to go off and leave me. Nobody except me to bother with. That's how I like it. You hear? Now go on. You've shown your Christian concern, and I've turned it down. There's nothing else for you to do."

She felt the tears stinging the corners of her eyes. "Papa, please—"

"Abe," he said, standing and walking toward the bookkeeper's desk, "did you get those receipts totaled up yet?"

Louisa flung herself out of the chair and dashed toward the stairs, covering her mouth with her hand. As she clattered down the steps, she heard him start coughing again.

Zeb walked into the agency and Abner immediately waved a telegraph message at him. "Western Union boy just brought this over, Zeb. Says it's urgent. Says it came from Nashville."

Zeb tore open the envelope and extracted the wire. He read it twice before the meaning penetrated. He puffed out his cheeks and his eyes went wide.

"What's the matter? Bad news from home?"

"Well, you might say that." Zeb tried to sort out the thoughts as they scrambled past his consciousness. He looked up at Abner. "I've got to go back, Ab. My wife's father died."

They filed slowly into the young attorney's office and seated themselves around the long table, the dark-suited men carefully holding the chairs for their wives. Louisa eased into her chair and felt Dub's hand rest lightly on her shoulder for a moment.

When they were all sitting, the bustling, nervous-mannered young man went to the head of the table and carefully stacked some documents, then seated himself. He cleared his throat and looked at them all. He tried to smile, without much success.

"Well, now that we're all here," he said, "I guess we'd better get started. As you may know, your father had filed a revised will with me quite some time prior to his death—"

"Revised?" said Junior, the oldest sibling. "I knew Papa had some kinda falling out with Dan Sutherland, but I didn't know anything about changes in his will." Junior peered a question at the rest of them. He looked back at the lawyer. By now a sheen of perspiration was visible on the young man's forehead. "Well?"

"Yes, ah . . . Mr. Caswell brought his former will to me at about the time he . . . he left Mr. Sutherland and asked me to make some, ah . . . some changes."

"What kind of changes?" Louisa said.

The attorney dabbed at his forehead with a handkerchief. "Yes, well . . . Why don't we just read the will, and I think everything will be self-explanatory."

Junior sat back in his chair with a frown covering his face, still staring at the sweating lawyer. The rest of them inched forward, their elbows on the table, and waited for the attorney to begin reading. Dub and Zeb were doing their best, Louisa thought, to maintain an attitude of respectful disinterest.

"I, Jacob Isaiah Caswell, being of sound mind, do hereby declare this to be my last will and testament . . ."

As the young man's voice droned on, Louisa studied Addie and Zeb from the corner of her eye. She had been watching them ever since their arrival for the funeral, two days ago. If Papa's death had affected Addie, she wasn't showing it. To Louisa, her younger sister seemed disinterested, somehow—apart. Zeb, on the other hand, appeared to be going out of his way to be the same old, glad-handing, smiling, good-humored fellow he'd always been. Courteous, proper, and well-mannered, he looked to Louisa to be a more prosperous, more confident version of the person who had left Chattanooga nearly four years ago.

But something had changed. Louisa couldn't miss the polite reserve between Zeb and Addie. Allowing for his solicitousness toward Addie's expectant condition, Louisa sensed a certain aloofness. Zeb treated Addie with the respect one might show an esteemed but distant relative. Louisa was worried about them, even though she couldn't put her finger on the exact reason why.

". . . do hereby direct that the remainder of my estate be distributed, *per stirpes*, among my three surviving children—"

"Do what?" said Bob, the younger brother. "What did you just read?"

The young lawyer wiped his forehead and cleared his throat. He looked around the table at them, then read again, in a quieter voice, "The remainder of the estate is to be divided among the three children Mr. Caswell mentions in the following—"

"I don't guess you can count, son," said Junior, leaning forward in his chair and carefully placing his folded hands on the table. "There's four of us: me, Bob, Lou, and Addie. Four."

The attorney's only reply was to begin reading again in a flat, weakened voice. ". . . my three surviving children: Jacob Isaiah Caswell Junior, Louisa Marie Caswell Dawkins, and Robert Wilkes Caswell. I hereby direct that—" The lawyer's voice faltered, then resumed. "—that Adelaide Margaret Caswell Douglas, by reason of her willful disregard for the peace and well-being of this home, be stricken from my inheritance, that her right to any proceeds of this estate be revoked, and that she and her heirs and assigns be specifically and perpetually enjoined from any of the benefits that they might otherwise have enjoyed." The lawyer's voice faded to a halt.

There was almost a minute of stunned silence. For the first time, Addie showed emotion. All color had drained from her face, and Louisa could see white half-moons beneath her fingernails as she gripped the edge of the table. Even Zeb had lost his usual self-assured air and sat with his mouth agape, staring sightlessly at the empty center of the table.

It was Junior who broke the hush. "Do you mean to tell me that you let Papa write his own daughter out of the will?"

The attorney's face had a strangled, desperate look. "Now, Mr. Caswell, you must understand that in the state of Tennessee, a person of good judgment can do anything he wants to his estate as long as—"

"Good judgment?" Bob said. "You call this good judgment?"

"No wonder Dan Sutherland and your daddy parted ways," Dub said. He put his arm around Louisa and softly patted her shoulder as she wept quietly into her handkerchief. "Dan wouldn't have been party to something like this."

They all stared accusingly at the young lawyer, who remained absolutely still, except to shrug.

"Mr. Caswell wanted it this way. I'm just the lawyer."

"Yeah," said Junior with a snort. "How much did he pay you, boy?"

"Now, Mr. Caswell—"

"I've got to get some air," Addie said, shoving her chair back from the table. She stood, took three steps toward the doorway, and crumpled in a heap of black satin and taffeta.

CHAPTER
24

*T*he young woman pushed through the door into Zeb's office and stopped short, her smile fading as she stared at Zeb's vacant desk. Abner got up from his desk just inside the front door and approached her. "Yes, Ma'am? Can I help you?"

"Isn't this Zeb Douglas's office?" she asked.

"Yes, Ma'am. He ain't here right now, though."

"Where is he?"

Abner studied her carefully. It was pretty obvious she was more than casually interested in Zeb's whereabouts. He added the columns in his mind and quickly decided he should tread with extreme caution. "Well, he got called back to Nashville, kind of sudden, Ma'am."

"It's 'Miss,'" she said. By now there wasn't anything left of the smile she'd worn coming in the door. "When did he leave?"

"Yesterday morning, Ma'am— Scuse me, Miss. I think he said it was some kind of . . . family emergency."

She stared a hole through him. "What kind of family emergency?"

Abner gave what he fervently hoped was a convincing shrug. "'Fraid I can't say, Miss. He got a wire, and he read it, and before you could shake a stick, he was out the door to the station."

Her features softened a trifle. "Well, I guess if he left in such a hurry as all that, maybe he wouldn't have had time to let me know . . ."

"Oh, I'm sure not, Miss," Abner offered in his most earnest manner. "He read that wire and lit out like a scalded dog— Scuse me, Miss. Anyway, he lit out right quick. I don't imagine he had anything on his mind but getting to Nashville quick as he could."

She looked at him thoughtfully for a few seconds. "Well, I'm sorry if I snapped at you. My mother is having a little social, and I came to invite Zeb; I guess I was pretty disappointed because I had no idea he was leaving town."

"Aw, that's all right, Miss. You didn't do nothing wrong."

She gave him another quick, hard look, then softened again. "Well, anyway, just tell him Miss Norwich came by. I'll talk to him when he gets back to Little Rock. I don't suppose he said when that would be?"

Abner shrugged again. "No, Miss, I'm afraid not. I'll sure tell him soon as I see him though."

"Well, all right." She gave him a quick smile, adjusted her hat, and left. Abner stood staring after her. He scratched his head and gave a low, worried whistle. "What's Zeb got himself into now, I wonder?" he asked the empty office.

Becky's mind was spinning as she walked back to her father's store. Gone again! She wanted to be angry with Zeb for yet another unexpected disappearance, but the man had said, after all, that it was a family emergency . . .

She thought again how little she really knew about Zeb Douglas. A tendril of shame tried to bloom in her mind, but she shoved it firmly back. She had allowed herself to cross the line with Zeb . . . once. It wouldn't happen again; she had promised herself that much. She knew better, and no matter how deeply she cared for him or he for her, she would not lose control again. It was a mistake, and it wouldn't be repeated. They were in love, and they had gotten carried away by the moment, but that was all there was to it.

Family emergency . . . Must be his mother, she decided. She wondered if Zeb favored his mother or his father. She hoped to meet them soon. She hoped that Zeb's mother would be all right. She also hoped that he would be back soon. She already missed him desperately.

As she swam back toward consciousness, Addie heard murmurs and ripples of voices around her. They reached her ears through the haze in her mind, and they seemed to come from all sides.

"Lou, you were the one that found him, right?"

"Yes. I went out to check on him a day or two after I went to see him at the store. He was in bed, looked like he must have died in his sleep. Had an asafetida bag tied around his neck."

There was a sad little chuckle. "Lot of good it did him."

"Too little, too late, I guess. She's trying to open her eyes."

Addie felt a hand taking hers, gently stroking it. "Addie, honey? How do you feel, sweetie?"

Addie blinked and tried to focus. Lou leaned over her, studying her face and stroking the hair back from her eyes.

"Well, hello there," her older sister said, smiling. "Nice to have you back with us!"

"Where's Mary Alice?" Addie's tongue felt thick.

"She's upstairs, taking a nap. She was acting kinda tired and fussy. I hope you don't mind me putting her down for awhile."

Addie shook her head. She looked around. "This is your house, isn't it, Lou?" Her sister nodded. "How long was I out?" Addie asked.

"Well, you kinda came around down at the lawyer's office, but you never really roused well till now, and that's been a coupla hours ago," Bob said, coming to stand behind Louisa and looking down at his younger sister. "We were getting worried, you being in a family way, and all."

Addie sighed. The lawyer. Papa's will . . . *by reason of her willful disregard* . . . It wasn't a dream after all. Papa had really disinherited her. The shame and hurt washed over her again, but it wasn't quite as overpowering this time—and she was already lying down. She felt like she ought to cry, but the grief seemed too deep for tears. It was more like a dull, dry ache, an emptiness inside her she had tried to forget. But now it had been shoved into her face, and there was no more avoiding it. Papa had put her out of his heart, and he had proved it by putting her out of his will. He had cut her off, just as he threatened on the day Zeb proposed.

Zeb . . . For a fleeting moment she wondered why he wasn't in the room, but it didn't quite seem important enough to ask about. He'd show up sometime, she assumed. She wondered how the news of the will had affected him. She had the vicious thought that he would probably leave, too, since there was no more hope of any dowry. She immediately reprimanded herself.

"Where's Junior?" she asked.

"Down at Dan Sutherland's," Lou replied. "Seeing if there's anything we can do about . . . the situation."

At that moment the front door opened. They heard steps in the hallway coming toward them. Addie heard the rustle of skirts, heard the murmured voice of Freda, Junior's wife, as she asked him a question. There was no audible reply, and then Junior was standing in the doorway of the bedroom. The defeated expression on his face told them everything.

Zeb had been walking for almost an hour, but his mind was still as snarled as a rat's nest. He just couldn't believe that Addie's father had actually cut her off. He'd known Jacob wasn't in favor of their marriage, but he just couldn't believe a father would . . .

He felt cast off and cheated. He felt sorry for Addie, guilty for what their marriage had done to her, and angry because he felt guilty. He felt responsible . . . And then, from nowhere, a vision of himself and Becky Norwich invaded his mind. Becky, with her shiny, golden hair fallen down around her bare shoulders. Becky, her blue eyes looking deeply,

deeply into his as he kissed her, as the pounding of his heart drowned out everything else except the feeling of his palms gliding over her skin—

Stop it! He grabbed his head with both hands, as if to clamp it in place—or perhaps to tear it off, to silence his restless and undisciplined mind once and for all. Zeb had never felt more wretched in his life. He had thought that in the days before their marriage, his uncertainty over his fate with Addie was the worst time of his life. But this . . . He was a battleground between duty and desire. There was no place he could go to escape the enemy inside his head; it was with him every waking moment, torturing him with rapidly alternating visions of rapture and wreckage. How could he even think of Becky Norwich now, when Addie needed him more than ever? But how could he forget Becky's agreeable smile, her uncomplicated, undisguised interest in him, her softness, her gaiety—and her lithe, glorious body, unfurled beneath him, then wrapped around him like a welcoming, warming blanket? Becky was his in a way Addie had never been, could never be. Where were the answers? What could he do?

He walked on. The gold band on his left ring finger felt unfamiliar and strange, and he thumbed it nervously as he went. He thought of praying but instinctively shied away. He was certainly in no position to approach God with his problems just now. Besides, he had gotten himself into this predicament; it was up to him to extricate himself.

He knew he ought to get back to Addie's sister's house, even though he really didn't want to. Addie must have come around by now; he needed to be there. At a time like this, surely there was something a husband could do—even a no-good like himself. He turned his feet back up the hill and began to retrace his steps, still thumbing his wedding ring, turning it round and round on his finger.

George was restless. It was the middle of a Sunday afternoon, and he didn't know what to do with himself. He thought about going upstairs and working on the model he had begun three months ago, a replica of the *U.S.S. Constitution.* He had started the ship on a whim after reread-ing the poem by Oliver Wendell Holmes, but the unpainted, unmasted hull had sat on his worktable, forlorn and abandoned, for weeks and weeks. Lately, he just couldn't make himself get interested in his models, for some reason.

What he really wanted to do was call on Laura Sanders Breck, but he wasn't quite able to go through with that either. After all, he had been with her late in the previous week. On top of that, he had escorted her to Jacob Caswell's funeral. *Cat that's always underfoot gets kicked sooner or later,* he lectured himself. In fact, he had imagined that she was the slight-est bit restive the last few times they were together. George thought she still liked him for the most part, though, and he was most anxious not to spoil anything by being too hasty.

So he fretted. He'd already gone over the *Times* twice. He tried to find a book to read, but nothing looked interesting. He thought about taking a walk, but the sky looked threatening, so that didn't seem advisable.

Pacing through the drawing room, his hands clasped behind him, he nearly collided with his father, who was trudging out of the hallway from the kitchen, carrying a brimming glass of buttermilk with cornbread crumbled into it.

"Watch it, Dad!" he said, shrinking back from the dollop of soaked cornbread that toppled from his father's glass.

"Watch it, yourself," Deacon Hutto said in a low grumble. "Moonin' around the house like a foundered cow. Why don't you just go see that woman before you fall down the stairs and break your neck, or somebody else's?"

George felt the blush stinging his cheeks as his father edged around him and made for his favorite Sunday afternoon chair. He hadn't realized his confusion over Mrs. Breck was quite so apparent. He watched thoughtfully as Dad settled carefully into the chair and began spooning the cornbread into his mouth.

"Well? What are you staring at?"

"Oh, sorry, Dad. I was just . . . woolgathering, I guess."

George's father grunted to himself as he swallowed another soggy piece of cornbread and chased it with a sip of buttermilk. George turned to go back the way he had come, then stopped and looked at his father. He swallowed, took a breath, then said, "Dad? When you were . . . Well, when you and Mother were courting, did you ever worry about, maybe spending too much time with her? Maybe wearing out your welcome?"

Deacon Hutto, a spoonful of cornbread halfway to his mouth, carefully put the spoon back into the glass. He looked at his pudgy, red-cheeked son for what seemed to George a full minute, but was probably only a few seconds.

"Son, I don't much know what you're driving at."

George nodded, shoved his hands into his pockets, and drifted out of the drawing room. Deacon Hutto shook his head, rolled his eyes, and dipped up another bite of cornbread.

CHAPTER
25

*R*emember the last time we walked along here?" Zeb said. He smiled at Addie as they ambled along beside the pond in East Lake Park. "Remember what happened that night?"

Addie's face wore the same vacant, burned-out look she had exhibited since the reading of the will.

"Hmm?"

"Don't you remember?" Zeb tried again, forbidding his smile to wilt. "I asked you to marry me, right here beside this lake."

"Yeah, now that you mention it, I guess you did."

It was barely March; the willows around the pond were still bare and the grass was still winter-browned, but it was one of those early spring days when the weather turned off so warm and the sky was so blue it defied a body to stay indoors. Still, it had required all Zeb's powers of persuasion to convince Addie to take a walk with him. He was beginning to wish he hadn't taken the trouble.

Since that day at the attorney's office, Zeb had been grappling within himself for an answer to his dilemma. All along, he knew what he should do, but the wrestling match was between that and what he felt like doing. He had fought and refought the same battles with himself—had captured and surrendered the same ground dozens of times. And today, out here in the lavish sunlight of early spring, he had resolved to finish the campaign once and for all.

228

Zeb felt the pressure of his next words building, pressing against the back of his teeth like captive steam seeking a release valve.

"Addie, I've been doing a lot of thinking since . . . everything's happened. The way I . . . the way we've been living isn't right, somehow."

She turned her face slightly toward him but said nothing.

"There's nothing left here for you now, anyway," he said. Somehow the words didn't sound as good out in the open air as they had inside his head, but it was too late for retreat. "Your father did the worst he could to you, and he shouldn't have, but he did, and nobody can change it now. So, what I want to say is—"

They had stopped walking. She was facing him now, her eyes on him, on his lips as they moved. It looked to Zeb like she was trying to see down his throat, to see the words as they formed inside him. Well, at least she was paying attention to something other than her grief.

"—I want you and Mary Alice to come to Little Rock. I want to get us all back together again. I don't want to live apart anymore."

Well, he had the words out at last. He tried to ignore the desperate moan of loss that drained away to nothingness inside him. He reached into himself and grabbed a smile from somewhere, trying to mash it into place on a face that wouldn't hold anything but a grimace. He wanted to do the right thing! Why wouldn't it *feel* right?

"When we get back to Nashville, let's just load everything up and head west." He reached out to take her hand. *Good-bye, Becky.* "I want our baby to be born in Little Rock. Addie, things can be good for us there. You'll see. I'll find us a—"

She yanked her hand away from him, as if he had smeared it with slime. Her lips were parted but not in a smile.

"Is that the best you can do?"

He stared at her.

"Do what?"

"This was what you wanted the whole time," she said. "You told me they sent you to Little Rock so you could prove to them you were good enough for the home office. But you never once meant to come back, did you?"

Their argument before his last trip back reared up again in his mind.

"Now, Addie, just hear me out this time—"

"My family and my life and my church and everything about me— it's never been good enough for you, has it? You had to change everything. Just bury it all and start over, didn't you?"

"Addie! That's not how—"

"Zeb, I told you before. I'll not set one foot in Little Rock, Arkansas, or anywhere else on nothing but your say-so."

The most frightening thing was how quietly she spoke. She had not raised her voice at any time, but the words stuck in his flesh like cockle-burs. She had fired from point-blank range.

He stuck his hands into his pockets. Not knowing what else to do, he turned and began walking again. She fell into step beside him. To a casual observer, they might have stopped to exchange remarks on the weather and then resumed their stroll. Zeb felt ruined inside, despoiled and aban-doned. And then he began to feel angry.

"It's really the same thing, you and Papa," she said, still in the same quiet voice. "Both of you have taken my life away from me and expected me to just go along. Well, I'm not going along anymore, Zeb. Not anymore."

So this was what happened when a man tried to do the right thing! A man puts his heart through the wringer for a woman, and he gets kicked in the teeth for his trouble! So this was how it was going to be, was it?

"All right, then. I won't mention it anymore." *And don't say I didn't try.*

Dub hauled on the hand brake as the automobile wheezed its last breath. "I'll get the bags," he said as he opened his door.

Louisa turned to face Addie and Zeb in the backseat. "I sure hate to see y'all go back so soon," she said, smiling at Mary Alice, who was seated in Addie's lap, disguised as a bundle of winter clothing. The child's face was barely visible through the tangle of her wraps. "When you gonna come back and see Aunt Lou?" she grinned at the child. "I'm sure gonna miss you, sweetie."

Dub opened Addie's door and offered her a hand. Behind them, a railroad agent strolled the platform, announcing their train. "Two o'clock to *Bridge*-port, *Tullllll*-ahoma, *War*-trace, *Murrr*-frizburruh, *Naysh*-ville, and all points west, now boarding on track number eight."

"Well, that's us," Zeb said, shaking Dub's hand. "'Preciate you bringin' us down here, Dub."

"No trouble."

"I need a hug from this young 'un before y'all go," Louisa said, taking Mary Alice from Addie and giving her a tight squeeze. "You make your mama and daddy bring you back to see me, now, you hear?" The child began squirming and reaching for her mother, a troubled look on her face. "Oh, all right, here's your mama, honey."

Louisa handed the toddler back to Addie. She put an arm around her younger sister. "Addie, don't worry. The boys and me'll work something out for you. What Papa did wasn't—"

"I know," Addie said. She gave Louisa a quick hug with her free hand. "I just don't want to talk about it anymore right now. We've got to go, Lou. Our train's been called."

"Need any help with the valises?" Dub said. "I can call a boy—"

"No, that's all right," Zeb said. "I got 'em. Bye." He hoisted the bags and followed his wife and child into the station.

Louisa watched them walk away into the crowd. Dub opened the car door for his wife, but she was still staring after her sister and her family.

"Lou?" he said after a moment, "can we go now?"

Naturally, Mary Alice was cranky the whole way home, and she refused to sleep. By the time the train pulled into Nashville at half past seven that evening, Addie was so frazzled, so crumpled with fatigue, that she could barely speak. Zeb's presence—when he wasn't restlessly pacing the aisles of the car—registered only as a brooding silence. She knew her words in the park had stung him, but she just couldn't make herself care. Addie doubted if they exchanged more than a half dozen words the whole way. That suited her fine.

When they had disembarked and Zeb had gathered the bags, he turned his face in her general direction and announced, "I'm gonna find a hack to take you and Mary Alice home. I've got to get back, so I'll just stay here and catch the next train west."

"Fine," Addie said. *If that's how you feel about it.* She hoisted the little girl on her hip, pressed a hand to the small of her back, and followed him off the platform and into the station.

The driver set the valises down just inside the front door. He touched the brim of his cap and turned to go. "Wait," Addie called, digging in her handbag, "don't I owe you something?"

"No, ma'am. Your husband, he done took care of everything back at the station."

"Well, all right then. Thank you."

"Yes'm."

She closed the door and set Mary Alice down. The child immediately began toddling down the hallway toward the bedrooms. "Da'ee?" she called, peering in one doorway, then another. "Da'ee?"

"Sweetheart, Daddy's not here. He's gone."

Still, Mary Alice methodically searched each room, then went toward the kitchen. "Da'ee? Da'ee?"

From some remote, tightly guarded place within her, Addie felt her convoluted sorrow rising. She dashed into the kitchen and scooped Mary

Alice into her arms, just as the sobs and hot tears started. She buried her face in her daughter's hair and sat down in a kitchen chair, crying and holding her child.

Mary Alice patted her mother's arm. She peered over Addie's shoulder, through the doorway into the parlor, where the valises still sat by the front door.

"Da'ee?"

The train rattled into Union Station, but Zeb was so dog-tired he knew nothing of it until he felt the hand of a porter on his shoulder.

"Sir? Sir? You better wake up, sir, unless you mean to ride this train all the way to Fort Smith. We're in Little Rock."

Zeb opened and shut his eyes several times in a groggy attempt to focus. He rubbed his face and gathered himself upright. The sunlight hurt his eyes. It looked like the afternoon of some day or other. Seemed like he'd been riding trains for a month.

He pulled his valise down from the rack and shuffled sideways along the aisle toward the doors. He could feel the cool outside air sliding through the mostly empty car. He wished again he hadn't packed his overcoat.

He stepped down onto the platform and began walking toward the cab stands. As he walked, he toyed absently with the ring on his left hand. Then he stopped and stared at it for a moment. He set down the valise. He pulled the ring from his finger and held it for a moment in his palm—delicately, like a soap bubble that had lit on his hand.

Then he dropped it down among the cinders and darkened gravel of the track bed. He picked up his valise and shoved his left hand into a pocket. Hunching his back against the cool wind, he walked off toward the cab stands.

CHAPTER
26

George strode along, feeling better than he had in days. In fact, he almost felt like whistling, and not caring what anyone thought. He allowed the smile inside him to creep across his face as he walked.

The weather had retreated from the warmth of recent days. A light breeze from the north was hurrying away the tattered scraps of the gray clouds that had poured a gentle night shower on Chattanooga. The wind was cool but bracing, and in the midmorning light, last night's rain gave everything a vivid, freshly painted look.

For some reason, George Hutto had felt odd and adventurous ever since awakening this morning. To his own surprise, his befuddlement of recent weeks had left him during the night. He was suddenly, unaccountably full of assurance about what he wanted. And what he wanted was to talk to Laura Sanders Breck and tell her, for once, how he felt about her.

At first, the notion seemed strange and risky. But instead of retreating from it, he had allowed himself to taste it, to handle it, and observe it from all sides. And the more he did so, the more reckless and dashing he began to feel. Why shouldn't he tell her? He was a grown man, after all! If a man cared for a woman, why shouldn't he say so? It wasn't as if she should be surprised, he told himself. He'd been accompanying her just about everywhere there was to go in Chattanooga these last three-and-a-half months, and she hadn't declined any of his invitations, as far as he could remember. Surely that entitled him to speak his mind—didn't it?

And so he had shaved and dressed and put on his coat. He had walked down to the office and told his father's secretary that he would be out all morning. What a delicious feeling, to deliver that news to Mr. Cox and turn and walk casually away, not even caring what Mr. Cox thought! George had especially enjoyed that.

And now he was approaching Mrs. Breck's street, and growing more confident with each step. He tried to imagine how her face would look when he said what he had come to say. Would she blush? Would she give him a demure, eyes-downcast smile? Probably not. She would probably stare at him with those coal-black eyes, blink once or twice, and then give her head a sharp nod. "Well, all right, then," she would probably say.

And that was all right with George. Everything was all right with George this morning because for the first time in his life, he knew what he wanted and knew what he was going to do about it.

There was a horseless carriage parked in front of Laura Sanders Breck's house, and that mildly surprised him as he rounded the corner and saw it. A thoughtful little crease appeared on his forehead, but he paced forward anyway. Probably a relative. It might even be a lady friend of hers. George had actually seen a few women driving about in the noisy contraptions.

Despite his newfound confidence, he felt his heart crowding into his windpipe as he stepped onto her front porch and removed his hat. Still, he had something to say, and he was going to say it.

It took Mrs. Breck an unusually long time to get to the door, and when she finally opened it, George was embarrassed to see that her hair was disheveled and she was in her dressing gown. He had never seen her hair down, and why was she in her dressing gown? It was nearly ten o'clock in the morning! He stammered and looked away. "I'm, uh . . . I'm sorry to come by so . . . so early, but—"

"George! I had no idea—" She clutched the neck of her gown and glanced back over her shoulder, toward the interior of the house.

He nearly bolted, right then. But then he remembered his earlier determination and decided to screw his courage to the sticking point, as the fellow said. He forced himself to look her directly in the eye, disregarding her flustered expression as he stepped firmly past her onto the worn Persian rug in her foyer. He was going ahead, and that was that. "Mrs. Breck, I have something to say, and I want you to hear me out."

And then, as he paused to begin his prepared remarks, he heard a muffled cough from within the house. A male cough.

George was completely befuddled and thrown offtrack. Everything he had intended to say to Laura Sanders Breck vanished like a mirage from his mind. He looked at her in confusion, and to his additional surprise he saw her covering her face with one hand. Based on his experience with her, he would have been equally prepared to see her standing on one foot and reciting "The Midnight Ride of Paul Revere." In fact, the whole scene was bizarre; he wondered fleetingly if he were still asleep in his bed and dreaming.

"George, come outside. We have to talk."

He allowed himself to be led back onto the front porch. She shivered as they sat on the swing, and George realized, without quite knowing how, that Mrs. Breck wore no clothing other than her dressing gown. Numbly, he added this to the rest of the weird facts quickly accumulating in his mind.

"George, I sure wish you hadn't had to find out this way." She sounded different: soft, almost. George had never heard her sound soft.

"George, you're a sweet man and a good one, and I've enjoyed your company. But . . . you don't know what you want—or at least you don't know how to ask for it."

But, wait. Let me say what I came to say . . .

"I've been on my own for a long time now," she said, "and I'm at the age where I can't wait much longer. And when someone comes along who *does* know what he wants, well— It's hard for me to turn that down."

George's mind began framing another objection but subsided. It was too late, he realized. That much, at least, was starting to seep through the fog. He peered at her, still confused. He had the impression that he ought to be leaving, that his presence was unnecessary—even undesirable. He stood and resettled his hat on his head. "Yes, well . . . I apologize for any inconvenience, Mrs. Breck. I regret calling on you at such an . . . awkward time."

She stayed seated, clutching the dressing gown to her in a vain attempt to shield herself from the cold air. She looked up at him with a pitying, almost beseeching look. "George, it's not your fault."

"Yes, well . . . Good day to you." He touched the brim of his bowler. "You'd better get back inside. You'll catch your death." He turned and walked down the steps. He walked almost to the end of the block before turning to look back at the house of Laura Sanders Breck. To his surprise, she was still on the front porch. She was standing, looking at him. He gave her a weak, tentative wave and continued on his way.

He walked into the office, past Mr. Cox's desk. The gaunt older man looked up in surprise. "I thought you were gonna be out all morning, George," he said.

George had begun removing his wraps. He turned about, a puzzled expression still on his face. "Yes, I did say that, didn't I?" Slowly he hung his coat and hat on a nearby rack. "Well, I'm back now. I expect I'll be at my desk the rest of the day."

Mr. Cox shrugged and returned to his work, and George shuffled back to his small, cramped office at the back of the warehouse.

Zeb hated to think about what his desk would look like. It would be a rat's nest of correspondence from the home office, policies that needed to be delivered—some probably with past-due premiums—and assorted other scraps and slabs of unfinished business that would all be screaming to be attended to at the same time. This was the worst part of leaving the office.

He put his key in the lock but found the door already open, somewhat to his surprise. As he entered, he saw Abner at his desk, busily sorting and stacking. "Well, hello, Ab! I didn't expect you to be here this early."

Abner grinned at him. "I had a feeling you'd be in this morning, and I didn't much want you to see the haystack that piled up on your desk while you were gone, so I'm doing a little baling here, is all."

Zeb sat down behind his desk and began looking through the stacks Abner had made, starting with the policies. Most of them were deliveries from the home office, but one or two looked like a policyholder had stopped making premium payments.

"Ab, who brought this one in? It looks like one somebody's trying to cough up."

Abner nodded. "Yeah, Hutchinson from over in Argenta told me one a his people said he couldn't make the payments any longer."

"Betcha two bits Mama wants a new cookstove, and this old boy is trying to figure out how to pay for it."

Abner nodded. "Probably. Trying to cut some corners."

"Well, I guess I'll have to go out with Hutchinson one more time and show him how to poke a policy back down."

This was just what he needed, Zeb thought: work to do, decisions to make, situations to handle. He could lose himself in agency business and take his mind off . . . everything.

The door jingled. "Looks like I'm not the only one who figured you'd be in this morning," Abner said quietly.

Zeb glanced up to see Becky Norwich standing just inside the entrance, staring at him.

"This ain't but the third time she's called this week," Abner whispered.

Ignoring the sarcasm in his secretary's tone, Zeb slowly pushed himself back from his desk and walked toward her.

"Morning," he said, trying to mean the smile he was showing. He wasn't ready for this—not yet. "What can we do for you?"

"How's your mother?" she said.

"Do what? My mother? Why she's—fine, I guess, but why—"

"I thought you went to Nashville because your mother was sick. At least, that's what he told me," she said, nodding toward Abner.

"Now, ma'am—I mean, miss—I never said nothing about anybody's mother. I said 'family emergency,' is all."

Zeb said a silent thanks for Abner's quick mind. Becky's voice was as taut as a telegraph wire; it wouldn't take more than a fingernail scrape across her veneer to expose her anger.

"I'm really glad to see you, and I'll be more than glad to explain everything," he said, careful to stop a respectful distance away from her, "but I've got more than a week's worth of catching up to do. Do you think I could call on you this evening, maybe? I've got a proposition to deliver to your father, anyway."

"Oh, you have, have you? Well, you just come right on over then, Zeb, and you and Daddy can have all the time you need because I'll be elsewhere!"

She spun on her heel and flung open the door, stomping off down the boardwalk.

Zeb closed the door behind her and then closed his eyes. Why did every problem in his life shove forward, clamoring for attention before he was ready? He sighed and turned around, barely catching the smirk on Abner's face before the secretary was able to swallow it.

"What are you gawking at? Don't you have a letter to write, or something?"

"Yessir."

Zeb wasn't sure what to hope: that Becky would make good her threat or that she wouldn't. He arrived at the Norwiches' near dusk, feeling jumpy as a green colt. He could have gotten there sooner, but he had walked around the block twice before he could make himself go to the door and knock.

He was so intent on the opening he'd rehearsed for Becky that when Pete Norwich answered the door, Zeb stared at him as if he were a stranger.

"Oh, uh, here. I brought the proposal I told you about." He fished the barely remembered sheaf of papers out of the breastpocket of his coat and proffered them to the older man, who regarded him with a sort of amused scowl. Pete took the papers without looking at them.

"Don't know what you did, son, but you're so far in the doghouse you may never see the light of day."

Zeb shoved his hands into his pants pockets and shook his head.

"Becky chewed you like an old bone when she got home. Even her mama couldn't get a word in sideways."

"Will she see me at all?"

"Shoot, boy, don't start me to lying. You gonna have to ask her your-self."

"I was afraid you'd say that. Well, lead the way to the wall. I don't smoke, and I don't want a blindfold." Zeb heard Pete's soft chuckle as he stepped past him into the house.

Hat in hand, he walked into the parlor. Becky was facing away from him, her head down and her arms crossed tightly in front of her. Mrs. Norwich had been saying something to her but broke off immediately when she saw Zeb enter. She withdrew into the kitchen, and Zeb heard Becky's father quietly close the hall door behind him.

"I didn't think you'd show your face," she said.

Zeb had been prepared for an interminable, frosty silence, and he felt ambushed by her quick words. "I . . . I guess I didn't think you'd be here when I did."

She turned to face him, her arms still crossed like a barricade in front of her.

"Well, I am." She stared at him.

Zeb felt her eyes on him. He wondered what she saw, and how much.

She was wearing a simple, long-sleeved cotton dress with a fine, blue floral print. Her hair was done up, but the inevitable lock was straying across her forehead. In the lamplight, he could barely make out the freckles across the bridge of her nose. He felt the soft place inside him, felt himself longing to open up, to let her in all the way. But how could he?

"Becky, I . . . I wish I could tell you . . . But sometimes, things are just not that easy—"

"I'll tell you what's not easy, Zeb. It's not easy being in love with you." In a more guarded voice, she said, "I've invested more in you than I can afford to lose, but I can't go on like this, Zeb." Her voice caught on the corner of one of her words, and she cupped a hand to her mouth. A moment later, she continued, still in a quiet voice. "I need to know where I stand with you, Zeb. I need to know if you regard me as anything more than an occasional good time."

"Now, Becky, it's not like that—"

"I need to know that I matter to you, that I count for something in your plans."

"But you do!"

"I won't be treated like a lap dog, to be petted or turned out at your whim. If I can't depend on you, Zeb, I'd just as soon not see you again." And with that, she strode into the kitchen. As the door swung open, Zeb had a glimpse of her mother and father, huddled together and turned away from the entry to the parlor, two conspirators caught in the act of keyhole peeking. Becky stalked past them as the door swung slowly closed.

Stunned, Zeb stared at the floor for a few seconds. Then he turned himself slowly about, with an almost aimless motion, like a heavy-laden barge drifting in a sluggish current. He placed his hat onto his head and showed himself to the door, hoping that he wouldn't have to speak to anyone on the way.

As he walked downtown, he glanced up at the night sky. There was a skiff of cloud, just enough to blur and dim the stars now and again. Zeb walked toward his lodgings, feeling like a lost soul doomed forever to wander between one burned bridge and another.

CHAPTER
27

By the time Beulah Counts had come and collected the fretting Mary Alice, Addie's pains had begun in earnest. Louisa brought in the large pan she had just scalded, along with a stack of freshly boiled towels.

"I'm so glad you're here, Lou," Addie said after her latest contraction subsided enough for her to speak. "Even with the doctor and all, it's sure good to have your help with this."

"Oh, honey, I wouldn't be anywhere else. You couldn't have kept me away last time, except for—"

"Yes, I know." There was a silence. "I sure wish Katherine could've known her cousins."

Louisa nodded, looking away.

"And I still miss Rose," Addie said. "She could make me feel safe, just by talking to me."

"Everybody needs to feel safe. But safe can be hard to come by sometimes."

The two sisters looked at each other, and their hands joined. Then Addie clenched Lou's knuckles as the next contraction ripped her in half.

"I wish that doctor would get here," Louisa said. "We're not gonna have the luxury of as much time this go-around."

The doctor, a youngish-looking man named Hodgkiss, arrived within the half hour, and, true to Louisa's prediction, the baby arrived only an hour or so later. It was a boy.

"You and Zeb talked about names?" Lou said.

Addie brushed back a sweaty lock of hair and shook her head. "I thought about it a time or two, but I guess we never actually got around to it."

The doctor, tending the baby in a corner of the room, glanced at Addie but said nothing.

"I guess we ought to send him a wire, at least," Addie said.

Louisa studied her younger sister carefully while she bundled up the soiled sheets. "Yes, I suppose. We can take care of that later though. You tell me what to say and I'll send it."

"Reckon I ought to name him after his daddy?"

"Well, he looks like his daddy, anyhow."

"Yes."

Louisa hoped Addie's flat tone was caused by her exhaustion.

Zeb glanced up at Abner. He was scribbling busily on an agency report form that had to be posted to the home office the day after tomorrow. Zeb glanced out the front window. The day was clear and mild. He knew he should be out with one or another of his agents—calling on prospects, running a debit, glad-handing policyholders. Or, at the very least, he should be working on the stack of applications they had received for processing during the last several days. He sighed. Time was when a stack of apps this size would have been plenty of reason for several days' worth of good spirits. He would have relished the prospect of preparing them for submission to the home office, would have gloated over the increase in commission income they represented, both for his agents and for himself.

For weeks and weeks he had fought a steadily losing battle with desperation. Becky had finally allowed him back in her presence, but it had taken all his persuasive skills to accomplish it. He had plied her with reams of letters, sent baskets of flowers and crates of candy. He had done anything he could think of to make her more kindly disposed. Her parents had even taken his part, he believed, so sincere had been his contrition for his mysterious ways. He had lavished her with every ounce of charm he possessed, and to his great relief he was at last able to reenter her good graces.

But even after he was back on firm footing with Becky, Zeb was not at ease within himself. Each time he would hold her hand, each time they laughed and smiled together in the familiar way that was so precious to him, Zeb felt guilt stinging his mind with visions of Addie, memories of the promises he had made and broken. He did his best to hide all this from Becky. Indeed, the passion they shared was as consuming as ever. On the few occasions they had been able to be safely alone together, her early reticence had melted away in his embrace, and they had tasted again the sweetness of each other's bodies. Indeed, they shared the guilty pleasure of these stolen moments as a secret they alone must keep; to them it became another evidence of the depth and intensity of the bond they shared.

But the harder he tried to straddle the fence, the less satisfied he was with the result. He feared that Becky would soon sense that he was hiding something from her. It had even begun to affect his ability to run the agency. Some days he could hardly make himself come to work. He was afraid that everything he had built in Little Rock would soon be in jeopardy, but he couldn't seem to summon the strength to care.

But all that was about to be behind him. Zeb had decided it was time once again to take charge of his life. Glancing surreptitiously at Abner and assuring himself that his secretary was still preoccupied with his paperwork, Zeb slid open the lap drawer of his desk and extracted the piece of cream-colored foolscap on which he had labored, off and on, all morning.

Dear Mrs. Douglas,

Surely it must have become apparent to you that the kind affection that once existed between us is now gone. I no longer desire to share this union with you. Accordingly, I request that you sue me for divorce as soon as possible. I will not in any way contest the dissolution of this marriage; indeed, I am anxious to have the business done at the earliest possible time.

Cordially,

Zeb. A. Douglas

Zeb stared at what he had written, momentarily unable to believe it had been composed by his hand. Yet there it was, on the same foolscap that he had used to send Addie a very different sort of letter not so very long ago. There beside the script lay his favorite fountain pen. The letters it had inscribed curved and dipped in the same elegant manner as usual; Zeb had always prided himself on his handwriting. The letters' appearance gave no sign of the darkness and finality of the words they formed. For a moment, a flicker of remorse tried to kindle in his heart.

But he sternly smothered it. He would not turn back the page, not again. All he had to do to steel himself for the task was remember the stealthy venom in Addie's words during their walk in East Lake Park. He did not deserve that. He had tried, had faithfully provided for her and Mary Alice—and gotten no thanks nor the slightest whit of understanding in return.

Didn't he merit some measure of happiness? Why should he deprive himself of the company of a woman who appreciated and understood him just because he had made an ill-considered union with someone else before meeting her? Was Addie's inner darkness his fault? Did he have responsibility for healing wounds that had existed since long before he had known her? In fact, hadn't he married her under false pretenses, of sorts? Had he known of the damage inflicted on her by her father's inflexible, uncaring prejudice, would he have allowed himself to be caught in the middle of it all? He didn't think so.

No, this was the right thing for him to do. He didn't care what anyone in Chattanooga thought of him—they didn't know his side, and wouldn't understand it anyway. The best thing for him was to put that life away—erase it as if it had never been. He would cease to be the person who had pursued and wedded Addie Caswell. Instead, he would fully embrace the life he had formed for himself in Little Rock. Everything behind him would drop away, like a useless cocoon. He would press toward the future—toward Becky Norwich. He would become the man Becky wanted him to be, and she need never know about the mistakes made by the man he had once been. Surely that was the best way now.

He folded the letter and reached for an envelope.

Ned Overby held his opened Barlow in his right hand and stared at the block of pine in his left, trying to see the shapes it held. He knew he couldn't start carving until he knew what the piece of wood wanted to be. Nobody had ever told him he should do this. Anytime he picked up a piece of wood, he tried to find the shape of its grain and the direction in which it seemed to be guiding his knife strokes. It made sense to him that he shouldn't try to fight the wood. He thought it surely made his work better.

Not that his carving was any great shakes. So far, none of the simple animal shapes he had finished had really suited him. They all seemed to fall a bit short in his eyes, but that didn't bother Ned. He knew he'd get better with time. It was just a matter of letting his hands learn which way to go.

The sun felt good on his face and neck as he sat propped atop the woodpile behind his house. It was warm enough that he didn't need shoes and still early enough in the summer that going barefoot was a novelty to be relished. Ned left his shoes inside when the weather allowed, to save wear. Lately, his shoes had begun to pinch, anyway.

Today was one of those rare, fine days when he didn't have extra chores to do. He had hoed the few scraggly rows of corn and pole beans just yesterday. There was plenty of wood chopped for the stove, and only two days ago he had made six trips down to the river and back, toting the heavy water bucket so he could refill the battered oak hog's head that served them as a reservoir. Perlie was running his trotlines on the other side of the river, around the mouth of North Chickamauga Creek. Ned would have to help him clean fish when he got back, but that shouldn't be until nearly sundown. In the meantime, all he had to do was soak up some sunshine and try to stay out of his mother's line of vision, or she was sure to dream up something for him to do. Seemed like she couldn't stand to see a body enjoying himself when she was busy—and she was busy all the time.

He heard the clanking of car couplings and the squeal of brakes echoing through the still woods. *They must be changing cars on the siding up by Orchard Knob,* he thought. A sudden desire stole over him to sneak into Chattanooga on one of the cars. He had heard his father talk about riding the rails as a younger man. A thrill of fear tingled his skin as Ned wondered if he was bold enough to do something similar. If he got caught, he'd get a whaling for sure—and that was just counting what his paw would do to him. He wasn't sure what fate awaited boys whom the railroad men nabbed trying to catch a free ride.

For a few minutes he tried to concentrate on what his hands were doing to the block of pine he held. But the shavings began to fall slower and slower as he spent more and more time thinking about the siding, just over the shoulder of Tunnel Hill and a little way through the woods. His mother would probably miss him, but she would most likely figure he was off in the woods somewhere. And if he got away with it, he'd have something to tell the older boys when school started again. Before long, he'd talked himself into it. He folded his knife and put it in his pocket, followed by the barely begun carving. Looking carefully around him, he climbed down from the woodpile.

Squatting in the darkest corner of the empty freight car, Ned began to think about all the things that could go wrong with this adventure, realizing that every single one of the looming possibilities carried with it the likelihood of a hiding, or worse. He could get caught leaving the car once it arrived in Chattanooga. He could fail to arrive home before his father. He could have judged wrong, and be sitting in a car bound for Nashville or some other foreign place instead of Chattanooga. Why hadn't he listened to his better judgment? Why wasn't he still sitting peacefully in the sun atop the woodpile, fashioning a turtle or maybe a bird from his block of pine?

But it was too late for such thoughts to do him any good. He was in for the whole ride, and he might as well see it through. To calm himself, he tried to do some carving, but the ride was too rough and he had to put knife and wood back in his pocket. He made himself as comfortable as he could in the dark, jouncing freight car, waiting to see where he would end up.

When the train finally squealed to its jarring halt, Ned crept to the partially open door. Though he knew he hadn't been traveling long enough to have gone very far, he was still relieved to recognize the silhouette of Lookout Mountain rising over the bustling freightyard. He peered carefully up and down the line and saw no one, so he scrambled quickly down from the car and burrowed into the nearest crowd.

He had been to Chattanooga only once before in his life, about a year ago. Perlie had allowed him to tag along when he came to town to sell his winter's take of pelts and had even let him squander an Indian-head cent on a piece of licorice. That dark-sweet taste was what Ned chiefly remembered about Chattanooga. But there would be no licorice today. He had nothing in his pockets of any value except his Barlow, and he would rather have sold some of his toes than his knife.

Walking along in the jostling crowds, Ned didn't understand how so many people could be in the same place at once. His closest experience of town life was Orchard Knob on a Saturday, and that was nothing compared to the masses of humanity now pressing all about him.

Passing the opening of an alley, Ned noticed some boys hunched in a circle.

"All right, sweethearts, here's the stuff I told you about. Anybody that wants some, show me your money."

The boy doing the talking looked a couple of years older than Ned, and he was considerably better dressed, as were most of the gang of about ten youngsters. Some of them looked younger than Ned, but the boy with the vial and the two or three gathered behind him looked older—maybe fifteen or so. As a few of the younger boys began digging in their pockets, Ned noticed a wicked smile flash from the vial boy to his cronies and back.

"You sure this medicine's gonna help me run faster?" one of the younger boys said, pinching a nickel between his thumb and forefinger.

"Guaranteed."

The smaller boy stepped up to him and held out his nickel, which quickly disappeared into the older boy's pocket.

"Hold out your hand," he commanded, pulling the cork from the vial. The younger boy obeyed, and the older boy sprinkled a few taps of the powder into his palm. "It tastes kind of bad, but it'll have you running like a spotted ape in no time."

Ned noticed one of the older boys smothering a grin.

Once the first boy had taken his dose, a line quickly formed. The older boy pocketed seven or so nickels and sprinkled each palm with the magic running powder.

"What do we do now?" said one of the younger boys.

"If I was you," said the vial boy. "I'd start running. Home."

This was met with a howl of laughter from the older boys and puzzled stares from the young customers.

"Fred, what'll your dad do when he finds out you swiped that stuff from the pharmacy?"

Fred grinned. "He'll never know. I pinched a little from three or four bottles so he wouldn't notice. But I reckon they'll notice, any time now," he said, nodding his head toward the younger boys.

Just then, one of the younger boys backed slowly away from the group, a concerned look on his face.

"Where you goin', Rob?"

"I'm, uh . . . I got to go," Rob said as he spun about and walked quickly away.

Fred and his buddies roared with amusement. "See? I told you! Ol' Rob's fixing to start running!"

"What's in that stuff anyway?" one of the younger boys said.

"Watch it, Shorty! Not that it'll mean anything to you, but it's called phenolphthalein."

"What's that?" said another of the younger boys. By now, two or three others had drifted quickly toward the alley opening.

"It means," said Fred between sputters of laughter, "that in about two minutes you're gonna have the worst case a green-apple two-step you ever had in your life."

The four older boys went limp with laughter, holding on to each other and slapping their knees.

Ned watched in fascination as the young boys hustled out of the alley. Evidently, that powder worked mighty fast. He was grinning at their retreating backs when he heard one of the older boys say, "Wait a minute, boys. We still got us a customer here."

Ned turned around and saw the four older boys looking at him in a way he didn't much like. He quickly took in the situation and began sauntering toward the alley opening with what he hoped was an unconcerned air.

"Where you going, white trash?"

Ned kept walking, a little faster. His ears burned with the insult, but he knew he didn't stand a chance against the four of them. He was about ten feet away from the street when he heard footsteps crunching rapidly behind him. He started to run, but hands grabbed him from behind. He flung himself forward, trying to wrestle free of their grasp.

"Lemme go! Lemme go! I ain't did nothing to y'all!" he yelled.

"Shut up, you little cow pie!" Fred aimed a fist at Ned's jaw, but he twisted away from the blow.

"Lemme go!" Ned scratched and kicked at his attackers. He was trying to get out of the alley, but they kept dragging him back. "Leave me be! I ain't hurt nothing!"

"Shut him up!" said Fred. One of the boys clamped a hand over Ned's mouth but promptly yanked it away.

"Little skunk bit me!"

George Hutto was walking aimlessly down Market Street, staring at the ground in front of his feet, when he heard the sound of a scuffle. He looked up and saw four bigger boys ganged up on one small, ill-clad fellow. For some reason, his memory flashed back to similar scenes from his boyhood, all the times at school and after church when the more daring, faster boys had made sport of him. Contrary to anything he was prepared for, his ire suddenly flared.

"Hey! Hey, over there! What's going on over there, you boys?"

Before he realized what he was doing, George had strode to the nearest of the older ruffians and seized him by the shoulder. He realized it was the son of one of the men in his Sunday school class.

"Freddy Stokes! What do you mean, picking on this boy so much smaller than you?"

CHAPTER

28

*T*he melee ended quickly as the four older boys released their captive and shoved their hands into their pockets, staring in guilt at their shoes. George looked around at the rest of them.

"Buck Tarfield! Don't you know any better?" Buck shrugged and looked away. "And you—Tommy Clayton! I've got half a mind to tell your father about this when I get back to the office!"

Tommy stared at George with big, round eyes. "Now, Mr. Hutto, we wasn't gonna hurt him, not really. We was just having a little fun with him, is all." The others nodded in earnest endorsement.

"Well, it didn't look like much fun for him," George said.

George realized, to his surprise, that he was enjoying this very much. He felt something kindling inside him, and it was welcome. Anything was better than the indistinct fog in which he had lived since that morning at Mrs. Breck's house. He was doing something that mattered. He was striking a blow in a just cause.

"You boys better skedaddle. Every one of you ought to be ashamed."

The four boys drifted off down the street, shoulders slumped and their hands still shoved into their pockets.

George looked down at Ned. "Now, son, what's your name?"

Ned hung his head and made no reply.

"You didn't do anything to make them mad, did you?"

The boy shook his head vehemently. George studied the small, bony form: the baggy, homespun pants with frequent and ill-sewn patches, the bare, dirty feet, the cracked, filthy fingernails, the matted hair. Even in the open air of the street, George could smell the small boy's unwashed body and the odor of bacon grease that clung to his clothing.

"Well, if I don't know your name, how can I help you get home?"

The boy dug a big toe into the dust of the street, but gave no reply except a shrug.

"Do you want to go home?"

A long hesitation, then a reluctant nod.

"Have you ever ridden in an automobile—a horseless carriage?"

Before he could stop himself, the boy looked at George with something close to excitement in his eyes. Then he dropped his face once again, giving George the same noncommittal shrug, accompanied by a slight shake of the head.

"I've got an automobile and . . . I was thinking of taking a short drive. If I knew what direction your place was, I could just drop you off there while I'm out."

The boy stole a cautious glance at his face. He jerked a thumb in a general easterly direction and said, "Yonder a piece."

"Do you live in Orchard Knob?" George quizzed.

"Other side a ways."

"How'd you get into Chattanooga so early in the day? You couldn't have walked here from Orchard Knob, unless you started awful early."

Again the suspicious silence.

"Well, never mind. The main thing's to get you back home again. Come on. My automobile's parked over at the livery." He started to walk away, then, on a sudden thought, wheeled around and stuck out his hand. "By the way, I'm George Hutto."

Without thinking, the boy shook his hand. "Ned Overby."

"Nice to meet you, Ned. Let's go."

Ned couldn't believe that human beings could travel so fast and survive. When Mr. Hutto had begun cranking the shiny, black contraption, Ned had his doubts. The engine had wheezed and coughed like an old man with consumption and flat balked at doing anything else, despite the sweating, earnest efforts of its owner. But then it had finally caught, somehow, and when the machine roared to life and smoke began pouring out of the exhaust pipe in back, Ned was awestruck.

He had heard the boys at school talk about the new vehicles, of course, but he had never been near one until now. He marveled at the way it just bowled along, all on its own. It was pretty bumpy, of course, and he had to hang on to the siderail to keep from getting tossed out, but my how it tore down the road! It would just leave a wagon in the dust! He was scared and enthralled, all at once.

They came down the hill west of Orchard Knob, and the big Caswell house came into view. He tugged at Mr. Hutto's sleeve and pointed. "You can let me out right there. My house ain't on no road—I'll walk from there."

"You sure?" Mr. Hutto shouted over the roar of the engine. Ned nodded. Mr. Hutto pulled over to the side of the road in front of the vacant two-story house, and Ned got out. "Thanks for the ride," he said, staring at the ground. "And . . . thanks for taking up for me back yonder."

"You're welcome, Ned. Older boys used to pick on me too. I remember how it feels."

Ned nodded, still unable to look at his benefactor. "Well, I best git." He crossed the road in front of the automobile and walked toward the woods behind the house.

George watched the boy duck into the tree line and gradually disappear into the foliage covering Tunnel Hill. He stared thoughtfully at the two-story frame house where no one lived anymore. He sat there for perhaps three or four minutes, remembering. Then he put the car in gear and turned it about in the road, pointing it back toward Chattanooga.

A germ of something was trying to grow in his mind. All the way out from town, he had been thinking about Ned Overby: wondering what his life was like, what sort of chances he would ever have. What about the other poor boys in the alleys and shanties, the ones who lived in lean-tos in the hollows and creek bottoms around Chattanooga? What would prevent their lives from being one long, desperate series of encounters like the one Ned Overby had had in the alley with the boys from the "good" families? George wanted to do something. He wanted to help change the balance of nature for the boys like Ned Overby who had no advantages.

George drove back to town and parked his car at the livery. He walked slower than usual on his way back to the office, but for once, his eyes weren't studying the ground in front of his feet. Instead, he looked around at the people he passed, as if seeing them for the first time in his life.

Zeb's letter—the first in a number of weeks—appeared identical to the many other letters Addie had received from him. She even felt a small thrill of anticipation when she took it from the box, but then she caught herself. Shouldn't get carried away just because he finally remembered to write.

It was on the same foolscap he always used, addressed in the same stylish hand. She closed the mailbox and went back into the house. Louisa was sitting in the rocking chair in the corner, reading from a storybook to Mary Alice while she held her sleeping baby brother.

"You get something in the mail?"

Addie nodded and smiled, despite herself. "Letter from Zeb."

Louisa grinned. "Well, open it up, for Pete's sake. Let's hear how he's doing. At least the parts you can read aloud."

Addie rolled her eyes. "Goodness, Lou. We're not exactly newlyweds anymore."

She tore open the envelope and began scanning the letter as she sat down on the divan. Louisa resumed reading to Mary Alice and her voice droned on, murmuring into the background as Addie's attention focused on the message from her husband. The salutation struck her as odd; to her best memory, Zeb had never referred to her as "Mrs. Douglas" before. And then, as her eyes scanned the first sentence, then the next, then the next, she felt her heart begin pounding out an alarm, felt her blood roaring a warning in her ears. She put a hand to her mouth and her eyes went wide.

"What is it, Addie? What's wrong?"

Addie got up and walked toward the kitchen. On her way past Louisa, she dropped the letter in her lap.

"Zeb's left me."

"What? What are you talking about?" Louisa grabbed at the letter.

Addie stood in the middle of the kitchen floor, hugging herself and gripping her elbows as she stared blankly out the window over the sink. In a way, she wasn't surprised. She told herself she had seen it coming, had known things weren't getting better.

But all during the past weeks and months, another voice inside her mind kept chanting, "Everything's gonna be all right, everything's gonna be all right . . ." It was that part of her, that illogical, hopeful, believing part that now lay wounded and dying, silent within her. She felt everything shifting around her, felt the world breaking apart and reassembling itself in jagged shapes. She thought she ought to cry, but at this moment she couldn't even do that. It was as if she was standing in the doorway, looking at herself. *This is what a divorced woman looks like. This is how a person feels who's just been abandoned.*

She heard footsteps behind her, then Lou's hand on her shoulder.

"Oh, Addie. Oh, my dear, sweet Lord, I don't know what to say."

Louisa hugged her. Addie felt her arms go up reflexively, felt her body returning the hug. But her mind was still standing in the doorway, watching from a safe distance.

NASHVILLE AUGUST 18 1903
ZEBEDIAH A DOUGLAS
IZARD ST. LITTLE ROCK ARKANSAS

WE HAVE A NEW SON STOP HAVE NAMED HIM
AFTER YOU AND PAPA STOP HOPE THIS IS ALL
RIGHT STOP YOUR WIFE ADDIE

Zeb stared at the telegram for a long time. By its date, it had been sent barely three days after he had mailed to Addie the last correspondence he ever intended to send her. Apparently, the two messages had crossed.

He felt almost as if the words on the yellow sheet had no meaning, as if they had been sent to him by mistake from a stranger. Then he crumpled the paper and tossed it toward the wastebasket in the corner of his room. It missed and lay on the floor beside the basket, slowly trying to open.

Part III

August 1903

CHAPTER
29

*A*ddie passed the next few days in a buzzing fog of murmured condo-
lences; she passed unseeing and unhearing through the tatters of
muted conversations. Most of the time she felt as if she had blundered
onto the stage of a play for which she neither knew the lines nor had the
script.

She was dimly aware of Louisa, of her concern and care. And of
course Beulah Counts fluttered around the edges of her consciousness in
a perpetual tizzy of Christian concern. There were many hours when
Addie had the sensation of watching herself pretending to be alive.

The children, though, were a different matter. They forced her awareness, demanded her involvement. Some mornings, the crying of little Jake
or the nagging and whining of Mary Alice were the only things that could
drag her from her bed.

A week or so after the arrival of Zeb's letter, Junior and Dub pulled
up in front of the rented house with a wagon and two muscular men.
Junior knocked on the door, and when she opened it, he said, "Addie,
we've come to take you home."

She fell into his arms and sobbed on his chest. She could speak no
words; she could utter only huge, heaving cries of grief and devastation.

Arrangements began to happen all around her: rail tickets bought, the
household goods loaded into the wagons and transported to the freight

yard for shipping to Chattanooga, Junior and Dub and Louisa loading her and the children into a hired car and driving them to the station.

They moved her, Mary Alice, and Jake into temporary lodgings at Louisa and Dub's house. When they had been there for perhaps two days, Dan Sutherland came to see her, at Junior's request.

The graying attorney sat across the kitchen table from her. Louisa sat beside her and Junior stood behind, a hand on Addie's shoulder.

"Addie, I know this is awful hard for you," Dan said, "but you've got to pull yourself together and think about the legalities of this situation. Your children are depending on you."

At Dan's mention of the children, something happened inside her. It was as if she suddenly remembered to start breathing again.

"No one—not even their daddy—can love those babies as much as I do," she said, staring into Dan Sutherland's faded blue eyes. "I'll do whatever I have to do to make sure they stay with me."

"I'm glad to hear you say so."

"Dan, he don't have a leg to stand on, does he?" Junior said.

"I don't know. I don't know what the grounds'll be. At this point," he said, looking carefully at Addie, "I don't even know who'll sue for the divorce."

"His letter said Addie should sue him," Lou said. "Why shouldn't she do just that? I mean, after all, he just dropped this on her out of the clear, blue sky! Why shouldn't she sue?"

Dan rubbed his chin. "Well, in the state of Tennessee, it's pretty hard for a woman who ups and wants out of a marriage to take her children with her."

"But she doesn't want out!" Lou said. "Can't you see that?"

"Of course I see that," Dan said, "but I'm trying to tell you how the courts'll see it. They'll see a man whose wife has sued him for divorce, and if he chose, he could present the case that she was the one who took the first action to end the marriage. That being the case, if he was to decide he wanted to keep the children, I know a lot of judges that would let him do it. Unless of course—"

"What are you thinking?" Junior asked.

"Addie, you say this came from nowhere?" Dan said. "You had no warning whatsoever? None?"

Addie pushed herself up from the table and walked away a few paces, hugging herself. She turned back toward them but kept her eyes on the floor. "Things hadn't been . . . real good between me and Zeb for awhile."

"How long?"

"Well . . . really since about . . . nine months ago."

Images flashed through Addie's mind: Zeb home from Little Rock; the presents he had brought for her and Mary Alice; the fondness they had somehow found for each other during that brief interlude; their passionate embraces in bed . . . Then, subsequent scenes: Zeb asking her to move to Little Rock; her angry refusals; his silent, brooding hurt . . .

She forced her eyes to meet Dan's.

"I'd say it was about then that things began to get worse."

Dan peered at her a few moments, chewing on a thumbnail.

"Y'all reckon Addie and I could have a minute or two in private?"

When Louisa and Junior had withdrawn to the parlor down the hall, Dan faced her.

"Addie, this is an awful thing to have to ask, but I've got to know: did you ever think Zeb might be seeing another woman?"

Addie felt the floor tilt beneath her, then right itself. Another woman! In all the dark confusion and blunt loneliness she had felt, despite her growing dissatisfaction with their marriage, Addie had never suspected Zeb of betraying his wedding vows. Zeb, who had placed such stock in knowing what the Bible said about everything, who had been so insistent that agreement on religious matters precede their marriage—how could it be that Zeb could do something so overt as violating the Seventh Commandment?

"I . . . I don't know, Mr. Sutherland. I mean . . . I never would have thought it of him, but—"

"Let me tell you what I think, Addie. I think the best thing you can do right now, at least until we know a little more, is to refuse to sue for divorce."

She looked a question at him.

"I think you need to wait and let him sue you. I think you'll stand a better chance of keeping the children."

"I don't understand."

"Addie, for whatever reason, Zeb doesn't want to be married to you anymore. My feeling is that there's another woman involved but leave that aside for now. If he wants out bad enough and you won't sue him, he'll have to sue you. And to do that, he's got to give grounds. This day and time, there's only a few reasons for divorce recognized by the courts of Tennessee: desertion, cruelty—which most men don't use—deprivation of conjugal rights, and adultery." Dan paused. "I'm making the assumption that none of these would apply to you."

"Certainly not!"

"All right, then. That's about it. If he sues you, he's got to prove that one of these fits. And if he can't prove it, he won't be granted a divorce. If, on the other hand, my guess about him is correct—"

"But, Mr. Sutherland, how would you ever find out? And if you did, how could you prove in court that—"

"Leave the lawyering to me. And my name's 'Dan' from here on. 'Mr. Sutherland' was my dad, and he died three years ago." He smiled at her and got a faint smile in return. "Now, like I was saying, if my guess is correct, you'll be granted a divorce, and no court in Tennessee would take your children away from you if he's involved with someone else."

"Then . . . I have no choice but to go through with this?"

He looked at her and sighed.

"No, ma'am, I'm afraid not. Unless, of course, your husband comes to his senses."

She turned away and looked out the window, once again cradling her elbows in her hands.

"I don't hold much hope for that, I'm afraid."

She stared out a window into Louisa's backyard. Louisa had taken Mary Alice outside, and for a moment Addie watched her daughter bobbing joyously back and forth between her aunt and the pile of toys she had heaped in one of the wrought-iron yard chairs—blissfully ignorant of the shambles her mother's life had become.

Addie thought of what her marriage had turned into and realized all she could feel was fatigue. She turned again to Dan Sutherland.

"I'll do whatever you say, Mr.— I mean, Dan. I've spent more time with these babies than he has, by a long shot. They know me—they don't know him. I mean to do whatever I have to do to keep them."

"All right." Dan settled his hat on his head. "I'll get to work."

As Dan walked toward the front door, Junior called him aside into the parlor.

"Dan, Addie's been left with little or nothing except what we brought back from Nashville. She may not can pay you much for the work you're doing, but you know I'm good for it, don't you?"

Dan gave Addie's oldest brother a direct look.

"Junior, I don't expect you'll see a bill from me for this."

"What do you mean, Dan?"

"Way I see it, your little sister's had a dang poor run of luck with the men in her life. Meaning no disrespect, but the day your daddy came to my office, I shoulda clubbed him on the head before I let him go down the street and write her out of the will. I guess this is something I can do to ease my mind on that score."

Junior stared at the lawyer for several seconds.

"Dan, I sure appreciate this."

"Don't worry. I might let you buy me a train ticket or two along the way."

And so it was that on a brilliant afternoon in October, Dan Sutherland received at his office a telegram from Little Rock, Arkansas. He had had to take certain actions that he personally found distasteful, but he had steeled himself to it by thinking of Jacob Caswell's daughter, abandoned first by her father and then by her husband. Sutherland knew a man in Little Rock who had a knack for acquiring information and an associated talent for making few ripples. He tore open the Western Union envelope and withdrew the wire.

> LITTLE ROCK OCTOBER 10 1903
> DAN SUTHERLAND, ATTORNEY
>   TALKED TO SECY STOP YOURE ON RIGHT TRACK
> STOP MORE LATER STOP SEND USUAL AMT STOP
> PURVIS

Dan leaned back in his chair. Purvis would keep digging until he either hit rock or the hole was plenty deep. He withdrew a bank book from a desk drawer and began penning a draft payable to A. Purvis, "for services rendered." He guessed it would probably be only the first of several such payments.

George Hutto walked through the rickety, abandoned warehouse, his footsteps echoing from the wide, knotty pine plank floor up into the dark spaces under the roof. The rafters were festooned with the untidy nests of sparrows and speckled, like the floor below, with black-and-white droppings. George stood in the middle of the floor, his hands in his pockets. He turned slowly through a full circle, his eyes roving everywhere through the big, empty structure. It would need a good deal of fixing up. The roof hadn't been patched in a few years, and the floor planking was buckled and water-stained in several places. They'd have to clean out all the birds' nests and haul off the three or four bales of moldering cotton hulking in the northwest corner. There'd be a good deal of carpentry too; there were numerous gaps between the wall slats and underneath the eaves, which explained the sparrow and swallow nests. Paint would be needed, and more lighting. They'd have to cut some good-sized windows. They'd have to heat the place, somehow. Then there was all the equipment they would need. And at some point he'd have to begin recruiting volunteers to teach classes and lead calisthenics and . . .

In his mind, George stepped away from the immediate tasks and allowed himself to peer past them. He thought about boys chanting in unison as they performed exercise drills, boys eating hot meals, boys huddled around men with open Bibles or literature books. George tried to imagine the building's appearance, its sounds, once he had succeeded in filling it with his vision. For just a minute or two he let himself savor the fulfillment of the mission. He needed to memorize the shape and taste of his future satisfaction to get ready for the plain old hard work it would take to make it real.

But even in the midst of calculating the difficulties, George's dream allowed him to feel reckless and capable; this idea of his was a good thing. He was coming to relish the sensation of inner certainty. Besides, other cities had had good success with the Young Men's Christian Association; why wouldn't it work in Chattanooga?

CHAPTER
30

Trusting as the moments fly,
Trusting as the days go by;
Trusting Him what e'er befall,
Trusting Jesus—that is all . . .

Becky wasn't much in the mood to sing about trust, which, it seemed to her, was getting harder and harder to come by. She mouthed the words to keep up appearances, but she couldn't bring herself to really think about what she was singing, as she knew she should. Mercifully, the song ended, and Woodrow Stark took up his station behind the massive, brown-painted pulpit. She was able to focus on the empty air just above his head and allow her mind to drift away from the service. Drifting was what she seemed to do best these days, anyway.

For the third time in as many weeks, Zeb wasn't at church. She had stood around the entrance longer than was decent, hoping to see him coming—but no. Becky just couldn't understand the man. One day he would be all smiles; warm, confident, and full of fun; and the next time she'd see him he'd be distracted and edgy, would hardly speak a civil word. Or, she'd go for days and not see him at all.

Becky felt her mother's presence in the pew to her left, sensed the looming worry in her erect posture, in the angle of her neck—cocked to allow her to study her daughter's profile without seeming to. Mother had the little New Testament she carried in her handbag dutifully cracked open to Brother Stark's text for the day, had a gloved finger laid on the verse currently under discussion. But Becky knew her mother's real attention was on her distracted, frustrated daughter. In the last few days there had been a few too many carefully disguised questions, a few too many jests left open-ended, capable of serving as the invitation to a mother-daughter talk. Yes, Mother was anxious about her little Becky. Oh, if she only knew . . . And, of course, there was Daddy, seated on the other side of Mother, arms across his chest, his head lowered in an attitude of bemused contemplation to disguise his boredom. She tried to imagine what he would be like if he suspected what she was really doing on some of those Saturday afternoons when she was "catching up the books at the store."

Becky had told herself she ought to have nothing more to do with Zeb—more times than she could count, she had told herself. But . . . when things were good with Zeb, they were *so* good. When he was right, when he was behaving in the manner she'd come to think of as "the good Zeb," something just loosened, came unwound inside her. There were times when they saw each other when his face would bloom like a starving man who'd just smelled a home-cooked meal; times when she felt she was his lifeline. It was good to be needed in that way, good to spend and be spent for someone she could sustain and provide for. In those moments, she felt herself to be a necessity to him, felt helpless to deny him anything he wished from her—and that had gotten her in farther than she'd strictly intended to go, much more than once. Even as she reviewed her indiscretions with him, though, there was a part of her that knew it couldn't be helped, a part that felt as if she already belonged to him in every way that mattered. Lying in Zeb's arms seemed to her the most natural thing in the world. Their lovemaking was to her like a secret conference in a world that would never understand a passion like theirs.

Why, that part of her asked, should she deny herself something that was so obviously right?

Because it *wasn't* right, the rest of her said. Zeb might be as good as the apostle Peter, but he wasn't her husband. Not yet. There were no promises between them, no commitments. She tried to hush the accusing voice inside her mind, but it wouldn't be stilled. There were things about the man she just didn't know, things she needed to know before she put much more stock in him—if, indeed, she hadn't already invested more in him than she could afford to lose.

". . . words of the apostle Paul as he writes to the church in Corinth," Brother Stark was saying in his dreary, endless voice. "He cautions them against the charms of this world and their former lives when he says, 'Know ye not that the unrighteous shall not inherit the kingdom of God?'—chapter six and verse nine. Hear the catalog of sins from which the gospel had rescued these folks: 'Be not deceived,' the apostle says, 'neither fornicators, nor revilers, nor . . .'"

At the word *fornicators,* Becky felt her face flush, hot and guilty. She prayed no one was watching her closely but felt as if all eyes must surely be upon her—scrutinizing her for any trace of reaction to hearing herself labeled. And then she was talking herself past it. *It's not like that with Zeb and me. We love each other, and we mean to stay together. It's not really like we're just doing . . . that . . . for base reasons.*

"Listen again to the warning of the apostle, folks," said Brother Stark. "'Flee fornication'—verse eighteen. 'Every sin that a man doeth is without the body; but he that committeth fornication sinneth against his own body . . .'"

Won't the man give it rest? Then the scold that lived inside her forehead took up the cry: *fornicate, fornicate, fornicate . . .* Laid over her gentle, softening remonstrances about the goodness of their times together, of the sweetness and, yes, the innocence of the love she shared with Zeb, was the jarring, sweaty ugliness engendered by that word, *fornicate.* The scold heaped coals on the furnace of her guilt, fanned the flames and shamed her with the heat of her own weakness. *You're a lewd woman, living in sin and too spineless to admit it to yourself.*

Becky felt the dull ache beginning behind her eyes, making a slow, pummeling progress down her neck and back until her body felt as if it had been hung like a ham in a smokehouse for a month of Sundays. She retreated into the pain, hiding her hurting mind in it as the words of the sermon drifted tonelessly over her head and out the open windows of the church house.

George shuffled through the reddish, rattling carpet of fallen leaves, doing his best to step past the broken limbs that littered the floor of the woods covering the flanks of Tunnel Hill. Why he hadn't stopped to change into more suitable clothing before coming out here, he couldn't imagine. Lately, though, he had found himself doing a number of incautious things. He was going to have to learn to adapt to his new-found bursts of impetuosity, he guessed.

Today his urge had taken the form of a sudden notion to try and locate the abode of Ned Overby. He had driven out from town and parked his vehicle behind the old Caswell place, then picked his way along the footpath that led back into the woods, up one side of the hill and down the other.

He felt a little silly, traipsing through the woods on a gray December afternoon when he really ought to be sitting in front of his grate at the office, but he had forced himself to continue with what he had planned. Since their encounter back in the spring, he had not been able to get the image of Ned Overby out of his mind: the bedraggled, defeated, vulnerable boy who scarcely spoke a half-dozen words. The Young Men's Christian Association of Chattanooga was nearly ready to open, and George was determined that Ned Overby would be one of its first members, if his family would permit it.

He finally emerged from the tangled undergrowth at the edge of the woods and laid eyes on the small, shabby dwelling by the railroad track. He nearly turned back. How in the world could he, who lived on practically a different planet from these people, possibly communicate what he had in mind for their son?

A woman came out of the door of the house as he approached and made her way toward the haphazard woodpile by the side of the house, a hatchet in her hand. When she was halfway to the woodpile, she noticed George's approach. She made as if to walk back toward the door. George tipped his hat and smiled.

"Hello, ma'am. Is this the Overby home, by any chance?"

She stared at him, taking a double-fisted grip on the hatchet. George slowed his steps, then stopped at what he hoped she regarded as a respectful distance.

"Ned probably hasn't told you about me, but one day this past summer—"

George suddenly realized that if he told Ned's mother about his ride in George's automobile, he might be getting the boy in trouble.

"—about the first week of June, I guess it was, I was out this way and . . . I asked your son about some directions. I was lost, you see, and . . ."

George felt his face flushing with the strain of inventing the fib off the cuff, and he hoped fervently the woman would let him finish before she sicced a dog on him, or threw the hatchet at his skull. He wondered what would come out of his mouth next.

"At any rate, we got to talking, and— This *is* the Overby house, isn't it?"

"My man ain't home right now," the woman said. "But I reckon Ned'll tell me if you're lying or not. Ned!" she shouted, never taking her eyes off the stranger in front of her. "Get out here! Ned, boy! You hear me?"

The front door squeaked and rattled, and George was immensely relieved to see the tousled head of the boy appear. Allowing for a few months of growth, George easily recognized him as the youngster he had rescued in the alley behind Market Street.

"Hello there, Ned! I was just telling your mother here about talking with you last June, when I saw you on the side of the road, through the woods, there." He stared at the boy, hoping he would pick up on the alibi and play along.

Ned glanced back and forth between his mother and George.

"Howdy," he said. The boy shoved his hands in his pockets and tucked his chin into his collar.

"You know this man?" the woman asked.

"Yes'm."

The hatchet now hung at her side. George hoped that was a good sign.

"Anyway, Mrs. Overby, my name is George Hutto. I live in Chattanooga, and I'm starting up a Young Men's Christian Association."

"We don't need no charity."

"Oh, no, ma'am! No, ma'am, nothing like that. This is just a . . . a sort of club, you see, for young fellows like Ned, there. Place to exercise, and read, and . . . well, just a place to come and sort of . . . associate with other boys and . . . well, I was just thinking about Ned, here, and . . ."

He had run out of words. He stood there with hat in hand, smiling like a fool at this poor woman who clearly didn't trust him as far as she could spit.

"Go on back in the house, Ned," she said in a low voice. When he had gone in, she hugged herself, cradling the hatchet with an odd gesture, as if it were an infant. She spoke, staring at the ground in front of George's feet.

"We make our own way, mister. We ain't got much, but we ain't beholdin' to nobody for what's here. It's a hard life, but it's all we know. I don't see much call for anybody puttin' notions in a boy's head—notions that ain't gonna do nothin' but let him in for hurt later on."

George blinked at her, the idiotic smile still frozen on his face. She knew! She knew there was another sort of life out there for some people; she just didn't think Ned could possibly aspire to it. She had completely circled him in her mind, and was already in the road in front of him.

"I understand your point, Mrs. Overby, and I won't try to talk you out of it . . . today, at least. But I wish you'd think on it some more, and maybe let me come back another time, maybe when Mr. Overby is here and we could talk."

Still hugging herself, she turned her head to the right and stared off in the direction of the place where the railroad tracks curved slowly to the left and out of sight behind the shoulder of Tunnel Hill.

"I ain't gonna say. Perlie's runnin' traps this time a year, and I never know when he's comin' or goin'."

George touched the brim of his hat and backed toward the woods.

"Well, good day to you, ma'am. I'll be on my way."

When he got back to the old Caswell place, he was startled to see two people standing beside his automobile. They had heard his rustling approach through the fallen leaves and were staring at him when he ducked from under the eaves of the woods. He realized he was looking at Addie Douglas and her oldest brother.

CHAPTER
31

*A*ddie's brother finally broke the silence.

"George." Junior nodded.

Like an animal trying to shake off a winter's sleep, George pulled his eyes away from Addie.

"Junior. Addie," he said, touching the brim of his hat.

"Hello, George," Addie said. She gave him a weary little wave that looked more like "good-bye."

"I hope my horseless carriage wasn't in the way, in the driveway there," George said. "I was just walking through the woods, and I had no idea anyone was here . . . that is, that anyone would be here when I—"

"It's all right, George," Junior said. "Me and Addie just took a quick drive out to look at the place. She'll be needing a place to live and all."

George felt himself gulping around the words he wanted to say.

"Addie . . . Junior, I've . . . I'm . . . If there's anyway I can help—"

"Thank you, George," Junior said. "We appreciate it."

"Yes, well . . . good day, then." He nodded at them and stepped past, going toward his car.

Junior stared after him for a few moments. "Funny time and place for him to be walking in the woods, don't you imagine?"

Addie shrugged.

"Well, what do you think?" Junior gestured toward the house. "Place is run down some, nobody living in it the last year or two. But I believe we could have it in shape right quick, if you'd be agreeable."

Addie tucked her hands under her elbows and looked at the house, the yard. So many ghosts here—so many old regrets hiding in the dark corners.

"Course it's a big old place, just you and the two young 'uns. Expect you'd need a hand now and then."

"I don't want to lean on anybody, Junior. I'm tired of that. I want to be on my own two feet, and the sooner the better."

"Well, I reckon that's up to you, Addie. But you know we're here anytime—"

She turned to him. "Oh, yes, Junior. You've done so much already. I don't know what I'd have done, if . . ."

He shrugged. "That's what family's for."

She turned back and looked at the house. Addie thought about *family*, about the varieties of loss that word summoned up within her: about Mama, and the sucked-dry look on her dying face; about Papa, and the way he had crumpled up around his anger; Louisa, and her cautious sponsorship of Addie's dreams, her ravaging grief at the death of her only daughter; and then, of course, Zeb . . . A drawn-out, dry longing twined its way through her heart as she looked at this cracked and peeling, untended, overgrown place where she had started. She wondered if it would also be the place where she finished. Beginning and ending. Grief and laughter. Disaster and rescue. That's what family's for. Who else would live in a place like this?

"Well," she said, "I guess we'll just make it work."

Zeb fumed and fretted over the sales report for the home office. All morning he had been in the foulest of moods, and he had already put this report off longer than advisable. But his unruly mind kicked at the traces and wouldn't pull the load.

That fellow with the battered black derby and the slippery eyes had been outside the agency when he got here this morning. This time he'd been walking away—maybe ten paces beyond the doorway of the agency—when Zeb saw him. Zeb recognized the nondescript slump of the man's shoulders even as he tried to lose himself among the passersby on the boardwalk. *Had he been in here—talking to Abner, maybe?* Zeb put down his pen and stared at his secretary, who kept his nose pointed toward the work on his desk.

Once or twice in recent weeks, as Zeb had walked across the street on various errands, he had thought he glimpsed the same man, seated at a table by the window in the chophouse across the street from the agency. One morning he could have sworn the stranger was lounging at a street corner near his lodgings when he came out to go to the office. Zeb had a mind, more than once, to go up to the fellow and ask him his business, but by the time he could summon the gumption to do it, the man had always slipped away.

This sneak-footed spying could only be Addie's doing! But how in the devil was a woman with two children and no inheritance paying for a gumshoe working in Little Rock, Arkansas? Why hadn't that blasted woman sued him for divorce, anyway? It had been nearly three months now—she'd had ample time! Did she cherish some fool notion of reconciliation?

He was swept by sudden, unaccountable longing to see Becky. He wanted to hold her in his arms, to smell her hair and remind himself that there was something good in his days, someone who understood and appreciated him.

But, no. Even that wouldn't do. In the state he was in, he was afraid he'd set off the worst in her. Probably say something harsh, or else she'd detect his distraction and want to know its cause. Becky Norwich certainly did not retreat into hurt silence—oh, no. She'd batter and harry and generally give him a piece of her mind until he'd be forced to lie again, just to preserve the general accord.

No, better to just get his mind on his business and wait a little longer. Surely, anyday now, Addie would wake up to the truth of the situation and release him from bondage. He picked up his pen and forced his eyes back to the sentence he had left dangling.

After lunch, just as he felt the walls of the office closing in on him, Gideon Plunkett strolled through the door. Zeb had just recruited Plunkett for the new debit in northwestern Pulaski County. Zeb stood and reached for his coat and hat.

"Abner, Mr. Plunkett and I'll be canvassing his debit for the rest of the afternoon."

This was good. Getting out of the office would force him to turn his attention to something besides troublesome thoughts. Normally, canvassing was not one of his preferred chores, but right now it looked like deliverance.

"Come on, Gideon. Let's go turn up some paying customers for you."

They walked outside. Zeb felt a pleasant glow at the respectful look with which Gideon Plunkett favored his new Oldsmobile with its unique, curved dashboard.

"Now, Gideon, the key to success in this business is activity."

Though Gideon Plunkett was probably at least ten years his senior, as far as the insurance business was concerned he was a debutante.

"You gotta see lots of prospects to make the kind of money you want to make, and this afternoon I'm fixing to show you how to find 'em."

Zeb grunted as he turned the crank on the front of the automobile, then he fiddled with the choke. Another turn, and the engine caught.

"Hop in," he said over his shoulder as he dashed around to the driver's side to switch the spark from the battery to the magneto. Then they were off, crow-hopping slightly as they pulled away from the edge of the boardwalk.

"Sorry about that," he yelled over the roar of the engine, "I'm still pretty new at this."

The Oldsmobile stuttered along the bumpy, chalky-white road northwest of town, and Zeb slowed as they approached the rickety bridge across the Maumelle River. He tugged the hand brake and brought the car to a stop, just as its front tires rolled onto the boards of the bridge runway.

"Gideon, we're about to enter your territory, here. You need to think of yourself as a farmer, and this as your field." Zeb waved an arm at the wooded river bottomland—choked with a tangled, brown undergrowth of last summer's lamb's-quarter and cockleburs—on the other side of the brown, sluggish stream. "What kind of crop you make depends on how well you cultivate your land, Gideon. And I'll tell you this: the only somebody that can limit the size of your crop is you. That's why the insurance business is the greatest one going, because a man's only limited by his own ambition."

Gideon Plunkett wore a serious look as Zeb turned back toward the steering wheel and engaged the transmission. They edged slowly across the bridge into Gideon's domain.

The first house they came to was a ramshackle, shotgun affair set back in a grove of bunchy elm trees about a quarter-mile along the road from the bridge. Zeb slowed and pulled to the side of the road. Gideon gave him a worried look.

"Now, Zeb, I know these folks here. This old boy don't do nothing but a little cotton chopping ever once in awhile, and besides that, they're colored. I doubt they can afford anything."

Zeb gave his new agent a patient smile.

"First rule, Gideon: never assume. Don't ever tell a prospect he can't buy; let him tell you. Come on, Gideon. You know these folks' name?"

"Uh, yeah."

"All right, then. You just introduce me, and watch what I do. By the end of the day, I'll have you talking smooth as silk to people you never saw before in your life."

A short-haired, yellow dog with ribs showing like barrel staves dragged itself from beneath the front porch steps and slouched toward them, wagging its tail between its legs.

"Don't reckon we'll get eaten alive, do you?" Zeb said.

A little boy, wrapped in a dingy blanket and nothing else, appeared on the porch.

"Hi, son!" Zeb said in a sunshiny voice. "Your mama or daddy around?"

The boy went back in and his place was taken a moment later by a heavy-breasted, big-hipped woman. Her feet were shoved into unlaced, badly scuffed men's shoes, and she wore a pink calico dress with an ancient, moth-eaten Army blanket pulled around her shoulders. She stared down at them with a face as blank as the grate of an unlit stove.

"Uh, Carlotta, is Arthur here?" said Gideon.

A younger child came out of the house and stopped short when she saw the two white men standing in the front yard. Tucking a finger in her mouth, she ducked behind her mother's skirts.

"Carlotta, I believe you already know Mr. Plunkett, here, and I'm Zeb Douglas. We're with the Dixie National Casualty Company, and we're out this afternoon looking for folks that are interested in protecting their families and saving up some money." He stopped speaking, smiling at her as if they shared some secret joke. Zeb could feel Gideon Plunkett's eyes flickering back and forth between him and the woman on the front porch, and he waited patiently, never allowing the pleasant expression on his face to waver. Whomever spoke first would cede control of this contest of wills. In a moment, her eyes flickered back toward the dark doorway of the house.

"My man he over to Mister Zeke's."

"Well, now, Carlotta, that's just fine," Zeb said, sounding like she had just given the winning answer in a spelling bee. "Mr. Plunkett and I don't really have time to talk today, anyway." Zeb saw the line of her shoulders relax slightly, saw the faint softening of relief in her face.

"Now, Carlotta, you know Mr. Plunkett here, right?"

He waited until she gave a short nod.

"Fine, then. Mr. Plunkett will be back over this way in a few days, and he's got some ideas I think you and Arthur'll be real interested in. It'd be all right if he took a few minutes to talk to you, wouldn't it?" Zeb began nodding as he said the last few words, still smiling directly at her. As he expected, she gave a short, quick shrug and a nod.

"Well, that's just fine. Mr. Plunkett, I guess we'd better get on to the rest of the folks we need to see today." Zeb tipped his hat toward the woman. "Thank you, Carlotta, and you be sure and tell Arthur we stopped by, all right?" Zeb turned and began walking back toward the road.

When they had reached the automobile, he turned to face Gideon Plunkett.

"Now, Gideon, I'd get back over here in about two days or so. She'll have her guard up some, but she'll be a little curious too. If I were you—"

"Wait a minute, Zeb! Them people back there ain't got two nickels to rub together! How in the name a Ned d'you expect me to get 'em to pay for an insurance policy when they don't have a pot to pee in or a window to pour it out of?"

"Gideon, I'll thank you to not use that kind of language around me." Zeb held Gideon's eyes long enough so he could see Zeb meant business.

"You're gonna have to listen to me, now, Gideon. I've been doing this for awhile, and I've called on lots of people, some that didn't even have as good a place as Carlotta's, back there. I'm telling you that there aren't very many folks I've found that can't come up with two bits a week for a five-hundred-dollar indemnity plan, especially if you sell it to them the right way and then show up regularly to collect the debit."

He walked around to the front of the Oldsmobile and put his hand on the crank.

"Shoot, man, I had people with nothing but a dirt floor looking down the road for me when I'd come to collect their payments, and when they handed it over, you'd have thought I was doing them the biggest favor they ever had in their lives."

Zeb grunted as he cranked the engine, then straightened once more and squinted at Gideon Plunkett.

"And in a manner of speaking, I guess I was doing 'em a big favor. You take a guy like ol' Arthur, back there," Zeb said, jerking a thumb back toward the shack in the elm grove. "Say he ups and dies one of these days, say, clearing timber and miscalculates and it falls the wrong way with him underneath—who's gonna take care of Carlotta and the young 'uns?" He peered at Gideon, who returned his stare for a few seconds, then nodded reluctantly, looking down at his feet and scratching his head beneath the sweatband of his derby.

"You see, Gideon? That's what we're selling, and that's how you gotta convince these people. You gotta put 'em in a bind, make 'em real uncomfortable, then show 'em the way out—for only twenty-five cents a week, which you'll be more than happy to collect for 'em, of course."

He cranked the engine twice more; it sputtered, then caught. He hurried around to switch the spark.

"Now, hop in, Gideon. We got more prospects to find."

With dusk settling red and pink against the deep blue of the western horizon, Zeb pulled in beside the boardwalk in front of the agency. By midafternoon, he thought Gideon Plunkett was starting to get the idea. The new agent had even talked his own way past a reluctant prospect or two.

Zeb felt good: competent and in control. He enjoyed seeing a new hire begin to learn how to succeed on his own.

He closed the door of the automobile. Abner was still seated at his desk in the front of the office. *What's he doing here at nearly half past six?* Zeb walked in the front door and looked at his secretary.

"Why you still here, Ab?"

Abner looked at Zeb like a cat who'd just swallowed the pet canary. Zeb glanced toward his desk.

Seated in front of it was Becky Norwich.

"Why, uh, hello, Miss Norwich," he said, taking a step or two past Abner's station. As Zeb passed Abner's desk, he heard the scooting of the chair and the quick steps, then the hurried closing of the door.

Becky stared at him. Her eyes were reddened tunnels of fear.

"Zeb, I'm . . . I think I'm going to have a baby."

CHAPTER
32

*O*h my land, now look what you've done!"

Mary Alice looked at her mother and rubbed her hand on the front of her smock, leaving a smear the same green as the pool of paint in which she stood. Addie propped her paintbrush against the sill and started toward her. Mary Alice began backing away.

"You come here to me, Mary Alice Douglas! I've been telling you all morning long to keep away from—"

"Well, looks like you're making progress."

Addie managed to snag Mary Alice's elbow. She looked up at Louisa, who stood in the doorway of the parlor.

"Some," she said, dabbing roughly at the little girl's dress with a rag. "I could do more if I didn't have to keep stopping to chase this one out of the paint." Mary Alice started to whimper.

Louisa stepped into the room, stepping around the puddle of green paint on the floor. She rolled up her sleeves and kneeled beside Addie.

"Come here, Miss Mary Alice, and let your Aunt Lou see what kind of a mess you're in."

Addie stepped away from them and went back to the sill. Junior had said something about getting wallpaper up later this week. The paint on these sills had to be dry by then. She dipped her brush in the pail and climbed back on the footstool. She painted several strokes.

"How you doing?" Louisa said.

Addie stretched, teetering slightly on the stool as she spread paint to the top of the jamb.

"I don't know. Some days I wake up and halfway expect to see Zeb in the bed next to me. Other days that whole life seems like something I'm trying to forget. And then, there are the days when I just want to lie there and go on sleeping. But I can't."

"No, you can't. I tried that. It didn't work."

Addie stepped off the footstool and dipped her brush. She held it over the pail and watched the puddling of the drip.

"I used to think I knew what my life was going to be. Once I married Zeb, I thought everything would take care of itself—that all the decisions were sort of made. Everything was settled." She looked at Louisa. "But it turns out nothing was. I just didn't know it yet." She raked the brush along the side of the pail, removing the excess paint. "There was a lot I didn't know."

"That's so for all of us."

"Oh, Lou. You've been through so much. I shouldn't go on about my troubles."

"I asked you, honey. And hurt comes in all shapes and sizes. Nobody knows what your load's like but you. Nobody knows mine but me. You can't compare them because you can't carry somebody else's."

Addie went to the window and began painting the other jamb.

"I know. But I don't think I could handle yours."

"Honey, I feel the same way. Oh, lawzy, Miss Mary Alice, just look at the mess on your shoes!"

The little girl gave Louisa a tentative smile around the finger stuck in her mouth.

"'S g'een."

"Yes, ma'am, it's green, and you'll be tracking it all over the place in a minute." Louisa settled Mary Alice on the floor and scrubbed the bottoms of her shoes. "Your mama'll skin you if she finds little green footprints on her kitchen floor."

Just then, Jake gave a fitful cry from the next room. Addie heaved a sigh.

"Awake. And hungry, I'll bet."

"So am I, come to think of it. Which reminds me. Miss Mary Alice, would you go out on the front porch and fetch that basket I left by the door? I brought us some lunch." Louisa watched the little girl scamper toward the doorway.

"Bless your heart," Addie said.

Mary Alice staggered back from the doorway, gripping the handles of the basket in both hands.

"Set it down here, sugar," Louisa said. She opened the lid of the basket and started setting out jars and plates and parcels wrapped in cheese-cloth.

"We can go in the kitchen," Addie said.

"No, let's just eat here on the floor, why don't we? It'll be like a picnic, won't it, Miss Mary Alice?"

Mary Alice grinned. She plopped down cross-legged on the floor, barely missing the puddle of paint.

"Have a pinnic," she said.

Louisa had brought a loaf of store-bought bread and a jar of homemade apple butter. She got out bread-and-butter pickles and red-rind cheese. She unwrapped a half-dozen slices of ham, all of them white-rimmed and marbled with fat. She pulled out a quart Ball Mason jar filled with buttermilk. It looked to Addie like enough food for a crew of field hands.

Addie cradled Jake with one arm to let him nurse while she ate. Louisa listened to Mary Alice's jabber and fussed over her and laughed with her and picked up the crumbs of bread and the shreds of ham the little girl scattered while she ate. Addie watched the two of them and thought about Katherine.

When they had eaten, Addie made Mary Alice lie down for a nap. The little girl moaned and fretted, but she stayed on the settee. Louisa told her if she was good and went to sleep, she'd leave a peppermint stick for her mama to give her when she woke up.

Addie changed Jake's diaper and bundled him up. She returned him to his crib and he was asleep in a moment. She went into the parlor, where Louisa had taken up a paintbrush and begun work on another sill.

"You don't have to do that," Addie said.

"I know."

For awhile the only sound was the swishing of the paintbrushes and the soft popping of the fire in the grate.

"What are you going to do?" Louisa asked.

There was a long quiet.

"I don't know."

"Any news from Dan?"

"No. Not in awhile. He just says he's working on it and to try to be patient."

"Easy enough for him."

"He's not charging me anything, Lou."

"I know. I shouldn't be so sharp, I guess. But I just hate to see you going through this."

"Dub's on the school board," Louisa said a bit later. "He could probably find you something."

"I'm . . . I'm not ready for that yet, I don't think."

They painted another while in silence.

"Honey, you've got to—"

"I know, Lou. I will. But not yet."

They painted until four o'clock. They finished all the window frames in the parlor and had a good start on the study when they heard the pop and clatter of Dub's automobile coming down the lane. Louisa laid a peppermint stick beside the still-sleeping Mary Alice. She gathered the remnants of their lunch into her basket and shrugged into her coat. Addie put her arm through her sister's and walked her to the front door. As Louisa straightened her hat on her head, she turned to give Addie a hug.

"We'll expect you and the kids for Christmas."

Addie gave her a surprised look.

"Oh, yes. It is next week, isn't it? Thanks, Lou. We'll be there. Mary Alice'll love it."

They looked at each other. Louisa gave Addie a peck on the cheek and ducked out the door. Addie went onto the front porch, hugging herself against the cold, and watched her sister go. She waved to Dub, robed and goggled behind the wheel of the auto. Addie went back inside and closed the door. She leaned back against it, still holding herself, and began to cry quietly.

"Oh, Lou! It's beautiful!" Addie stood and held out the bedspread, letting it fall to the floor.

"I've heard it called 'candlewicking.'"

"I've never seen anything done this way," Addie said. The spread was powder blue; its smooth surface was decorated with intricate, curving lines of tufted stitching. "Where did you find it?"

"An old German lady over by Brown's Ferry makes them. Looks like she does pretty well."

Mary Alice was playing with the doll she had just unwrapped when she noticed the bedspread piled on the floor at her mother's feet. She rolled herself up in it, cradling her doll in the bend of her arm.

"Night-night," she said, squinting her eyes shut. Everyone laughed.

"Well, better get started cleaning up this mess," said Dub, gathering the torn wrapping paper from around his feet. "Robert, come help me."

The boy sighted steadily down the barrel of his new popgun.

"Son."

Robert sighed and propped the gun in the corner. He shuffled toward his father, kicking scraps of paper into a drift in front of him as he came.

"Why don't Ewell have to help?" Robert said.

"'Why *doesn't* Ewell,'" Louisa said.

"Never mind about that," Dub said. "Stuff all that into this sack here."

The rest of the day was spent in getting ready to eat, eating, and recovery from eating. For Christmas dinner, Louisa baked a goose and chestnut dressing to go with it. There were yams, mashed potatoes, cranberry salad, apples fried in butter and brown sugar, green beans and limas from last summer's canning, plum and rice puddings, and the obligatory fruit cake.

Once, Dub leaned toward Addie to chuck little Jake, in her lap, under his chin.

"Boy, I bet you wish you had you some teeth so you could eat some of this."

"He'll be eating more than his share before too long," Addie said. She spooned small portions of mashed potatoes and yams into the baby's mouth. He smacked his gums and rolled his tongue at the unfamiliar sensation.

After dinner Addie and Louisa cleaned up the dishes while Dub sat by the fire and read his new book. Mary Alice, Robert, and Ewell chased each other up and down the stairs and through every room of the house, shooting and being shot by the popgun.

Just after dark settled, they heard the sound of carolers in front of the house. Addie and Louisa quickly bundled the younger children, and they all went to stand on the front porch.

It was a sizeable group, maybe twelve all together. They clumped under the gaslight by the sidewalk and sang "Silent Night." Addie could see their breath puffing white in the light from the lamp. They finished the song, then struck up "God Rest Ye, Merry Gentlemen." At the end of that, Dub invited them all inside for hot spiced cider and cocoa. As they trooped in, wiping their feet on the doormat, Addie realized one of the singers was George Hutto.

"Hello, George," she said, reaching out to take his wraps and add them to the stack in her arms.

The sudden warmth of the house steamed his glasses as he looked at her. He fumbled them off, blinking and squinting as he wiped the lenses on a wrinkled handkerchief. "Why, uh, hello Addie. Nice to see you."

"Y'all sounded good out there."

"Oh. Thanks. Some of the people from church came by, asked if I wanted to sing. I figured, why not?'"

He settled his glasses back on his nose. He gave her a tiny smile and a shrug. She nodded, then tried to find something else to look at. After a few seconds, he followed the other carolers toward the steaming bowl of cider on the dining room table.

Addie piled the wraps on a settee in the parlor and went back toward the dining room. Few of the men would look at her. The women tried to study her without seeming to. None of them would give her more than the flicker of a smile before busying themselves with something else.

She felt someone touch her elbow. It was George.

"Addie, ah . . . I just wanted to say— Oops!"

Someone jostled his arm in passing, sloshing some of the hot cider onto his cuff. He swiped at it with his hand as Addie hurried into the kitchen and found a cup towel. She came back into the dining room and blotted the spill.

"Thank you," he said, watching her work.

"Don't mention it."

"Anyway, I was saying . . . I'm awful sorry about your—your situation. If there's anything—"

"Thank you, George. That's real kind of you. I think that's got it." She made a final dab at his cuff.

"Yes, that's fine. Thanks."

She went back into the kitchen and occupied herself there until the carolers left. Then she found Mary Alice's coat and hat.

"Dub, I'm ready for you to drive us back, if you don't mind."

Louisa's face held a question, but Addie didn't feel like acknowledging it.

She bundled herself and her children into Dub's Duryea, their presents piled between them and around their feet. Addie threw her new tufted bedspread around the three of them as Dub released the brake and they started down the sloping street toward the main road.

"Want us to pick y'all up for church on Sunday?" Dub said when they were getting out at the house.

Addie paused, then went up the steps to her porch.

"No, I guess not," she said over her shoulder. "I expect I'll go on out to Post Oak Hollow."

Dub shrugged and nodded. He carried their parcels into the house, then said good night as Addie closed and locked the door behind him.

CHAPTER
33

Zeb had never spent a more miserable Christmas in his life.

He went to Becky's house, of course, on Christmas Day. How could he refuse? In the state she was in, there was no telling what she'd do or say if he didn't agree to whatever she proposed. He arrived at the Norwich's door bright and early, wrapped parcels in hand. Pete answered the door with a hearty "Merry Christmas," and Zeb breathed a little easier. He'd half expected to be staring down the muzzle of a double-barreled shotgun.

He went inside. Becky's mother bustled around the table, setting out china and crystal. She gave him a big smile.

"Hello, Zeb! Merry Christmas!"

"Merry Christmas to you, Mrs. Norwich. Here." He held out one of the presents.

"Oh, honey, would you mind just taking it into the parlor and putting it under the tree? I'm trying to get the table set right quick before we open presents."

"Yes, ma'am." *Well, another hurdle cleared,* he thought. No problem there, evidently.

He set the presents under the tree and removed his coat and hat. He hung them on pegs in the entryway and went back into the parlor. At the same time, Becky came into the parlor from the kitchen entrance carrying a double handful of punch cups. When she saw him, she hesitated—so slightly that he might not have seen it if he hadn't been looking for it—then gave him a wide smile.

"Merry Christmas," she said. She arranged the cups around a porcelain punch bowl resting on a side table, then came and took his hands.

"Merry Christmas, yourself," he said. He leaned toward her. She backed away, laughing.

"Zeb, not here! What'll Mother and Daddy think?"

What, indeed? "Sorry," he said.

"Come into the kitchen and help me for a minute," Becky said, pulling him after her.

He went in. Becky handed him a fistful of silver forks and a polish cloth and told him to get busy. Mrs. Norwich hurried in and out, taking platters and plates and saucers to the dining room. She and Becky kept up a constant barrage of comments about what needed to be done next for the table setting, the turkey browning in the oven, the various pots and pans bubbling and steaming on the stove. You'd have guessed they were fixing to entertain the governor and his cabinet, Zeb thought.

You'd have also guessed Becky had absolutely nothing on her mind but the preparations for the Christmas meal. He watched her, waiting for a hastily wiped tear; a trembling lip; a long, unfocused glance—something to betray her state of mind about her . . . inconvenience.

But it wasn't there. It just wasn't. As far as Zeb could see, she was the perfect hostess, completely intent on enjoying the perfect Christmas dinner with her perfect beau and her perfect parents. She clearly hadn't said anything to either of them. And right now, it looked like she'd figured out a way to keep the secret even from herself.

At first, Zeb was relieved. They all went into the parlor and passed around the presents. They took turns opening their parcels. Becky and Ruth exclaimed over each prize, and Zeb and Pete traded wry comments.

When Becky unwrapped the matching parasol and bonnet Zeb had found for her at Simpson's, both she and her mother squealed with delight. It was her ideal color, of course: a pale blue that just set off her hair, eyes, and complexion.

"Now if you'd of just thought to buy a few days of sunshine for her to try out that getup," Pete said.

Becky had gotten Zeb a new valise for work. He grinned and held it up.

"Mr. Norwich, there's a pocket in here for that new policy I'm gonna sell you." Pete made a disgusted noise and shook his head.

But after awhile, Zeb felt his enthusiasm ebbing. The more Pete grinned and laughed and joked, the more Becky and Ruth took on over everything, the worse he felt. Maybe they really knew, after all. Maybe, in a little while when he was relaxed and unsuspecting, the three of them were going to close in on him and . . . do something drastic. Maybe all this Merry Christmasing was a cover for the coming ambush.

By the time the meal was over, Zeb thought he was about to have a running fit. He felt like he was standing in the far corner of the room watching the wooden smile on his own face and listening to the lame words coming from his mouth. It was as if he were pointing at himself and hollering, "Liar! Humbug! Scoundrel!" The voice in his head was so loud he was surprised they couldn't hear it.

As they finished their pecan pie and coffee, Becky's mother said, "Becky, why don't you let me clean this up? Zeb looks like he could use a walk."

Zeb looked at her, but he couldn't detect anything in her face but good humor. He hoped his smile disguised his clenched jaw.

"Well, I can see to myself, Mrs. Norwich. I'll wait for Becky—"

"No, you two go on. If I get in too deep, I'll make Pete help me."

"Now, wait a minute here—"

"Oh, Pete, you hush. Go on, now. Shoo."

They walked nearly half a mile before either of them said anything. Finally, Becky said, "How you doing?"

He gave a tight little laugh that hurt his throat.

"Seems like I ought to be asking you that."

They took a few more paces. They both had their hands shoved deep in their coat pockets, their faces locked straight ahead.

"Well?" she said.

"Well what?"

"Why don't you?"

"Why don't I what?"

"Why don't you ask me how I'm doing?" Her voice was rigid. She sounded like somebody hauling on the reins of a horse about to bolt.

"All right, then. How are you doing?"

The sniffles started then, quickly followed by the long, quavering breaths.

"Oh, Zeb. How in the world should I know?"

After a minute he realized his jaw ached from clenching. He took a deep, slow breath.

"Looked like you were doing pretty well back there, with your folks."

"Well, of course. You think I can afford to let them see how I really feel?"

"No, I guess not. I just— It surprised me, I guess, that's all."

"Zeb, what are we going to do?"

There it was. He'd known it was coming, but still he chewed it back and forth, trying to pin down some words to put beside it, something that had a chance to seem right to her and to him at the same time.

He looked back over his shoulder at the capitol dome, dull white against the dull gray overcast. He wondered what it would feel like to be able to just launch yourself toward it, like a bird. Just jump up and keep on going and going, the wind rushing past your face and the ground dropping away.

You could forget how to fly, though, maybe. You could get fifty, a hundred feet off the ground and then the knowledge of how you got there could just leave you as quickly as it came. That was the trouble with flying, he guessed. You might forget, but the ground didn't.

"Becky . . . I—"

"Don't."

Now he stopped walking. His face swung around to look at her. "Don't what?"

"Don't say it. Not now. Not like this. I don't want it this way."

"What did you—"

"It's cold. Let's go back."

And she turned around, just like that, and started walking back the way they'd come. He could either stand and watch her go or hurry and catch up with her. She walked, without slowing, without a backward glance. Just walked like someone who had someplace to get to and was in a hurry to do it, and he could either come on, or go somewhere else, or stand out in the weather; she didn't care which.

"What you doing there, boy? Lemme see."

"Nothing."

Ned quickly shoved the wood in his pocket and folded the Barlow. He hadn't heard his paw coming up behind him. That was why he liked to sit out behind the woodpile; it was usually private.

"Whadda you mean, boy? Take that nothin' outta your pocket and lemme see it."

Ned dug out the pine block. It was trying to be a squirrel, but he couldn't get the hindquarters to look right. He handed it to his father. Paw would probably laugh about it, he figured. Ned wouldn't look at him.

"How'd you get the tail to look like that? All bushy, just like a real one?"

Ned shrugged, still looking down.

"Say, this is good, boy. Real good." Perlie chuckled. "Shoot, I didn't know you could do something like this. I guess you got your granddaddy's eye."

Ned risked a glance at his father. "My grampaw?"

"Yeah, your mama's daddy. You should of seen him, boy. He could carve out a dove that looked like it'd fly off if you stomped your foot. He could make a mallard hen that'd fool a drake. He was a carvin' fool."

"How come I never seen him?"

"Died 'fore you's born. Gun went off when he was cleanin' it, way back in the mountains somewhere, in a winter huntin' camp. Wound went bad and poisoned him." Perlie smiled and shook his head. "He could sing too. Taught me half the songs I know. And whistle? He could mock a brown thrush better'n anythin' I ever saw."

"Wished I'd of known him."

Perlie looked at the squirrel, rubbed his hand over its tail. He handed it back to Ned. "Yeah, he was somethin'. Your mama used to say I only took up with her to have an excuse to be around him. Shoot, everybody liked it when he was around."

"What was his name?"

"You mean you didn't know? I thought sure we'd told you. You're named for him. Ned. He was Ned Hutchins."

Ned looked off toward the river, dull and gray in the winter light.

"Paw, you reckon I could help you some with the traps next time you go out?"

"Well, sure, boy, if you want to."

Ned took the Barlow out of his pocket and thumbed open the smaller blade. He worked at the squirrel's flank, crosshatching it to look like fur.

"I do. If it's all right."

He could feel his father looking at him.

"What's on your mind, son?" Perlie's voice was quiet. Ned liked it when Paw talked to him like that, like it was just the two of them and they were telling each other things nobody else needed to hear.

"A man came by here awhile back, in the fall. From Chattanooga."

"What happened?"

"Nothing, Paw. He was just a man I . . . helped one day." Ned felt his ears tingling a little bit with the fib, but it was the same one the man had used, so he kept going. "He told Maw he was starting a club—a club for boys, in town."

"Ned—"

"It don't cost nothing to go," Ned said quickly. "And they'd teach you things. And you could see books."

"And you don't want to go among them town boys without proper shoes."

Ned carved a few strokes. "No, I don't reckon I do."

"What'd your mama say about it?"

Ned shrugged.

"Well, I don't know. I'll talk to your mama," Perlie said after a long wait. He chuckled again and ruffled Ned's hair. "I wish you'd look at that. Just like ol' Ned Hutchins." Perlie's footsteps crunched away toward the house.

Lila knocked on the backdoor. She looked down at herself and wiped at the front of her coat. She heard footsteps approaching from inside the house. The door opened, and Louisa stood there, smiling at her.

"Hello, Lila. Thank you so much for coming. Come on in."

"Yes'm. Thank you." She climbed the steps and stood in the kitchen of the big house. There was cabbage cooking, and some other smell Lila couldn't exactly place. The kitchen was too warm and close to be wearing her coat, but Louisa hadn't told her where she should put it, so she just left it on.

"I don't know how to thank you for this," Louisa was saying. "This big old place is just too much for me, by myself. I just loved Cassie—I guess you know her, don't you?—but she moved to Memphis. And I haven't been able to find anyone else who's worked out."

Lila didn't know Cassie; she went to a different church, and she lived in a different part of the Negro section. But Louisa would think all the coloreds knew each other.

"Anyway, I'm just so glad you came by. You know how much we all loved your mother-in-law."

"Yes'm."

"Rose was the sweetest thing, and so good to Addie. My father wasn't ever the same after she was gone."

"Yes'm."

Louisa looked at her. Lila kept her eyes down.

"Lila, I know my father wasn't very . . . easy to work for. I'm sorry."

There was a pause, like Louisa thought she was supposed to say something. Lila waited.

"But I hope you won't think we're like he was. Like he got toward the end, anyway, God rest his soul."

"Yes'm."

Another pause.

"Well? Do you want to take a look around? See what needs doing?"

"Yes'm. I guess we better."

Louisa showed her where the pots and pans and knives and such were. She didn't expect her to do much cooking, she said, unless there was some kind of doings. Mostly she needed her for dusting and cleaning once or twice a week, Louisa said. And washing and ironing on laundry days. Louisa took her through the dining room, showed her where the silver was kept. She wouldn't have to trouble herself with that unless there was a big dinner or something, Louisa told her.

They went through the drawing room and the parlor. Lots of furniture and corners to gather dust, Lila decided. The big downstairs bedroom wouldn't need much, Louisa told her, except every now and then the mattress needed a good beating and airing. Next was the entry hall. A staircase led up and around a bend to the next story. Take a long time to dust and mop that staircase, Lila thought. They went up the staircase, and Lila noted the chandelier hanging in the center of the stairwell. She could see the cobwebs and dust on it. She'd need a long stick to reach the chandelier, she figured.

Upstairs were the childrens' bedrooms and the nursery. There was also a small library, but Louisa said Dub wouldn't even let his own boys in there unless he was on hand to supervise.

"When he's had some of his men friends over and they get in there smoking their cigars," Louisa said, "I'll make him let you in the next day to clean it out. But that's all you'll ever do in there." Lila smiled and nodded her head.

At the next door they passed, Louisa paused with her hand on the knob, then went on. Her face changed, fell.

"That was Katherine's room," she said.

"I'm sure sorry, Miz Lou."

"Oh, thank you, Lila. Goodness, it's been, what, nearly four years now?"

"Anythin' need seen to in there?"

"No. That room stays closed."

"Yes'm."

They went back downstairs. "Can you come on Tuesdays and Thursdays?"

"Yes'm."

"What time can you be here?"

"Well, Mason go to work at seven, and time I get the children to school . . . Half-past eight, I guess, if that's all right."

"Oh, that's fine. Can you start day after tomorrow?"

"Yes'm. I reckon."

"Oh, and . . . I pay three dollars a week. Extra, of course, if I need help with a party or something."

"Yes'm. Thank you."

Lila started home. Three dollars. Their oldest boy needed some new shoes; patches and paper stuffing was about all that held his old ones together. And if she had a piece of calico, she could finish that dress for little Clarice. And some new ticking for their mattress would sure be nice. Three dollars.

The wind was cold. She pulled her coat around her; it didn't help much, old and thin as it was. Maybe someone would come along and give her a ride.

CHAPTER
34

A basketball bounced against George's shins as he walked across the south end of the gymnasium. He picked it up and tossed it back to the boy who had been chasing it.

"Sorry, Mr. Hutto."

"That's all right, Tim." George watched as little Tim Dobbins dribbled back across the crowded floor, dodging through the calisthenics class toward the game in progress under the single goal on the north wall. Ever since that team from the Buffalo YMCA had played an exhibition game here just before Christmas, the boys had been wild about the new game from up north. They'd nearly warted him to death until he got the goal installed and some balls bought. He needed to find some volunteers to start a league, he guessed.

A Bible class was in session in the meeting room. George stepped inside quickly and closed the door against the noise of the gym. A few of the boys looked up at him as he stepped quietly along the back of the room toward the office. He slipped out his watch. Rev. Stiller was running over time, as usual. Some of the younger boys in the back were swinging their legs and staring at the ceiling. George wondered if he ought to give that young Baptist preacher a try for the next class. He'd heard the man held the view that a sermon should be strictly limited to an hour's length. Maybe he'd know how to liven things up a little for the boys.

George stepped into the office and sat behind the desk. The last stack of receipts still sat where he'd left it yesterday at lunchtime. He sighed. He needed to work down here full time, it seemed, to keep up with all the paperwork. But it wouldn't do the club any good for him to let his business die for lack of attention, either.

He heard the noise of the Bible class breaking up. He needed to say something to Rev. Stiller, but he had to get these receipts signed and posted to the donors. His door opened. He looked up, and there stood Ned Overby with a rough-looking character that could only be his father.

"You Mister Hutto?" the man said.

George stood and held out his hand. "Yes, I'm George Hutto."

The man wiped his hand on his pants leg and shook George's hand. "Overby. Perlie Overby. Ned here says you know each other."

"Ah, yes. Hello there, Ned. I was pretty lost one day out close to your place, and Ned got me back on the right track."

"Well, he knows the country pretty good, I reckon. Anyhow, Ned told me about this here club. Says there's book reading, and such."

"Yes, we've got several classes of various kinds." The pungent smell of Ned and his father—a mixture of bacon grease, tobacco, and body odor—was rapidly filling the small office. George stepped from behind the desk and held open the door. "Can I show you around?"

"That'd be fine, I reckon," Perlie said. "All right with you, boy?"

Ned shrugged and nodded.

George walked across the meeting room. "The Saturday boys' Bible class just left. Maybe you saw them as you came in." He opened the door to the gymnasium. "And out here we've got all kinds of exercise classes: calisthenics, weights, boxing—"

"Yeah, a boy needs to know how to take care of hisself, that's for sure."

"And Mr. Allen from the Carnegie Library comes over once a week to teach literature and loan books to the boys."

"Ned can read pretty good, can't you, boy? Now, uh, Mr. Hutto, I just wanna make sure of somethin'. We ain't got much in the way a money—"

"Oh, no, Mr. Overby. Some of the boys pay dues, but the YMCA doesn't exclude any boy on the basis of payment."

"Ned said it didn't cost nobody nothin'." Perlie's eyes flickered darkly toward his son. "Didn't you say so, boy? Now, we ain't interested in no charity."

Ned looked back and forth from his father to George.

"Of course not," George said, trying to think of something. "We've . . . we've got lots of jobs that need to be done around here, and I'd expect Ned to help out with his share, just like the others."

Perlie scratched his beard. It made a coarse, grating sound. "Well, then, in that case . . . I think he's pretty set on it, if you'll have him."

Ned was looking up at George. It was the first time George had ever been able to tell the boy really wanted something.

"I'd be especially happy for Ned to be here, if he wants to be."

Perlie looked at his son for a long time. "I guess that settles it, then. When can he come?"

"Why, he can stay here today, if you like. I can even bring him home."

"No, now, I'd hate to put you out like that. His two good legs got him here; they can take him home."

"No trouble at all. I've got another boy that lives out past Orchard Knob, and I can drop Ned off along the way."

"All right, then. Ned, boy, you pay attention to what Mr. Hutto says, you hear? You mind."

Ned nodded. George could see, even through the grime, the flush of excitement in the boy's cheeks.

He walked to the door with Ned and his father and waved Perlie on his way. When he closed the door and turned around, several of the boys were looking at Ned. They stared until they noticed George watching them, then they quickly went back to what they were doing.

Dan Sutherland looked at the telegram and shook his head. He looked at it again and rubbed his temples. There it was, plain as Western Union could make it. He ought to be pleased, or at least satisfied for his client. He'd hired out to protect Addie Douglas's interests, after all.

But he wasn't pleased and he wasn't satisfied. He was put out, was what he was, put out with the whole sorry world. This Douglas boy had seemed like a decent enough fellow. And Addie was dead-set enough on him to go up against her bullheaded Methodist of a father. Even without her father's approval, two young people could have made a worse start. And now this.

What went wrong? Something always did, seemed like. Church-going people or not, moneyed or not, town folks or country, people just had a hard time not treating each other poorly if you gave them enough time and chances. And you never knew, that was the thing. What started fair ended up foul; what started with love and promises ended up in spite and lies. People fooled you. Fooled themselves, most likely. He'd seen it often enough, he ought to be used to it by now. But he wasn't.

Dan folded the telegram and tucked it into his breastpocket. He went to the chair in the corner and got his hat. "Louis, I'll be out for awhile," he said as he passed the clerk's desk. "Ring up the livery and tell 'em to get my sulky hitched up." He paused in the doorway. "Oh, and draw up a check for three hundred dollars, payable to Albert Purvis of Little Rock, Arkansas. In the memorandum, put 'final payment.' I'll sign it when I get back."

Addie stared at the words on the yellow Western Union sheet. She thought she'd been prepared for this; for weeks now she'd imagined herself sitting at this table or at Mr. Sutherland's desk, hearing news like this.

She'd imagined herself crying or shouting or angry. But she'd never imagined what she felt now, with the proof in front of her. It was as if she sat at one end of a huge, long room, and Mr. Sutherland was at the other. She stared at the words until they blurred, but all she felt was a cold, hard void.

LITTLE ROCK JANUARY 17 1904
DAN SUTHERLAND, ATTORNEY
    CONFIRM SUBJ Z DOUGLAS CONSORTING WITH
WOMAN HERE STOP CAN PROVIDE TIMES AND
PLACES IF NEEDED STOP REASON TO BELIEVE SHE
IS WITH CHILD STOP
    SEND USUAL AMT STOP PURVIS

"Addie."

She blinked and looked up at him.

"Addie, I'm sure sorry to be having to bring this to you. But you had to know. For sure."

"Yes, sir, I— With child?"

"Yes, I'm afraid so."

"Who is this Purvis person?"

"That doesn't matter, Addie. He's just a man who finds out things for me sometimes."

She nodded. She swallowed, then brushed back a stray lock of hair. She looked around. "Jake . . . where's . . . I'd better—"

"Addie, now listen to me. We're going to have to sue him on the grounds of adultery. He'll be found at fault. And the way the laws read— here in Tennessee, anyway—he won't be allowed to marry this woman as long as you're alive. I don't know for sure what they'd do about it in Arkansas."

"Not marry?"

"That's right."

Addie thought about that for a minute, and then she was thinking about this other woman who was—who might be—carrying Zeb's child. Once he was divorced, he was banned from marrying her? She hadn't known that. But then, she hadn't spent much time thinking about the legalities of divorce. Not until Zeb informed her of his intentions, anyway.

Then she started to be surprised at herself for being able to form such sensible thoughts at all. Why, she might be a judge herself! What if Zeb had to come before her bench, plead his case in her court? What would he say? Would he apologize? Beg for clemency? Or would he list her sins against him, the ways she had driven him to this other woman's arms? No one thought of himself as truly wicked, did he? Surely Zeb had reasons that seemed fair in his own mind. What case would he present?

She realized Dan was saying something. He was looking at her strangely. "Addie, I need your approval to go ahead with this."

"My approval?"

"Yes. You have to have what the law calls a "nearest friend." A man to act on your behalf."

"Oh, of course."

"Might as well be me, I figure."

"Yes."

"All right, then." Mr. Sutherland got up from the table. "I'll be on my way. Need to get the papers drawn up." He turned his hat in his hands and gave her a studying look. "Addie, I'm real sorry about this. I'd sure never wish any of this on anybody."

"Yes, sir. Thank you."

"You want me to send for Junior? Or your sister?"

"Oh, well . . . yes, I guess that'd be nice."

He gave her one more long look. He put on his hat. He leaned over and took back the telegram. "I'll need this for evidence. You sure you're all right?"

"I'm— Yes."

He touched his hat brim. "Good day, then, Addie. I'll be in contact with you soon."

"Thank you, Mr. Sutherland."

"Now, I told you—"

"Oh, yes—Dan. Thank you, Dan."

"That's better."

Zeb walked into the agency and saw the man at Abner's desk. Abner looked up. "Well, speak of the devil. Zeb, somebody here to see you."

The man swiveled around. He held a light brown derby in one hand and a thick-looking envelope in the other. "You Zeb Douglas?" he asked.

"Yes. I don't believe I caught your name?"

Zeb stuck out his hand, and the man slapped the envelope into it.

"Legal papers, Mr. Douglas." He stood, put on his derby, and quickly walked out the door.

Abner stared after him for a few seconds, then looked at Zeb.

"What in thunder was that all about?"

Zeb looked at the envelope. There was no writing of any kind on the outside. He thumbed open his pocketknife and slid the blade under the flap. The first thing he saw on the sheaf of papers as he unfolded it was the seal of the State of Tennessee. The next thing he saw was the large, ornate printing across the top: "Bill of Divorce."

"Zeb? You all right?"

"Oh, I . . . yeah, Ab, I'm fine. I just . . ."

He wandered back toward his desk, his hat still on his head, his coat still buttoned. He sat down. His eyes swept back and forth across the close printing. There were blank lines in the document, and someone had penned, in a very neat hand, the words "D. L. Sutherland as nearest friend of the plaintiff, Adelaide Caswell Douglas." The same careful scribe had written Zeb's name in the blank reserved for "defendant." Zebediah Acton Douglas. He hadn't seen his full name written out like that since the announcement of their engagement was printed in the Chattanooga paper.

". . . sues on the aforenamed plaintiff's behalf for the cause of adulteries committed by the aforenamed defendant . . ."

Zeb had a sudden image of the man with the old black derby. What had he seen? Zeb clenched his jaw, trying to think what kind of scum would take money to spy on another man's private business. What had been relayed to Chattanooga to be pawed over by some lawyer? Zeb wanted to punch the derby man in the face. He wanted to make somebody pay, right now. This wasn't supposed to be the way it happened.

What in the world was he going to tell Becky?

He had to get out; he needed to think. He shoved the papers in the bottom drawer of his desk, all the way to the back. He pushed himself away from the desk and strode toward the door. He was vaguely aware of Abner's upturned, surprised face, and then he was outside.

He walked quickly, his arms swinging. He didn't know where he was going, and he didn't care. A horse pulling a dray down Cumberland Avenue shied and splashed water on him, and he barely noticed. He walked until he came to the railroad tracks fronting the river bluff, and he turned west. The wind hit him in the face and made his eyes water.

He came to the crossing of Water Street and North Ringo Avenue. He could see the trestles of the railroad bridge across the Arkansas River. His breath was coming harder now, and he was walking slower. He needed to stop somewhere. There was a small, mean-looking saloon on the northwest corner. The faded sign over the door named it "The Golden Horseshoe." He'd never been in a saloon in his life, but now seemed like a good enough time to start.

The first thing he noticed inside was the quiet, and that surprised him; he'd always imagined saloons as noisy. When his eyes had adjusted to the semidarkness, he saw an empty stool next to the plank bar. He straddled it and propped his hat on one knee.

"What'll you have?"

What does a man order in a saloon, anyway? "Beer," Zeb said.

The barkeep turned around and did something, then swung back and clumped a heavy glass mug onto the bar in front of him. Some of the beer slopped out and ran down the side of the mug. Zeb looked at the drink. It didn't look the way he'd generally heard beer described; it had a meager layer of suds on top, like dirty dishwater. He picked up the mug and took a tiny sip. The taste was bitter; he wrinkled his face but swallowed it anyway.

The barkeep was staring at him. "That'll be a nickel."

Zeb fished a five-cent piece out of his pocket and flipped it on the bar. It vanished under the barkeep's grubby fist.

Well, I've paid for it; might as well drink it. He picked up the mug and took a half dozen large swallows, trying not to taste, just get it down. He set down the mug and took a couple of deep breaths, then turned it up again until he'd drained it.

A thought flew through Zeb's head, a memory of his father. Daddy would've never set foot in a place like this. But then, Daddy wouldn't have gotten himself in such a mess, either. Zeb waggled the mug at the barkeep and dug out another nickel.

What was he supposed to do? Zeb guessed he'd need to talk to a lawyer. But did it matter? Once the divorce was done, he'd be shut of Addie, and good riddance. This whole thing was his idea to begin with, wasn't it? He was getting what he wanted, in a manner of speaking. He might just let her have her day, if that was what she wanted. Not even give her the satisfaction of darkening the courthouse door.

But . . . were there penalties for not showing up? What could they do to him if he didn't defend himself? Yes, he needed a lawyer.

One that didn't know Pete Norwich, preferably.

He was starting to feel a slight teetering sensation, somewhere in the center of his skull. It wasn't unpleasant, to tell the truth. He was sitting in a saloon drinking a beer and holding his problems out at arm's length, where he could see them. That's all it was—a problem. He'd solved problems before. He took two large gulps of beer and slapped another nickel on the bar.

Abner glanced up from his paperwork and saw her just as she stepped onto the boardwalk in front of the agency doorway. He had a quick thought of hiding but realized she was already too close; he'd never make it. He bent to his work and waited for her to come in, feeling a little bit like a condemned man listening for the step of his final escort. The door jangled. He met her with the best smile he could gather up.

"Afternoon, Miss Norwich."

"Good afternoon, Abner. Where's Mr. Douglas?"

"Well, now, I don't know, just exactly. He left outta here about an hour and a half ago, I guess, but he didn't say where he was going."

That didn't set well, it was easy to see. She had a light blue parasol in her right hand, and she was staring real hard at Zeb's desk and tapping that parasol across the heel of her left palm. Abner didn't think he wanted to know what she might do with that parasol if she had Zeb here right about now.

"Didn't say where he was going?"

"No, Miss, he sure didn't." She'd dropped all notions of smiling by now. Abner devoutly wished he was somewhere else.

"There's his valise, on the floor beside his desk. He didn't take it with him?"

"No, Miss Norwich, I guess he didn't."

"So he wasn't going out on business. Did he take anything with him?"

"No, not a thing. Except his hat and coat. And he—" Abner had a sudden desire to bite his own tongue.

"And he what?" The question came out quick, like a hen pecking at a june bug. She was looking at him now, and it wasn't a friendly look.

"Aw, nothing, really, Miss Norwich."

"And. He. What?"

"And . . . he'd just come in a minute or two before he left, so he never even took them off. His hat and coat, I mean."

She got a white, pinched-looking place around her lips. "Abner, did Mr. Douglas do or say anything else before he left?"

Keeping his eyes on the parasol, Abner said, "Yes, I guess—I guess there was one other thing. He . . . he looked at some papers right before he left."

"Papers?"

CHAPTER
35

*A*ddie drew her head back slowly, slowly, until she could look into Jake's face. His eyes were closed and he breathed in soft, sudden puffs. She stood as gingerly as she could and carried him to the bed, careful to step over the squeaking board in the doorway. She reached the side of the bed and leaned over with him, so gradually that the muscles in her back started to complain. She got him onto the mattress and pulled her arm from beneath him, watching his face for any sign of disturbance. Just as she pulled her hand from beneath him, he gave a little whimper. She froze. His eyes never opened. She covered him with the Dutch doll quilt and tiptoed from the room.

Finally. Jake had been cranky all morning, needing her every second. And naturally, Mary Alice had seen to it that Mama's attention had to be divided. After a meager lunch of toast and milk, she'd made Mary Alice go to her bed for a nap. But only after nearly two hours of alternated rocking and walking had she been able to get Jake to sleep.

Addie felt like lying down herself. But she was afraid if she stopped moving or doing, she'd fall down in a hole so deep she'd never climb out again. It was hard today; the sadness was on her like a lead-lined overcoat.

She went to the window and pulled aside the curtain. The winter sunlight lay thin on the late afternoon. She let the curtain fall back in place and looked around the parlor. Her eye fell on the Bible her Epworth

League class had given her as a wedding gift. It lay on a side table at the end of the horsehair sofa. She went over to the table and picked up the Bible. The binding was still stiff, almost like new. She carried it to the armchair near the window. She sat down and put the Bible on her lap. She thought about trying to pray but decided she lacked the strength to wrestle with the Almighty.

She opened the Bible, spreading the pages out from the center, handling them like fine linen.

> And Jeremiah said, The word of the LORD came unto me, saying, Behold, Hanameel the son of Shallum thine uncle shall come unto thee, saying, Buy thee my field that is in Anathoth: for the right of redemption is thine to buy it. So Hanameel mine uncle's son came to me in the court of the prison according to the word of the LORD, and said unto me, Buy my field, I pray thee, that is in Anathoth, which is in the country of Benjamin: for the right of inheritance is thine, and the redemption is thine; buy it for thyself. Then I knew that this was the word of the LORD. And I bought the field of Hanameel my uncle's son, that was in Anathoth, and weighed him the money, even seventeen shekels of silver . . .

Her eyes drifted on down the page. She read God's promise to the imprisoned prophet: his real estate investment was to be a sign that even though Babylon was about to destroy Jerusalem and enslave her people, houses and lands would again one day be bought and sold in Judah. But it sounded like that day was on the far side of a lot of suffering and trouble.

Addie leaned her head on the back of the chair. She didn't want Zeb's money, not really. Come to think of it, he didn't have anything she wanted. She wanted to be completely free of him. Maybe she didn't want to leave him with any excuse, any way to take credit for whatever she might do or make of herself. Her children had his name; that was enough. It was more than you could say for the poor child being carried by his paramour.

She guessed she needed to tell Dan Sutherland. As far as she knew, the lawyer was still planning to get everything he could from Zeb. No point in that, as far as she could see.

Of course, that also meant she'd have to do something about her own support that much sooner. The little bit of money Junior had loaned her was about to run out, and she strictly did not want to live off her brothers and sister, however willing they might be to help out.

She pushed herself up out of the chair. Dropping the Bible onto the side table, she wandered back through the house. She arrived at the door to her bedroom. She hadn't even made up her bed today; the sheets and quilts still lay tangled up, just as she'd crawled out of them this morning. She could see the edge of her new bedspread, draped haphazardly along one side of the bed.

Addie went over to the bed and picked up a corner of the spread. She ran her thumb along the line of the tufting, then bunched the material in her hand. Didn't seem to be all that much to it. Maybe she ought to go out and talk to the old German woman at Brown's Ferry, see if she ever needed any piecework.

Orange light slanted through the windows. Nearly sunset. Part of her wanted to just let Mary Alice sleep, wanted to go and sit in the parlor and let the house fall dark around her and do pretty close to nothing for as long as she could. But she guessed she'd better try and find something to feed the child, or she'd wake up hungry and scared and twice as hard to manage as before her nap.

Her steps sounded dry and insubstantial, creaking on the floorboards as she walked back toward the kitchen.

Becky smelled him before she saw him. He'd slid off one side of his bed, it looked like; he was crumpled between the bed and the wall. The front of his clothes was sodden, she guessed with his own vomit.

"Lord, help us all," she said. "Is this what we've come to?"

One of his eyes tried to open, but couldn't. "Becky. Oughtta not use . . . Lord's name in vain."

"Oh, is that what you thought I was doing? No, Zeb, I believe that was about as sincere a prayer as I've ever said." She tossed the divorce bill onto his chest and stood over him with her arms crossed.

He fumbled for the papers a second or two before he could grasp them. He held them up and tried to look at them. His head lolled back and he moaned. The arm holding the papers fell limply to one side. "How'd you get hold of this?"

"You'd better not worry about that. That's the least of your problems, don't you think?"

"Becky—"

"Zeb, how could you! You lied to me—and to your wife, too, looks like. If my father knew—"

"No! Now, Becky . . ." He struggled, then pulled himself into a sitting position. He grimaced and grabbed his forehead, like he was afraid it might come off. "Becky, what good's it gonna do for you to tell Pete?"

"I'm not sure it'll do any good," she said. "But if it got you a good horsewhipping, it might be worth it anyway. If I could see that before he turned me out of the house—" The rest of it lodged in her throat. Then the sobs built up enough force to break the jam. She sank down on the foot of the bed and held her face in her hands, and the desolation poured out of her in a sour-tasting flood. "Oh, God. Please, God, help me."

In a little while, he got himself onto his feet. Holding on to the wall, he made his way to the washstand. He splashed some water on his face and wiped it on his sleeve. He weaved back toward her and sat heavily on the bed beside her. He tried to take her hand, but she pulled it away.

"I'm not in the habit of holding hands with somebody who smells like puke."

"Becky, now listen to me. I've . . . I'm sorry. I never meant for you to find out this way."

"Oh. When were you planning to let me know?"

He kneaded his forehead. "I don't deserve anything from you but a cussing, I guess."

She got up and walked across the room, hugging herself. "Zeb, what in the world am I going to do? I'm carrying your child, and that's bad enough, but I let myself go too far because I loved you, and I thought you loved me. And now I find out—"

"I do! Becky, I do love you, that's what I want to say. I love you, and . . . and we'll work this out. I'll stand by you, Becky. I will."

She turned and looked at him. "Like you stood by your wife?"

For awhile he just sat there, staring at the floor. "Becky, I've made some bad mistakes. I've done some wrong things." He looked at her. "But loving you wasn't one of them. Addie, she—"

"That's her name?"

"She never saw me the way you see me. She never could." He stood, and for a second she thought he was going to topple. But he balanced himself, then came toward her. He put out a hand, and for some reason she didn't understand, she took it.

"Becky, I just need some time to think. There's a way out of this, I know it. I just have to figure out what it is. I promise, I won't leave you. I couldn't."

She looked at her hand in his. Then she looked into his face. "Well, you better get to thinking, Mr. Douglas. I'm nearly two and a half months gone, and before long I won't be able to keep our little secret anymore. So you'd best come up with something good, and do it mighty soon." She pulled her hand from his and walked to the door. "I'll be waiting to hear," she said, and then she left.

Mary Alice was squirming again. She wanted to lay her head in Addie's lap. So, for at least the third time that morning, Addie peeled back her bonnet and Mary Alice lay down. The heels of her shoes clomped loudly on the pew as she stretched her legs.

Then Jake began to fret. He couldn't be hungry; she'd fed him just before the service started. She jogged him up and down and tried to get him to take the fooler in his mouth, but he just spat it out every time she plugged it in. She blew little puffs of air in his face. That distracted him for a minute; he blinked and tried to see where the strange sensation was coming from.

It was hard to pay any attention at all to J. D.'s sermon, though she was trying. He'd employed a chart today, a tattered sheet tacked onto the wall behind the pulpit. J. D. had his main points daubed onto it with tempera paint. He couldn't talk his wife out of one of her good sheets, Addie guessed, even if it was for the Lord's work.

There was a big red cross painted in the middle of the sheet, representing the cross of Christ. On the left side of the cross were the laws of the Jews, the Old Covenant; and on the right side, the laws of the Church, the New Covenant. It would have been a tedious enough sermon even without the two children to entertain. J. D. cited two or three Scriptures for every law on both sides of the cross. His main point was supposed to be the superiority of the New Covenant over the Old, but Addie was about to get to the place where she'd vote for either one if it would help J. D. to finish what he had to say and let her take herself and these children home.

"Well, brethren, the Lord's established his New Covenant kingdom, and he's set its laws in place. They're good laws, laws meant for our protection. But before we can get the benefit of those laws, we've first got to enter that kingdom.

"We've got to hear the word and believe it, for faith cometh by hearing—Romans ten, seventeen. We've got to repent of our sins and our former ways of life, and confess the name of Jesus before men, for with the mouth confession is made—Romans ten and verse ten. And brethren, we must be baptized for the remission of our sins, 'For as many of you as have been baptized into Christ have put on Christ'—Galatians three, twenty-seven."

Getting close to the end for sure, now. As best Addie could tell, there wasn't a single person in the room old enough to make sense of J. D.'s words who wasn't already a baptized member of Post Oak Hollow Church. But he had to give his altar call, just the same. You never knew, an unbaptized sinner might've slipped in the back door without him knowing it.

The congregation stood to sing the final hymn. Addie roused Mary Alice and got the bonnet back in place, after a fashion. She bounced Jake on her hip until the final chorus slid to a halt and the crowd started to disperse.

"Good to see you, Addie."

"Morning, Sister Clay. Good to see you too."

"That little one there is just growin' up a storm, isn't he?"

"Fussing up a storm, anyway."

Sister Clay grinned and wiggled a forefinger at Jake, who twisted his face away as if he'd been insulted. The old woman patted Mary Alice on the head and gave Addie a final look before moving away down the aisle toward the back door.

That last look was what Addie dreaded—the pitying, pious look. *Poor woman, raising those two precious children without a daddy . . .* She knew the thought came from a good place, a well-meaning place. But it was also a constant reminder of things she wished she didn't have to think about. Things they all knew, too, but would never speak of. Not to her, at least.

The back door was open now. Addie bundled the blankets tighter around Jake and checked to make sure Mary Alice's coat was buttoned all the way up. She shuffled along the aisle, balancing Jake on her hip with one hand and holding onto Mary Alice with the other.

"Mama, we go Aunt Lou's?"

"No, honey, not today."

"Aunt Lou's." Mary Alice whimpered. "Go Aunt Lou's."

"Sweetheart, not today."

"Why not?"

"Just because."

"Go Aunt Lou's."

"No."

Lou and Dub and their boys would be leaving Centenary Methodist about now. They'd visit with the people Addie had known all her life, they'd speak a complimentary word about the sermon to Rev. Stiller at the back door. They'd walk down the tall flight of concrete steps to the sidewalk and have a nice stroll along Georgia Avenue until they came to their street. They'd go in the house and smell the roast or whatever else Lou had baking in the oven for their Sunday dinner.

Every now and then, Addie wondered why she kept on coming out to this dingy little whitewashed clapboard building in the middle of nowhere, Sunday after Sunday, where the people knew her only as the woman Zeb Douglas had left—if they even knew that much about her. Dub and Lou would gladly come out to the house and pick her up. They'd take her and the children with them to church in the lovely old building downtown, then to their house for a delicious lunch Addie wouldn't have to cook. There would be other sets of arms to hold children, cousins to distract them, a fire already laid in the hearth.

But something reared up stubborn inside her every time she thought about it. Going back to the Methodist church seemed to her like just one more way of admitting she'd been wrong about everything all her life. *Well, Zeb's not around to tell her what to think anymore, so maybe now she'll come back where she belonged in the first place . . .* It was too easy, some-how—too expected. She wouldn't let her weight down on it.

And would things really be much different at Centenary Methodist? Wouldn't she get the same pitying looks? Wouldn't the same tut-tuts be whispered behind her back? She released Mary Alice's hand so she could mind her skirts going down the outside steps.

"Sister Addie, we're ready whenever you are," Dink Gilliam said as she turned to help Mary Alice down the steps. His wife and four children were already in the buckboard. Addie was glad; as cool as it was, she hadn't relished the thought of standing in the churchyard making conversation until her ride was ready to leave.

She handed Jake up to Dink's oldest daughter and took his hand to make the step up into the wagon. Dink lifted Mary Alice up to her. He climbed in on the other side and the springs complained loudly. "Get up," he said, and his jug-headed bay leaned into the traces.

"Nice weather, for February," Maud Gilliam said awhile later as they clattered over the Cellico Creek bridge. Addie smiled and nodded.

"Mama, look at him. He's smilin' at me," said the daughter who was holding Jake. Addie hated to tell her it was probably just a gas spasm.

"Brother J. D. sure had a good lesson today," Maud said.

Addie nodded again. She hoped Maud didn't ask her opinion; she was too brain-tired to be up to the polite fib she'd have to tell.

"Mama, 's go Aunt Lou's," Mary Alice said, jouncing along in the bed of the buckboard between Addie's knees.

"No, honey. I already told you."

"You mind your mother, sugar," said Maud, giving Mary Alice a fond, admonishing look. "You want to be a sweet little girl, don't you?"

Mary Alice looked at Maud as if she'd just suggested asparagus for dessert.

"I got me one of those new turfed bedspreads," Maud said. "Have you seen 'em?"

Addie shook her head, confused. "Turfed?"

"Yeah, you know—a row of turfing on a smooth background." Maud gestured in loops and circles.

Tufted, Addie guessed. "Oh, yes, I got one for Christmas from my sister."

Maud looked a little disappointed. "I found it up by Brown's Ferry."

"The German woman?"

Maud nodded. "Land, she's sure got the business. The day I was there, they was two in line ahead of me and more comin' behind. These turfed spreads are all the fashion nowadays. Wished I'd of thought it up."

"I guess so. I sure like mine."

"Me too."

Addie was relieved to see her lane coming up. Dink hauled up in front of her porch and got off to help them down. He set Mary Alice on the ground and handed Addie down. She turned and took Jake from the daughter.

"I wish I could keep him all the time. He's so sweet," the girl said.

Addie smiled up at her. "You'd get tired of him pretty quick, honey."

"But he's so sweet."

"Well. Thanks for holding him."

"Need me to do anything 'fore we leave, Sister Addie?"

"No, thank you, Dink. We're fine."

Dink climbed back in the wagon. He slapped the reins lightly on the bay's rump, and they trundled off. "Come home with us some Sunday; I'll show you my bedspread," Maud called as they pulled away.

Addie smiled and nodded. She waved, then turned toward the house. "Come on, Mary Alice, let's get inside. It's cool out."

CHAPTER
36

*L*ila spread her palms on the small of her back and grimaced as she tried to stretch the stiff muscles. Her head ached too. She'd sat up late last night, trying to finish Clarice's dress. It was about all she could handle this morning to scrounge up some day-old cornbread for the children to eat on their way to school.

She was worried about Willie. Deacon Green had sent a note home with their middle boy saying he'd been getting into a lot of scrapes lately, during recess and after school. It was a shame, the principal said, because Willie was smart enough to do anything he wanted to do; he just didn't want to stay out of trouble, looked like. Deacon Green thought Willie's parents ought to know.

She talked to Mason, but his answer didn't go much past whipping the boy again. So far, that hadn't done much good.

Lila had hopes for Willie. Something told her he was special. Now, Mason Junior was a good son, respectful and hardworking, levelheaded. And the two girls minded and were good to help with the chores and their baby brother.

But Willie had something extra. He was more than just able; he had a gleam about him. That mind of his just naturally stayed about a half a jump ahead of everybody else. Hadn't he been talking like the grown folks since he was two years old? Didn't he remember every story he'd ever heard anybody tell, and couldn't he tell it just like they did, their voice and movements and expressions and all? Oh, he could shine, Willie could—when he wanted to.

Lila didn't want Willie to end up working in a foundry or a railyard. He could do more than that, be more. She just knew he could. Of course, he could also end up a lot worse.

Lila climbed the steps up to the Dawkins's back door. She raised her hand to knock, but the door yanked open.

"Oh, Lila, thank goodness you're here! I just got a call from Mamie O'Dell and the Women's Study Group was supposed to meet at Lucy Hawkins's today but Lucy's sick and Mamie wants to know if they can come here instead and I don't have a thing ready but I told her yes and oh there's so much to do. Come in, come in, I need you to start dusting the parlor while I try to figure out what in the world I can fix right quick to go with the tea and coffee . . ."

"Yes'm."

The preacher's voice droned in and out of Ned's ears like the buzz of grasshoppers in the bushes on a summer afternoon. The boy on his left had his chin on his chest, and a little spot of drool had begun to wet the front of his shirt. The one on his right had turned to the boy on the other side and was whispering something behind his hand.

Ned hoped the preacher didn't notice the pile of wood chips growing in front of his chair. He probably wouldn't, all the way on the back row.

He reached down to scratch his ankle. The shoes were still new enough to chafe. Most of the other boys had stockings. That would help some, Ned guessed. But he wasn't likely to get any. And stiff shoes were better than barefoot.

He turned the wild cherry block in his hand, eyeing it critically. He didn't like the curve of the dove's breast. He shaved off a little here and there, then a little more. He looked at it again and thought about the dove he'd seen yesterday near sundown, perched on the dogwood branch just under the eaves of the woods across the tracks from his house. The dogwoods were about ready to bloom, and the redbuds. He was glad the warmer days were close.

Ned wished he knew how to paint. If he did, he could cover the finished carving with the soft, pink-brown of the mourning dove's plumage, its belly a few shades lighter. He could paint in the black eyes, tiny and round as drops of water in the delicate head. He might even try the black spackling of the wing bars, the dark primaries outlined in white, folded against the bird's body.

The boy on his right snickered. "Hey, peckerwood," he said, his hand cupped so it sent the whisper toward Ned. "Peckerwood. Where'd you steal that Barlow?"

Ned kept his head down, his hands moving steadily over the block of cherry.

"Hey, we're talkin' to you, peckerwood," said the boy on the other side, leaning past the boy on Ned's right. "You ever learn to talk?"

Ned's eyes flickered at them. Town boys. The one next to him was smaller, but the one on the other side was bigger. Ned had watched him in boxing class. When Mr. Fairchild wasn't looking, he'd rabbit punch his opponents.

"You better say something, peckerwood," the bigger one whispered, "or we'll catch you after class and give you some talking lessons." The boy on Ned's right snickered again.

"I ain't did nothin' to you." Ned looked nervously toward the preacher.

"'I ain't did nothin' to you.'" The smaller boy imitated Ned's voice. "That how your peckerwood mama taught you to talk?" The two boys smirked.

"Taught him to talk like she taught him to bathe," the bigger one said, and they giggled some more.

Ned felt the back of his neck tingling and getting hot. His knuckles were white where he gripped the wood. He nearly cut himself.

"Let us pray," said the preacher. All the boys bowed their heads. During the prayer, one of the boys reached over and thumped Ned's ear. He heard them laughing quietly. When the prayer was over and everybody was hurrying out of the classroom, the big boy got between Ned and the preacher and grabbed a handful of Ned's shirt.

"Come on, peckerwood. Let's go outside."

"Ned. Can you come here a minute?"

It was Mr. Hutto. He was standing in the doorway of his office, looking right at Ned and his two tormentors. Ned looked up at the big boy, and he had a disgusted expression.

"You got lucky today, peckerwood," the boy said in a low voice, turning Ned loose. "But I'll be around." He and his smaller companion slouched out of the classroom, their hands shoved in their pockets.

Ned walked over to Mr. Hutto. Mr. Hutto was watching the two other boys leave. Then he looked down at Ned.

"What have you got there, Ned?"

Ned ducked his head. He shrugged.

"Please, Ned. Let me see it." Mr. Hutto held out his hand.

Ned dug in the pocket of his overalls and removed the carving. He put it in Mr. Hutto's hand.

"Sorry, Mr. Hutto. I won't carve in Bible class no more—"

"This is pretty good, Ned. How long have you been doing this kind of thing?"

Ned shrugged. Mr. Hutto didn't say anything for a long time.

"Ned, I've been thinking about finding someone to start an art class. If I could, would you be interested in taking it?"

Ned looked up at him. "Yes, sir. I reckon."

Mr. Hutto handed Ned the dove. "Here. You'll want to finish it, I expect."

"Yes, sir." Ned stuck the wood back down in his pocket.

"I need to go out to Orchard Knob on some business. You want to ride home in my car?"

Ned shrugged, then nodded.

"Come on, then. Let's go."

Dan Sutherland smelled a rat. It was nearly the middle of March and Zeb Douglas still hadn't filed a response to the divorce complaint he'd been served in late January. Dan didn't know what kind of law they practiced in Arkansas, but any fool with a shingle and half sense ought to know Zeb stood to lose big if he didn't contest the issues.

He scribbled a note and hollered for his clerk.

"Louis, take this down to the telegraph office and have them send it right away. Oh, and here—" He took a twenty-dollar gold piece out of his vest pocket and handed it to the clerk. "Along with the note, cable as much as this'll buy to the same recipient."

Louis looked down at the note. "The Purvis fellow again?"

Dan nodded. "Hurry up, now. It's getting toward evening and the Western Union office'll be closed before too long."

Louis went out, and a few seconds later Dan heard the front door open and close.

What might a man do if he was in the kind of pickle Zeb Douglas was in? Dan leaned back in his chair and reached into his humidor for a cigar. He didn't light it, just rolled it around in his mouth while he stared at the ceiling.

Becky stared out the hotel window at the stand of scraggly yellow pines across the street. She hoped Zeb would remember to bring back the soda crackers she'd asked for. He'd sure been gone long enough, seemed like. But what else could she do except wait? Even if she felt like going out and hunting for him, she hadn't learned enough about Texarkana to have any notion of where to start. And right now, the thought of standing up and walking around in the dust and noise of this tacky little town was almost enough to make her stomach turn inside out. In fact, nearly anything was enough to make her stomach turn inside out. She hoped this phase of the pregnancy would pass soon.

Waiting on Zeb. That was pretty much her life, ever since that night when she found him passed out drunk in his flat.

When he came to her house a few days later and smiled himself past Mother and Daddy, she already had a feeling what he was going to say. As they turned onto the street in front of the house, her hand on his arm, he told her he had two tickets bought. They could leave for Texas in three days' time, he said. Nobody would have to know anything.

"What about your divorce?"

"I've got that all taken care of."

Part of her wanted to press for details, and part of her didn't care, as long as she had some choice besides staying in Little Rock and facing the shame of watching people's faces as they found out the truth about her. Two rail tickets to somewhere else. Maybe it was better not to know.

An elopement, Zeb had called it. More like a getaway, or a self-imposed exile.

She heard his step coming down the hallway. She turned away from the window just as his key rattled in the lock. The door swung open and there he stood, all smiles, one hand holding up a little white paper sack and the other hand behind his back.

"Hello, there, lovely lady. I brought you something."

"Did you find some crackers?"

"Sure did." He handed her the sack, then brought out the other hand. "And one more thing." It was a sheet of paper covered on one side with ornate printing. He laid it on the foot of the bed with a little flourish.

A marriage license.

"Well?"

He was grinning like a possum in the henhouse. Like he'd just handed her the key to a chest full of diamonds and rubies.

"Oh, Zeb, I—"

"You're what? You're ready to go hunt for the first justice of the peace we can find? Well, whenever you're ready, we'll just go and get this thing officialized."

She looked at the license, then at him. One corner of his grin started to wilt just a little bit.

"Becky? You're . . . you're still my girl, aren't you?"

She dragged out part of a smile from somewhere. She crossed the few steps to him and put her face against his chest. His arms went around her, and a moment later, hers went around him.

She was happy. Wasn't that what she was supposed to be feeling right now?

"Becky, it'll be all right. You'll see. Everything's gonna be all right."

Yes. Happy. That had to be it.

Addie watched as Lou braided Mary Alice's hair. The little girl sat perfectly still in her aunt's lap, her eyes flickering around the room to see who might be noticing all the attention she was getting. Dub sat by the window, reading the newspaper. The boys were outside; Robert was trying to teach Ewell how to hit a baseball.

"Lunch sure was good, Lou," Addie said, stretching her arm along the back of the settee. "Thank you again for having us."

Lou made a dismissing sound. "Family's family. You're always welcome."

"I was wondering—could you take me over to Brown's Ferry sometime, to that lady who sold you my bedspread?"

"Mrs. Langfeld? Sure, I guess, if you want to."

"I wonder if she'd show me how she does that tufted stitching. It doesn't look too hard."

Louisa gave Mary Alice's braids a final tug and pat. "There you go, Miss Mary Alice. You look just like a little milkmaid now. Go play."

Mary Alice slid down from Louisa's lap. "I wanna see 'em." She dashed from the parlor and up the stairs toward the mirror on the second-floor landing.

"That girl's as vain as a peacock," Louisa said, smiling after her.

"Well, you're not helping her any," said Dub from behind the paper.

"Oh, you hush, Dub. Nobody rattled your chain."

"She loves the attention," Addie said.

"It's mutual," Dub said.

"What if we go to Mrs. Langfeld's Tuesday?" Louisa asked, giving Dub the evil eye. "What time would you want to go?"

"Oh, doesn't make me much difference, I don't guess. Just not too early. It's hard for me to get the kids ready much before nine."

"Why don't you just bring them here and let Lila watch them while we go? She gets here between eight-thirty and nine."

"Well, but if Jake gets hungry—"

"Then we'll bring him with us. Mary Alice can have the run of the house. Lila's the sweetest, most agreeable thing you ever saw. Mary Alice'll be fine till we get back. And then you and I can get caught up on things on the way there and back."

"Lila? Isn't that—"

"Mason's Lila. Rose's daughter-in-law."

"You want me to have Jimmy pick you up?" Dub said.

"I guess," Louisa said. "Brown's Ferry's a little too far to walk, and I just hate the streetcars."

"I'll have him come by your place first, Addie."

"Thanks, Dub."

Bertie Langfeld didn't look anything like Addie had imagined her. For some reason, Addie always thought of Germans as big people. But Bertie was a small, sharp-faced woman who looked at her with quick eyes and spoke in jerky sentences that almost sounded like barking.

"You want to see the tufting, *jah?* So. I'll show you. But. Only this once. I got good business, *jah?* I don't give no more free lessons."

Stacked all around the room were bolts and bolts of cotton broadcloth of nearly every color Addie could imagine. Bertie gathered up a pile of cloth draped over a chair and seated herself.

"So. The design you trace, *jah?*"

Addie could see the lines penciled on the broadcloth. She nodded.

"You stitch in the design." Bertie made several quick, precise stitches, leaving the thread in loops. Then she took up a pair of scissors and snipped a few inches along the line of stitching, severing the loops and leaving a neat row of wicking.

Bertie looked up at her. Addie nodded again. "Yes. I see."

"So. You finish the design, you got a nice tufted bedspread. Some people they use thicker stuff for the rugs. But me. I do the bedspreads."

"Thank you, Mrs. Langfeld."

Bertie gave her a quick, tight-lipped nod. Her eyes flickered back and forth between Addie and Louisa, who stood quietly off to one side, gently bouncing Jake in her arms.

"I heard about what happened," Bertie said. She shook her head. "Him running off on you like that. Bad thing. You pick out some cloth to take with you. To get started."

"Oh, Mrs. Langfeld! I couldn't."

"*Jah.* You take some cloth." She laid aside her work and walked to one of the stacks of broadcloth. "This one. You take the peach. Get you some nice cream-colored thread. Make a nice bedspread. Very popular. So." She thrust the bolt toward Addie.

Addie looked at Louisa, then back at Bertie. "Well, Mrs. Langfeld—"

"Bertie. Here."

Addie took the cloth. "How can I ever thank you?"

Bertie's shoulders twitched a shrug. "You got babies to feed. Go. Make a nice bedspread."

They walked out onto the front porch. Jimmy was waiting in the Oldsmobile, his hand in the same position on the steering tiller it had been in when Addie and Louisa went inside. He saw them come out and leaned over to crank the engine.

"Thank you so much, Bertie," Louisa said. "You've been so kind to my sister."

"Yes, thank you," Addie said. They went down the steps and reached the car just as the ignition caught. Jimmy rushed around to open the door for them.

"You have any trouble, you come back," Bertie shouted over the din of the auto. "I maybe help you. Just a little more, *jah?*"

CHAPTER
37

I wish you'd look at that," Louisa said, nodding toward Jake. "He's trying to see where the sound's coming from."

The baby writhed in Addie's lap, twisting his face toward the front of the auto. At first, Addie had expected the noise of the engines to frighten him, but from the first time Dub had picked them up for Sunday lunch in his Curved Dash, Jake had been fascinated with every one of the loud, smelly contraptions he encountered. This morning, when Jimmy came to fetch them, Mary Alice had stayed on the front porch with her hands over her ears, but Jake had acted like he was trying to jump out of Addie's arms and crawl into the driver's lap.

They turned off the road into Addie's lane. "Isn't that Dan Sutherland's rig in front of your house?" Louisa said, craning her neck.

"Looks like it might be."

As they got closer to the house, they saw Dan get out of the sulky and walk around to his horse's head. He held the halter as the chestnut tossed its head and tried to back out of the traces.

"Stop here, Jimmy," Louisa said, leaning over the seat. "This car'll spook Mr. Sutherland's horse."

"Yes'm." Jimmy eased off the throttle and pulled on the hand brake. He started to get out.

"That's all right, Jimmy. We can manage," Addie said.

"Yes'm." He touched his cap as Addie stepped onto the ground.

Addie helped Mary Alice down and gripped Jake with the other arm. He made an irritated noise and tried to climb back into the Oldsmobile. Louisa handed out the bolt of broadcloth. Addie waved to her as Jimmy backed slowly down the lane. She turned and walked toward the house. Jake tried to climb over her shoulder and get back to the auto. She made Mary Alice carry the cloth so she could wrestle with him.

"Getting so you can't take a peaceful drive out into the country anymore," Dan said when they reached him. The horse had quieted, but Addie could still see the whites of its eyes as it rolled them toward the receding noise of the car. Lather dripped to the ground from where it nervously tongued the bit.

"Sorry, Dan."

"Oh, that's all right. I guess I'll have to give in and get me one of the clattertraps, pretty soon. Scare somebody else's horse, for a change." He touched the brim of his hat. "Good to see you again, Addie. How you doing?"

"Fine, thank you."

He looked at her. "Really?"

"What brings you out, Dan?"

"Why don't we go inside and sit down? I'll tell you all about it."

"Do you have any candy?" Mary Alice said.

"Mary Alice!"

Dan laughed. "Well, yes, ma'am, it just so happens I do." He looked a question at Addie. She rolled her eyes and nodded. He reached into his breastpocket and took out a shiny peppermint stick. "How's that?" he said, leaning over to Mary Alice.

She grinned, then dropped the cloth and took the stick. She turned around and flounced up the front porch steps. Jake made a noise and reached toward his sister.

"No, sir, not until you've got a few more teeth," Addie said.

"I'll get this," Dan said, bending to pick up the cloth.

They went inside. She put Jake on the floor in the nursery and went into the parlor. Dan sat on one of the armchairs, his legs crossed and his hat on his knee.

"Would you like some coffee? Or, I've got a spice cake."

"No, thanks, Addie. I've got things waiting on me back at the office."

She sat across from him, on the settee. "Well, what brings you all this way on a workday?"

He looked at her. "Addie, Zeb's gone."

"Gone?"

"Left. Lit out. Him and that other woman. Got a telegram from my man down there yesterday evening. A couple of weeks ago, looks like, he drew all the money out of his bank accounts, bought two railway tickets, and neither he nor the woman have been seen in Little Rock since."

It was several moments before any words would form in her mind. "Where?"

"Don't know. My man couldn't find that out."

So somebody really could do this, Addie thought. *They could share your life, father your children, and then they could just leave, just vanish. They could pack up and go and never look back.*

"What'll I . . . How can—"

"Addie, he's been served the papers. If he doesn't appear in court, the judge will rule in your favor on every element of the complaint." He waited for awhile, watching her. "Still, I think I'd advise one more thing, just to make sure we've covered ourselves."

"What?"

"There's a thing called constructive service. Usually, it's applied when a party wants to sue for divorce, but the spouse can't be found. That's not exactly where we are; we sued him and served him, but now we can't find him. What I'd do is I'd take out ads in the newspapers. I'd post notices in the courthouse, whatever. Just to make double sure he can't come back later and say he didn't know our intentions."

"But he's not in Little Rock anymore."

"No, but there's plenty of folks there who knew him, and the woman too. Word'll get back, I bet. If anything can flush him out, this is it. And if it doesn't, we haven't lost anything."

"We haven't?"

He looked at his hat, dusted it with the heel of his hand. "You know what I mean, Addie."

He stood up. "Well, I've got to get on back. No rest for the weary, I guess."

"I guess not."

"Addie, I'm—"

"I know, Dan. Thank you. It's all right. I'm all right. Just go on and do what you need to do."

"Well. All right, then. Good day to you."

"And to you, Dan. Thank you for coming."

"Least I could do."

He left. Addie stayed on the settee, thinking about constructive service. An odd term to apply to a divorce proceeding. What would Dan's notice say? Would the Little Rock newspaper carry a catalog of all her hurts and grievances? No, probably not. There would probably be a long paragraph made up of a single sentence, salted with lots of semicolons and wherefores and parties of the first part aforesaid. It would say exactly what it needed to, most likely; it would achieve exactly the aim Dan Sutherland had in mind.

But the words wouldn't tell anymore about the truth of Zeb and her than the label on a tin of powdered milk would tell you about a cow. Dan's words would be proper but not accurate. They would be like a screen; they would protect, but they would also conceal.

She tried to imagine herself writing the notice. If she got to choose the words, what would they be? *Adelaide Caswell Douglas is divorcing Zebediah Acton Douglas on the grounds that she has no choice. He loved her, and then he didn't, and there was nothing she could do about it, so why bother to try?*

She couldn't even tell you when it started happening, could she? Couldn't pinpoint the hour or even the week when her weight of expectation and unfulfilled hopes started to drag him down and make him wish for something else, someone else—which he found, as it turned out.

What was she like, this other woman? What was the shape of her hands, her face? Did she resemble Addie in any way? For a minute, Addie wondered if she'd feel any better if she knew Zeb had left her for someone who reminded him of his wife on a good day. But somehow she doubted it. Doubted a man would do that, and doubted it would make her feel any better to know.

Adelaide Caswell Douglas wishes to announce her permanent disengagement from the man formerly known as her husband. May he rest in peace, amen.

She wished it were that easy.

She heard an automobile popping and backfiring, slowing as it neared her lane. Why would Lou be coming back? She got up and went out onto the front porch.

It wasn't Lou. The car had stopped at the opening of the lane. Someone got out of the passenger side and crossed in front of the car. A boy. He waved to the driver and walked down her lane.

Ned Overby. So the car belonged to George Hutto; he was bringing Ned back from a meeting at that new boy's club he'd started in the old cotton warehouse downtown.

Addie hurried back in the house, to the kitchen. She found an apple and quickly sliced off a hunk of the spice cake. Wrapping the food in a dish towel, she went back to the front porch. When she came out, Ned was just stepping off the lane to cut across her yard toward the woods.

"Hello, Ned. How about a treat?" She held up the bundle.

He glanced toward her, then turned and walked over to the porch. He wouldn't look at her. He never did.

"There's an apple in here, and a piece of cake. Thought you might like a little snack for your walk home."

He shrugged and nodded. She put the bundle in his hands.

"Thank you, ma'am."

"You're welcome, Ned. Tell your mother and daddy I said hello."

"Yes, ma'am." He shambled off around the corner of the house.

She turned to go back inside and noticed George's car was still stopped at the opening of the lane. He waved, and she returned the wave. He pulled a little way into the lane and stopped, then backed onto the road to return the way he'd come. He waved once more and drove off toward town.

Louisa opened the door and paused in surprise. Lila stood there, all right, but a little boy was with her.

"Good morning, Lila." Louisa's eyes went to the boy.

"Willie with me today. He won't be no trouble, Miz Lou."

"Well, certainly, but . . . shouldn't he be at school?" He didn't look sick.

"No'm. Not today. He won't be no trouble."

"Well . . . of course." She stood back from the door and they came inside.

As he passed her, Willie slid a look up at Louisa, a look somewhere between curiosity and distrust. He appeared to be about nine or ten. He clearly had his mother's features, and he was as neat and scrubbed as she would have expected any of Lila's children to be, but something told Louisa he would bear watching. She smiled at him and he looked away.

He took a little too much interest in his surroundings, she thought, just a shade too observant.

"Lila, the drapes in the parlor need to be taken down for cleaning today."

"Yes'm."

"And if we have time, I'd like to air the mattresses in the boys' room."

"Yes'm."

"This where y'all eat at?" Willie said. He stood in the kitchen doorway, staring at the polished dining room table.

"Hush, now, Willie," said Lila, moving to him and taking him by the shoulder. "You come on and help me. Stop botherin' Miz Lou."

She pulled him after her toward the parlor, but not before Louisa saw his scowl.

All morning long, Louisa found excuses to check in on Willie. Once, as she approached the doorway of the parlor where Lila was working, she heard the boy's whining voice, then Lila speaking to him in short, sharp words. "You should have thought of that before you sassed Deacon Green. Now get over here and hold this." Louisa must have paused in the doorway without realizing it; Willie and Lila noticed her and quickly busied themselves with the drapes.

At lunchtime, Louisa went into the kitchen and asked Willie if he'd like some cathead biscuits she had left over from that morning's breakfast. Willie and his mother sat at the little breakfast table by the window, sharing a section of cornbread Lila had brought and some warmed-up black-eyed peas and buttermilk Louisa had given them. He shook his head. "Don't like no cathead biscuits," he said. His mother gave him a tight-lipped stare. He ignored her and took a swig of the buttermilk in the Mason jar they were using for a glass. He put it down and licked the white froth from his upper lip.

Louisa wished she had some old toys the boys didn't use anymore, something she could give Willie to pass the afternoon. But she'd cleaned out all the old stuff in the last Christmas toy drive for church.

Early in the afternoon, she climbed the stairs and started down the hallway to the boys' room, where Lila was tugging the mattresses off the beds. The door to Katherine's room was open. She stepped inside and there was Willie, standing in the middle of the floor, looking around as if he owned the place. He turned around to look at her.

"Willie, you need to get out of here, right now."

"Whose room this?"

"My daughter's."

"What's her name?"

"Katherine. Now you get—"

"Where she at?"

"She's—passed on. Now will you go back where you belong?"

"My meemaw passed. My cousins moved into her house."

Louisa took a quick step to him and pulled him toward the doorway. "You get out of this room. You don't have any business in here. This room stays closed."

He shuffled down the hallway toward the room where his mother was working. Louisa stood with crossed arms, watching him go. He turned and looked at her just before he stepped through the doorway.

There was a time, Zeb thought, when he knew what he wanted and how to get it. Had it really been so long ago, or did it just seem that way? And since when had the days gotten so heavy and long and useless?

Last night he'd dreamed about his mother. She was out in the hillside field behind the old house back in Georgia, and she was trying to plow the red clay with some kind of contraption made of boards nailed together. He kept trying to tell her to give it up, but it was as if he wasn't talking. He couldn't even hear himself.

That was the strange part of the dream, he'd decided, maybe the part that caused him to wake with sweat drenching his pillowcase: he could hear every sound except his own voice. He could hear the rooks croaking in the pines at the crest of the hill; he could hear Shep yapping at a squirrel in the woods below the house. He could hear the grunts his mother made as she tried to force the pitiful and rude wooden thing through the soil. But when he tried to talk to her, there was nothing. And somehow, in the dream, he knew there was no point in going to her either. He wasn't really there. Not in any way that could do anybody any good.

He'd started to just tear up the telegram from Ab, just tear it up and throw the pieces away and pretend he'd never gotten it. But Becky would've known, somehow—seen it in his face, maybe. He'd had to tell her.

And it was as bad as he feared—maybe even worse. For a long time, she said nothing, but he could see it working up inside her, twisting her in knots. And when it came out, oh, it was bitter.

She railed at him, called him names he never knew she'd heard. She'd never see her mother and father again, never be able to look them in the face, and that was only if the public shame didn't kill them outright, she said. By now everybody in Little Rock thought she was a flat-out whore who'd stolen another woman's husband and did he think for one minute she'd have given him such encouragement as she had if she'd known the truth about him? And now here she was, stuck in some pitiful little boarding house room in Texas with an illegitimate child in her womb and a man who'd lied to her every step of the way and her name on a marriage license that meant pretty close to nothing and the worst of it was she had no place else to go. And then she crumpled onto the floor at the foot of the bed and sobbed.

He was afraid to get close to her, much less touch her. So he sat on the little stool in front of the scarred maple dressing table and listened to her cry and tried to think of some way things could get any worse. The stool was short and his knees stuck out. As he tried to look anywhere but at Becky, his eye swept across the table's vanity mirror, and he had the absurd urge to laugh; he looked like a grasshopper, ready to jump.

His mind slewed around like a hog on ice. He was probably supposed to say something, but right then "I'm sorry" seemed about like spitting on a house fire. Maybe he ought to hang himself, or go to Little Rock and let Pete Norwich give him that horsewhipping Becky had talked about. Something extravagant, something to even things up.

That was three days ago, and she'd barely said a dozen words to him since. Each morning, he'd half expected to wake up and find her gone. But she'd been there in the bed beside him. Using her back like a fence, but there, all the same. She wouldn't go out of the boardinghouse, would barely go downstairs to meals.

Well, there had to be some sort of prospect going, even in a catch-as-catch-can place like Texarkana, he decided. He'd gotten up this morning and dressed and shaved like a man with places to go. Becky lay in the bed and stared at him like she thought he was crazy, but he went right on. Went down and ate a good breakfast and came back upstairs with some dry toast and weak tea. He set the food on the bedside table, kissed Becky on the top of the head, put on his hat, and left.

It was a little on the warm side this afternoon. He'd have liked to loosen his tie and unbutton his collar, but it was more important to make the right impression.

This morning he'd had a pretty good conversation with a cotton buyer who was thinking about hiring an agent. Zeb didn't much like the idea of working for somebody else, but the money he'd brought from Little Rock wasn't going to last forever.

He stood on the street corner and tipped back his panama to mop his forehead. About halfway down the block to his right sat the columned façade of a bank, and right across the street from the bank was a barbershop. Zeb headed for the barbershop.

There was always some kind of prospect going. You just had to know where to look.

CHAPTER
38

*A*t first, Addie wasn't sure what it was. It didn't look exactly like anything she'd ever seen. But when she picked it up and turned it over in her hand, it was as plain as anything that it was a fish.

Or more like the distilled, concentrated idea of a fish—a fish shown the way it might think of itself, if you could imagine such a thing. How could wood be made to do the things this piece of wood did?

She'd found the smooth, polished curve of linden lying on the corner of her porch, in the same place she had taken to leaving treats for Ned Overby on the days George Hutto drove him back from the YMCA. She'd found it last Tuesday morning as she was sweeping; she guessed it had lain there since the previous Saturday. The linden, almost bone-white, made little contrast with the whitewashed porch planking. If she hadn't scooted the carving with the broom, she might never have noticed it.

She smiled as she looked at it now. She'd placed it on her mantle in the parlor. It soothed her eyes from the strain of her candlewicking. The flow and bend of it invited her hand like an old friend.

She was almost finished with this bedspread. Just one more corner of the pattern to stitch and then it would be ready to wash and dry and take to Dub.

She was still surprised at how quickly the spreads sold. She could tell, at first, that Dub only let her put the spread in his store as a family favor—or maybe to keep from having to put up with Lou's displeasure. But it sold within the week. After she gave Dub the store's share—over his protests—she still had more than three dollars left over. And the next piece sold just as quickly. And the next. Dub soon stopped trying to act like he didn't care about the money and started asking her how soon she could get the next bedspread on his shelf. Mr. Peabody had recently offered to start having one of his boys drive out with her cloth and thread and notions, and he let her know if she needed a few days on credit, that'd be just fine.

Addie was leery of credit, though. She liked the thought of the money in the ginger jar in the back of her closet, and she especially liked knowing all of it belonged to her, to do with as she saw fit. Credit muddied the water.

The Ingraham clicked and rattled, then struck. Ten o'clock—the mail was probably here. She finished out the row she was on and laid aside the cloth. She went to the front door, brushing her hand across the fish's back as she passed the mantle.

She stepped out onto the front porch. A meadowlark sat on the top rail of the lane fence. Its black necklace puffed out, dark against the yellow breast, every time it piped. She came down the steps, and the meadowlark blurred away toward the tree line.

The sound of hammers battered at the clear midmorning air. James Potts had sold off a piece of his pasture fronting the road, and somebody was building a big house on it. Every fair day since early spring she'd been waking to the sound of the project, first the sawing and shouting as they cut down enough of the big sweet gums and ashes to make a notch in the woods for the house to sit in. She'd watched as they leveled the plot, then watched the frame go up and the clapboard siding wrap slowly around the house. Now they were nailing down the roof planking. One of these days, Addie knew, she needed to find out who her new neighbors were going to be. Not that she minded neighbors. It'd be a comfort, in a way. And it would sure be nice if they had a little girl about Mary Alice's age. Take some of the pressure off.

Good. Her summer *Delineator* was in the mailbox. Beneath it was an ivory-colored envelope addressed in a very decorative hand. She ran her thumb beneath the flap and opened it. An invitation to Callie Watson's wedding.

Addie looked down the road, tapping the invitation against her palm. In a little while, she dropped it into the pocket of her apron and started back toward the house, thumbing through the *Delineator* as she went.

The magazine was a bit of an indulgence, she guessed, but one she thought she could afford. Looking at the smart fashion plates and reading the elegant descriptions of each costume allowed her to dream a little, to imagine herself able to pick and choose among the delightful outfits for herself and her children, just like the ladies in town who lived on Cameron Hill, whose daughters went to Epworth League and whose husbands came home every night to sit in an armchair and smoke and read the paper. The *Delineator* was an hour or two of pleasant escape, delivered to her mailbox four times a year. Not a bad bargain for twenty-five cents per annum.

She went back in the house and dropped the magazine on the side table near her sewing chair. She promised herself a nice, long read after lunch—after she finished this spread.

Addie put the last stitches in her work just before noon. Miraculously, though Jake woke up, he was content to coo and gurgle up at the ceiling of his room until she had tied off the last thread and clipped the final row of wicking. She got him out of bed and carried him on her hip into the kitchen, calling up to Mary Alice to come down and get something to eat.

She fed the children and herself and got them both interested in some toys. She went into the parlor and settled herself in her chair, then reached for the *Delineator*, when she felt something rub against her thigh. It was the envelope in her apron pocket.

She sat back in the chair with a sigh. She'd managed to forget all about Callie Watson and her wedding until just now. She took the invitation out of her pocket and laid it on top of her magazine. She looked at it, cupping her chin in her hand.

She'd known Callie since she was born; the Watsons sat in the pew behind the Caswells at Centenary Methodist, Sunday after Sunday for years. She really ought to go to the wedding. She reached over and thumbed open the card. "William Jefferson Briles," the groom's name was. Addie didn't recollect any Brileses. The boy's people must be from somewhere else.

Addie wondered where they'd live after they were married. Would William Jefferson Briles settle in Chattanooga, become a partner in his father-in-law's business? Would he and Callie move into the family pew? Would he be a class leader someday, or even a messenger to the Conference? Or would he follow some strange dream, drag Callie hither and yon, and leave her the day she finally gathered enough gumption to say, "no more"?

Lately, there were whole days at a time when Addie didn't think about Zeb—when she didn't wonder what he was doing, where he was living, whether he and this other woman had any friends, any fun, or if they were even still together. Days when she didn't try to figure out where she'd gone wrong, what signs she'd missed, how she could have done better by him, or by herself, or by somebody.

She turned the wedding invitation over in her hand a few times, then tossed it onto the table beside her magazine. She'd send a gift by Lou. A nice tufted bedspread, most likely. She picked up her *Delineator* and started looking through the ladies' evening dresses. Here was one: "Absolutely guaranteed to make the lady wearing it the very cynosure of any gathering, and the gentleman on whose arm she enters the envy of all the swains present."

George slowed as he approached the lane, then clenched his jaw and turned the wheel, aiming the auto toward Addie's house. Ned looked at him, a question on his face.

"I'll just take you on up to the house this time."

She came out onto the porch, holding the little baby boy. Her daughter trailed behind her, holding onto her apron strings. George braked to a stop and took the car out of gear. Ned got out.

"Well, I guess I'll see you next time, Ned."

He nodded and started toward the trail to his house. She was smiling down at the boy.

"Ned, how about taking a loaf of bread to your mama for me?" she asked. "I've got you a slice already buttered, with some honey on it."

Ned shoved his hands deeper in his pockets but didn't show any signs of leaving without the bread. She went inside and came back out with a bundle wrapped in cheesecloth and Ned's slice balanced on top. "Here you go." She handed it to him, and George saw the quick way she glanced away from Ned, toward him. A sliding-away look, like she might be feeling a little bad about something, but not bad enough to say anything out loud.

Ned took the loaf in one hand and the slice in the other. He started to take a bite, but stopped long enough to mumble, "Much obliged."

"And thank you for the fish," she said. "I've never seen anything quite like it. Will you carve something else for me sometime?"

Ned's chin fell onto his chest, and he gave what might have been a nod. A flush crept up his neck. He shuffled off around the corner of the house.

Her eyes swung back toward George. He was still sitting behind the wheel of his car, and when she looked at him, he suddenly realized he had no notion of what he might talk to her about.

"George Hutto." She gave him a slow, greeting nod.

"Addie." He touched the brim of his hat.

"Fine day for a drive."

"Yes, I guess it is." He jerked a thumb over his shoulder. "Somebody building a house across the road from you."

"Pretty good-sized one too."

"Yes, pretty good sized."

The little boy grabbed a fistful of Addie's hair and tried to put it in his mouth. She craned her head away from him. "Jake, now stop that." She reached up and pulled the chubby arm away from her hair. He made a squalling sound and tried to snatch his hand away from her.

"No, sir. You stop that," she told him. He squalled some more.

"Well, I guess I'd better get back," George said, looking away as he worked the gear lever.

"All right, then," she said, still wrestling with the little boy. She gave George a sort of distracted wave and went back inside, grabbing at Jake's hand.

George backed carefully down the lane. Today was Saturday. Why hadn't he asked her if he could pick her up for church tomorrow? She seemed in pretty good spirits, considering all she'd been through. But maybe that was how it was with most folks—they absorbed the bad in life, then went on. Maybe Addie was going on, that was all. Just doing what people did.

He backed out into the road and put the auto in low. As he drove past, he glanced at the house going up across the road from Addie's place. This wouldn't likely be the last house built out this way. He'd heard James Potts was going to divide up a good deal more of his land. Probably a good move, what with the government starting on that dam out by Hale's Bar and all the talk of the army camp going in just a few miles east. He wouldn't be surprised if more and more of Chattanooga crawled out this direction.

George felt a vague kind of sadness, thinking of Addie alone in that big house of her daddy's, just her and the two little children for company.

Come to think of it, what made him turn in at her lane today? What did he think he was going to say or do?

Today was Saturday. In a week's time he'd be back out here, picking up Ned Overby and bringing him home again in the afternoon. Maybe he'd pull down Addie's lane again. Maybe they'd talk some more. Maybe next time her little boy wouldn't be quite so cantankerous. Maybe he'd ask for his own slice of bread with some honey on it.

"Old Leather Britches" started running through George's mind. Pretty soon, he was drumming his fingers on the steering wheel of his car and whistling as he drove back into town.

Addie broke off a corner of the communion wafer and passed the tray to Sister Houser, seated to her right. She had a pretty good spot today, fairly close to the front and no dippers or chewers ahead of her. One Sunday, she'd been late and had to sit at the back, beside Will Tucker. She didn't know if he noticed her turning the communion cup as he handed it to her, and wasn't sure she cared. It was nearly enough to make you stop taking communion. No use complaining to J. D. or any of the elders, though. They'd just send her to Matthew 26:27 and Luke 22:20 and say the Lord only authorized a single cup when he instituted the Lord's Supper, and if it was good enough for the Lord and his apostles it was surely good enough for his church. Addie had thought once or twice about asking them if they thought any of the apostles chewed tobacco.

Addie knew she was supposed to be meditating on the sacrifice of Christ on the cross as she partook of the communion, but her mind was an unruly thing today. As she took a demure sip from the cup and passed it to Sister Houser, she had the guilty realization that she'd been trying for the last little while to remember where she'd put Mary Alice's pinafore that needed mending. She sat a little straighter in the pew and tried to imagine the scene at the Crucifixion: Jesus on the cross, his woeful eyes turned to the stormy heavens; the Roman guard on his knees, realizing this was the Son of God; Mary leaning on the shoulder of the apostle John, her newfound son; Peter and the other men somewhere a little distance off, trying to figure out whether to run or pray.

Poor Peter. Addie could easily picture the look on his face—that scared, confused look men get when they suddenly realize they are about to have to do something they never thought they'd have to do. She remembered the first time Zeb was around when Mary Alice got a soiled diaper. He'd called from the other room, announcing the problem. "Well, there's some diapers right there on the floor by her bed," Addie had answered from the kitchen. A minute later when she went into the room with Zeb and the baby, he'd been sitting there, looking from that pile of diapers to his newborn daughter, looking like he couldn't decide whether to bawl or break for the front door. She'd laughed at him till she had to sit down on the edge of the bed to catch her breath, then shooed him out of the room and gone about her business with Mary Alice.

That was in Nashville, in that little bungalow that had been the servants' quarters behind the big house on Granny White Pike.

Jake twitched in her lap. She looked down at him, sleeping with his fist bunched in front of his face. Mary Alice was leaning into her side, her face sweaty where it was scrunched against the bodice of Addie's dress. She brushed a damp strand of hair out of her daughter's face. Sister Houser looked down at Mary Alice and smiled at Addie. She smiled back. They held each other's eyes for a moment, the old woman and the young one, as the cup moved steadily along the line of the pews somewhere behind them.

The organist mashed a dense hedge of chords out of the bank of pipes at the back of the church, and everybody stood up, sidling along the pews toward the center aisle. Louisa spoke to the people on either side of her, then noticed Callie Watson standing near the end of the pew, faced by a small half-circle of women. She moved toward them.

"Callie, I was so happy to get your invitation in the mail," she said. "I sure hope you sent one to Addie." Louisa kept her eyes steady on Callie's face so she wouldn't have to decide what to do about the looks the other women would be exchanging at the mention of her sister's name.

"Oh, yes, ma'am, I sure did."

"Well, fine. Guess you and your mama are busy as beavers these days, getting everything ready."

"Yes, ma'am."

"Well. I'm happy for you, honey." She patted the girl's hand.

"Thank you, Mrs. Dawkins."

Louisa walked away. "Ma'am," Callie had called her. "Mrs. Dawkins." When, exactly, had she crossed over from "Louisa" to "Mrs. Dawkins"? She felt a faint sadness and, at the same time, a wry amusement at herself. The thought came to her that it had been a good little while since she and Dub had pleasured themselves with each other. If he wasn't already asleep tonight when she got in bed, she might just do something about that.

George was about to step into the center aisle, but he saw Louisa Dawkins coming and waited for her. As she passed, he gave her a polite little nod and a smile, but she must have been thinking about something else; she didn't acknowledge him.

Something Rev. Stiller had said was troubling him. At the time it had seemed an offhand remark, really, just an aside from the main gist of his sermon. But it was stuck in George's mind like a cocklebur in a horse's tail, and he couldn't shake it loose.

Rev. Stiller's text today was from St. Matthew, the fourteenth chapter. He was talking about Christ's provision for his followers, starting with the feeding of the five thousand and continuing with his rescue of the terrified disciples from the storm on the lake. He'd said something about how, usually, preachers liked to berate St. Peter for the lack of faith that caused him to start sinking when he tried to imitate his Master's miraculous walking on the water. "But when you think about it," Rev. Stiller had said, "St. Peter was the only one who had sufficient fortitude to step out of the boat."

He'd gone on then, talking about Christ's love and compassion, about how it was displayed even for those who didn't understand his mission, like the five thousand, or his power, like the storm-spooked apostles. But George had stayed back in that tossing boat, pondering Rev. Stiller's chance comment. He tried to imagine himself, like St. Peter, seeing Jesus stride across the waves and asking boldly for the ability to join him. No, he decided, it was a lot easier to place himself with St. Andrew, St. John, and the others, fearfully gripping the gunwales of the bucking boat and staring wild-eyed at their crazy fishing partner as he climbed out of the boat in the middle of a roaring gale. Or, even more likely, somewhere at the back of the crowd of five thousand, grateful for the fish and the bread, but otherwise mostly confused about what had just happened.

He was at the door. He nodded at Rev. Stiller and said a complimentary word or two about the sermon. The pastor shook his hand and said he'd see George next Saturday at the YMCA, which reminded George he'd never had that talk with Rev. Stiller about the Bible class, nor had he approached the young Baptist minister about coming in to teach. George smiled, settled his hat on his head, and picked his way down the steps of the church.

Willie felt his stomach grinding. He was glad Bishop Jefferson was talking loud, so the noise from his stomach wouldn't make Mama look at him from the sides of her eyes like she did sometimes. It wasn't his fault his stomach was empty and church went too long. But Mama would probably look at him anyway. And Clarice would laugh at him.

Willie bet the white folks were already out of church, maybe home by now. He didn't know why colored folks wanted to string church out so long. He looked up at his older brother, Mason Junior, sitting all serious and still with the choir. Just for a minute, Willie wished he could be sitting up there with his brother, out from under Mama's elbow. But up front like that, he'd have to be still too. Everybody would be able to see him. No, that was no good.

He wished there'd been more to eat this morning than a half pan of cornbread that he had to share with his brothers and sisters. Not even any milk to wash it down, just water. Mama said hush complaining. Daddy didn't say anything, just went on shaving at the kitchen sink. Daddy usually didn't say much. Even when he was reaching for his razor strap.

Willie listened to Bishop Jefferson. Not the words, really, just the sound of them. That was about the only thing he really liked about church—the way Bishop Jefferson half spoke, half sang his words. Willie liked the rhythm of it, the way the words dipped and swooped and rumbled around low right before rising up all of a sudden, like trumpets blaring. Willie liked it that colored folks talked different than white folks. Put their words together different.

His stomach growled again. He liked to listen to Bishop Jefferson, all right. But Willie wished right now he'd finish on up so they could go home.

The pains hit about halfway through the service. As he helped Becky down the front steps of the small white church building, Zeb wondered vaguely what it was about him and women and babies and church services.

He stopped thinking about that when he saw the crimson stains on the back of Becky's dress as he helped her into the seat of the hired surrey. "Honey? Is something wrong?"

"When was the last time you looked at a calendar?" she said. "It's only the seventh month, Zeb." Her breath was coming in quick, shallow pants.

Fear dried his mouth as he yanked the horse around and slapped its rump with the reins. He had to think a minute to remember where he'd seen the small, squarish, two-story frame building that housed the hospital. He prayed there was a doctor around on a Sunday morning.

Part IV

April 1909

CHAPTER
39

*A*ddie walked to the window and peered as far as she could down the
lane and along the road toward town, trying to see some sign of
Dub's headlights. Nothing. She paced into the parlor and looked at the
mantel clock. Half past eight.

"Mother, when are they coming home?"

"I don't know, honey. Your Uncle Dub said he'd be back by dark."

"It's been dark a long time."

"I know."

"Why aren't they back?"

"I don't know. Why don't you go finish your lessons?"

Mary Alice turned away and went back toward the kitchen, her head
down. Addie's voice was sharper than she intended. Her anxiety was
infecting Mary Alice, most likely. Addie was trying to keep ahead of her
worry, but the later it got, the more it gained on her.

The telephone made its rattly ring. Addie stepped quickly into the
entryway and pulled the earpiece off the hook. "Hello?"

"Addie, it's Lou. Dub and the boys just left for your place. He told me
to call and tell you, so you wouldn't worry."

She felt a rippling flash of relief, followed quickly by aggravation.
"What kept them so late?"

"Dub said the traffic down the mountain was real bad after the races
were over. He said they got back as quick as they could."

"Well, all right. They're on their way?"

"Yes. Dub said Jake had the time of his life."

"I don't doubt it. All right, then. Thanks for calling."

Addie replaced the earpiece on its hook. She wouldn't have agreed to this at all, but Dub promised he'd keep Jake with him every minute of the time. For weeks and weeks now this auto race foolishness had been the only thing you heard anybody talking about; it had even crowded out the prohibition vote as a topic of conversation. But now that the commotion was over and Louis Chevrolet and all his millionaire sporting friends were packing up to go back wherever they'd come from, maybe things would settle down to normal again.

She stuck her head in the kitchen. Mary Alice was hunched over her school tablet in the pool of light from the hanging bulb. "That was Aunt Lou. They're on the way home."

No acknowledgment. Well, let her have her mad; she probably deserved it.

Addie went back to the parlor and inspected her day's work. Two more spreads ready to ship to Mr. Lawlis. It was a lucky day for her when the Chicago businessman happened into Dub's store and saw her bedspreads. He'd let her know more than once he'd be happy to take more than the two spreads per month she'd been sending. But Dub had helped her get started, not to mention he was family. She wasn't about to throw him over for some fancy dresser from up north, no matter how promptly he paid.

She heard the sound of Dub's Model T. She went to the front door and stepped out onto the porch.

Dub pulled up in the yard and the doors flew open. Jake and his cousin Ewell chased each other around and around the automobile, imitating the sound of racing cars.

"I'm T. J. Gates, from the Buick Racing Team," Jake hollered.

"And I'm Loueee Chevrolaaaaay," shouted Ewell.

"All right, you two," Dub said. "The races are over; time for the cars to go back in the shed."

Jake stopped in the middle of the yard and windmilled his arms, still making race car noises.

"Jake, you better tell Uncle Dub 'thank you,'" Addie said.

"Thank you!" he yelled, without turning around.

"Thanks, Dub, for taking him," Addie said.

"No trouble, Addie. We had a big time, didn't we, boys?"

"What do you hear from Robert?" Addie said. "How's Vanderbilt?"

"Fine, except for the classes." Dub laughed and shook his head. "Takes after his daddy, I guess."

"Well, Jake, you better get in the house," she said. Jake immediately took off on another lap around the Model T.

"Ewell, get in the car, son. We better get home. Sorry to be so late, Addie. The traffic—"

"Yes, Lou called. Jake! You better get in this house right now, young man, or I'm fixing to flatten your tires!"

Jake sputtered up the front steps and sprawled on the porch at her feet. "I'm out of gas, Mother."

She waved at Dub as he backed out of the yard, then bent over and poked the boy in the ribs. "Out of gas, huh? Out of gas?"

He giggled and squirmed, trying to evade her tickling. She got him up and pointed him toward the front door. "I don't guess Uncle Dub fed you anything, did he?"

"Sure did. They had barbecued turkey legs up there, and lemonade, and cider, and corn on the cob, and—"

"All right, all right. I get the picture."

"Oh, you should've seen it, Mother! All those cars, and the engines just a-roaring, and the dust flying out from under their wheels when they made the turns—"

"I'll bet you were in hog heaven."

"There were even some drivers from Chattanooga. Uncle Dub knew 'em. Eddy Kenyon, and Charles Duffy, and—"

"And you'd best get those clothes off and get ready to get in the tub. You've probably got dust in places you can't even show decent folks."

"—and the Buick Racing Team! All the way from Detroit, Michigan, Uncle Dub said. And Louis Chevrolet. He's French. Mother, where's Detroit, Michigan?"

"North a ways. Now get on upstairs."

"Oh, Mother, it was just bully, is what it was. Bully all the way down to the ground!" He pounded upstairs, shedding clothes as he went. She looked after him, shaking her head. He'd be talking about this for weeks, most likely. She'd be surprised if he slept a wink tonight.

A little while later, she went to the kitchen. It was getting late. Mary Alice needed to be getting ready for bed. "About finished, dear?"

"Yes, ma'am." Mary Alice closed her book and sat with her hands in her lap, staring down at the dull blue cover of the McGuffey Reader.

"What's wrong, honey?"

Mary Alice sat very still, not even moving her eyes. Addie was fully prepared to hear about how she'd hurt Mary Alice's feelings with her sharp tone just before the phone call came from Lou. She was prepared to respond to why Jake got to go to the car races with Uncle Dub and Ewell and she had to stay at home and do her schoolwork. But she wasn't quite ready for what her daughter actually said.

"Sarah Frances Tanner says I don't have a daddy."

"Do what?"

"She does. She says I don't have a daddy." Still, Mary Alice wouldn't look at her. "At recess today, she said it. And at lunch she said it to Lucy Wilkes. She told her I don't have a daddy."

Addie felt as if a place in the center of her chest was emptying. She stepped to the table and quietly pulled out a chair, then sat. She put her hands on the table and laced her fingers together, then spread them out, palms down. She took a deep breath and let it out slowly.

"So Sarah Frances said that, did she?"

"Yes, ma'am." Now she raised her eyes to her mother's. "Why doesn't my daddy live with us, like Sarah Frances's and Lucy's?"

"Sweetheart—" *Where on earth to start?* "Honey, do you remember your daddy at all?"

She pursed her lips. "Just a little. I remember some sparkly paper. Was that Christmas?"

Addie gave a sad little smile and a nod. "Yes, dear, that was Christmas. Anything else?"

She twisted her mouth back and forth, then shook her head. "No, I think that's all."

"Honey, your daddy traveled a lot. He was gone more than he was home, even after you were born. And then, one day—"

The old hurt surprised her, sidetracked her with its sudden intensity. As if it had been waiting for a chance at her, and this was it.

"One day, he decided he didn't want to come home anymore."

"Was he mad at us?"

"Oh, no, sweetheart, not a bit. Not at you, anyway. No, don't ever think that."

"Was he mad at you?"

A place in her throat was starting to ache. She swallowed. "I guess he was, in a way. Maybe not mad, exactly, but . . . I guess he was just sad, maybe."

"Did you do something bad to him?"

"No, I didn't. At least . . . if I did, I didn't know what it was."

Mary Alice's forehead wrinkled. "Mother, was he ever around after Jake was born?"

"No, honey. He wasn't."

"Well, what'll Jake do? He won't even have shiny paper to remember."

No, not even that. "I . . . I don't know, honey. I don't know."

She reached across the table, put a hand on her daughter's arm. "Mary Alice, now listen to me. What happened with your daddy and me wasn't your fault. And it's none of Sarah Frances's business, or anybody else's. You're a sweet girl, and I love you, and you just remember that. All right?"

Mary Alice looked at her a long time. "Yes, ma'am."

"All right, then. You'd better go get ready for bed. School tomorrow."

"Yes, ma'am."

She dragged her books and paper off the table, tucked them under an arm, and wandered out of the kitchen, toward the stairs. Addie watched her go until she rounded the corner. When she heard Mary Alice's feet on the stairs, she put her face in her hands.

She wondered why her own hurt hadn't taught her how to soothe her daughter's. *You'd think I'd know something to say to her,* Addie thought. But Mary Alice's wounds were in a different place, had a different shape. And then Addie felt the raw and livid place inside her, the part of her that felt insulted that her daughter should even notice the lack of a man who'd cared so little for her—or if he did care, it wasn't in any way that made a practical difference. *Just one more way I'm not good enough,* she thought. *Just one more thing he's done to me: leaving me here to explain something to a nine-year-old girl that her twenty-nine-year-old mother has never been able to explain to herself.*

She got up from the table and wandered over to the sink. She'd tacked a calendar to the wall above the sink, beside the window that looked out onto the backyard and the tree line beyond. Peabody's Dry Goods sent them out; they had a different illustration for each month of the year. The illustrations were in the style of the old Currier & Ives prints; this month it was a party scene, men and women playing croquet or some such game in the foreground, and a group gathered around some kind of table in the background. A church social, maybe. There wasn't a title to it. The men were all wearing top hats, and the ladies' dresses were old-fashioned, flared affairs with huge sleeves ballooning between the shoulder and elbow. And they were all wearing gloves. Didn't look too practical for croquet, come to think of it.

Mary Alice's birthday was coming up in a few weeks. Addie would make her a great big cake and invite all her little school friends over. Maybe she'd pay Ned Overby a little extra, get him to stay after his wood chopping and turn the crank on the ice cream bucket. She'd think of some party games the little girls could play, and she might even try to sew a special frock for Mary Alice to wear, just for the occasion. Maybe she'd see if Lou would loan her Lila's services to decorate and get ready for the event.

She stared out the window at the dark yard, the darker trees. She found herself thinking of Carolina Clark.

Her name was Carolina, like the state, she said, and she was very particular about the correct pronunciation. She was from somewhere up north. She came to Chattanooga when Addie was still a little girl to be the second wife of John Larimore Clark, a wealthy landowner whose first wife died from consumption. Addie remembered the first Sunday John Larimore Clark brought his new wife to church at Centenary Methodist. Addie remembered that even as a child, she thought of Carolina Clark as a small woman, and very pale. She wore big, wide-brimmed hats to church.

Carolina had odd ways, even for a Yankee. She was rarely seen outside the big, three-story house on Walnut Street that she shared with her husband and stepfamily. Some said she almost never left her own room. She was subject to headaches and would spend weeks at a time in bed with the curtains and shutters drawn.

But one of her strangest habits was that she never went anywhere or did anything, indoors or out, without wearing gloves. Naturally, most of the women at Centenary Methodist wore gloves to church. But even at meals, people said, Carolina Clark kept her hands concealed in gloves of silk or fine linen.

On a Sunday afternoon in the middle of the summer, right after dinner, Carolina Clark got up from the table and announced that she was going to her room for her usual nap. The servants were away, her husband was traveling on business, and the children were in their rooms upstairs. Sometime that afternoon, Carolina rose from her bed, removed her Sunday clothes, walked outside, and threw herself down the eighty-foot well in the backyard. When her body was removed a few days later, all she was wearing were her white silk gloves.

That was what everybody knew, but what nobody said. At her funeral service, the preacher spoke of her as "a quiet woman who troubled no one." But the thought of her troubled Addie, even as a young girl. What would make anybody want to do what Carolina Clark had done, she wondered. What dark voices whispered to her from the well, and why didn't anybody else hear them, or know? Why wasn't there anyone to shoulder a corner of Carolina Clark's quiet desperation?

Addie suddenly felt very tired. She had some spreads she ought to work on, now that the house was quiet, but the thought of going into the parlor and threading her needle seemed arid and burdensome. She thumbed the button by the door to switch off the kitchen light. She tested the lock on the front door, then went to her room, turning out lights on the way.

The man across the desk picked up the carvings as if he were handling Babylonian pottery shards. He held them up this way and that way, looked at them from every possible angle. He was a big man; his face was red and sheen with perspiration. His hands were beefy, but he handled Ned's work like an acolyte might handle sacramental vessels.

"He's got drawings?"

"Yes, right here." George laid the leather portfolio on the desk between them. He was proud of the portfolio. He'd ordered it from one of the catalogs Professor Gaines suggested. Ned had grinned for a whole day when George gave it to him.

The man opened the portfolio. His lips made little pursing motions as he looked at Ned's drawings. He would flip quickly through several sheets, then pause, slightly squinting one eye or stroking his upper lip as he studied a piece more closely.

"The style is a little naive, of course . . . that's to be expected. But, my! What a sense of line." As he looked at the drawing, one of his hands strayed to the carving he'd been examining: a deer springing over a log. George smiled. It was hard to keep from touching Ned's carvings.

"Oh, so he's done some charcoals . . . Hmm . . . Yes."

He closed the portfolio and looked up at George. "Well, Mr. Hutto, I must admit I was dubious when I received your first telegram. If Percy Gaines weren't an old friend— But it appears to be just as you and Percy say. The boy is very, very talented."

George leaned back in his chair. "Well, Professor Koch, I— It's good to hear you say so."

"May I speak with him?"

"Oh, well . . . he isn't here. That is, he didn't—couldn't come with me."

Professor Koch arched his eyebrows.

"His father needed him, you see. It's spring, and that's the time Perlie—Mr. Overby, the boy's father—when he sells his hides, and—"

Professor Koch had bridged his fingertips and was staring at George with a blank expression.

"Well, at any rate, Ned couldn't come with me to New York, you see. I was hoping you could look at his work and tell me— And you have, of course, and so . . . I was hoping . . ."

Professor Koch looked at him a bit longer, then cleared his throat with a delicate sound. "Mr. Hutto, you must realize. Our institute has certain standards."

"Yes, of course."

"To be considered, each candidate must undergo a personal interview by the faculty."

George nodded.

"He must agree to the terms and conditions of enrollment. He must be made to thoroughly understand what we expect of our students."

George took a handkerchief from his pocket and dabbed at his lips.

"Still . . ." Professor Koch took up the deer carving. He ran a palm over the deer's back, ran a fingertip along the delicate, perfect curve of the neck. "I suppose, given the geographic challenges involved . . ." He put down the carving and aimed a forefinger at George's chest. "The tuition for the first quarter must be completely prepaid."

"Oh, yes, sir. That will be no problem."

"And we'll need letters from a teacher, and from Percy, and—"

"Yes, I've already spoken to them, Professor."

Professor Koch leafed through the portfolio some more. "Yes. Extraordinary eye this boy has."

George leaned back in the chair again, and smiled.

CHAPTER
40

*B*ecky?"

Zeb stepped inside and let the screen door bang shut behind him. He looked in the parlor, but she wasn't there. He called her again. No answer. He heard the hissing noise from the kitchen and smelled the acrid odor of burning beans. He turned the corner and saw the bluish cloud rolling out of the saucepan. He wrapped a dish towel around the handle and carried the pot to the sink. He opened the window over the sink to let out some of the smell and smoke.

"Becky? You here?"

He quickly went through the rest of the rooms, but he didn't see her until he stepped through the backdoor into the small yard. She was sitting on the ground under one of the elm trees, staring at something in her lap.

"Becky, your beans burned," he said, moving toward her, trying to pretend to himself that he had no reason to feel relieved. Of course she was still here; where else would she be?

She didn't look up at him until he was maybe three steps away, and when she did, he saw she'd been crying, and that the thing in her lap was a crumpled telegram.

"It's Daddy," she said in a voice raw from weeping. "He's real sick."

Zeb stood there, looking down at her, trying to think of something to say that would seem right. He wished he could hold her, but he doubted that would be anymore welcome than usual.

"Well, uh . . . what's wrong with him?"

"His heart."

"He in the hospital?"

"Not now. He's at home. Mother says the doctor mainly wants him to rest and gain some strength, but—"

"Honey, I'm sorry."

"Zeb, I've got to go."

"Well . . . sure. Sure, you do. I'll go buy you a ticket, first thing in the morning." There was another question waiting to be asked, but he wasn't sure if he really wanted to hear the answer. "Uh . . . you want me to come?"

She studied the telegram for a long time. "I don't think so, Zeb," she said without looking up. "It's probably better you didn't."

He nodded to himself, trying to figure out if he was relieved or disappointed. A few days to himself might not be too bad. And Becky needed to be with her mother, that was certain. And the thought of being back in Little Rock still wasn't too appealing. That wouldn't be any easier for Becky, he guessed, but it was her daddy, after all, and she had to go.

"What do you want to do about supper, Becky?"

It was a little while before she answered. "I've got some beans on."

"I guess you didn't hear me awhile ago. They burned. I took the pan off the stove and put it in the sink."

"Oh . . . I'd just put them on when the Western Union boy came to the door."

"Yeah. Well, how about going down to the hotel? They've usually got a pretty good—"

"Zeb, I don't know when I'll come back."

He thought about making a joke of it but found he didn't have the strength. "I, uh . . . Well, how long do you think you might have to stay?"

"I don't know, Zeb."

He stuck his hands down in his pockets and swallowed. He nodded some more. "I guess you need to stay as long as your mother needs you, then."

She stood up and dusted the back of her dress. She nodded at him. She looked at the telegram one more time, then folded it up. "However long that is. I just don't know."

He tried without much success to convince himself that she was just talking about the uncertainties of her father's health. He wanted her to tell him exactly when she was coming back. He wanted to hear her say she was sorry she had to go off and leave him alone like this, and she loved him, and she'd get back just as soon as she could. He wanted to make her promise to come back, promise she wouldn't pull Little Rock and her parents' home around her like a shroud.

Most of all, he wanted to believe he had something coming from her—that somehow, she ought to want to be with him enough to make this separation as brief as possible. But when he looked far down inside and let himself think about everything that had happened, it was hard to make much of a case for that.

He realized he was staring at the tops of his shoes. He took a deep breath and straightened. She was watching him. He gave her a smile. She looked away.

"Well, you want to go to the hotel?" he asked.

"I guess so. Yes, that'd be fine."

She crossed the yard and went up the steps to the back door. She turned and looked back at him. "You coming?"

There wasn't any place in Humble where you could go to get away from the flat, dirty smell of crude oil, Becky thought. Even when they walked through the ornate double doors of the Lone Star Hotel, the smell followed them in like a drenched cat on a rainy day.

The restaurant was crowded with the usual mix of roughnecks, rig foremen, drilling engineers, and speculators. They found a table that was almost clean, and Zeb waved down a harried busboy and talked him out of two menus. She didn't know why they needed menus. She always got the pork chops with yams and boiled cabbage, and Zeb always got the ham with black-eyed peas and rice. He was running his finger up and down the offerings, though, just like somebody here for the first time.

She watched him over the top of her menu. His eyes danced back and forth between the bill of fare and the roomful of people. He was always working, always prospecting everywhere he went. They'd been here less than six months, and she guessed he could probably call half the people in the room by name. That was Zeb's gift, such as it was. He could make you think he'd never met anyone whose company he enjoyed more than yours, and it didn't matter if you were a grimy roustabout or one of the company bosses in a linen suit and panama hat.

She knew she ought not complain; he made good money. The oil business wasn't really that much different from the insurance business, he told her, once you learned the terms and got the hang of it. Zeb had sure enough landed on his feet. Looking at him like this, you'd never know he'd had a minute's worth of trouble in his life.

A large, red-faced man came up and clapped Zeb on the shoulder. "Buy you a beer, Zeb?" Becky could smell the drink on the man's breath from where she sat.

"Now, Colonel, you know I don't drink," Zeb said, his eyes darting at her. "'Wine is a mocker, strong drink is raging, and whosoever is deceived thereby is not wise'—Proverbs twenty and verse one."

"Well, I don't know about that, Zeb. You reckon the Lord minds all that much if a bunch a hard-working men have a little drink or two at the end of the day? You wouldn't mind if he had one, would you, there, Missus?" The man was leaning over the table toward her, grinning. She gave him what she hoped was a noncommittal smile and renewed her study of her menu.

Zeb shifted uneasily in his chair. "Say, Colonel, have you had a chance yet to think about that Caddo prospect I showed you the other day?"

"Yeah, I took a look at it. Come on by tomorrow morning and we'll talk some more." The man nodded at Becky and weaved between the tables in the direction of the doorway. Zeb watched him go for a few seconds, then looked back at her. He grinned and shook his head.

"Colonel Dickson's liable to say anything to anybody. He doesn't mean anything by it, though."

"I'm ready to order, if you are."

Zeb flagged a waiter. "Teddy, I'll have the ham plate with black-eyed peas and rice." He glanced at her, and she nodded. "And Mrs. Douglas'll have the pork chops with boiled cabbage and yams."

The waiter nodded as he scribbled on a dog-eared note pad, then hustled toward the kitchen.

"Maybe I can get you on the eight-oh-seven, day after tomorrow," he said a minute or two later.

"Just do the best you can. I'll be ready early. I wouldn't even mind leaving tomorrow afternoon. I can sleep on the train."

He nodded, toying with his silverware. He was doing his best to act unconcerned. She knew she probably ought to say something, but she couldn't think of a good enough reason to want to, somehow.

Part of it was the worry about Daddy. But not all of it, no matter how much she tried to pretend otherwise. She and Zeb lived in silence more and more, like two neighbors with a hill between their houses. The hill was getting harder and harder to climb. Or maybe it was becoming less worth the trouble.

Sometimes, lying in their bed at night or at odd moments during the day, she tried to imagine how it might have been if she hadn't lost the baby, or if they'd been able to have another one. Maybe the joy of a child would have distracted her from all the ways her life didn't quite match expectations. She wondered how Zeb would have acted as a father. Would he have doted on their baby? Would he have made up a silly name, as Daddy had done for her? Would she have found in his fondness for his children a reason to remember her fondness for him?

"Sarge," Daddy had called her, until she started school and Mother made him stop. He used to say that when she cried as a baby her face looked just like a drill sergeant he had when he was in the state militia. Becky had always felt a little sadness after he quit using his pet name for her; it was a small, sweet loss to be treasured. A few times, on the sly, he still called her "Sarge"—but never when Mother was around. Becky wished she were on the train to him right now, wished she were far away from this muddy, humid little town with its overhanging pigpen smell and its crowds of oil-smeared, noisy men.

Zeb was staring at the tabletop. He saw her watching him and gave her a quick smile. She tried to answer it.

"Well, I wish they'd hurry up, don't you? I'm hungry."

Becky shrugged and nodded.

"Honey, I'm sure your daddy's gonna be all right."

"I hope so."

"Shoot, with you and your mother both taking on over him, he'll be back on his feet and down at that store before you can say 'Jack Robinson.'"

There was a shout from the tool-pushers in the corner. The barkeep, a dour Black Irishman named Rourke, stared hard at them with his hands on his hips.

"I may be gone awhile, Zeb."

"Yeah, you said that." He wouldn't look at her now.

The waiter brought their food. He clumped the thick, white porcelain plates onto their table; he put Becky's pork chops in front of Zeb and his ham in front of her. They slid the plates across to each other and ate, mostly in silence. The noise of the dining room swirled around them but left them untouched, other than maybe giving their silence a convenient excuse.

"Lila, can you hold this end? I'll tack it up."

"Yes'm."

The bunting was blue, Mary Alice's favorite color. Addie tried not to think about what she'd paid for it, even after Mr. Peabody's special discount. "For one of my best customers," he'd said. She tapped a tack through the fabric and into the top corner of the doorframe, then scooted the footstool over to the other side. She took the other end from Lila and tacked the other side into place. She got down from the stool and backed up a few steps. Yes. The effect was just right; it gave the parlor doorway a festive frame.

Mary Alice came bounding down the stairs. "Mother, is my white crinoline dress clean?"

Addie glanced at Lila and got a nod. "Yes, honey. Lila's got it hung up in my room. I want to do a little work on the hem before you put it on." Mary Alice made an impatient sound. "Don't worry, Mary Alice; there's enough time before your friends get here."

"I can see to it, Miz Addie," Lila said.

"Oh, could you? That would be wonderful. Then I could go finish icing the cake."

"Yes'm." Lila went toward Addie's room.

"My needles and thread are on the vanity, Lila."

"Yes'm."

There was a knock at the back door. Addie went back through the kitchen and opened it. Ned Overby stood there, his stained plug hat in his hand.

"Ma'am, the wood's chopped."

"Thank you, Ned. Just a minute, and I'll get your money." She turned to go, then turned back. "Ned, if I paid you an extra twenty-five cents, could you stay long enough to help me move a table into the parlor for Mary Alice's party?"

"Yes, ma'am, I reckon. Oh, and ma'am? He wanted me to ask you if his mama was ready to go yet."

Addie looked in the direction of Ned's thumb and saw a colored boy leaning against the corner of the house with his hands stuffed in his pockets.

"Oh, hello. You must be Lila's boy."

He nodded. "I come to get Mama when she ready."

"Almost, uh—what's your name?"

"Willie."

"Almost, Willie. She's just finishing up one more thing for me before she goes. Have you got a way to get home?"

"Yes'm." He jerked his chin toward the woodpile. A lop-eared sorrel mule stood there, tethered by a halter rope, its nose down in a patch of clover.

"Well, fine. Ned, can you come on in and help me with that table?"

"Yes, ma'am."

"Willie, would you like a cool drink or anything?"

Willie shook his head. Addie looked at him; he reminded her of Rose. Something about the set of his jaw, maybe.

She and Ned pulled the settee and an armchair to one side, then wrestled the big oak pedestal table from the dining room into the parlor. She went to her closet and found some coins; she gave two quarters to Ned and a silver dollar to Lila, who was at the kitchen table finishing the hem work on Mary Alice's dress. Her eyes widened when Addie gave her the dollar.

"Miz Addie, that's an awful lot of money for no more than I done—"

"Now, Lila, don't argue with me. I want you to have that. I couldn't have gotten ready for this without you."

"Well, then . . . thank you."

"You're welcome. And Willie's here to take you home, when you're ready."

"Yes'm."

She sent Mary Alice up to her room with her party dress and walked with Lila to the back door. They went outside and saw Ned, Willie, and Jake all gathered beside the mule. Ned and Willie were talking, and Jake was pestering the older boys and the mule, by turns. "Jake! Leave that mule alone!" Addie said.

Willie saw his mother coming and began untying the rope. Grabbing a handful of the mule's mane at the base of its neck, he slung himself up onto the animal's back. He used the rope as a rein and headed the mule toward where his mother stood on the back steps. Lila put an arm around her son's waist and scooted herself on behind him.

"Thank you again, Lila. I appreciate you coming over."

"Yes'm."

"Tell my sister thanks."

Lila nodded. Willie clicked his tongue and pulled the mule's head around. He gave it a little kick and got it going toward the lane. Addie watched them leave. Lila sat sideways on the mule's bare back, holding on to her son's waist. Addie felt sorry for her; it was a long ride to Chattanooga, twisted halfway around like that.

She saw a quick movement from the corner of her eye and turned her head. Ned was holding onto Jake and taking something away from him.

"Lemme go! Lemme go, Ned!"

Addie went toward them. Ned released Jake, who bolted toward the tree line, bawling as he went.

"Jake! You come back here!" Addie called, but he kept running.

She looked at Ned. He was holding a palm-sized rock.

"He was fixing to throw it at the mule," Ned said. "I just took it away from him, is all."

Addie sighed and shook her head, staring in the direction her son had gone. "What am I going to do with that boy?"

CHAPTER
41

Ned cinched the strap around his books, and when the teacher rang the bell, he was the first one through the door. He walked at a good clip down the sidewalk and turned right along Ninth Street. He needed to get to the YMCA and find out whatever it was that Mr. Hutto wanted to tell him. Then he had to catch the trolley out to the Orchard Knob end of the line.

He stuck his hand in his pocket and felt the note the girl had brought from the principal's office during geometry. "See Mr. Hutto after school at the Y," it read. "He has some news for you."

"Ned! Ned Overby!"

He looked around and saw Willie Lewis trotting toward him. *Guess the colored school must get out the same time we do.*

"Where you goin', Ned?"

"YMCA."

"What you goin' there for?"

"Man wants to tell me somethin'."

"What?"

"If I knew, I wouldn't have to go."

"What y'all do at the YMCA?"

"Different stuff. Basketball, calisthenics—"

"What's that?"

"Exercises. And there's Bible classes, and other stuff."

"How come you in such a hurry?"

"You ask a lot a questions."

"You ask a lot a questions," Willie said in a perfect imitation of Ned's voice. "How come you white folks so tetchy about somebody just wanta know somethin'?"

"Ain't tetchy. Just not used to answerin' so many questions from somebody that ain't my mama."

Willie laughed. Ned thought he ought to be mad about it, but he couldn't quite get there, somehow. He grinned at Willie. "Ain't you got someplace you oughta be goin'?"

"Yeah. The YMCA. I want to find out what them calisthenics is."

"Well, I ain't doin' no calisthenics today. I'm goin' to talk to Mr. Hutto, then I gotta get home."

"Who's Mr. Hutto?"

"He runs the place. He's the one got me set up with my art lessons."

"Art lessons? They teach you about that too?"

Ned nodded.

"You an artist?"

Ned gave a loose-limbed shrug. "Shoot, I don't know. I just like to do stuff, that's all."

"What kind of stuff?"

"Draw. Paint a little. But I mainly like to carve."

"Who started you out doin' that?"

"Nobody. I . . . I just always did it, I reckon."

They walked along awhile before Willie said anything else. Willie had a loose, springy way of moving, as if every part of him had a mind of its own and only decided at the last second it wanted to come along with the rest. Ned wanted to find a piece of wood for Willie. Blackjack oak, maybe, or hickory. Yes, hickory. It would render Willie's angles so much better.

"How long you been working for Miz Addie?" Willie asked.

"'Bout three years, I reckon."

"She pay you good?"

"All right, I guess."

"I'm gonna get me a job, and when I done saved up enough money, I'm gonna ride me a train all the way to New York City."

Ned gave out a snort. "What you gonna do in New York City?"

Willie wore a funny look that seemed like it started out to be a smile but wound up somewhere else. "Things I can't do here," Willie said.

A few boys leaned against the walls beside the main entrance of the Y. There was a game of mumblety-peg going on on one side of the doorway, and some of the smaller boys had scratched out a circle for marbles on the other side. Ned walked up to the boys lounging against the wall.

"Hey, Ralph."

"Hey, yourself."

"Mr. Hutto in?"

"Yeah. He just got here." Ralph's eyes flickered toward Willie.

"Okay. I'm supposed to go see him."

Ned opened the door and started inside when he heard Ralph say, "Where you think you're going?"

He turned around. Ralph stood in front of Willie, blocking his way.

"I was going inside with my friend, here," Willie said, nodding toward Ned.

Ralph looked a question at Ned. Ned shrugged.

"Niggers ain't allowed," Ralph said. A couple of the other boys near the doorway slowly uncrossed their arms and stood away from the wall, watching Ralph and Willie with narrowed eyes.

"Ain't gonna stay but just a minute," Ned said. "Mr. Hutto asked me to come by after school."

"He ask this coon to come with you?" Ralph said.

Ned studied his shoe tops. "Just ran into him on the way."

"Well, if he knows what's good for him, he can just—"

"What's the problem, boys?"

Ned felt his chest loosen with relief. It was Mr. Gaines, his art teacher. "Mr. Gaines, I'm here to see Mr. Hutto. Willie came along with me. He just wanted to see what goes on here at the YMCA."

"Oh. I see." Mr. Gaines looked at Willie for a few seconds. "Ralph, you other boys. You have something to do?"

"Yes, sir," Ralph said. He shoved his hands deep in his pockets and slouched inside. Two of the other boys followed him, looking at Willie out of the sides of their faces as they passed him.

"Now, ah—what's your name, son?" Mr. Gaines said.

"Willie Lewis."

"Now, Willie. The boys do have a point. This is for white boys only. I guess Ned forgot to tell you that."

Willie looked at Mr. Gaines for a second or two, then let his head drop. He nodded, looking down at the ground.

"Well, fine. Why don't you just wait right over there, in the shade of that tree, and I'm sure Ned's business won't take long."

Willie was walking away before Mr. Gaines could finish what he was saying. He watched Willie's back for a moment, then flashed a big smile down at Ned. "You better come inside, Mr. Overby. Mr. Hutto's got some news I think you'll want to hear."

Ned followed Mr. Gaines inside.

Where you goin', white trash? Come on, peckerwood. Let's go outside . . .

The voices snickered and sneered in his head. They were all he could hear, and all he could see was the way Willie's head hung between his shoulders after Mr. Gaines spoke to him. What was the difference, really, between him, walking back to Mr. Hutto's office with his art teacher, and Willie, turned away at the door? He didn't dress any better than Willie— shoot, Willie's clothes were probably cleaner. He wasn't any smarter, most likely. From the minute Willie walked up to the woodpile at Addie's, holding the halter rope of the mule he'd borrowed to come fetch his mama, Ned had known here was somebody he could talk to. From the way Willie held himself, Ned could tell here was a quick mind that wanted to see out, to know what there was to know. Ned could see it the same way he could see the agility of a deer in its hindquarters, the same way he could see the shape of a blue jay's flight in the spread of its wing.

But Ralph couldn't see it, nor the other bullies. Even Mr. Gaines couldn't see it. The man who'd taught Ned to let himself really see what he saw—he was as blinded by Willie's dark brown skin and nappy hair as the rest of them. It confused Ned, put him off. He wondered what else he didn't understand that made perfect sense to the rest of the world.

Mr. Hutto was standing at the doorway of his office. "Ah, good, Percy. You found him."

"Here he is."

They were both grinning at Ned like he was a prize hog. What was going on?

"Ned, come on in and sit down, won't you?"

Ned shrugged himself into one of the oak chairs in front of Mr. Hutto's desk. Mr. Gaines sat beside him, in the other chair.

Mr. Hutto laced his fingers together and leaned across at him. "Ned, Mr. Gaines has been telling me you're doing some really good work. He says you've got a lot of talent with your art."

Ned looked at the corner of the desk and said nothing.

"In fact, he tells me he thinks your work is good enough to get you into a special art school where you could learn from some of the greatest artists and teachers in the country."

Ned felt his forehead wrinkling.

It was still wrinkled fifteen minutes later when he walked out of the office.

He stepped outside and was surprised to see Willie sitting under the tree. He'd figured Willie'd be long gone after what happened when they got here. He walked across the yard and Willie stood up. He looked at Ned and cocked his head to one side.

"What happened?"

"They just told me I'm goin' to New York."

George didn't know when he'd felt so good. When he locked the front doors of the Y and started his walk home, he was still wearing the grin he'd found when Ned Overby left his office.

"He doesn't think it's real," Percy Gaines had said when Ned walked out.

"He'll figure it out soon enough when I hand him the train tickets."

"I'd like to be a fly on his shoulder when that boy gets off the train in New York City," Percy said.

George rounded the corner of Eighth and Georgia. He looked up and saw a swallow wheeling around the cornices of the Milton Building. He stopped for a minute to watch the bird arc back and forth across the purpling sky. It looked like it was kissing the corner of the building before darting out again, dodging and tumbling and always circling back to the same place.

Ned Overby was going to get his chance. He was going to find out what he was capable of, and if the reactions of Professor Koch at the Institute were any gauge, that was quite a bit. George wondered where Ned might go, what he might see. He wondered how living in New York would change him.

Would the tumbledown shack where his family lived ever seem like home again? Would his father's rough, good-natured voice come to sound strange in his ears? George's walk slowed as he considered. It was the right thing, wasn't it, to extend this opportunity to Ned Overby? Didn't Ned have the right to find out what was inside him? Didn't the world have the right?

When George went up the front steps of his house, his mother was sitting in the huge white wicker armchair on the porch. It was dark now, and Mamie had set a coal-oil lamp on the small side table by the chair. Candle bugs flittered all around the light. It was a pretty warm evening, but Mother had a woolen afghan draped over her shoulders. George smiled at her. Her poor old eyes looked faded and watery. She smiled back at him.

"What are you doing out here, Mother? It's getting dark."

"Just sitting. It's nice, sometimes. Just to sit."

"Aren't you getting cold?"

"I hadn't noticed."

"I'll go find Mamie—"

"Sit down with me a minute, George."

He perched on the edge of the footstool.

"Honey, why don't you sit in the swing? You look like a toad on a toadstool."

"I'm fine."

She shook her head and gave him a sideways smile. "You put yourself in such awkward places, trying to accommodate. You always have."

"Ma'am?"

"Nothing." She leaned back against the chair and let her head fall to one side. "Lots of lightning bugs tonight."

George looked out across the front lawn. The tiny yellow-green lights flickered on and off, hanging almost motionless in the humid air. He nodded.

"Your father always liked to look at the lightning bugs. But he never wanted anybody to know he did."

"Why not?"

"I don't know. But he'd sit out here and watch them. Sit here in the dark for hours. And if I said anything about it or anybody else came out on the porch, he'd clear his throat and say how late it was getting, and go straight in and get his nightshirt on."

George gave her a puzzled smile.

"I guess he thought it was foolish for a grown man to enjoy lightning bugs." She shook her head. "But I never thought so."

"Why didn't you just tell him?"

She looked at George. "Good question. There were lots of things I never got around to telling him."

They sat for a minute, watching the lightning bugs.

"I'm sending Ned Overby to art school in New York," he said.

"Who's that?"

"They live out past Orchard Knob. Perlie Overby's his father."

"The fellow that used to work odd jobs for your father?"

George nodded.

"He's got a son that's an artist?"

"Yes, ma'am. A good one, looks like. The Peabody Institute took him sight unseen."

"And you're paying for it?"

George nodded. "I can afford it, Mother."

"Of course you can." She tilted her head and gave him a narrow-eyed look. "What do you want, George?"

"Ma'am?"

"You heard me."

"Well . . . I guess I want to see him get a chance to—"

"I'm not talking about Ned Overby, honey. You. What is it you want?"

George stared out at the lightning bugs. They reminded him of brakemen's lanterns, signaling a train to a siding far away in the dark. They blinked on and off at him, flashing a cool, mysterious code he couldn't follow. They were like tiny stars set in the stillness above his lawn, guiding lights to some destination he hadn't guessed. Couldn't, most likely.

"I don't know. Haven't thought much about it, I guess."

He wouldn't look at her, but he knew she was looking at him. He just watched the lightning bugs and listened to the moist, settling dark.

"New York?"

Ned nodded.

"And all you've got to do is say yes?"

He nodded again.

Perlie took a deep breath and let it out with a funny little whistling noise. He stared out the front door like he was waiting for somebody.

Ned cut his eyes at his maw. She was whipstitching a torn place in a flour sack quilt. She gave no sign what she'd heard.

"Well, son, that's sure a long ways off."

"He'll pay for it, he says."

"I ain't talkin' about the money," Perlie said, scratching his head. "It's just . . . none of our people's ever done nothin' like this, and . . . I don't know." Perlie got up and walked over to the door. He leaned against the frame and stared out into the night.

"Where's Brother going?" Percy said. "How come he's leavin'?" The little boy came over and stood in front of Ned. "Where you goin'?"

"Be quiet, Percy," said Mary.

Ned looked at his father. How could he explain to him what he didn't understand himself? He had no more notion than a goose what he'd do once he got to New York. He was as confused and uncertain about all this as anybody. When he thought about all those people rushing here and there and all that racket and all those buildings blocking the sky, he felt as jittery and shy as a hoot owl in the sunlight. But beneath that, beneath the commotion and the stir ran a low, steady voice that told him this was right, it was his time. Even in Mr. Hutto's office back at the Y, while he was listening and figuring out he was being offered a chance he'd never even had any excuse to dream about, something was off in a corner of his mind, whispering to him that he was going to grab this thing like a prize and run with it as far and as fast as he could.

How could he make his father hear that voice? How could he tell a man who'd never even been as far as Nashville that he wanted—needed—

to go to a place that scared him and pulled him like a magnet, all at the same time? Shoot, Ned had never been to Nashville either. And then he was ashamed and angry because he could look at the man who'd raised him and sung to him and given him a Barlow for Christmas and see that he wasn't as big as he used to be. And the worst of it was, he didn't know for sure if he was angry at his father for being less than he had been or himself for knowing it.

His mother was still stitching the quilt. Her hands never paused; her eyes never left her work.

"I'll be all right, Paw. I will."

His father's face swung slowly around, and the way he looked made Ned want to run, or hit something, or bury his face in Paw's chest. Then Perlie smiled, and Ned's throat started to feel like he'd swallowed a green persimmon.

"Well, boy . . ." Paw shrugged and gave a real slow nod. "Yep. Just like ol' Ned Hutchins."

Ned heard the snap of the thread as his mother leaned over to bite it.

CHAPTER
42

George was tired. As tired as the stiff, blotched, late-summer leaves of the ash tree in Addie Douglas's front yard. He hauled on the parking brake and killed the engine. The August air hung limp and heavy, even though it was only nine in the morning. He hoped Ned remembered that today was the day his train left for New York. George sure didn't want to have to tramp back through the woods to his house.

He got out of the car and walked to the edge of the yard, staring into the woods. He tilted his hat back on his head and looked up at the sky. It was blue now, but by midday there'd be a dull, whitish dome of humidity blanketing everything.

"George?"

He turned around. Addie stood on the front porch.

"Oh. Hello." He touched his hat brim. "Came to get Ned, carry him to the train. Didn't mean to disturb."

"You're not; don't be silly. Would you care to sit till he comes? I've got some coffee."

"Well . . . thanks. Yes, I guess that'd be all right." He ambled back toward the house.

There was a cane-bottomed rocker at the corner of the porch, near the swing. He sat in it. A minute later Addie came out of the house carrying a wooden tray with two steaming cups.

"Cream and sugar?" she said.

"No, thanks, just black."

He took a cup and saucer from the tray and balanced it in his lap. She set the tray on one end of the swing and carefully sat down on the other end. He slowly brought his cup to his lips and blew across the top of the hot coffee. He took a careful sip.

"Going to be hot again today, I expect," she said.

George nodded.

"Where's Ned going?"

"New York."

Her eyes widened. "New York City?"

He nodded.

"Whatever for?"

"He's going to art school." George felt a little bloom of pride. He took a small sip.

"Well, I'll say to my time . . ." She blew on her coffee. "How'd he ever manage that? I mean, he's surely very talented, but—"

"I'm sending him."

As soon as he said it, George felt a little ashamed. Or, not ashamed, maybe, but embarrassed, as if he'd put himself forward when it would've been better to keep quiet. He waited, taking a sip of coffee.

"Well, George. That's really something. Really generous of you."

George gave a little shrug. "Ned's a fine young man. He deserves a chance."

She was looking at him. He tried to meet her eyes, but couldn't. He drank some more coffee.

There was a crash inside the house. She put her cup and saucer on the tray, splashing a little coffee into the saucer. She got up from the swing and hurried into the house. "Jake!" he heard her call out as she opened the door. "What are you doing?"

The swing swayed slowly back and forth from her leaving. George watched the ripples bounce back and forth across the black surface of her coffee. The cup rattled against the saucer, but it didn't tip. He heard voices inside the house: Addie scolding and her little boy whining in protest. In a little while she came back out onto the porch.

"That young 'un might not live to see his seventh birthday," she said.

George smiled. "How's your daughter?"

"Oh . . . she's fine, I guess. Considering."

It sounded like she had more in mind to say, but when he looked at her, she'd turned her face toward the road.

A brown thrush trilled in some rhododendrons at the edge of the woods.

"I sure am sorry, Addie. For everything you've been through."

She gave him something not quite like a smile and then minded her coffee.

They heard footsteps, then Ned came around the corner of the house. He was carrying a burlap feed sack cinched at the neck with a piece of rope. He wore a white shirt buttoned to the neck and a pair of blue bib overalls, so new and stiff the legs barely bent when he walked. He set the sack down on the ground near the porch and shoved his hands deep in the pockets of the overalls.

"Hello, Ned. Mr. Hutto tells me I'm going to have to find a new hired man," Addie said.

He either ducked his head or nodded; it was hard to tell which.

"Do you have everything, Ned?" George said.

"Yes, sir." He nudged the sack with the toe of his brogan.

There was a short, quiet moment. "Wait here," Addie said, and went back in the house. She came back a couple of minutes later carrying a black leather valise. "Here you go, Ned. I've been meaning to give this to you anyway. You might as well use it to carry your things to New York."

She handed him the valise. He reached up to take it, and George could see the flush creeping up his neck.

"Thank you, ma'am." He opened it and began transferring items from the sack.

"One more thing," Addie said. She went back into the house.

"Here are your tickets, Ned. All your transfers and everything. You remember what I told you about changing trains in Philadelphia?"

"Yes, sir."

"Professor Koch said he'd be waiting for you at Grand Central. I've described him for you—"

"Yes, sir."

There was so much more George wanted to say to him. He wanted to tell him to relish this chance; it wasn't likely to be repeated. He wanted to tell him not to be afraid of the strangeness of the place and the people; that was only a matter of experience and circumstance anyway, and besides, if you set a New Yorker down in the middle of the woods and told him to find his way home, he'd be just as lost as somebody from Tennessee who found himself in the middle of Manhattan. He wanted to tell Ned to cherish the gift he had, to hone it and nurture it and let it turn the world on its ear.

"I know you're going to do just fine, Ned. I've got every confidence in you."

Ned studied the toes of his shoes. He nodded.

"Yes, sir. I'll do my best."

Addie came back out onto the porch, and in her arms were a jar of some kind of preserves, a loaf of bread wrapped up in a cotton dish towel, a jar of pickles, and a hunk of yellow cheese.

"Now, Ned, I think you've got enough room in the valise to pack most of this stuff. That's a long train ride, and I expect you'll get hungry, so I just grabbed a few things." She started handing the food to him. "I know your mama probably gave you some good stuff, but just in case—"

"Yes, ma'am. Thank you. I'm obliged."

"Oh, now don't be silly. I can't have you going all the way off to New York City and starving on the way. There. I think that'll fit, don't you?"

"Yes, ma'am."

"I tell you, Ned, I just don't know if I can let you go or not. Who's going to chop wood and do chores for me?"

Ned scuffed his toe in the dirt.

"Willie Lewis, ma'am."

"Who?"

He looked up at her for an instant, then back down at the ground. "Willie Lewis. He says he needs a job."

"Lila's boy?"

"Yes, ma'am."

"Well." She smiled at him, then at George. "I guess that settles that."

"Ned, we'd better get going," George said.

"Yes, sir." He picked up the valise.

Addie leaned over the porch railing and gave Ned a quick, hard hug.

"Ned, I just know you're going to do really well at that school. One of these days that fish you made me will be worth—oh, I don't know—a hundred dollars."

His cheeks were beet red.

"Yes, ma'am. Thank you, ma'am."

George went down the steps. He turned and looked back at her. "Thank you, Addie. For helping him out."

"Oh, goodness! He's done far more for me than I've ever done for him."

George smiled. "Well, I'm not so sure about that."

She gave him a tiny smile in return. "I'm always glad to help when I can."

"Yes. I believe that's right," George said. He ducked his head then and pushed his glasses up on the bridge of his nose. He went to his car and started it. Ned tossed his valise in the backseat, and they backed out and headed down the lane.

I need to get in touch with Lila, she thought. *I need to see if Willie can come to work.*

The air coming through the train window was hot but better than nothing. It seemed to Becky as if the closer she got to Texas, the hotter and more stifling the air became. But it was August, after all, and the air she'd left behind in Little Rock wasn't any better, that she could tell.

At least Daddy was doing better; that was one thing to be thankful for. Maybe now that he was back on his feet for the most part, Mother could manage on her own. And with her tainted daughter gone back to Texas, maybe she wouldn't have to endure quite so much polite silence from her acquaintances.

Neither of them had asked Becky if she was going back, but neither had they invited her to stay. She wasn't sure if it was because they respected her choice or because they were too ashamed to admit it existed. She tried to remember if they'd even talked about Zeb while she'd been home. She didn't think so. But every so often, Becky could tell by her mother's look that she was wondering. Or maybe trying to figure out where she and Daddy had gone wrong.

When they'd gotten to her platform at the station, Daddy had squeezed her arm. "Well, Sarge," he'd said, leaning close, "I guess you better get on back to Texas."

Another time, Becky might have teared up. But too much had changed, somehow. She'd smiled at him and kissed him on the cheek. She'd reached past him to hug Mother. And she'd turned and stepped up into her car. Just like she knew what she was doing.

She looked out the window. The train was rolling through the soggy bottom country east of the Red River. They'd probably cross into Texas in the next hour or two. Just off the railroad right-of-way, in the corner of a cotton field, stood a row of unpainted shotgun houses. Half-naked colored children chased each other in the bare dirt yard of one of the houses, and a heavy old woman sat on a keg by the front door of another. The old woman watched the train as it went by.

Becky wondered where the old woman had been, what she'd seen. Had she ever left somewhere and come back? Or had she lived all her life beside the tracks, watching other people come and go but always staying in the same place herself? Did she ever look at the windows of the trains as they passed, wondering about the people sitting behind the glass?

You could lose either way, Becky figured—going or staying. It was just a question of which loss you thought you could tolerate. At least Zeb had enough share in her shame that he couldn't look down on her. That was something, she guessed. Maybe it was enough, for now, enough to bring her back. Beyond that, it was hard to say.

Zeb left the telegraph office, trying to ignore the heavy feeling starting up in his chest. Still nothing. He hadn't heard a word from Becky for the three months she'd been gone, except for the terse wire she'd sent from Little Rock, notifying him of her safe arrival.

It wasn't right, what she was doing. That was the thought at the front of his mind. It contended with the thought at the back of his mind, the one that kept saying he didn't deserve anything good from her or anyone else after all he'd done. But didn't a man ever get through paying for his sins? When did enough get to be enough?

He decided to go over to the hotel, drink a cup of coffee, see what was going on. This time of the afternoon Colonel Dickson and some of the other big wildcatters would usually be there, smoking cigars and lying to each other about their prospects and the production from their wells. Zeb picked his way across Front Street, tiptoeing around the muddiest places. Somebody ought to do something about the streets. He might need to talk to the mayor. Grady wouldn't do anything much on his own, but he'd be glad to let Zeb or somebody else with a little gumption take the lead. That was the way things got done around here.

The hotel lobby was quiet, but the blue smoke of Cuban cigars was rolling out of the restaurant. Zeb strolled in, letting his eyes adjust to the dark. "How about a soda, Mr. Rourke?"

"Usual?"

"Yes, sir."

Zeb slapped a dime on the counter while the barkeep spooned the dark brown syrup into a glass and squirted it with seltzer water. "There you go," he said, sliding it across to Zeb.

"Thanks. Keep the change."

The oil men were at their usual corner table. Zeb walked over. One of them spotted him. "Hello, Zeb. Pull up a chair."

He scooted in and set his drink on the table. Colonel Dickson looked at him. "Zeb, you still drinking that Waco sugar water instead of a man's drink?"

Zeb shook his head and grinned. "Now, Colonel, you know—"

"Yeah, yeah." He winked at his cronies. "I said I'd never trust a man that wouldn't drink with me, but I don't believe ol' Zeb cares a rip what I think."

"Looks to me like you don't care either, Woodrow," said one of the others, "long as the deals he sells you keep making oil. I tell you what, Zeb, you bring your next prospect over to my office, and I'll let you drink all the Dr. Pepper you can hold and never say a word about it."

Some of the men chuckled.

"Well, what you got going, fellas?" Zeb said.

The man to Colonel Dickson's right, a big German named Schott, gave a theatrical shrug. "Dickson got all the production tied up. What else for us 'cept borrowing money from Dickson, and him tighter than bark on a tree?"

Colonel Dickson took a long drag on his cigar and aimed a stream of smoke at the low ceiling. "You boys keep singing that old song, you're gonna break my heart." He flicked a thumbnail-sized ash onto the floor, then cocked his head at Zeb.

"Tell you the truth, Zeb, me and the boys are glad you happened in here this afternoon. We were just talking about you."

Zeb saw some of the others nodding and watching him. He took a slow drink of his soda and set it on the table.

"Must be an off day, you fellas don't have any better topic for conversation."

"Zeb, you're a capable fellow; we all know that. And you're honest. Least I've never caught you lying to me."

"Don't believe you will, Colonel."

"Fact is, Zeb, we need somebody like you for a little venture we're putting together. Somebody who knows how to put in a day's work, knows how to talk to people." The Colonel leaned toward him. "And somebody who won't forget who he's working for."

They were all looking at him now. He pressed himself against the back of his chair, sat up straight.

"A little venture?"

"Yessir. The kind that'll make you enough money to not care if you ever sell another deal to me or anybody else."

"I'm listening."

"You like to travel, don't you, Zeb?"

Nearly an hour later, Zeb stepped out onto the boardwalk in front of the hotel and squinted into the late afternoon sun as he settled his hat on his head.

It was a lot to think about, he had to admit. If this Ranger oilfield was half as big as some of the Colonel's scouts thought, it would generate an unimaginable amount of activity. Why, a discovery that size would make fortunes for hundreds of people. And to be the agent that brought it all together . . . The man that pulled that off would be in the history books.

He could just get on a train tomorrow and go, they told him. Stay in the best hotels back east, hobnob with the moneyed people. Represent the interests of the consortium in all the right places. And earn himself the same cut of the profits enjoyed by each of the other men gathered around the table. It sounded real good.

Especially right now, with things at home being what they were. Just get on the train and go. Come back when he wanted to—with enough money to do as he liked.

Coming toward him was a parcel-laden woman followed by a little girl. The little girl was fussing with her bonnet, asking for her mother's help. Zeb stepped aside to let them pass on the relatively dry margin of the street. Just as they reached the place he stood, the little girl's bonnet fell off in the mud. Zeb scooped it up and flicked off most of the mud. He put it back on her head and tied the ribbons under her chin. He gave her a smile and stood back.

"Thanks, mister," the mother said.

Zeb touched his hat brim, and they went on their way. He watched them go, thinking about Addie and his little girl. About the son named for him, the child he'd never seen.

It was the same old dream, and it was a good one: follow the rainbow till you find the pot of gold. It was out there, just over the next hill. You just had to keep moving. Once you found it, everything would be all right. And even if you didn't, there was always another hill to climb. He shook his head and shoved his hands deeper in his pockets. He resumed his walk home.

He climbed the steps to the front porch and reached in his vest pocket for the house key. He put it in the lock, but it was already unlocked. Odd. He never left the house unlocked during the day. He went inside and immediately smelled her.

Becky came into the parlor.

"I hired a buggy to bring me from the station," she said. "I didn't want to bother you at work."

He looked at her, reaching inside himself for some feeling, something a man might say when his wife came home after three months.

"How's your daddy?"

"He's going to be all right."

"Well." He nodded, not quite able to look at her, not quite able to look away. "I'm glad you're home."

She stood there for a second or two, gripping her elbows. She crossed to him, put a hand on his shoulder, and gave him a dry, quick peck on the cheek.

"Me, too," she said. "Sit down and rest awhile. I'll fix us something to eat."

EPILOGUE
September 1920

*A*ddie watched through the window as George drove down the lane. He pulled up in the yard and got out, then walked around toward the front of the car. He was squinting at something on the left front fender. He bent over and used the sleeve of his coat to scrub at whatever it was. She smiled.

She stepped out onto the front porch. "You take on over that car like it was a baby."

He grinned over his shoulder, pushing his glasses up on the bridge of his nose. "Well, they get good money for these rigs nowadays. Fellow oughta take care of it, don't you think?"

"I've got some coffee brewed."

She went in and gathered the coffee things. She sliced a few pieces of pound cake and arranged them on a small plate and added that to the tray. When she came back out, he was sitting in the ladder-backed chair. She set the tray on the table and seated herself in the cane-bottomed rocker.

"Busy day?" she said as she leaned over to pour into his cup.

"Thanks. Yes, I suppose it was." He scooped his heaping spoon of sugar and dolloped the cream.

"How's that new man working out?"

"Jennings? Oh, I think he's going to be fine. He's a bright one, learns quick. Wish I'd have hired someone like him years ago."

She balanced the saucer in her lap and laid her palms around the cup. The air was just cool enough to make her savor the warmth.

"You cold? We can go inside," George said.

"No, it's nice out here. I love the fall evenings."

He nodded and took a sip of his coffee. "Course, it was nicer when there weren't houses across the road to block the view."

"Well. Progress."

He made a dismissing sound.

"Had a letter from Jake."

"When? Today?"

She nodded. "Would you like to read it?"

"Sure would."

She went in the house, to the bedroom. It was still lying where she had put it after reading it, on the bedside table atop her Bible. She took it to him.

He looked at the envelope, then took up the letter. His eyes ran back and forth across the single page. From this angle, she noticed the smudge on the back of the letter. That was Jake all over, not thinking of the grease on his hands before sitting down to write. She was surprised enough he'd written. He'd been gone for two months now, and this was the first communication he'd sent.

"Sounds like he's doing pretty well," George said. He folded the letter back into the envelope and handed it to her. "Detroit's the place for him, Addie."

"I guess."

"Long ways off, though, isn't it?"

She smiled, looking at Jake's spidery, impatient handwriting on the envelope. "I just hope he doesn't go any farther."

George looked at her. "Addie, you've done a good job with him. He's a good boy."

"Thank you. And you've helped."

George shrugged. "I haven't done much."

"You've been here when he needed you. That's a lot."

"I was glad to do it."

"I know. And he knew, too, even if he never had the words to tell you."

He took another careful, slow sip from his cup. *Yes, you could have done more, George,* she thought. *You could have always done more. But then, anybody could say that. Anybody could always know they could have done more. You did what you could; that was the point. You did your best with what you knew, and you prayed it was enough. Not what you knew, because you never knew everything you needed to know—at least, not at the doing. But sometimes, maybe, it worked out, it was all right. Maybe that was enough grace to go on.*

"You ever think about him?" George asked. "Still?"

She looked at him in surprise. "Are you still worried about that?"

"Not worried." But the color was rising in his cheeks. "Just wondered, is all."

She set her cup and saucer on the tray and leaned back in the rocker, closing her eyes. "Oh, I guess I'll always think about him. Every time I look in my children's faces, I will." She looked at George. "He wasn't bad all the way through, you know. There was a lot in him to like . . . to love."

George studied his coffee cup. She could see his jaw working in and out.

"I wish him well," she said. "He's had his share of trouble, too, I expect."

"Yes, I imagine so."

"I wish he could see his grandson," Addie said. "He'd be proud of him, I think."

"Well. Maybe someday he will."

"I don't know. I just don't know."

The sadness was coming toward her, kicking up the dust of remembered hurts, missed chances. She sat forward in the chair to lean over and pinch off the corner of a piece of pound cake. She put it in her mouth and offered him the plate. He took a small corner of the same piece and ate it. She set the plate back on the tray and retrieved her cup and saucer. George took a sip of his coffee. She took a sip of hers.

"Well, I'd better get on home," George said, after a longish silence.

"Yes. The dark falls quicker these days."

He got up, dusted a few cake crumbs from the front of his vest. "Thanks for the cake and coffee."

"You're welcome." She got up and walked with him toward the porch steps. "Will I see you tomorrow?"

He looked at her, showed her a tiny smile. "Oh, I imagine so."

She nodded. "Well. Good evening, then."

He touched his hat brim. He walked to his car and got in. He cranked it and backed carefully around. She watched him drive down the lane to the road, watched him until he had climbed the hill toward town and disappeared on the other side.

She hugged herself and leaned against the porch post. The lights were yellow in the windows of the houses across the road. She stood there until the evening purple edged over into full dark. She picked up the tray and carried it back inside.

Acknowledgments

I must first thank Pam Wilson and her mother, Frances Acuff, for entrusting to me a portion of their family effects and memoirs concerning Cynthia Hatchett Simmons, on whose life this book is loosely based. In many respects, Addie Caswell Douglas's experiences and thoughts are what I imagined Mrs. Simmons's might have been, although there are significant differences between the facts of Mrs. Simmons's life and those I have constructed for the main character in this book.

Next, I wish to thank my mother and father, Marjorie Thomas Lemmons (deceased) and C. G. Lemmons, for providing me with fascinating historical data about my own ancestors and certain artifacts of their daily lives that aided me in adding authenticity to this story. Perhaps it goes without saying (but shouldn't) that they have also provided me with the lifelong sense of heritage, which kindled and sustained my interest in telling a story of the type in this book.

Thanks are also due to Terry Browder for sharing his expertise in American quilts. Any technical errors in the quilting scenes presented in this book are certainly not to be laid at his door.

I must also express appreciation to Dr. Leonard Allen of Los Angeles and Dr. Douglas Foster of Abilene Christian University for their assistance in helping me gain some insights into the interdenominational climate that existed at the turn of the century in the middle South.

Most of the hymns quoted and alluded to in this story were gleaned from the pages of *Great Songs of the Church, Revised Edition,* edited by Dr. Forrest McCann and Dr. Jack Boyd and published by ACU Press.

The Chattanooga-Hamilton County Bicentennial Library graciously provided me with a valuable list of resources. Chief among these were the books of James W. Livingood and John Wilson, two eminent local historians. I must also thank Andrea E. Cantrell, head of the Research Services Department of Special Collections in the library of the University of Arkansas at Little Rock, who provided great assistance with historical data important to the story. I also express appreciation to Thomas T. Taber III, administrator of the Railroad Historical Research Resource Center in Muncy, Pennsylvania, for providing me with actual railroad timetables for the period and locale in which this story is set.